Praise for
GHOSTED

"This master of immersion journalism opts to give us a novel about a young man who makes a living writing suicide notes. Yes please."
— *The National Post*, "Most Anticipated Books of 2010"

"Grimly funny, terrifying and tender."   —*Montreal Mirror*

"The unique voice heard throughout *Ghosted* is so heartbreakingly authentic. This is a voice whose wry tones are surely as addictive as the drugs abused by the tormented characters in *Ghosted*. This is a story that you never want to end."   —*The Ottawa Citizen*

"It leaves you stunned. But then you realize you have just read a terrifying but moving and life-affirming paean to love, friendship, devotion, determination and all those other characteristics that make human beings such wonderfully fascinating creatures in real life and in richly imagined novels like *Ghosted*."
—*The Edmonton Journal*

"The characters of *Ghosted* compose a rogue's gallery like no other. Most are drug addicted, hopelessly self-destructive, dangerously suicidal or just plain psychotic . . . It is exceedingly difficult to top a hotdog-selling, poker-playing, cocaine-addicted writer of suicide notes whose adventurous, bar-hopping girlfriend Willy is partially paralyzed, confined to a wheelchair and addicted to heroin."
—*Calgary Herald*

"In *Ghosted*, love and friendship are real and just as powerful as addiction and nightmares. Despite what the narrator might say, redemption isn't just something c⸍ ⸍ ⸍ ⸍ ⸍ ⸍ to bad novels."
                                                                          ⸍ ⸍ ⸍ ⸍

"Bishop-Stall is a major talent. H⸍ coke seeping down the back of done a line in your life . . . an un⸍ and impossible to ignore."   —*Now ⸍ ⸍ ⸍*

"A savage, heartfelt, exhilarating first novel . . . What makes this high-concept premise work is the book's a) heart, and b) voice. Which may, in the final analysis, be one and the same thing."

—*Toro Magazine*

"One finishes *Ghosted* amazed by Shaughnessy Bishop-Stall's ability to cram three or four novels' worth of incident and characters into one book. Impressive, ambitious and exhausting, *Ghosted* is a novel for those who don't scare easily." —*Globe and Mail*

"*Ghosted* is not for the faint of heart—in places it's an unflinching exploration of depravity. But it is, above all, an often funny, always optimistic parable of victory over demons of despair, the ghosts of our failed selves."

—Linden MacIntyre, author of *The Bishop's Man*

"Bukowski craggy and Hornby sweet . . . a smart book about smart guys who can't stop from acting dumb. The real pleasure, though, is in the lines: funny sad, funny strange, and funny zing! A hell of a first novel."

—Andrew Pyper, author of *The Killing Circle* and *Lost Girls*

Photo: Goran Petkovski

SHAUGHNESSY BISHOP-STALL'S first book was an account of the year he spent in deep cover, living with the homeless in Toronto's infamous Tent City. *Down to This: Squalor and Splendour in a Big-City Shantytown* was nominated for a number of awards, including the Pearson Writers' Trust of Canada Non-Fiction Prize, the Drainie-Taylor Biography Prize, the Trillium Book Award, and the Toronto Book Award. He was a journalist for fifteen years and has also worked as an actor. He currently teaches writing at the University of Toronto. *Ghosted* is his first novel.

GHOSTED

Shaughnessy Bishop-Stall

Soft Skull Press

This is a work of fiction. Names, characters, places, and incidents are the product of the author's imagination or are used fictitiously. Any resemblance to actual persons, living or dead, is entirely coincidental.

Library of Congress Cataloging-in-Publication Data
Bishop-Stall, Shaughnessy.
Ghosted / Shaughnessy Bishop-Stall.
    p. cm.
ISBN 978-1-59376-295-7
1. Ghostwriters—Fiction. 2. Drug addicts—Fiction. 3. Suicidal behavior—Fiction. 4. Losers—Fiction. 5. Toronto (Ont.)—Fiction. I. Title.
PR9199.4.B533G48 2010
813'.54—dc22

                                        2010010917

"Fire Lake" Written by Bob Seger, © 1980 Gear Publishing Company (ASCAP).
Used By Permission.

"Atlantic City" by Bruce Springsteen, © 1982 Bruce Springsteen.

Cover design by Adrian Kinloch
Interior design by Neuwirth & Associates
Printed in the United States of America

Soft Skull Press
An Imprint of Counterpoint LLC
1919 Fifth Street
Berkeley, CA 94710

www.softskull.com
www.counterpointpress.com

Distributed by Publishers Group West

10 9 8 7 6 5 4 3 2 1

For Dr. Kate,
the Wasko boys,
and the late, great
Mr. Q.

For my money, that's the best song ever written about going to hell. Can you hear it now? The scratch of the grooves in the record, then piano and acoustic guitar, that strong steady backbeat, those first haunting lines . . .

Bob Seger—long may he run—should get me to write his epitaph:

Here lies a man who wrote the best song ever about going to hell.
So let him rise.

That First Mistake

Introducing:
Mason, Chaz, Warren,
and a little bit of Fishy

1

MASON DUBISEE dodged a booze-propelled bullet on the day he was born.

His father came in to the hospital room smiling—a bottle of champagne cradled in his arms. He looked at his wife and newborn son, tore off the foil, and cranked the wire. Angling the bottle heavenward, he pushed with his thumbs.

The cork shot out with incredible force. It ricocheted off the ceiling, a wall, then rocketed into the pillow an inch from Mason's infant cranium.

His father told the story for years to come. Grinning with pride, he'd pass around the infamous cork: "I swear to God, he dodged the fucking thing."

It was a feat that would prove more difficult as Mason's life went on.

Thirty years to the day since that very first bottle, Mason opened his eyes—and saw water pipes. They were painted white, against a white ceiling. It took him a moment to realize he was somewhere comfortable and quiet. There was nobody kicking him, or trying to grab his stuff, or banging on the door. He wasn't too cold, and he was barely hungover. There was a pillow beneath his head, and when he rolled onto his side, it smelled like a new stuffed animal.

He looked at the far wall: exposed brick, power-washed clean. There were silver and bronze specks in the bricks and in the grout, and they sparkled beneath a skylight. Against the wall was an ancient curliqued radiator, painted deep chestnut. The floor beneath it was hardwood, also dark, giving way to ceramic tiles—midnight blue and mottled—demarcating the kitchen area.

It was a thousand-square-foot loft. If he kept turning around in bed like this, he could see every corner of it. According to Chaz, it used to be a belly-dance studio.

After a while Mason was ready to get up. Or rather, down. The bed was fairly high—not so much that you'd injure yourself if you fell out, but enough that it would hurt to land. There was a three-step ladder, with storage space beneath. A captain's bed, it was called. Mason kind of liked that. He kind of liked everything right now. It was his thirtieth birthday and here he was: waking up in a captain's bed. He had an open concept, a skylight, and hardwood floors darkened by the sweat of amateur belly dancers. The day was full of possibility.

He climbed down and pulled on a pair of boxers. They were green, with penguins on them. He stood in the middle of the room, light spilling in from all directions. There were two large windows at the front, looking down onto Spadina Avenue—and one at the back that opened onto a flat tarmac roof. He surveyed the apartment, flecks of gold dust in the air.

By one of the front windows stood a simple oak desk, by the other a seating area with a burgundy couch, two easy chairs, and a TV, then a shelving unit, a cabinet, and a dresser, all empty. Mason's to fill.

Other than the duffel bag by the door, the only proof of habitation was on the table in the centre of the room. Mason pulled up a chair and studied it: Johnnie Walker Black—almost empty—two glasses, a rolled-up twenty, an ashtray surrounded by ashes, white residue, playing cards, poker chips . . .

How much did you lose?

He wasn't sure, but he knew he hadn't won—Chaz was better than he used to be.

Mason picked up one of the glasses and walked into the kitchen area. The icy ceramic felt good on the soles of his feet. There was a

coffeemaker on the counter. He looked at it for a while, but there were too many buttons. He opened the fridge: beer and an open box of baking soda. He poured himself a glass of water, dug into his duffel bag for paper and a pen, then crossed the room and sat down on the sunlit couch. He wrote:

To Do List—Monday

He wouldn't usually have known the day of the week, but today was a day for cognizance, for new beginnings. He underlined *To Do List*. Then *Monday*. Then he looked out the window.

He was sitting on the couch in his underwear staring out the window when Chaz came in. "What's the headline, pigeon?"

"So what? You don't knock?"

"Not till you start paying rent." He walked over to the table in the centre of the room, slung his jacket over a chair, then started gathering up the cards. Chaz was sort of a neat freak.

"How much did I lose last night?"

"Two and a half."

Mason's heart rate doubled, his skin got cold. "Thousand?"

"Don't worry," said Chaz, stacking up the chips. "I know where you live." He went into the kitchen area to get a dishcloth.

Until yesterday it had been five years since they'd seen each other, but Chaz looked much the same. He was wiry, and there was a slickness to him, like shiny leather. Mason was well-worn suede—barrel-chested, beaten in, rough around the edges.

They'd been friends since they were kids. And now, as adults, they came on like men who'd gotten away with something, tough guys who liked to dance. Both were handsome in certain lights— dim ones mostly—which fit their lives just fine.

Chaz was wiping up the ashes. "You got some rhino coming, right?"

Other than being better at poker, this was another way he'd changed. It used to be Chaz only talked like a whacked-out gang-ster when he was drunk, but now he was like Jimmy Cagney on Ritalin. "I'm in a good mood," he'd said the day before, by way of explanation. But Chaz's mood was often good. He was the least haunted smart guy Mason had ever met.

"Rhino?" said Mason.

"You might have called it something else." Chaz threw the dish-cloth into the sink. "But if it's a problem . . ."

"No. No. You're right, I've got magazine money owing, from like three different stories. I just got to give them an address."

"Well, you got one now." Chaz spread his arms, indicating opulence as he walked across the floor. Then he sat down in one of the easy chairs.

"Yeah. Thanks for this."

"I was just going to say, if it's ever a problem—I mean, I don't know what it's like in this town, as far as the writing biz goes and all . . . but if you're short, I can set you up."

"No thanks, Chaz."

Chaz shot him a sharp glance, then rubbed his hands together and looked around at the apartment, surveying the reno job that he himself had done. "I wasn't talking about dealing—not a bindle-stiff like you."

"Then what *are* you talking about?"

"*Hot* dogs," he said, as if he'd burned himself happily—the emphasis on *hot*.

Mason waited.

"Uncle Fishy, he's got this Dogfather thing."

"Do me a favor." Mason stood up. "A moratorium on the Chaz-speak. I've got no clue what you're trying to say." He went to find a shirt.

Chaz called after him. "It's just what I said: my Uncle Fishy has a Dogfather thing."

"What's a Dogfather thing?" Mason dug into his duffel bag. "And since when do you have an uncle named Fishy?"

"That's what they call him. He's a bit simple, but he's family. Got all sorts of family I never met out here . . ."

Mason tossed clothes in all directions.

"Anyway—Fishy's got these ideas: one of them's the Dogfather Hot Dog Company. It's a *theme* thing, right? And the cart would reflect that—the 'Dogmobile.' It's like a state-of-the-art, pseudo-mafioso hot dog–stand kind of thing."

"That's a terrible idea."

"Well, either way, I gave him money for a prototype."

"You're kidding me." Mason pulled on a T-shirt.

"What can I say? It's his dream. All he needs now is a Dogfather."

"You mean a hot dog salesman."

"Think of it as research on the human condition."

"There's no way I'm selling hot dogs, Chaz."

"Then I hope your game gets better."

"Fuck you."

Chaz held up his hands in surrender. Mason sat back down.

"What about that book you were writing?"

"Almost finished," said Mason.

"Hasn't it been like six years now?"

"Five."

Chaz looked at him. "So what do you plan to do?"

Mason reached for his to-do list. He turned it so Chaz could see. "Any ideas?"

"Number one: *Shave.*"

Mason scraped his fingers down his bearded cheek.Chaz walked to the chair where he'd slung his jacket and took an envelope from the pocket. "Here," he said, tossing it to Mason.

It was full of twenties. "What's this for?" For a moment he thought Chaz had remembered his birthday.

"Basics, buddy: food, stuff for the apartment, razors . . . I'm strapping on jets to Montana. See a guy about a can opener."

"You're cracking safes now?"

Chaz just grinned. "I'll be back on Wednesday. And by the way, the liquor store is . . ." but Mason wasn't really listening. He knew where the liquor store was. Chaz was under the impression he'd just arrived in Toronto. After all, why would your best friend come to your town, then wait a month to look you up?

" . . . Oh, here." Chaz reached into the other pocket, pulled out a cell phone and tossed it to Mason. "I'll get you a landline when I'm back."

"Thanks," said Mason. He suddenly felt embarrassed. "I'll have the rent together soon."

"Good to see you, kid," said Chaz.

Mason just nodded. That's what Tenner used to say. He'd called them both kid.

* * *

This side of Spadina was Chinatown, but on the other side of the road was Kensington Market—six square blocks of mom-and-pop shops from every culture you could think of: Portuguese butchers, Korean grocers, Jamaican candlestick makers—the smell of barbecued sardines, mangoes, and pig's blood mixing in the air.

Mason picked up a dozen disposable razors, ten oranges, five T-shirts, four pairs of underwear, a coffee, and an empanada, and when he got back to the apartment, he still had almost $480 left over. He disrobed and took the razors into the bathroom. As the steam rose he looked in the mirror. When Chaz had opened the door, what would he have seen? A world traveler? A drifter? A vagrant with a thrice-broken nose?

One more and it'll be back in place.

He plugged the sink, made a lather with the soap, and turned off the taps. "Out of the cold just in time," he said. But a voice inside him muttered something else.

He soaked his beard, then realized he had no scissors. With this kind of scruff, a dozen razors and you still couldn't find your face. Mason went to get his knife.

An hour later he was sitting on the couch eating an orange and watching *Judge Judy*, the first item on his to-do list done, his cheeks still stinging.

He hadn't watched TV for a while, and nothing made sense. Judy was cool, but everyone else in the courtroom made him sad or angry. At a quarter to three, he turned off the TV. The world was quiet. He was thirty now.

He began to shuffle cards, looking at the wall. It had all been mirrors, Chaz had said, floor to ceiling for the belly dancers. He'd agonized for days, then stripped it down to the brick. Mason could picture them now—all those Toronto girls in sweatpants and sports bras, undulating toward him. He shuffled the deck for a long, long time. Eventually he got up, intending to eat another orange, but instead he left the apartment.

It was after five when he got back, and he'd acquired a few more of the basics: midrange champagne, a ghetto blaster and a stack of used CDs, a steel sword—somewhere between a cutlass and a

saber—with a dog-faced dragon on the blade, a sharpening stone and scissors, toilet paper, a cheeseburger combo from the Harvey's right there on the corner, a pack of Camel Lights. There was $280 left in his pocket.

He took a beer from the fridge, plugged the ghetto blaster in, put on *The Best of the Animals*, and finished his fries. He opened one of the windows. The bottom pane slid up high enough that he could sit on the ledge drinking his beer, looking at Spadina.

His was the top of a three-storey red-brick. The apartment on the second floor was still being renovated. On the street level was an electronics store and a porno shop—then a narrow alley, Harvey's, and the Lucky Save Convenience on the corner.

The neighborhood used to be Jewish, Chaz had told him, but they sold most of it to the Chinese—and soon thereafter the city decided to turn Spadina into an expressway, which only made it halfway down its planned route from the superhighway at the top of the city before it stopped—killed in its tracks by an enlightened group of urban activists, political academics, artists, hippies, Chinese businessmen, and Jewish gangsters.

Across the street from his window were bars and Cantonese restaurants; and, on the corner, the new MHAD building: the Mental Health, Alcohol, and Drug Center. It no doubt added a little something—not that the neighborhood needed much. The original saviors of Spadina were still out there, showing their stuff: marching down the street with placards protesting shark's fin soup—*Sharks are great! / But not on your plate! / Sharks are great / But not on your plate!*—past blankets on the sidewalk covered with DVDs, restaurant managers throwing fortune cookies, deals going down in the doorways . . .

On the median, conceptual art loomed: Corinthian columns rising from the concrete. Atop each column was a figure: a chicken made out of chicken wire, a steel horse, a plastic dog, and so on . . . Beneath the plastic dog stood a flesh-and-blood man—eyes focused on the sky, hands circling in the air, tugging—flying a kite that wasn't there. A woman weaved out of the Palm Tree Tavern into the line of shark supporters. There was yelling and laughing. A cop car pulled onto the sidewalk. His siren gave a squawk—anyone's guess as to who was in trouble.

Mason got another beer from the fridge. Through the back window he could see the green roof of the library. He poured himself a glass of Scotch. Sure, it was new-leaf-turning time and all that, but it was also his birthday. Just because Chaz wasn't here didn't mean he couldn't celebrate. He'd never remembered Chaz's birthday either. He walked from the back windows to the front ones. *The Best of the Animals* was over. He put on Billy Idol. The sun was going down. He lit a cigarette.

Soon everything glowed—the ember and the smoke, the violet exhaust rising from the street, twilight refracting off windowpanes. Through the music and the traffic he could hear his heartbeat. He picked up the cell phone and looked at it. He knew quite a few people in this city by now, but only one number.

It's your birthday, bub. Dial it up.

2

MASON AWOKE to find that his body had stopped working.

He tried to breathe, but the air only got halfway to his lungs. He tried to swallow and choked. It felt as if there was a block of dry wood in his mouth. He tried to raise himself off the mattress, but his arms shook and he fell back.

Water.

People had told him this would happen—that one day he'd reach a certain age and wouldn't be able to do the kind of things he'd always done, but he tended not to listen to people who said things like that. And even if he had, he wouldn't have taken them so literally.

Water!

He managed to scootch to the edge of the bed. He saw the word *scootch* in his head, then the scales on a viper's belly, his mean dry tongue. And now he was falling, like a snake from the bough of a tree.

When he woke again, he was lying on the floor beside the captain's bed. There was something beneath his head: a piece of lined steno

paper. He pulled at it—his to-do list, streaked with spittle and blood. On the back it read:

Thanks for the party, chump.

There seemed to be a wind blowing. Slowly, he rose to his knees. It looked as if a meteor had hit the apartment. The window by the desk had been shattered—in the frame, a circle of shards like teeth in a tiger's mouth. The floor was strewn with broken glass, underwear, cigarette butts. The TV was gone. One of the chairs had been smashed to kindling. It looked as if someone had tried to light it.

And now, as if punishing him for not getting *water*, something inside Mason started playing a reel of the night before:

Clicks, flashes: faces. He knows some of them, but barely, from shelters, soup kitchens, alleyways, the shantytown down by the lake—others he doesn't recognize.

A pile of cocaine. Someone laughs. It billows up in a cloud.

Mason beheading champagne bottles with his dog-dragon sword—running the blade up the seam in the glass—the tops, cork intact, shooting across the room, the neck cut cleanly, champagne everywhere, golden and bubbling.

"And now . . . the Five-Gallon Bottle Dance!" Mason grabs a hat off someone's head. People gasp, but Mason has already begun—mixing five kinds of booze in the stranger's hat. He begins to glug it down.

The stranger grabs the hat. His face contorts. Booze spilling over both of them.

Mason hits PLAY on the ghetto blaster. He steadies a wine bottle on his head, his arms stretched out for poise and glory, then bends his legs and begins to kick in time to the music, dropping to his knees for the finale.

The bottle exploding on the floor, his legs still circling through red wine and glass. Bright streaks of blood . . .

Click: someone throws a punch.

Flash: chaos.

And now it was morning: Mason on his knees again—sun rays streaming through the skylight, everything dry: the stains on the floor, the tongue in his mouth.

Water, you asshole!

This was no ordinary hangover. He made it to the sink, but every sip came up again. And then he just kept heaving—nothing in him but blood and bile and breath. He was at the point of accepting defeat, maybe even death, then decided to seek professional help. There was a clinic on Yonge Street that took you even without a health card. Mason had gone there for an infected dog bite his first day in town.

He crawled across the floor and found his jacket. It was stuffed under the couch—the cell phone and the last of the money still in the pocket: enough for a cab there and back.

In the hall, atop the long straight flight of stairs, he wavered for a moment trying to balance between gravity and the banister. He reached for the rail and began the descent.

Once outside he clung to a lamppost, waving for a cab. Then he noticed something in the gutter, surrounded by a shimmering circle of broken glass. It looked as a coffeemaker would, had it been thrown from a three-storey window.

A taxicab was honking. Mason lurched toward it.

The clinic was in a mall. The woman at reception looked bored.

"I need help," Mason gasped.

"What exactly is the problem, sir?"

"I think I turned thirty."

"Take a seat," she said.

When the doctor saw him, she pressed her fingers against his throat. At first glance she looked too young to be a doctor. But close up, like this she had the scent of self-assurance, and her hands were steady. "I'm Dr. Francis," she said, then slipped a stethoscope beneath his shirt. "Breathe deeply."

He inhaled, the cold metal on his chest, and started to giggle. "Are you really a doctor? You look so young."

She pushed her chair back.

"You're about to vomit," she said. And then his guts were in his throat. "There's a bathroom across the hall."

Five minutes later he was back.

"Sorry about that." Mason took a seat.

She looked at his eyes without looking in. His head was clear

from the purging, and now he could see how smart she was—a disturbing kind of intelligence.

"Really," he said.

"Really what?"

"I'm really sorry."

"You've got tonsillitis."

"Really?"

She sighed and turned to some papers on her desk. "Probably it's been there for a while and you haven't noticed. We'll get you some antibiotics." She wrote a prescription and handed it to him. "There's a pharmacy past the food court."

"Okay," said Mason. "Thanks."

"Take this, too," she said, and put a pamphlet in his hand. It was blue, with a chimpanzee on it.

Through the food court, past the Source, the Royal Bank, and the Yarn Barn, Mason finally reached the entrance to the Pharmasave—but things were starting to shake and swirl again. A sign hanging from the ceiling suggested there was a bathroom around here somewhere. He looked at it for a while, then turned and threw up on the roots of a small palm tree.

After getting the antibiotics, he found the bathroom, swallowed a pill with water from the tap, and staggered into one of the stalls to heave some more, his body pressed against the cold tiles.

Businessmen came and went, washing their hands and faces after lunch.

When he could move again, Mason found the blue pamphlet in his jacket. He looked at it. The chimp, both mad and endearing, had a bottle in one hand, a syringe in the other, its eyes intense and bewildered. The billowing letters above its head said: GET THE MONKEY OFF YOUR BACK! Then, at the chimp's feet: TO BOOK AN ASSESSMENT CALL 1-800-TO-MHAD, OR VISIT OUR CENTRAL LOCATION. He put the pamphlet back in his pocket, then steeled himself and stood—out of the stall, across the mall, and up to the sunlit street. A taxicab pulled to the curb.

He almost reached home, but on College, just a block from his apartment, the traffic jammed and his stomach churned once more. He tossed the driver a ten and climbed out of the back seat.

Mason figured that he, as much as anyone, knew how to be hun-

gover—but this was something new. Staggering down an alleyway he came to a grassy courtyard and threw up again, his nose and eyes streaming. In front of him, on the other side of a chain-link fence, was the back of his apartment building. Behind him was the library, patrons reading and studying on the other side of a giant window. He crawled away from his puke then collapsed, limbs stretched in every direction.

He awoke to a woman shouting.

"Help me!" she yelled. Mason lifted his head from the soft dirt smell of the courtyard. He craned his neck until he could see a skinny woman and a fat man struggling on the other side of the chain-link fence.

Not now, thought Mason. But the woman kept shrieking, and even from this distance he could see sweat on the fat man's head.

Yes. Now.

"Stop! Thief!" yelled the woman.

Stop thief? Do people actually say that?

He got up on his elbows and crawled across the grass. Grabbing hold of the chain-link fence, he pulled himself up to a kneeling position. "Hey! You better stop that, buddy . . ." Neither the thief nor the woman in distress took any notice. Mason couldn't get to them without climbing over the fence, and that seemed improbable. He dug into his jacket pocket, pulled out his new cell phone, and called 9-1-1.

"Police, fire, ambulance?" said a voice.

"Police," said Mason.

"Police," said a voice.

"There is a woman being robbed by a fat man in progress—right in front of me. There is a fence between us. Otherwise I'd—"

"Where are you, sir?"

"Behind the library. Wait . . ." He tried to focus. "Them—they're in the alley. At College and Spadina, the southeast corner."

"Police are on their way."

By the time Mason got the phone back in his pocket, the robbery had transformed into a baffling argument. And now the victim seemed more like a crackhead with financial issues. "That's my fucking money!" she yelled, as the man shuffled off. *A fat man in*

progress, thought Mason. The angry woman swiveled on her heel, looked at Mason, then stomped away in the other direction, her ponytail bobbing down the alley.

Now that they'd left, he noticed something else there at the back of the building: a giant poppy seed fedora on wheels. There was a sign on the side: HE'LL MAKE YOU AN OFFER YOU CAN'T REFUSE! And then he heard the sirens.

The cops looked at Mason clinging to the fence. His T-shirt was streaked with vomit—over that, a grass-stained jacket. There were twigs in his hair. At midnight on the weekend this might have been okay, but it was 3 P.M. on a Tuesday. They stepped out of their car. One was in uniform, the other in a pinstriped suit.

"Can you stand up, sir?" asked the uniformed one.

"If I could stand up, I would have climbed the fence," said Mason.

"Okay, sir. We're coming around to get you."

It occurred to Mason that when figures of authority called him *sir* it generally ended badly.

They didn't bother with handcuffs—just put him in the back of the cruiser.

"I'm the one who called you," he said. He'd been taken from alleys and put in cruisers a number of times before, but never so ironically. "I was almost home, you know?"

"It's three o' clock on a Tuesday," said the one in the suit—his moustache the *V* of northbound geese, skin like dark mahogany. He was sitting in the passenger seat.

"You're arresting me for the time of day?" said Mason. "What is that—like a temporal infraction or something?" He laughed, then coughed up bile, fluorescent and stringy—a glowing nest on his lap.

"Here's the thing," said the mahogany one. "We can write you up for public drunkenness and hold you till tomorrow. Don't want that, right?"

"Where's your uniform?" said Mason.

"But due to the state you're in, and considering we found you like this, we can't just let you go."

"Are you a detective? Don't you have a murder to solve or something?"

"What we *can* do," said the detective. "Particularly in light of the reverse peristalsis—is take you to Emergency."

Mason nodded. For a while now he'd suspected his life was out of his hands. This just seemed to prove it.

At the hospital they put him on a gurney in a hallway and left him there with a bottle of water. After a couple of hours he felt like he might be able to stand up, and eventually he did. He walked out of the hospital and flagged down a taxi.

As he glided through the streets, Mason realized he'd been thirty for only a day, and already he'd traveled by three different taxi cabs, a cop car, and a hospital gurney. It was an amazing world to live in. He gave the driver the last of his money, climbed the stairs to his apartment, then onto his captain's bed. The wind was blowing across the room. He closed his eyes. A young leaf dropped from his hair and settled onto the pillow.

3

AS FAR as hot dog carts went, it *was* pretty cool—a three-wheeled hybrid truck, all chrome with a serving window that opened and closed by remote control. It came equipped with a sink, grill, cooler, electronic cash register, and even a surveillance camera. And you could store things in the hollow fiberglass crown of the fedora. On its hatband in large letters were the words THE DOGFATHER.

Mason had decided to make the best of it. He'd sell hot dogs in the open air, work on his novel at night. He'd get a membership at the Y and exercise every day. He'd pay Chaz for the damages, the rent, the gambling debts. He'd meet a girl, be a prince again— virtuous and clean, charming in a humble way. Five years was long enough.

For the moment, however, there was a lot to keep track of: all-beef, chicken, veggie, buns, drinks, ice, condiments, propane levels, oven mitts, plastic serving gloves, fire extinguisher . . . And apparently there were city inspectors—hot dog watchdogs—who came around to check on all this.

Then, of course, there was Fishy Berlin—a man with a face to fit his name, keeping his fishy eye on things. At least Mason had talked him out of the dogfather outfit—arguing that it made no logical or aesthetic sense for a man serving hotdogs to wear a hat when he was standing beneath a larger, more impressive, poppy seed one.

As the morning wore on, the smell of propane, grilling wieners, and car exhaust combined in a very particular way. Mason was still queasy from his birthday party, and the effort not to puke soon became distracting.

"My first day," he said when the dogs started burning. And for the most part, people were understanding.

He'd set up at the edge of Matt Cohen Parkette, named for the famous writer who had called Spadina the center of the universe. It wasn't really a park, though—more a strange extension of space making up the gap where Bloor and Spadina didn't quite meet. The Dogmobile was parked next to a stone sculpture of giant dominoes that stood and leaned like alien headstones. Embedded in the nearby tables were large granite chessboards. Sunlight reflected off passing windshields. Everything was framed by sharp angles, slants of silver, black and gray—and among them, a dishevelment of people: a woman and two men drinking out of the same paper bag, students slumped against the concrete planters, no energy left to keep reading. This was the lip of the famous writer's universe—the intersection where, for some reason, Spadina Avenue ended and Spadina Road began.

By 6 P.M. Mason had sold forty-two hot dogs, given away four, and burned eleven. He packed up—not exactly the way Fishy had shown him, but close enough. Then he got behind the wheel, waited for a really big break in the traffic, and pulled out onto Spadina.

Driving an oversize three-wheeled fiberglass hat through rush hour traffic was stressful. He only had to make it six blocks, but just before College came an inexplicable Gothic castle—right there in the middle of the avenue. It wasn't easy trying to maneuver an already wobbly motorized fedora, dodging spaced-out students, bouncing over streetcar tracks, in a looping circle around a looming castle.

By the time Mason reached College, the chopped-up banana peppers were strewn across his feet. He turned into the alley and

pulled in next to Chaz's silver '68 750cc Norton. It was painful, parking the poppy seed Dogmobile (with its lawn mower engine) right there beside it.

There was a new pane of glass in the window. Chaz was standing in front of it, backlit by the setting sun. His motorcycle helmet was on the counter, next to a new coffeemaker.

"Hey," said Mason, more than a little sheepishly.

"How's the wiener business?" Chaz had not forgiven him yet, but the idea of Mason selling Mafia-themed hotdogs had done a lot to improve his mood.

"Not too bad."

"I'm glad." Chaz knocked on the glass. "Gotcha a new window."

"I see that."

"I figured you could do without a TV for the time being. Anything else missing?"

Mason decided not to mention the sword with the dog-faced dragon—just shook his head.

"Well, I got you something else," said Chaz, and cocked a thumb toward the desk. There was a laptop on it. "It's an old one, but it should work for book writing."

Mason walked over and flipped it open.

"Happy birthday," said Chaz. "Try not to lose it. I hooked you up with Internet and a landline, too." There was a phone on the table next to the couch. Chaz picked it up to check for a dial tone. Then he went to the fridge for a beer. "I got a question for you, Mason." He sat on the couch. "How'd you find enough degenerates to trash this place in just one day? I mean I know you're good, but . . ."

"This city's full of them." said Mason.

Chaz shrugged and took a sip. "Well, don't ever go buying from somebody else again. It makes me look bad." He tossed a baggy onto the coffee table.

"Chaz . . ."

"That's about seventy hot dogs. I'll put it on your tab." He got up, walked across the room and picked up his helmet. "And try to find the TV, will you?"

After he was gone, Mason picked up the baggie of coke. Flick-

ing it, he held it to the light. It was just like Chaz: Even pissed off, he couldn't help doing favors for people. Mason walked over to his duffel bag and dumped it out on the floor. Then he gathered up his beaten-up spiral-bound notebooks—ten of them. He put them down next to the computer and pressed the power button. It made a ghostly sound, like breath in another dimension.

Notes on the Novel in Progress

Things to figure out:
Who *(or what)* is narrating? Can we trust him? Inconsistent POV?
Is there more than one street in this city?
To research:
Intensive care units, troglodytes, palominos, shark's fin soup.
Possible title:
The Center of the Universe

4

MASON WAS scraping the grill when a vast shadow fell—as if a mountain had suddenly risen between the Dogmobile and the sun. He looked up. A large man in mirrored sunglasses stood before him.

"What can I get you?"

The man's head turned from side to side—surveying the grill; the counter; the square plastic bins of relishes, hot peppers, onions; the display of soda cans and water bottles; the rack of potato chips. It was like those scenes when the Terminator enters a room, his robot brain scanning the new environment. It occurred to Mason that a hot dog watchdog might act in such a manner, and he was glad to be scraping the grill: "Would you like something, sir?"

"It's very clean," the man said, still looking around. "It looks new."

"Thank you," said Mason.

"But why is it a hat?"

"That's a good question."

"It's okay," he said. "I think I like it. There's something contained about the whole idea—though I don't really get it." He seemed to be talking to himself more than to Mason.

"Would you like to try a hot dog?" said Mason.

"Try. Exactly," said the man. "I'd like to *try* one."

"Okay then," said Mason. As he turned the dog on the grill, he glanced again at his customer: a dark business suit, pressed neatly, with a blue handkerchief jutting out of the breast pocket. His hair was streaked with gray. There were deep lines in his face that seemed incongruous with the oval shape of it.

Is this what a hot dog watchdog looks like?

He tucked the dog into a bun and placed it on the counter.

"Something to drink with that?"

"Not just yet," said the man.

"Gotcha," said Mason, though he didn't at all.

Usually—insofar as the habits gained over two days of work could be described as *usual*—Mason would have turned to the next customer or otherwise distracted himself by wiping down the counter or something. It seemed invasive to watch a man dress his dog. But it was one thirty, past the lunch hour rush, and he couldn't help but look.

Holding the mustard bottle tightly, the man painted a careful line of yellow along one half of the bun. He then did the same on the other side with the ketchup. He looked up and caught Mason watching him. It didn't seem to bother him. "I'm glad you have squeeze bottles," he said. Mason just nodded. The man put the bottle down and began flipping open the condiment containers. He counted out four rounds of sweet pickle and laid them across the ketchup. Then four slices of raw onion went along the mustard line. "These are very well cut," he observed.

"Thank you," said Mason.

The man closed the bun carefully. He put the plate down, then closed the lids of the condiment containers. "I'd like a Sprite." Mason got him one. The man handed him $5. "Please keep the change."

"Thanks," said Mason, but the man wasn't listening. He was lifting his hot dog, slowly, as if about to take a bite. Just before it reached his mouth, he opened up the bun and looked inside.

He closed it again, closed his eyes for a moment, then turned and walked away. A half block down, without breaking stride, he dropped the hot dog into a garbage can.

5

THE BIG weird guy had made him nervous. And Fishy always watching from across the street didn't help. For days Mason turned wieners, sweating over the grill, waiting for the hot dog SWAT team to descend. Then, as he was packing up the cart one afternoon, he saw the big weird guy walk by.

"Hey!" he said. "Excuse me!" But the guy kept on walking. Mason left his post and caught up to him at the corner. "Excuse me," he said.

The man flinched. He was wearing his sunglasses.

"I'm sorry to bother you," said Mason.

"All right," said the man.

"I've just got to know: Are you a hot dog watch—are you a cart inspector?"

"I'm a computer programmer. What's a cart inspector?"

"It doesn't matter."

"All right." He turned away from Mason to cross the street.

"It's just . . . you didn't eat your hotdog."

The man stopped.

"The other day—you bought a hot dog from me, but then you threw it in the garbage without even trying it."

"I *did* try."

"Excuse me?"

"I'm very sorry for any trouble I caused you."

"No, it was no trouble . . ." Mason didn't know how they'd gotten to this point. "I'm sorry."

They stood looking at each other.

"Okay then . . ." said the man.

"I've got to get back to my cart," said Mason.

They nodded once and went their separate ways.

When Mason arrived home, Chaz was sitting on his couch drinking a beer.

"How you doing, daisy?" His mood had improved substantially.

"Just because you have a key doesn't mean you can let yourself in. Only in case of emergency." Mason tossed his jacket onto a chair. "It's in the tenant's act and everything."

"It *was* an emergency." He gave the bottle a lift. "Insufferable thirst."

Mason pulled out a wad of cash wrapped in an elastic band. He tossed it onto the couch.

"This before or after Fishy?"

"I don't trust that guy."

"That's okay. He doesn't trust you either."

"*My* name's not Fishy."

"No, Mr. Dubious, it ain't. But you still gotta pay him." He picked up the wad of cash. "Tell you what, let's play for it."

Chaz was a dealer who didn't do drugs, a gangster who disliked violence, and except for Mason's beer, he barely ever drank—but he liked the cards almost as much as Mason did. "Look at it as a bundle," he said. "Like the cable companies offer you: rent, drugs, poker debts, all in one easy payment plan." He grinned. "C'mon, dogboy. Don't you want your spinach back?"

"That doesn't make any sense," said Mason. But the cards were already in his hands.

Notes on the Novel in Progress

To consider:
Why the fuck are you still writing this thing?
What is it even ABOUT?

To research:
Heroin. Horse thievery. HOW TO WRITE A FUCKING NOVEL!

To keep in mind:
Breathe. Some days are better than others. Do NOT try to write after losing at poker.

Possible title:
Five Years Wasted

6

It was warm for the middle of April, especially standing over an open grill. Mason was strung out and pissed off after his bad night at cards. He'd lost it all and was starting from scratch with another fucking hot dog.

He could feel himself sweating, and his back ached in that way that seemed to come right from his heart and liver. He'd read somewhere that those were the only two organs with the ability to regenerate completely—each cell reborn, if you could just find a way to make it happen. It gave him more hope than he probably deserved. He cracked open a bottle of water, his eyes closing as he glugged down half of it.

"I've got a lot of fears," said a voice.

Mason opened his eyes.

"I am scared of heights," said the large man with the sunglasses. "I'm scared of tunnels. Of public places, intimacy, spiders, germs. I'm scared of sunsets, dreadlocks, short people, odd numbers, the color orange . . ."

"The color orange?" said Mason.

"Actually—any color that's not primary disturbs me. But orange the most. I don't like things mixing together. That's why I threw out your hot dog."

"Oh."

"I had to tell you that."

"Okay. Thanks."

"I'm sorry if this is awkward for you," said the man, staring intently. "It's difficult for me, too. I have a profound fear of speaking to strangers."

"Then, well . . . why are you?"

"It's important for me to face my fears." And now Mason could see how much effort this was taking—how the man's huge body appeared locked in place. "And also you seem like a nice guy."

Mason, unaccustomed to people telling him things like that, took a long drink of water. Then cleared his throat. "Why did you look?" he said.

"What do you mean?"

"The hot dog. Before you took a bite—you looked in the bun. Is that what did it for you?"

The man nodded. "It's a tricky balance. I like the way hot dogs taste."

"Why don't you give it another shot?" said Mason.

Again the man nodded, more to himself than to Mason. "I could come back in the afternoon."

"Sure."

"When there aren't any crowds. Okay then." He held out his hand, steady and practiced. "My name is Warren."

A wave of nausea flooded over Mason. He looked down at the counter until it passed. Warren's arm was still outstretched.

"I'm sorry," said Mason, taking off his plastic glove. "I used to have a horse by that name." He shook Warren's hand. "I'm Mason . . . He was a good horse."

"Oh, good." They looked at each other. "Well, it's good to meet you, Mason. I'll come back after lunch."

Then he walked away—Mason's dead horse hanging in the air.

Notes on the Novel in Progress

Life is a room: You're born in a room, die in a room, sit in rooms that glide across the land.

From the moment of birth, the world expands outward, and so does the protagonist—from boy to rebel to traveler to hero.

And then, one day, it starts to shrink again (traveler to drifter to living in a box) until the universe is just a room again.

The room as narrative device:

First—fill it with stuff. Now look around; the objects in the room will turn into stories.

When all the stories are told, the room is empty.

When the room is empty, the story is over.

To research:

Phobias, horse trailers, caves, GPS guidance systems.

Possible title:

Room to Move

7

BY HIS second week as the Dogfather, Mason felt he was getting a handle on things. He was burning fewer hot dogs, not drinking as much, and doing less drugs. He'd looked into getting a gym membership and had even worked on the novel a bit.

The hot dog job wasn't that bad—kind of like being an open-air, lunchtime bartender. People were in a fairly good mood and kind of dopey since the snow had melted, as if they were still stretching after hibernation. They'd comment on the Dogfather thing, make a lame joke—often quite accurate (*You guys laundering money through this thing?*), then hang around and whine good-naturedly about their lives. Mason listened and sometimes offered advice. He watched the girls walk by and waited for Warren, who remained his most interesting customer.

They'd figured out a system so that Warren could eat his hot dog. Mason kept a bag of romaine lettuce in the cooler. He applied a line of ketchup to the sausage, laid out four spears of onion, wrapped it all in lettuce, and put it on the counter. All that was left for Warren was the mustard and the pickles. The lettuce leaf held the juices in. Then, on a whim, Warren added two slices of yellow banana pepper.

Looking inside the bun, where all those colors and textures were touching each other, Warren had an unsettled feeling. But this time it was more butterflies than nausea. He took a bite.

"I was thinking about the color orange," said Mason, as Warren continued to eat. "You're right—I don't much like it either. It's shrill, isn't it? Caution signs, religious cults, convicts . . . and those guys—what are they called? Those guys who are always marching?"

Warren wiped his mouth. "The Orangemen?"

"Right." Mason laughed. "The Orange Men."

Warren nodded as he ate. He seemed appreciative. It was a rare quality, this willingness to turn someone's irrational fears into rational theory. The hot dog finished, he crumpled up his napkin and dropped it into the garbage. "So, Mason—you're a writer. Where can I read your work?"

"I dunno . . ." said Mason. It was an embarrassing thing to talk

about, especially while serving hot dogs. "There's probably some magazine stuff online . . . I'm working on a novel."

"What's it about?"

He hated this question, mostly because he didn't have a good answer. "A bunch of stuff . . ."

"Like what?"

"I don't know: horses . . . memory . . . different kinds of freedom. It's kind of complicated. And it's about a room that moves."

"Oh."

"But actually I'm not sure about that now . . ."

"Oh?"

"And there's all this stuff that happened in the past—there's like three different time frames, and one of them is still unfolding. It's kind of an adventure story. It's hard to explain . . ."

Warren nodded. "What's your last name again?"

Mason told him. Warren wrote it down. Then, as if in return for this information, he said, "I've fallen in love."

"Really?"

Warren nodded. They looked at each other. Mason felt he had to say something more.

"What's her name?" It was a lame question, and he was thankful when Warren, instead of answering, asked for a bag of chips.

"What kind?" said Mason.

"Dill pickle."

He handed them over.

8

It was midafternoon on a blustery day. Fishy Berlin was watching him. Mason could see him on the other side of the street, his fishy arm around a lamppost.

Warren walked up to the window. The wind blew his hair sideways.

"I Googled you," he said. "Got some stories you wrote off the Internet . . . I hope you don't mind."

"Oh, sure, that's okay."

"They were good."

"Thanks. You want a hot dog?"

"Please."

Mason put one on the grill.

"Why aren't you writing any more?"

"What do you mean?"

"All those stories were old. And you're—well, you're selling hot dogs."

"I told you," said Mason. "I'm working on a novel."

"How long have you been doing that?"

"I dunno. Five years."

"How much have you been paid?"

"That's not how it works. It's not like you can just . . . What?"

"Here's the thing." Warren took a breath. "I think you should put the novel aside, just for now, and write something else."

"Thanks for the advice." He placed a bun on the upper rack.

"It's not advice. It's an offer: I want you to write something for me."

Mason turned the wiener on the grill.

"I want you to write me a love letter."

"Sorry, Warren, but I don't really feel that way about you. Maybe with time . . ."

Warren stammered out a laugh. "No—for me to give to someone." Mason wrapped the hot dog in lettuce. "I'll pay you $5,000."

Mason turned the heat down on the grill. "You're kidding."

"It won't be an easy sell," said Warren. "I'm a strange person"

Mason placed the hot dog on the counter. Warren pulled an envelope from his pocket and put it down next to it.

"That's a $1,000 advance, plus $5 for the hot dog, and I'd like a Sprite too, please . . . so actually you owe me a dollar."

"Excuse me?"

"That's how it works. You'll get the rest on receipt of an acceptable manuscript. You should know this stuff, Mason." He reached for the mustard.

Mason put the Sprite on the counter, then opened the envelope. "This is crazy . . ."

Warren took off his sunglasses. He looked at Mason. His eyes were large, rimmed with pale, white skin. "Please listen to me," he

said. "This is between you and me, and it is not a joke. I need you to take it seriously. Are you able to do that?"

Mason nodded. At that moment a dark-skinned man in an orange sweater appeared. He asked for a veggie dog. Warren picked up his hot dog and Sprite, and the wind picked up his napkin.

"Wait!" said Mason, startling the vegetarian. "I . . . I still owe you a dollar."

"Next time," called Warren over his shoulder. "I trust you, buddy."

People rarely told Mason they trusted him. It was the way to his heart.

Over the next four days Mason learned more about Warren than he ever wanted to know about anyone. The story of Warren's life had a strange ebb and flow. What at first glance appeared a string of disturbing, seemingly unrelated events took on a jagged sort of sense when seen through Warren's fears—crippling hesitation followed by leaps of faith, sometimes panicked, sometimes brave.

He was born in '57, he said, just outside of Boston—an unsure boy in a self-conscious suburb. He grew fast and large and always felt out of place.

In junior high he tried out for the basketball team with the express purpose of overcoming his worsening fears—of crowds, of kids, of echoing spaces. He was already tall, and that carried him through tryouts. He got rid of the ball as fast as possible and had the makings of a good guard. But then, in the first quarter of the first game, in that big bright gym, he freaked right out. Somebody passed him the ball, and he just held on to it, frozen and shaking, like Superman with a lump of orange kryptonite. He fell to the floor and the game was stopped.

After that he was a pariah. They came up with new names for him all the time: Weirdo Warren. Frankenballs. He fought back once. Two young men beat him to the ground, and then everyone dog-piled on. A girl in stilettos (he was sure she didn't mean to do it) stomped clumsily onto his groin. The left testicle burst—his freakishness complete.

His family moved to Florida. He read a lot, went to university, but quit to work with a newly established branch of the International High Commission on Refugees. He learned to travel and to control his breathing. He was freaked out all the time, and the world was his. In Mozambique he fell sick. Small worms started crawling out from behind his eyes. He went blind and almost died and fell in love with one of the nurses. By the time he could see again, his fear of the dark—once unbearable—had disappeared. But so had the nurse. And then all he wanted was to be in love.

Mozambique was the wrong place for it. When an eleven-year-old boy kicked a sick dog in the head right in front of him, Warren threw him onto a pile of tires. A hidden tire jack, broken and sharp, went through the boy's ribcage. There was death all over the place, though, and Warren returned to the States without being charged.

He started drifting. He'd never been a drinker, but one night he found himself in an Oklahoma bus depot bar on open mike night. He drank a bottle of Baby Duck champagne, got on stage, then spent the next three years traveling up and down the East Coast as a stand-up comic. Mason found this difficult to picture.

"Were you, um . . .?"

"Funny?" said Warren.

Mason shrugged, half apologetically.

"What? You don't think I could be funny?"

"I'm just asking. What kind of bits did you do?"

"Bits?"

"Or whatever . . ."

"Mostly they were, you know, personal anecdote stuff—honest things about my life, but with a humorous slant . . ."

Mason tried to imagine it: *Right onto a tire jack . . . I mean really! You can never find one when you need it! Did I mention I'm short a testicle? Trust me: Girls just love it. They're like, Oh! Didn't Hitler have that? By the way, I have a fear of people looking at me. No, I'm serious—can you please stop looking at me!*

Canadian audiences were particularly receptive to Warren's brand of counterintuitive, confessional humor. He scored a two-month gig at a racetrack outside Toronto, rented an apartment, won $6,000 on the trotters, quit comedy, enrolled himself in a computer programming course, got a job, and now—six years later—had fallen in love with a woman named Carolina.

Nowadays he liked to read and go for walks. His favorite thing was to walk down to the lakeshore when the fog rolled in. He spent a lot of time alone.

"I guess you're right," said Warren. "I wasn't very funny."

9

MASON SHUFFLED cards and drank, thinking about Warren. Usually, neurotic people drove him kind of crazy, but Warren was different. Right from the start he'd confronted his fears, even as his life had become more dangerous—a hostile world of stilettos, worms, and broken tire jacks. Mason could identify with that. Not that he himself had ever been a fearful person—quite the opposite—but, like Warren, he'd sought out danger, had decided early on that middle-class life would make him soft, and set out in search of trauma. And now here he was—a drunken, traumatized thirty-year-old hot dog salesman writing love letters to people he'd never met. And still he wasn't particularly scared. But he *was* impressed by Warren.

People had this romantic view of facing down their fears, as if only good could come of it. Warren could testify otherwise, and yet still he kept on doing it. Case in point: this love letter Mason was supposed to be writing. It was a ballsy move on Warren's part. At every step—approaching Mason, commissioning the letter, delivering it to a woman named Carolina—it must be freaking him right out. The least Mason could do was start to write . . .

He put the cards down, then carried his drink to the desk. He sat down and picked up a book of matches. With his right hand he pushed the leftmost match out and around the edge of the book, turned it in his fingers and struck down at the flint. The match head burst into flame. He lit his cigarette and then a candle.

He didn't bother blowing out the match, just threw it over his shoulder, where it smoldered, then flickered out. Mason laughed out loud and took another drink. He trayed his smoke, did a line, then turned on his computer.

His job was not necessarily to put Warren in a true light—a

multiphobic, unitesticled, manslaughtering ex-comedian looking for love—but rather a *good* light. The trick was not to freak the lady out. There'd be plenty of time for her to get to know him.

So what could he write about?

It's a love letter, *Einstein. Write about Love.*

"You know what I think the problem is?" Mason flipped the bun, then took it off the grill.

"What's that?" said Warren.

"Carolina. You haven't told me anything about her. It'd be easier if I knew who we were in love with."

"Hmmm . . . That *is* a problem."

"What do you mean?"

"I just don't know her that well."

"I thought you were in love with her."

"Well, I know her *that* well."

"I've already got a headache, Warren."

"Sorry."

"What does she look like?"

"She's beautiful."

Mason waited.

"Caucasian. Brown eyes. Five foot nine."

"Well, that's romantic."

Warren took a moment, then spoke: "Her eyes are almond shaped, like a cat's—but with only two eyelids, of course. Cats have three, you know? I think it's called the nictitating membrane."

"Now *that* I can use," said Mason pulling an invisible pen from behind his ear to scribble it down: "*No* nictitating membrane."

"She's got a small mole on her upper lip."

"Okay . . ." *Scribble, scribble.* "Got it."

"She's very pretty."

"Good enough. So what does she *do*?"

"She works at a video store."

Mason looked at him. Warren looked back.

"Is that how you know her, Warren? She rents you videos?"

"You sell me hot dogs."

"Good point. What have you talked to her about?"

"Mostly videos . . . What?"

Mason took a breath. "Okay. Well, what movies does she like?"

"I know this . . . her favorite movies are—let me think. *Chariots of Fire*, *Pretty in Pink*, and *First Blood*."

"Really?"

"Those are all good movies. Have you seen *First Blood*? It's an excellent film."

"Great. This has been really helpful, Warren. Thanks."

10

MASON WASN'T getting anywhere writing about love. Writing about Warren could scare her off, and he hadn't exactly got a clear picture of Carolina. So what was left?

Feelings.

Feelings?

How does he make her feel?

Mason started to type.

You make me feel big without being huge and cumbersome. You make me feel like a tough guy in a bar, instead of a moving mountain that steps on trees and toes.

You make me wish I could be stronger.

Too close to that Nicholson movie: "You make me want to be a better man." Gag.

Carolina behind the counter,
You make me feel like Rambo before the crummy sequels.

Short and sweet.

Not worth five grand, though.

Mason sat there, drinking and shuffling cards, bereft of inspiration. Finally he reached for the phone. Twenty minutes later, Chaz was at his door.

"Howdy, popstand. What's the haps?"

"I'm writing a love letter."

"Aw shucks, for me?"

"Nope."

"Who else are you acquainted with?"

"People."

"You're a half-wit."

"Play some cards later?"

"You're already into me for too much dough. And little lambs eat ivy."

"Well, that's why I called you." From his desk drawer, Mason pulled out the thousand Warren had given him. "I'm making some money."

"That's from hot dogs? Maybe I should switch jobs."

"Aw, c'mon. Drug dealing suits you." He passed him half the cash. "We'll play for the rest later. Just leave me some powder, okay?"

"Sure enough," said Chaz. He put the money in his pocket and tossed a baggie on the desk.

After Chaz left, Mason did a long, thick line and tried to imagine what would make someone fall in love with Warren. He wanted Carolina to envision him in some seemingly real yet romantic light—what he was, but also what he'd been, and what he *could* be.

"You don't look so good," said Warren.

Mason broke off some lettuce. "I missed my morning workout."

"Oh."

"Tell me, Warren." Mason's head throbbed." Why don't you write this thing yourself?"

"Writing scares me."

"You don't say?"

"It's not like some other fears, where I've just got to find the will to step up. It's more like eating when you're nauseous." Mason handed him the hot dog. "Every word is a new struggle."

"That's what writing is."

"Do you want this gig or not, Mason?"

Mason nodded. "Yeah, I want it. I just need more material . . . Or maybe less—there's so many ways to go . . ."

"How about this?" Warren was dressing his dog. "Why don't you write me a few different letters? Then you don't have to worry about it being perfect. I can choose what parts to use. It's not like I'm going to just hand over whatever you give me, right?"

"All right." Mason handed him a Sprite.

"Tell me," said Warren. "Why did you start writing in the first place?"

"What do you mean *why*?"

Warren seemed to think about it, then changed his question. "Well, if it's so difficult, why do you keep doing it?"

11

WARREN'S QUESTION lingered unpleasantly, since Mason struggled with the suspicion that narcissism played a considerable role in his desire to write. In earlier days, he'd been obsessed with being cool. He roamed the world in search of ways to prove just how cool he was. But it's a tree-falling-in-the-forest type of thing. It doesn't matter how many trains you hop, how many rabbits you skin, how many rafts you build, how many bar fights you almost win, how many times you crouch in the shade of your own duffel bag—boots beaten and dusty, the desert burning behind you, waiting for that next ride to anywhere—if nobody's there to see it.

And so he'd learned to write in order to document his own coolness, his guts—his good-looking, good-lighting, good-karma-hair days—the stuff that would sell a man to pretty girls and a fickle god so they'd take him as a hero.

But Mason didn't care what people thought of him anymore. Wash your clothes in enough gas station bathrooms, break enough of your own vows, and eventually you don't give a shit—which is too bad, because the desire to impress people at least keeps you connected to the world somehow. And it's hard to write a book

when you don't give a damn about the reader. Warren had been right: It was time to put the novel aside—to write something for a man who loved the reader madly. But how to make her love him back—to *show* him to her?

Try it in the third person?
And why not present tense?

Warren in Love—Third Person, Present Tense

He is on a train. The air outside is burning with brush fires, pulsing and crackling in the twilight. People are stuffing the broken windows of the railway car with blankets and shirts to keep out the smoke. There are goats in the aisle. The smoke swirls in, a chicken flaps out, aflame as it shakes to the ground.

He is on a dark beach. It has been storming for days—huts collapsing, people huddled in fear. The ocean is bleeding, rusted red and frothing, yet somehow he is pulling fish from the shallow churning waves. He cooks them up, sparks rising in the air. He is carrying medicine through a desert. He is going mad from the heat and nobody ever speaking his language. He is jumping from a cliff into aqua blue waters. An ugly dog follows him, won't leave him alone, so he can't even get on a plane and go home—because of the dog; it's the closest he's come so far to love.

And would you believe that *he* is this same man, hunched over this desk—bad hair, unsure eyes, trying to write a love letter—a big man with vague dreams and desires stuffed into a suit? He knows no one can see him. No one could possibly see, by looking at him, the things he's done. The thoughts he's had. All that bravery and fear. It's as if it's not even him. As if you wake up a new person every day—no credit at all for the life you've lived. He feels huge and invisible, as if the universe itself finds him cumbersome, irksome, baffling, boring—as if every time he tries to do something strong, his big hands and thudding brain mess it up . . .

Who's that? It feels as though there's someone out there, in the fog. For a moment his heart jumps, not in fear but hope. He straightens his back, narrows his eyes, stabs at the keyboard with confidence—trying to look as if there is magic in his head.

The next morning Mason printed all the letters he'd written, spread them on the table in the middle of his apartment, and read them again. Over the past few days, he'd written five versions, altogether. But nothing looks good with a cocaine hangover. For the most part it is a horrible ghost of emptiness. Then there are those rare moments of *all right*: those random, leftover bursts of energy, fortitude, drive. And suddenly you're out the door.

Mason rounded the block three times. He could have headed for the hills, but instead he stayed close—thinking, sick, and energized. So when he was ready, he was already there, up the stairs, back to the desk, *all right*, and ready to focus. He pushed the letters together and looked at them anew.

One thing he'd learned over the years: Trying to mythologize yourself rarely had the desired effect. Why had he thought doing it for somebody else would be any different? It was time to write the truth.

So Mason sat down for one more letter: "Warren in Love—Take Six."

It began like this:

I've got a lot of fears.

12

TWENTY DAYS after first they'd met, two weeks after Warren had paid $1,005 for a hot dog and a Sprite, he gave Mason another $4,000 for ten pieces of paper.

"Aren't you going to read them?"

"Later."

"But—"

"Six letters, Mason. At least one of them's *got* to be good. Don't you think?"

It was a gray day, with a heavy warmth in the air.

"You want a hot dog at least?"

But the big man, nodding a sort of thanks, was already lumbering off down the street.

Mason put the envelope of money behind the counter, picked up a scraper, and started on the grill.

Warren walks west on Bloor Street. The low clouds swirl overhead, rumbling, and then it starts to rain. Light at first, but within minutes it becomes a downpour, streaming across his sunglasses. He holds the envelope inside his jacket, his heart beating against it, and walks on—the clean water cascading over him. He loves the rain. The only thing better: thick night fog.

They were sitting at the table in the open concept loft.

"I sold a story," said Mason.

Chaz put his finger on top of the money. "You're flapjacking me, shore leave."

"What happened to popstand?"

"You got a stack like this, standing on dry land? You're a sailor on shore leave."

"And I'm flapjacking you?"

"Damn straight."

"Are we playing or what?"

"Deal 'em up."

They traded about a thousand back and forth for a while, then went out on the town with it, hit a few bars. Mason made out with a girl in a bathroom, Chaz dropped some jerk's cell phone into his own pint of beer, and they watched the sun come up from the roof of a pool hall.

It was a beautiful day.

Notes on the Novel in Progress

The story is the thing. Without the story you got nothing, chump. Look out the window. Spadina is gingerroot salesmen on the steps of a synagogue. It is lingerie for a dollar, fake trees in real earth, giant chickens made out of chicken wire on storey-high pedestals in the middle of the avenue. It is a Gothic cathedral right there, in the middle of the avenue. It is a madman with an invisible kite, fighting the winds in the middle of the avenue. It is screeching tires, growling outpatients. It is a dead pig, slipped off a truck

in the middle of the avenue. It is *not* the middle of the road. It is a drastic, aching, redbrick surprise.

Possible title:

A Drastic Aching Redbrick Surprise

13

It was a new world—a debt-free one. And other things had changed, too. Since watching the sunrise with Chaz, Mason had done his damnedest to get his act together. He hadn't done drugs in four days. And so he was barely hungover when two police-men—one in uniform, one not—walked up to the Dogmobile.

"What can I get for you?" said Mason, his head down, fiddling with a bag of buns.

"Mason," said one of them.

"Dubisee," said the other.

He looked up, a bun in each hand.

They were definitely familiar: a blurry, irksome memory, seen through metal diamonds—chain link, then the back of a cruiser. "I'm Detective Sergeant Flores," said the plainclothes one, skin like mahogany.

"Are you kidding?"

"About what, exactly?"

"I don't know. I'm trying to run a business here."

"Okay."

"I've sobered up a lot since . . . since last time."

"We're not here about that, Mason."

In retrospect, Mason preferred *sir*.

"Do you know a man named Warren Shanter?"

"Captain Kirk?" said Mason.

"Not Shatner. And not William! Warren Sha—"

"You mean Warren?"

"Yes, that's what I said."

"I didn't know his last name was Shatner."

"It's not."

"Sorry," said Mason. "You guys make me nervous."

"That's fine. We just want to know how you knew Mr. Shanter."

"I don't know."

"You don't know how you knew him?"

"Knew?"

"What?"

"You said *knew*."

"Warren's deceased."

Mason's hands felt awful with the stupid plastic gloves on. He took them off and dropped them.

"Are you okay, Mr. Dubisee?"

The stench of burning plastic filled the air.

"What happened?"

"There was an incident . . ." said the detective.

"Your gloves are melting," said the officer, scribbling in his notepad.

Mason scraped at the toxic, bubbling mess on the grill. "Why'd you come here?"

"We saw your name on some papers in his apartment—figured we should talk to you." The officer scribbled.

"Papers?"

"Some articles off the Internet."

"Oh yeah." Mason scraped. "Warren wanted to read some of what I wrote."

"Why would he do that?" *Scribble.*

"I don't know . . . we were friends." *Scrape, scrape.*

"You said you didn't know how you knew him." *Scribble. Scrape.*

There was a gentle pop, then a sizzle, as water fell from Mason's eyes onto the red-hot grill. "I sold him hot dogs."

"Are you all right, Mason?"

Mason watched himself open a bottle of water and pour it onto the grill. "What about the funeral?" he said, the steam billowing upward, a large impatient spirit.

When the cops were gone, Fishy came over. He'd been watching from across the street. "What was that about?" he said, looking off down the sidewalk.

Mason looked at Fishy's profile—bulgy eyes and flappy lips, then a flat, stubbly chin. He didn't answer.

Fishy turned his head. "I asked you a question. What was the fuzz doing here?"

"You actually call them *the fuzz*?"

Fishy lowered his gaze, and Mason glimpsed some hatred back there, behind the stupidity.

"It was nothing," he said.

"What kind of nothing?"

"The kind that isn't something."

"You think you're smart, don't you?"

Mason wanted to hit him. He wanted to yell, "My friend is dead, you fishy fuck!" What he didn't want to do was help him out, or ease his worries. "They were looking for someone," he said. "An ugly guy with bulgy eyes. I told them I didn't know anyone who fit that description."

"You better watch yourself," said Fishy.

Mason shrugged. It was a bit too late for that.

14

ON THE day of Warren's funeral, Mason decided not to open the hot dog stand. He drank a bottle of wine in his underwear, washed down two cheese sandwiches with a pot of coffee, then put on the black suit he'd bought in Kensington Market.

There were at most a dozen people in the pews, a closed casket on a platform below the dais. He hadn't meant to reach the front, but walking down the aisle it was as if he'd forgotten where he was going—and now the priest was standing right there.

Mason sat down, the only one in the first row. He barely even knew Warren, for God's sake, and here he was: best man at the funeral.

It quickly became clear, however, that the priest knew Warren not at all.

"Take solace in God," he said, "And have faith in his fairness. I cannot give you answers, only this: Take stock of your tears, and

know the Almighty sheds them with you." Mason heard no one crying behind him—nor from above. As for him, there'd been that moment with the cops when his eyes had teared up, but mostly he was confused. He didn't even know how Warren had died, and *Father* here wasn't dropping any hints.

"Please welcome," said the priest, "Ms. Amanda Shanter—Warren's sister. She's come all the way from Florida, folks." He said it like she was singing at the casino or something. But to no applause. A woman was coming down the aisle. "Also," said the priest, "following the ceremony there will be a wake at the Sheraton Plaza Hotel, in the Red Room, courtesy of Ms. Amanda Shanter."

She was big like her brother but sensual and openly sad. The priest did an awkward two-step, until finally Ms. Shanter was alone on stage.

She unfolded some papers. Both her dress and hair were shiny black, midlength, curving inward. Her lips were red. She cleared her throat, staring at the mike as if it were a large wasp buzzing at her mouth.

"They found this on my brother's desk," she said, then flattened the papers and began to read:

I've got a lot of fears.

I am scared of heights and tunnels. I am scared of crowds and being alone, of speed and paralysis, of dawn and dusk and so many lights between.

I am scared of spiders and Janet Jackson, of needles, bonfires and middle initials, of the earth speeding up so that gravity kills us and the birds explode in the trees.

I am scared of drought. I am scared of drowning—of tidal waves, heat waves, electromagnetic radio waves, the signal passing through our bodies; the static, the snow, the wind that blows through your sleep so it feels like you've fallen awake in your bed, the terror of hitting the waves.

I am scared of things mixing together. I am scared of them blowing apart: summer leaves off the limbs of trees, arms and legs strewn across a battlefield, the dispersion of words—how they fly from your mouth like swallows, then dust into the atmosphere, never to be heard from again. I am scared of Easter and Easter Creme Eggs, of chickens and omelets and

the Intifada. I am scared of gummy bears and grizzly bears, of nudity and hand grenades, of waking up faceless and famous, homeless and nameless. I am scared of being thoughtless.

I am scared of my own thoughts.

I am scared of worms and wormholes and black holes and vacuums; of lightning and thunder and bad theater; of practical jokes and leprosy; of guavas, iguanas, and coconut trees. I'm scared there's nothing out there, not even darkness—beyond the skin of our universe, the sum of our days—not even the absence of something.

I am scared of caves and bridges; of hospital rooms and Gothic castles; of gallows, gambling and public speaking; of basketball and Armageddon; of Judgment Day and Jerry Lewis; of Huey Lewis and horses. I am scared of getting lost—of getting caught and tranquilized, stuffed in a cage, and sent to Rikers Island. Or Mozambique. Or The Hague. I am scared of being found out.

I am scared of love and happiness. I am scared of the first kiss—but more than that, I am scared of the second. My body quakes, the Earth's tectonic plates coming together like granite wings.

I am scared of never asking, never knowing, never breathing—a full, knowing breath. I am scared of writing, of never writing this. I am scared of giving it to you.

But also I am brave as hell. I look, and then I leap.

I hope to see you when I land.

Who wants to break the news about Uncle Joe?

You remember Uncle Joe,

He was the one afraid to cut the cake.

The
Second

Introducing:
Tenner, the Warrior Monk,
and the Day of the Swallows

15

MAYBE IT all started then, on the day of the swallows.

That was five years ago now, not long after Mason's twenty-fifth birthday. He'd been out of the country a few months, rambling and writing travel stories for various magazines. He'd come home for Tenner's funeral.

Things had changed in his absence. His mom had sold the house in Vancouver and bought a ranch in the interior of British Columbia with her new husband. Also, Mason's girlfriend of four years had started sleeping with a spoken-word performer. On Mason's return she tried harder to explain spoken word than why she broke his heart.

After they buried Tenner, Chaz split for Toronto. Mason said he'd be along soon. But before he could follow, he was expected to make an appearance at Aunt Jo's eightieth birthday party. He went up a few days early, to get a feel for the ranch—a sudden lonesome cowboy. He'd decided to write a novel.

By the day of the party, though, he was still on the first chapter and the relatives were arriving. Many of them he hadn't seen in almost twenty years—since his own father's funeral. The ranch house was large—three levels, with seven bedrooms, and still there were going to be cousins sleeping on the floor. With each new arrival Mason sequestered himself further. By noon he was on the roof.

The house had been built by a German couple. Or rather, by

a German man while his wife hid beneath the blankets in a mid-size Winnebago. She hadn't realized how large the house would be until the logs arrived. "Trees don't even grow that big," she said, in German, and took to her bed.

When her husband was done, there was a solarium, a greenhouse, a paddock, a barn, a game room, and a wine cellar with two hundred bottles of fine red. "It's all for you," he said. Then, three weeks later, he died of a heart attack. The German wife sat in her new log mansion, drinking the wine. By the time she was done, only seven bottles were left in the cellar. Their bodies were flown to the Rhineland.

Mason's mother didn't hear this story until after they'd bought the place.

"What happened to the seven bottles?" said Mason.

Up on the roof, he drank champagne. The house was on a steep hill overlooking 120 acres of grazing land, sparse forest, and creek beds. The view was remarkable. In fact, he could hear a half dozen of his brethren remarking on it from the veranda below.

He heard his name being called. A few more times, then he shuffled over to the edge. Rupert, his mom's new husband, was looking up at him. "Swallows," he said.

Mason swallowed. "What?"

"I need your help."

Moments later they were standing on the large deck off the kitchen, looking up. There, clinging to the wall below the eaves, were a dozen round nests.

"They're swallows' nests," said Rupert.

"So?"

"They're shitting all over the deck."

"So?"

"So this is where we're having dinner. Your Aunt Jo says she hasn't lived eighty years just to watch four generations of her family covered in shit."

"Okay."

"We should knock 'em down. You've got to do that anyway with swallows."

"But they've got babies . . ."

"Nah. They're just making the nests. Babies won't come for another couple weeks. They're just making the nests now."

"Are you sure?"

"Yep. I'm going to take everyone to the lake. You get it done, okay?"

Once they were gone, Mason popped open another bottle of champagne. In the greenhouse he found a ten-foot bamboo pole and sported it like a javelin to the deck. But even on a chair he couldn't reach the nests. Back in the kitchen, more champagne, down to the games room for a pool cue, then up two flights of stairs to the westernmost bedroom. He opened the window and stuck out his head.

The nests were only about five feet above him. It was an awkward angle, leaning out, scraping upward with the cue. He couldn't really see what he was doing, but it appeared to be working, bits of brittle nest falling onto his head. He swung the cue a bit more, scraping a wider arc. Then he flinched as something hit him—a flurry of wings—another and another. From the surrounding treetops the swallows were diving at the window. He ducked back into the room. Their talons scratched the glass. He caught his breath. There was debris in his hair, and he shook it to the floor. Then, slowly, he leaned back out, looking up.

Half the nests were gone, others broken to various degrees. Something flickered in the corner of his eye, at the end of the line—something moving, emerging: a tiny pair of feet.

He stopped breathing. The nest was crumbling like an avalanche, feet flailing above him, legs like matchsticks. An infant bird slipped into the air. Then fell.

He saw feathers damp like hairs on a newborn's head, beak like a nose, eyes pulsing beneath lids. His hands were out now, the body falling slow—a fetus with a parachute, a floating baby dinosaur. But still he couldn't catch it, his fingers stiff and stupid. He looked down and saw the body drop. Bouncing once, it landed hard, among the broken nests. And then he saw the rest of them— squirming on the deck below.

Too many moments later, Mason stood among them—a pool cue in one hand, a bottle of champagne in the other, nestling birds dying at his feet.

Harder to take, though, was the aerial offensive—not because the swallows, diving from the birch trees, were trying to kill him, but because they couldn't. No matter how they tried, their scratches, like unreturned kisses, made everything hopeless.

On the wall above him six nests remained, then a line of dark circles—too many ellipses, the shadows of a half dozen heads. Mason looked down. Inches from his foot, a tiny body pulsed, a heart on cedar. He took a breath, then stomped down with the heel of his cowboy boot. The sound was popping and wet.

As he moved across the deck, crushing birds beneath his feet, Mason wished for two things: that he'd start to cry, and that he'd finish before they came back from the lake.

If only the day had ended there.

16

AFTER THE service came to a close, it was hard to move, as if he were asleep and panicked at the same time, trying to wake from an awful, truthful dream. He stepped out of the church, into the bright sunlight. The Sheraton Plaza Hotel wasn't far and he decided to walk.

Cutting through the churchyard, he came upon a dead squirrel. He picked it up, put it in a garbage can, then crossed the street, went into a store, and bought a pack of cigarettes. He walked on. Before he knew it he was there.

The Red Room was large and seemed even larger with so few people in it. Mason shook hands with the priest who was standing just inside the door, then excused himself to wash the dead squirrel off his hands. He did a long, thick line on the toilet tank, looked in the mirror, said, "Please let me offer my condolences. Con-*do*-lences." Back in the Red Room he made his way to where Ms. Shanter was standing.

"Please let me offer my condolences," he said. They shook hands. "Can I buy you a drink?"

"The beer and wine is free."

"If you don't mind me saying," said Mason. "You seem like him . . . in a good way. I liked Warren a lot."

"Oh," she said. "How did you know him?"

"This is going to sound like nothing at all—but I sold him hot dogs."

She started to laugh. "Oh jeez. I'm really sorry!" she said, dabbing her eyes with a napkin. "Are you serious?"

"I . . ."

"Really? The one person who talks to me at my brother's funeral and he sold him hot dogs?"

"Um . . . Yes."

"Well, okay then."

"I'm sorry."

"It wasn't *your* fault," she said. "You're just trying to be nice."

"I dunno." They stood for a moment. "Can you tell me . . ." he looked at her until she met his eyes. "Can you tell me how he died?"

She picked up a plastic glass of wine. "Specifically? Far as I can tell, he drowned in that lake of yours."

Not my *lake.*

"How?" said Mason.

"They say you can drown in six inches of soup." She was looking at the ceiling.

Mason took a glass and drained it.

"That thing you read . . . ?"

She looked at him. "It was beautiful," she said. He didn't know how they usually were, but her eyes seemed deep with confusion. "Don't you think?"

Mason shrugged.

"I didn't know he could write." She put down her glass. "I guess it made me see him differently. But so did killing himself."

Mason felt his guts drop; only his knees were holding them up.

Ms. Shanter turned to take in the rest of the room. "Do you know these people?" she said. Mason looked around for someone who might be Carolina. Then for the first time it occurred to him—maybe she didn't exist. He turned, pushing through the

doors, across the foyer, then outside past rows of Doric columns. *Fast as you can*, he thought, through the rotunda then into the back of a cab. He called up Chaz as he headed for home.

There are those who say you can't play good poker with only two players. They're either ignorant or scared—the same people who tell you dueling never solved anything, don't pick up hitchhikers, everything in moderation. At least that's how Mason and Chaz saw it. For them, heads-up Texas hold 'em was a perfect one-on-one battle: Ali vs. Frazier, Borg vs. Becker. Man against Nature.

Chaz knew every backroom boozecan in the whole damn town, and yet here the two of them sat, facing off across the table in Mason's apartment, time and time again. It wasn't about the money, and it was all about the money—a tactile, moving entity, flowing between them like breath, inspiration, and purpose.

Mason cut lines while Chaz shuffled. He snapped the cards down, lifting them in a riffling bow, then together like ice floes colliding—into one hand, three stacks splitting, over and under. Mason snorted a line.

They cut for deal. Mason took the cards. Shuffled twice, not fancy but so fluid and natural you barely noticed him do it. It was as simple as pressing his hands together. It often gave others at the table a vague feeling of unease, imperceptible and nagging. Chaz knew why. It was because everything else Mason did came off as unnecessarily elaborate, overly difficult. Only when shuffling did he seem in control.

"Stacking the deck?" said Chaz.

Mason used to let that get to him, Chaz using his own dead father to mess with Mason's focus. But he'd have done the same— any way under the skin was fair game.

Chaz's dad was known as Tenner because he'd bet on anything— stars in the sky, chicken wings in a pound, words in a newspaper headline, or that he could get himself on the front page the very next day. "Let's put a tenner on it," he'd say.

To Chaz and Mason, he was like the last of the old-time men— with scars, stories, and secrets. He was born on Vancouver's west

side before the yacht clubs and coffee shops, even before paved roads. There was a photo of his father, Chaz's grandfather, on a horse in the front lobby of city hall. He'd ridden it there from his boondock house, just for a drunken laugh.

Tenner had spent his life doing things for a drunken laugh. He'd had a few steady jobs—helped build bridges, ran a crew of high-wire guys for the telephone companies. At work he wore a saber in his belt, just for the hell of it, and nobody suggested he shouldn't. At various times he was a biker, a gangster, a mercenary, a drinker, and always a player.

When he caught Chaz and Mason and other underage boys drinking beers in the back alley, Tenner drove to the liquor store in his '59 Galaxy and came back with a gallon jug each of Ruby Red, Slinger's Grape, and Bounty—"The Taste of Exhilarating Adventure."

"If you mugs can siphon this and keep on breathing, than you deserve to be boozers," he said. Mason took this cryptic challenge to heart. He outdrank them all and was the last one found, in the bushes by the yacht club, just as the sun was coming up.

"A soft spot for this one," said Tenner, as he lifted him up. Somehow, through all the red wine and vomit, Mason heard him, and he loved him like a hero.

After school, Tenner taught Mason how to play poker with the big boys. Chaz sat there grinning as Mason lost his allowance, then his textbooks and gym clothes. He learned how to laugh when he lost, how to walk home without his shirt, a fire in his guts.

When Mason was seventeen, Tenner threw a poker party. All Chaz's gang from high school was there, as was Tenner's crew—roughnecks from the old days. Mason showed up drunk and high on mushrooms. Chaz was busy with some girl in the living room. Tenner said Mason could play, and he took a seat between Sam the Chinaman and Straight Ron, smoke circling up through yellow light, chips clicking together like coins.

He lost, lost again, and kept on losing. The mushrooms amplified everything—the sting of the loss, the smirk. He wanted more than anything to impress Tenner, and instead he was almost out of money.

When it came to his deal, Mason gathered up the cards. Tenner

was holding court—telling a trademark story. Mason, meanwhile, had found the aces, slipping one in every sixth card as he shuffled. And now he was dealing them, snapping them down on the felt. As he dealt the second round, Tenner reached his arm across the table. He laid his hand on the deck.

"Let me deal it out," he said, interrupting his own story.

It was supposed to be down, but Tenner turned the next one up.

"That's a deuce for me." Flip. "A cowboy for Sammy." Flip.

"Crabs for Lou . . .

He lifted the next card slowly then slammed it down in front of Mason.

"*BOOM!*"

The ace was face up. Tenner reached over and grabbed Mason's down card.

"*BOOM!*" he said, turning another ace.

Sam the Chinaman pushed back his seat. Mason's mushroom high was now a sweating, heartbeating hell. The faces around him were morphing from good ol' boys to demons who'd finally got a hold of him. He was only seventeen, but that's how it felt: *finally*. And *done for*.

Tenner stood up and put his large hand on Sam's chest. With his other hand he pointed his finger like a pistol at Mason. "And *boom*," he said.

The air went out of the room.

"If you're going to stack the deck, you should at least learn how to do it."

Mason tried to talk, made no sense. Then he was up, pushing through the party, out the door, escaping into the night air.

He never cheated again. It wasn't the humiliation, the fear of being gutted, or a sudden injection of ethics that did it. It was Tenner's disappointment.

Tenner deserved a kick-ass, blaze-of-glory kind of death. Instead, the doctors kept cutting off pieces of his liver until finally he died. Chaz was too broken up to talk, so Mason delivered the eulogy, and he told that story. In a church full of goons, poker players, fishermen, Vietnam vets, hunters, and good ol' boys, he confessed that Tenner's sharp eye had turned his son's stupid friend into an honest man.

When Chaz left town after the wake, he ended up here, with the Toronto Berlins. He'd heard plenty about them over the years, but didn't know how much to believe. There'd been a split in the family before he was born. It turned out that the Toronto contingent didn't have Tenner's dilettante spirit. They were gangsters through and through.

Chaz figured it would have made his dad happy—the reunification of the Berlins. So he set to work. And now he was pretty much running things.

Mason tried to carry Tenner's legacy in a different way. The plum incident was a good example. Just last week, Chaz had invited him to a house party an actor friend was throwing. There was plenty of booze and pretty people and, on a counter in the kitchen, an arrangement of very small plums. Mason began to hold court in the kitchen, Tenner-style, eventually turning his attention to the bowl of fruit. "I'll bet I could put eight of those in my mouth," he announced.

The first six went in okay, the seventh a bit trickier. While attempting to push the eighth and final plum past his gums, plum number one slipped from the pack into his windpipe. And there he was: eyes suddenly bulging, a horrible, panicked wheeze coming from his throat. He grabbed at people, hands flailing, gesturing toward his fruit-filled face, but they just laughed. He tore at his mouth, jaw jammed tight, then began to pound on his cheeks to crush the plums, to make some room. It seemed to work, and then he was pulling them out, desperately—like babies from a fire. But plum number one would not dislodge. The actors laughed as he ran out of air.

This, he thought, *is how you go? Death by fucking plum!* That gave him enough of a jab—sent him lunging across the kitchen, gut first into the edge of the counter. The plum shot out, hitting the window above the sink with a squishy thud—a champagne cork flashing through Mason's mind.

Just then, Chaz had entered the room. "I almost died," gasped Mason.

"What else is new," said Chaz.

The others were cheering and laughing. He felt like a complete idiot, and Chaz was right: It was not a new sensation.

And neither was this one: the feeling of losing at cards—the smoke rising, chips skimming across the table, Chaz's eyes flashing, his taunts, clubs and spades, a heartbeat, music, silence, the bet and raise and then call . . . It was easy to get under his skin, into his head, open it up, letting stupid things through: mushrooms and Tenner, funerals and plums, then Warren and birds and birds and birds . . .

And money.

By 4 A.M. he'd lost it all. And now Chaz was gone and Mason was left with that soul-destroying combination of panic and emptiness that often came with a big-money loss. Then something ran right over it. The rush of playing was dead, the drugs would only do so much, and so here he was, point-blank thinking of Warren:

Did he need the letter to do it?

Or did he do it because of the letter.

Either way, you sort of killed him.

Fuck that! It was him. *He played you from the start.*

Just go to the cops. Tell them about the five grand.

Five fucking grand! He could have paid a helluva lot more than that. It's not as if he was saving up for anything . . .

That's a terrible thought! I need a drink.

You should sleep.

How the hell am I going to sleep?

You should write.

I need another line.

17

WHEN THE sun came up, Mason was in his underwear standing in front of his desk, shaking, drugs dripping down his throat. He heard a voice: "It's all yours. It's all yours. It's all yours, sweetie pie . . ." Outside the window at the apartment's far end, he saw a man on the roof with a cat on a leash. And he was talking to it: "It's all yours. It's all yours . . ." The sun was rising behind them. Mason wanted to talk to someone. He thought maybe the

roof-cat man had been sent for this purpose, so he rapped on the window. The cat looked up but the man didn't. Mason banged the window harder. Still nothing, and the sky was filling with rose-colored light. He left his apartment, pushed open the fire escape door to the roof, and stepped out into the morning. The door clicked behind him. Locked.

The roof man and the leash cat were nowhere to be seen. Standing on the dirty tarmac he looked out on the city, burning time before he'd have to face facts: He was fucked-up, locked out, and stuck on a roof in nothing but his underwear.

At least they were boxers. Unfortunately they were red, with monkeys on them. *Monkeys.* He felt like he was falling over. He steadied himself, then walked carefully to the edge of the roof and sat down. Everything felt undone—not just unraveling, but like he'd left things hanging, forgotten them all over the world: a kettle boiling in Honduras, a van double-parked in Chicago, his mother's birthday, a soldier hanging off a bridge by his fingers, hot dogs burning on the grill . . . and more profound, buried, unnameable things. But trying to locate these abstractions seemed silly. There was enough to figure out right here, in the present, nearly naked on a third-storey roof.

He looked around. The roof itself didn't offer much—not even a loose brick he could use to break the window. There was the fire escape, of course, down three floors to the back alley. But then what? People were on their way to work now. What would he do? Stand there in his monkey underwear, begging for a quarter to call a locksmith?

Atop the Mental Health, Alcohol, and Drug Center rose a large moving billboard. Mason knew it well, as he could also see it from inside his apartment. *Oh, the inside—those were the days.* On the billboard was an apparently dissolute, frowning woman. Above her, black letters read GRAY SKIES ARE GOING TO CLEAR UP . . . The sign revolved, and as it did, the woman turned from sad to joyous. SO PUT ON A HAPPY FACE! Then, beneath it: TO BOOK AN ASSESSMENT, CALL 1-800-TO-MHAD, OR VISIT OUR CENTRAL LOCATION.

He thought of monkeys again, and the pamphlet with the drunken, stoned chimpanzee. He looked down at his boxers, then

GHOSTED

57

at the giant manic woman on top of the building across the street. And then Mason saw the path ahead of him: down the fire escape, through the alley, across the street, and into the MHAD building.

It was a good plan for a lot of reasons. Shimmying down the escape, he commended himself. Time out in the open would be limited—just the few seconds it took to cross the street. And once on the other side, he was practically there—he just had to make it through the gates, across the yard, and in through the sliding doors. If you couldn't be strung out and mostly naked in the center for madness and drugs, where could you? They probably wouldn't blink an eye.

People out on Spadina, though, they sure were blinking, and it was taking him longer than he'd foreseen to cross—it was a very wide street, after all—parked cars, two lanes heading north, a turning lane, two sets of streetcar tracks, two lanes heading south, then another row of parked cars. *That's nine lanes of traffic, for God's sake!* Plus, he'd stepped on some glass in the alley, so now he found himself hopping as he tried to cross the street. It was like *Frogger* (if, instead of a frog, the video game had featured a full-grown man in red monkey underwear). Tires screeched. A bell clanged. Mason looked up to see a streetcar full of people staring down at him. It seemed everyone—not only on the stalled streetcar, but driving and on the sidewalks, too—was talking into a cell phone. He thought maybe they were talking about him, even reporting him to someone, then decided he was just paranoid. Being too high with too little clothing will do that to you.

There was a woman on the grass in front of the MHAD building. She was humming, a Ms. Pac-Man towel tied around her neck like a cape. As he passed she frowned, then smiled, like the lady on the billboard. There was a large ashtray on either side of the entrance, and a man was checking them both, the automatic doors opening and closing as he paced back and forth. Mason prepared himself—then timed it right and made it past the ashtray man, through the open doors.

It was a big foyer with a semicircular desk in the middle. There were other people in the background, in and out of doorways, but Mason focused on the large desk, striding straight toward it. Since calling an $800 bet against three kings, six hours earlier, it was

the first thing he'd done with real conviction. His appearance, no doubt, would trick them into thinking he was mentally unbalanced, or a drug addict. They'd be compelled to help him out.

Then he saw the woman behind the semicircular desk and realized he'd misjudged the situation. It wasn't exactly panic on her face—more emergency resolve. Like the people on the street, she was muttering into a handset, but hers was a walkie-talkie, and she was looking right at him. So this was the answer: Apparently there was *nowhere* you could be strung out and mostly naked. He'd have to play it cool—take it down a notch.

"Good morning," said Mason. "I would like to book an assessment."

There was something humming next to him. It was the woman who'd been sitting in the grass. She was holding the Ms. Pac-Man towel in her arms now. She stood on her toes to speak into his ear.

"She eats ghosts," said the woman, then tied the beach towel around his shoulders, like a cape.

"Thank you," said Mason. She stepped aside, still humming, and a man in uniform took hold of his elbow.

18

CHAZ WAS waiting for him in front of the building, dangling his keys like a sadistic jailer. "Nice outfit."

Mason was in sweatpants, running shoes and a yellow hoodie, the Ms. Pac-Man towel tucked beneath his arm. "They didn't have a lot of selection," he said and took the keys from Chaz.

"Why didn't you just call me?"

"Things got complicated. I'm okay, Chaz. Really."

"All right. You let me know if you're not."

Chaz left, and Mason let himself in.

All things considered, it could have gone worse. A doctor had "formed" him, which meant they were allowed to keep him in hospital, against his will, for up to seventy-two hours. Fortunately, though, it hadn't taken long to persuade them he was neither a threat to himself nor to others. He explained about the sunrise, the

cat on the leash, and the difficulty crossing Spadina. They'd given him some clothes, then put him in a room with nothing but his thoughts—not even a doorknob.

It had only been one night, but a lot had happened in that empty room. By morning the thought of Warren meant something different. All his thoughts, in fact, had shifted.

After a small breakfast, a nurse named Danny had sat down and talked to him. They would let him leave, he said, as long as he booked an assessment and follow-up. "Usually you have to wait a few weeks, but we can get you in sooner."

"Great," said Mason.

They'd written down some information, given him some more pamphlets, then let him use the phone to call Chaz. It all seemed like a lot of trouble just to get back into his own apartment—but now, finally, he was home again.

His new outfit smelled like someone else. He took off the clothes, folded them—along with the Ms. Pac-Man beach towel—and put on some of his own. He walked to the center of the room and sat down on the floor, trying to cross his legs lotus-style, closing his eyes. After a few minutes he got up, poured a glass of whisky, and drank it down. Then he yelled, for no reason at all. It shocked the hell out of him. In the front window's reflection he saw the surprise on his own face, and he started to laugh.

Notes on the Novel in Progress

To keep in mind:

Transformation. How does the main character change over time?

Possible insert:

A typical day for our (anti?) hero.

To research:

Funerals. Antipsychotic meds. Card tricks. Different types of squirrels. The amount of cocaine you can do before your heart explodes.

Possible title:

Life After Birth

19

MASON WAS quietly stunned by his inability to run a business even as simple as this one. It had got to the point where he was dragging his fiberglass fedora to the Matt Cohen Parkette just in time for lunch, then packing it up when he got itchy or hit the sweats—usually between 3 and 4 P.M. He was making barely enough to cover his costs. Fortunately, Fishy didn't come around much since the fuzz had been there.

Some days Mason didn't work at all. He slept and slept. Waited until the weight of his body ached against the mattress so much that he had to stand up. He drank several glasses of water, pulled back the curtains. Let the light shine in. He looked at the day and felt like he might throw up. He got dressed and went for a walk. There was a small park in the middle of Kensington Market that reminded him of Richard Scarry's Busytown—every kind of folk doing every kind of thing—mohawked punks playing guitar, old Chinese women doing tai chi, a man on a unicycle being chased by small children, a circle of fishmongers smoking from a hookah, painters with their easels and watercolors, young Wiccans with their sticks and stones, fire jugglers juggling, dealers dealing, drummers drumming, drinkers drinking, all together in the same small frame.

There was a statue of the actor Al Waxman there, and Mason sat beside it on a bench, staring at the birds as they pecked in the grass. He found a newspaper box that suited him, and then a diner or restaurant, ordered a coffee, then another, something to eat. He lingered over the most disturbing newspaper articles, reading some of them twice. He finished his meal, left the newspaper and a ten-dollar tip, and walked back toward his apartment.

He stopped at the liquor store, then the Lucky Save to get some poppers—amyl nitrate disguised as an ancient Chinese remedy. Most of the convenience stores in Chinatown had them—little brown vials beside the cash register: *impulse purchases.* Mason, impulsively, bought a half dozen. Then he dialed Chaz's number.

While he waited, Mason tried to think.

He knew how to win. It was all about the Warrior Monk. The Warrior Monk won because he didn't care. He was careful, carefree, and ruthless. His head was always in the zone. Sometimes Mason felt like that before he played—that perfect mix of clarity and confidence, and then the cards were like quick love notes passed into your hands. You could fight demons or bullets with hands like those. That was how you won.

But poker is a cruel game, most of it played before the cards are even dealt. The more you care, the more you lose. The more you lose, the more you need to win, the more you care, the more you lose. That is called being "on tilt," and it is a vicious cycle—the opposite of Zen. Mason had been on tilt for a while now.

The only way to break the cycle was to not care. But no matter how he tried, he just couldn't trick himself into it. He owed so much damn money . . . *A Warrior Monk wouldn't care about such things*. But a monk didn't have to worry about the rent. A monk didn't have to worry about his drug habit and how much all this booze cost and keeping the condiments fresh.

Mason did a line, then cracked open a popper and inhaled deeply. The coke and nitro mix sent shivers through his brain stem. The rush was intense, and for a moment he felt something more than Zen. He felt kingly. Godlike. Powerful.

And then Chaz arrived.

After a while, Mason was losing. He'd bought back in twice for $1,000. Chaz had humped his chair as he counted it out, and now he was composing an opera. Its main theme involved Mason's lack of prowess: mostly in the ways of courtship, lovemaking, rational thought, and Texas hold 'em. Right now his aria went something like: *"Why is he so bad? Tell me tell me tell me, why so bad, at ev-ry-thiiiiiing?"* Chaz had a mountain of chips.

There was $200 in the pot and the flop was yet to be dealt. Mason had an 8 and an ace. They both checked.

Mason dealt it: 8, 8, 2.

He checked. Chaz bet $800.

Mason sat there. His measly hand had become a great one. Three 8s would kill just about anything. So he pretended to think as Chaz worked on his opus—alternating tenors building: *"The sad man thinks (watch him think watch him think watch him think) nothing to do (to do to do to do) but go all in or fold! Already lost $3,000 toniiii-ight (he should fold he should fold he should fold . . .) But no! His stupid heart—his hot dog cart! He'll lose it all—never get laid again (he should go all-in, go all-in, go all-iiiiiiiiiiiiin . . .)!"*

"All in," said Mason.

The sudden quiet had nothing to do with the calculating of odds—just Chaz trying to figure out a suitable operatic bridge. Mason was feeling good. He was about to win—big time, as long as Chaz went in. Sure he'd still be down, but his losing streak was over, and he could work from that blessed, fragile point.

"Another tragic mistake! The hot dog hack has done it again, done it again, done it again . . ."

Chaz was trying to get a read on Mason, who stared steadily back at him until finally Chaz ended on a lame, ill-thought note— *"He's blown his load!"*—and pushed his chips all in.

Mason turned his cards, for three 8s. Chaz flipped a jack and ace, for nothing. "Flippin' deal 'em out," he said.

There wasn't a straight or a flush to be had. "What happened to all the singing?" said Mason, then turned up a jack.

Chaz pointed his finger at Mason. *"One more jack, and you're my bitch (my bitch my bitch my biiiiitch). How lucky, it iiiis, that I alreeee-ady-like-you."*

Mason laughed, because the final crescendo was better than he'd expected—and also there was no way they'd hit another jack. The odds were astronomical: like finding God in a bowl of Shanghai noodles.

"Eat it up," said Mason and flipped a jack.

Neither of them moved or breathed a word.

Chaz had left with all the money. The Warrior Monk was dead.

Mason couldn't trick himself into not caring. Just two weeks, and he'd lost every dollar of Warren's five grand. All that blood money. He could have paid off Chaz, worked less on hot dogs, more

on his novel. It made him furious. The only way to ever win was having enough to lose.

That's how Chaz did it. It bugged him how much money Chaz made. And the fact that Chaz didn't snort the stuff himself made it even lousier. Mason had vowed he'd never become a dealer, but he'd broken a lot of other vows—that's what happened if you went around vowing haphazardly like a carefree, careless monk. So what had he become instead?

A vagrant. A cokehead. A drunk.

A guy who sells hot dogs.

A lousy gambler. A hack.

Yeah, that's way *better.*

As he had another drink, as he did another line, as he shuffled the cards, Mason's anger grew. It had been expanding slowly since his night in that empty room. But now it grew in spades, and as it did its focus shifted from Mason, to his predicament, to the late Warren Shanter. It rose up and set upon the dead man like a dog who'd been kicked in the head.

He screwed you over.

He lied to you. He took advantage of your kindness—your desire to help people. And he turned you into a chump.

A love letter, for Christ's sake! You are *a chump.*

And Warren knew it.

He used you. He bought and sold you. The money's all gone and so is he, and now you're going to hell.

What else is new?

The question is, What are you going to do about it?

The anger snarled around him. The wind was blowing outside, banging against the windows. Across the street the MHAD billboard turned. A drink, a line, a shuffle. The wind, the snarling, the pieces turning . . .

Then click—the image snapped into place

And suddenly he could see it: his very own billboard.

He put down the cards and walked to the desk. The sun was rising. A car alarm went off. Mason looked out the window. The man with the invisible kite was there, his arm tugging at nothing. Mason sat down and began to type.

Are you at the end of your rope,
or do you plan to be?
Contact www.ghostwriter.com

So life ain't worth living?
And your writing skills suck?
Try www.thelastword.com

Given up hope?
Don't give up your legacy.
Go to www.eternalspin.com

Ready to throw in the chips?
Shock and awe them all.
Check out www.prosetodieby.com

So you're going out in a blaze of glory,
Let 'em know why.
Go to www.weneverknewye.com

The gray skies may never be clear,
But at least your letter should be.
Contact www.GhostMason.com

Hell, what do you have to lose?

Who wants to tell old Aunt Sarah?
Joe's run off to Fire Lake.

The
Third

Introducing:
Sissy, the Doc again, the Cave,
and the QT room

20

"You can call me Sissy."

"Is that your name?"

She glanced around as if checking for spies in the fluorescence. There was a Harvey's burger joint in the building next to where Mason lived, and he loathed going in, though sometimes he had to—for morning grease salvation. But this one was possibly the worst Harvey's in existence. Those in the know called it Ho-vees. Those in the know were hookers, johns, junkies, dealers, cops, and a few purgatorial employees.

"My dad named me Circe. Like from the *Odyssey* . . ."

Mason hoped she hadn't noticed him wince. He couldn't picture a less Circe-like woman. There wasn't a tempting thing about her.

"I guess he thought it was funny or something." She took a small sip from her little peel-back cup of apple juice. "He's a poet."

"I don't much like poetry."

"Then you'd hate my father. He's actually kind of famous . . . You know what the kids in school used to call me?"

Mason waited, hoping he wouldn't have to say "What?" He took a sip of his milk shake and swallowed. "What?"

"Circle," she said, eyes leveled, as if daring him to laugh. She was the roundest person he'd ever met. "Just call me Sissy, okay?"

"You got it."

It had been over a week since he'd discovered the website: TheWay-Out.com. The home page read *"A forum for those with final thoughts."*

There was a "Hall of Infamy" with bios of Spalding Gray, Sylvia Plath, Hunter S. Thompson; a "Do it yourself" section (which Mason had skipped); and then, at the bottom, a classifieds page. It contained the same sort of ads you'd find at the back of an urban weekly. But here even the most banal of announcements carried an ominous tone:

FOR SALE: MATTRESS, COUCH, AND TV (AND SOME OTHER
THINGS) — AVAILABLE IMMEDIATELY.

WANTED: CARVING SET, PREFERABLY SILVER
WITH IVORY HANDLES.

CAT-SITTER NEEDED.

Mason realized his own ad need not be detailed. The site itself would supply the necessary context. And so he kept it simple, and vague:

PROFESSIONAL GHOSTWRITER AVAILABLE, FOR NOTES
AND LETTERS. RATES NEGOTIABLE.

Then his new email address: GhostMason@hotmail.com. All messages sent to this address would be automatically forwarded to his primary account.

By "rates negotiable" he meant "as much as you've got"—his theory being, if someone required his services, then, logically, they'd have no use for money.

Sky's the limit, he'd thought, then shivered.

But now, with this round girl sitting across from him, holding nothing but apple juice, the limit seemed a helluva lot lower. Somewhere near the fluorescent lights.

"Is this really the best place to talk about this?" He fished with his straw for the milkshake dregs, then pushed the cup away.

"We're not even talking about anything," said Sissy. "And yeah, this is the best place. Everyone in here is either loud or passing out, so they don't listen to anything. And they don't look at you like you're disgusting."

Her girth spilled over one and a half Harvey stools. Her hair

looked as if she'd colored it with a mix of oil and watery rust. It fell over her eyes, and the acne on her cheeks and chin looked like it had dripped there from her bangs.

"You sure you don't want a burger?" asked Mason.

"I don't eat fast food."

"Well, I'm going to get one for myself, okay?"

She shrugged, and Mason walked to the counter. "High School Confidential" was playing out of fuzzy speakers. It was evening outside, but here in the yellow light, people carrying trays back to tables, glaring and grumbling, it felt like lunchtime in a homeless shelter. He was regretting his decision to come here sober.

Mason paid his money and picked up the tray—a bacon burger, an apple juice, and a Diet Coke. He turned and looked at Sissy, who was looking down at the metal table in front of her. And suddenly this—on the surface much better than many he'd lived—felt like the most depressing moment of his life.

"I got you another apple juice," he said, putting the brown tray on the yellow table.

"Oh, thanks."

He sat down. "What can I do for you, Sissy?"

She looked at the empty juice container in her hand, placed it on the tray. "I dunno."

"Well, you contacted me."

"Well, you posted the ad."

They looked at each other. It might have been his imagination but, for an instant, Mason thought he saw the glimmer of a joke in her eye. He took a bite of his burger, then another. He wasn't hungry at all. Sissy reached for the apple juice.

"Back in a second," said Mason. He went into the bathroom, into a stall, dumped some powder onto the toilet tank and did a quick line. Within moments he was back at their table.

"Okay." Sissy looked up at him as he laid out his terms. "Here's the deal: I don't want to know your last name. I don't want to know where you live. I don't want to know how you're going to do it." He stopped, letting that last one echo. This was how he'd practiced it.

"What *do* you want?" said Sissy.

"I want to know everything else—enough for me to write a good letter. And at least $5,000 . . ."

He'd decided this was the best way to do it. If she made like this was nothing, he'd finish the sentence "as a retainer . . ." then go ahead and raise his fee.

"What do you mean, at least?"

"The more you can pay, the more time I can spend with you," he said. It just came out—so sickly intuitive, so base and brilliant. He felt the coke move through him.

"How do I know if you can even write?" said Sissy. "I mean . . ."

"It's all I do!" said Mason.

It was like a bark, and they both went quiet. Sissy slowly peeled back the tin foil seal and looked into her apple juice. "Me, I don't do anything."

To: Sissy84@hotmail.com
From: GhostMason@hotmail.com
Subject: Portfolio and Invoice

Sissy,

In answer to your (valid) question, Can I write?, here are some samples of my work. I am also attaching an invoice per our agreement.

-- Mason D

It had taken Mason a half dozen attempts to come up with these two sentences, then the invoice attached:

Invoice #005:
$6,000 payable, in person, to author for services rendered.
Payment will be made by Sissy, in two installments:
    1) half upon receipt of this invoice
    2) remaining half upon acceptance of manuscript.
Both payments will be made in cash.

They'd decided on this amount, awkwardly, after Sissy had declared, "I've got *some* money."

The attached portfolio included five writing samples. Mason had meant to just glance over what he was going to send to her, but then he'd had some drinks and sat there reading all of it.

There were two short stories he'd had published (one about a teenage security guard who buries his beloved father behind the factory he's hired to guard, and the other about a drunken American who becomes the mayor of a small Mexican town because they think he's Santa Claus), a feature magazine article about a deaf bull rider with whom Mason had spent a week on the circuit, the first chapter of his novel in progress (though he still wasn't happy with it), and the letters he'd written for Warren.

By the time he'd read it all, Mason was so high, it felt like the floor was beating beneath his feet, sending dull rhythmic shocks up into his gut. He did lines until the floor, his feet, gut, and heart pounded as one. Then he emptied some tobacco out of a cigarette, cut the last of the powder into it, tapped it down, gave a twist with his fingers and smoked it as hard as he could. He pressed SEND, drank three ounces of Scotch in two large gulps, then stared through the screen till the sun came up.

21

1. I feel isolated and alone.
2. Music is a gift from God.

He reread the section heading:

Socrates #4
Respond to these statements using the following model:
N = Not true at all
S = Somewhat true
E = Extremely true

"I don't get it."

The man (Mason had already forgotten his name) looked up from the desk. "What part?"

"What does *somewhat true* mean?"

"Oh, that. Just answer best as you can."

1. I feel isolated and alone.
2. Music is a gift from God.
3. I would very much like to belong to several clubs.

"By 'true' do you mean *applicable*?"

"What?"

"Like somewhat *applicable*, or not *applicable* at all?"

"Sure. Yeah. Do it that way."

Mason turned back to the questionnaire.

4. If I were a sculptor, I would not sculpt figures in the nude.
5. I sometimes drink more than I should at social functions or sports events.
6. The top of my head feels soft.
7. I have never urinated blood.

"Wow."

Silence.

"This is a weird section."

"Uh-huh."

8. At times I hear so well it bothers me.
9. I believe I dream in color.
10. I have little or no fear of the future.
This completes Socrates #4.

"Are there any more like this?"

"Excuse me?"

"For, um, Socrates #4?"

The man put down the file he was looking at. "You want more of them?"

"Do you *have* more?"

"Let me see." He picked up a spiral-bound book and flipped some pages. Then he started to read: "'This section is culled from a list of five hundred Socratic statements. They are designed to,

among other things, disrupt the subject's pattern of answering questions by rote. They also supply the trained Socratic analyst with a unique spectrum of personal information.'"

"So there's five hundred more of them?"

"Four hundred and ninety, apparently."

"Do you think I could get a copy?"

"What for, exactly?"

Mason imagined five hundred different people blurting out the first thing that came to them. He pictured their thoughts, scattered somehow throughout his novel. "I don't really know," he said.

"I'll tell you what," said the man. "You've still got . . ." he looked at the notebook—"nine more sections to complete your assessment questionnaire. Finish those, and I'll make a note—right here in your chart—that you're interested in acquiring the full list of Socratic statements. Okay? That way, when you come in for your assessment with the doctor, she might be able to help you with that."

"I thought this *was* my assessment?"

"This is just the preliminary," said the man, as if Mason was qualifying for the Olympics. "Go ahead and finish them up."

The rest of the sections were what he'd come to expect: lists of redundant questions regarding alcohol consumption and drug use:

> How much per day / per week / per month?
> How much alone / with friends / in bars?
> From mason jars / in the backs of cars?
> In a little how town / with up so floating / many bells down?

Then those old chestnuts, regarding the effects of such use:

> I have missed work or a work-related deadline.
> I have fought with friends or family members.
> I have experienced anxiety or memory loss.
> I have locked myself out, wearing red monkey underwear.

I Agree. Strongly Agree. Disagree. Strongly . . . On and on, till the nameless man said he was done.

22

Sissy thought for a while, then finally said, "I used to like horses."

This was in response to Mason asking her to tell him about herself.

"I read all sorts of stories about girls and their horses, and boys and their horses, when I was a kid. Do you remember that scene in *The Black Stallion*, at the beginning, when the Black Stallion is in the ship, and they're being so awful to him? All I dreamed about was having a horse like that to save. Are you even listening?"

"Yes . . ." said Mason. His skin felt itchy, as if there were flies on his neck. He, too, had once liked horses.

"So have you seen that movie or not?"

"I have." They were quiet. Then Mason said, "How about *The Man from Snowy River*?"

"I haven't seen it. Is it good?"

"I shouldn't have said anything."

"What?"

"I'm sorry. I think it's just this place. Do you think we could go somewhere else . . . Somewhere with a tree, maybe?"

"I don't know . . ." Sissy lifted up her little plastic cup. "I've still got some juice left."

"So bring it with you!" He said this like it was a daring idea.

Sissy thought for a moment. "All right," she said.

"Okay then. Great!"

"But I don't want to sit on the ground."

"No way. Near a tree, maybe. But definitely not on the ground."

"We could find a bench."

"A bench would be perfect!" He ushered Sissy and her apple juice out of the Ho-vees, into the cold sunlight and traffic outside.

They found a park with a bench near a tree. It was at the bottom of a grassy hill. They sat down. Mason waited for Sissy to catch her breath. Eventually she pulled an envelope from her pocket. "Your money," she said. "And I also brought you this." She handed him a folded piece of paper.

"What is it?" asked Mason—distracted by the weight of the envelope.

"It's one of my dad's poems."

He was about to take it, then stopped: "I don't want to know who he is."

"His name's not on it.'

"I might recognize the poem."

"I seriously doubt it."

He unfolded the paper.

CIRCE AND THE STALLION

You remember the waves like breath, but never will
See the ocean, the stables where the gods keep them
Pawing, their hooves sparking aqua blue, snorting hot breath from
Massive lungs, the stables, the ocean, the heat, the waves, all the same
    and so
You never even sweat.

But you guess at being a girl once, running breathless
Placing things in a box, an island with walls you could fill
With toy soldiers, a purple toenail, a funny sketch of your mother
You might have drawn, had you not become more lovely, so unearthly
You put the island in its place.

And when eventually came the stallion, it was indistinguishable
From the waves it crashed upon the shore breathing and beaten tough
With the burning of its own lungs, it sighed your name and made you
    run
For the first time, down to the edge of the water, the island, the earth,
    the box, the page
You picked up and wrote.

You rode it down the shore, in circles, Circe,
Then stumbled finally
On brine-covered, salty, wind-whipped glass.

The critics had loathed it, but Sissy loved the poem. She'd read it over and over, imagining herself on the back of that horse. She begged her father for riding lessons, and finally he relented.

On her thirteenth birthday, her father drove her out of the city, down gravel roads, to an enclave of paddocks and stables surrounded

by elm trees. "It was Utopia," she said. Standing in wood chips with six other girls, she waited on the horses. The woman who'd told them to wait was barely a woman—only seventeen or so—but she was the coolest, most beautiful person Sissy had ever seen in real life. Before she pulled it into a ponytail, her straight dark hair touched the waist of her riding pants. Her dark eyes were like cool coal, and the coil of rope swung down from her shoulder into her hand as she turned toward the stables. *I want to be her*, thought Sissy. And for a moment she didn't think at all about the other girls standing in the wood chips, the normal skinny six of them.

She didn't even give them much thought later that night, as she lay sobbing on the rug at the foot of her bed. She was accustomed to their sort of derision, and it was nothing compared to the shame she felt in the lovely face of the coal-eyed cowgirl. *She* was the kind who could save a wild stallion from a sinking ship, make it to shore still breathing, stand up, and meet his dark horse eyes with hers, mount him bareback and gallop o'er the glistening sand. Whereas Sissy was the kind who couldn't even hoist her fat round self onto a saddled, half-asleep nag. She'd tried, again and again, kicking and kicking her monster legs . . . and by the time the horse lady had managed to get a shoulder under Sissy's large butt to help hoist her up, the Normal Six were already laughing. Then she was on top of the old nag named Venus, tears welling in her eyes, reaching hopelessly for the reins.

"Here they are," said the horse lady. Her hands grasped Sissy's, and Sissy began to sob, thirteen years old, already slumped on the back of her dreams.

23

THE FILE was thick—full of all those answers he'd given. Mason could guess, more or less, what was on the first page:

Name: Mason Dubisee.
Age: 30.
Occupation: Writer / Hot dog vendor.

Health Card #: Not available.

Treatment for: Alcohol and cocaine.

Use in past 60 days: Extreme.

Duration of heavy to extreme use: 5 years, approx.

Arrests, parole, or court appearances: None.

Psychiatric history: Formed once. May 4, this year. Less than
   72 hours.

Drinks per week: 84.

Cocaine per week: 4.5 grams.

Willingness to decrease use: Unclear.

Risk to self: Moderate.

Risk to others: Low.

Managing day-to-day life: Moderate difficulty.

Isolation or feelings of loneliness: Quite a bit.

Depression, hopelessness: Quite a bit.

Fear, anxiety, panic: Quite a bit.

Confusion, loss of concentration, memory: Quite a bit.

Mood swings, unstable moods: Quite a bit.

Uncontrollable, compulsive behavior: Quite a bit.

Impulsive, illegal, or reckless behavior: Quite a bit.

Manic, bizarre behavior: A little.

Openness to treatment: Unclear.

Would like to belong to several clubs: Very unclear.

"You don't recognize me, do you?" said Mason, a half smile on his face.

The young doctor looked up from the file. "How are your tonsils?"

"Oh," said Mason. "They're okay. Thanks."

She turned back to the file.

Mason looked around. There was indirect light coming through the window. If one were to look out, across Spadina, one could see Mason's apartment building. He made a mental note to close his curtains.

The office was sparse. A few books, a framed picture of a girl with pigtails, some bottles and pill containers. On the wall was a diploma, a poster from the 1970s advertising cod liver oil (YOU ARE MY SUNSHINE!), and a laminated sign: NO NUTS ALLOWED!

Mason laughed.

The doctor looked up.

"Is that a joke?" he said, pointing to the sign.

"No. I'm allergic to nuts."

"Oh."

She turned back to his file.

"So what would happen? If like, I brought a bag of chestnuts in here?"

She put down the file and looked at him.

"Just asking . . ."

She sighed. "I carry an EpiPen at all times, but I'd rather not have to use it. So please refrain from bringing bags of any kinds of nuts in here. Do you think you can manage that?"

"Yes." Mason looked down at his lap.

The doctor picked up the file.

"It says here you came to book an assessment in nothing but your underwear."

"But I did book one."

"True."

"It's actually a chimpanzee, you know?

"What?"

"On the pamphlet you gave me—'get the monkey off your back.' It's actually a chimpanzee."

"Yes, I know."

She had a knack for making him feel stupid, but for some reason Mason liked talking to her.

"I thought you worked at that other place."

"The other place where I was working?"

"Uh-huh."

She closed the file and pushed back her chair. "Let's start over," she said. "Mr. Dubisee, I'm Dr. Francis. I am a family doctor, but I am also an addictions counselor. The model we use here at MHAD is one of harm reduction. Do you know what that means?"

"I think so."

"There are various kinds of help I can offer you, depending on what your goals are. What are your goals?"

"I'm not really sure."

"Okay. Well you did take the step to come here—so that's something. Tell you what: I'll present you with some possibilities. How about that?" Mason nodded. She leaned forward and opened his file. "Based on your history and level of use, I could recommend you to a medical detox." Mason swallowed. "It generally takes between five and ten days, during which time you would be in our care, under constant surveillance. It can be a difficult process, but highly effective. Unfortunately, spaces are limited, and we couldn't find you a bed, if you were interested, for at least another month."

"Oh," said Mason.

"One thing I would not recommend is that you quit cold turkey— at least not the alcohol. The cocaine, you can walk out of here and never touch it again—and physically at least, you should be fine. The alcohol is another matter. People die from stopping all at once. If you choose to go on the list for detox, I could find someone to counsel you until a place comes available. Does that interest you?"

"What about you?"

"Excuse me?"

"Could you counsel me?"

"Well, we can see about that. For now I need to know if you're interested in a medical detox."

"I think so."

"Well, all right then. We'll get you on the list, and how about you come in next week for a session, okay?"

"With you?"

"We'll see."

"What about the statements?"

"Excuse me?"

"From the questionnaire. Socrates #4."

Dr. Francis just stared.

"The guy who did the assessment said that if I came back, you'd give me some more Socratic statements."

She looked down at his file. "That's what this note is about?"

Mason nodded.

"You're kidding? I'm used to people trying to negotiate for drugs...."

"I've *got* drugs."

That looked almost like a smile on her lips.

"What do you want them for?" she asked.

"They're funny."

She took off her glasses. She *was* smiling. "Okay, Mr. Dubisee. If you don't mind sitting in the waiting room, I'll get you fourteen Socratic statements. That's two per day. Come back next week and we'll see about a refill."

"Can you make them random?"

"That's how they come," said Dr. Francis.

24

ON THE bench at the bottom of the hill, sporting an orange coat made round by her girth, Sissy looked like a giant gourd displayed in a farmers' market. Mason waved as he approached, then felt foolish for it—even more when she waved back.

"You look nice," he said, sitting down next to her.

"You look kind of like hell."

"Thanks."

"Tell me about the guy."

"What guy?"

"The one you wrote the letters for."

"I'm not sure . . ."

"You can tell the next one about me."

That creeped him right out, and to fend off the feeling he started to talk. He told her about Warren coming to his hot dog stand.

"You sell hot dogs?"

"Not as many as I should . . . but yeah." He told her about Warren's proposition, but left out the love letter part.

"So did he do it?" asked Sissy.

"Yeah. He did."

Mason expected her to ask how, but instead she said, "Did you like him?"

He looked down. There were three small daisies between his feet. He felt exhausted and queasy.

"Forget it," said Sissy. "You don't have to answer that."

11. *It matters to me what other people think.*
12. *Potable water often tastes salty.*

As far as Mason could figure it, Sissy wanted her suicide note to accomplish three things: to surprise people with the good things she'd done, to shock them with the bad, and to make them feel shame for how poorly they'd treated her.

Listening to her, it occurred to him that the good things she'd done were not much better than what he might put on a list of his own, and the bad ones nowhere near as bad. Her maltreatment by the populace, however, was a whole other story. Or rather, it was the story he had to figure out how to write. It was subtle, brutal, and seemingly unending—a string of scenes like the one she'd first described to him: young Sissy sobbing on the back of Venus, the Normal Six laughing with their mouths open.

"But don't write about that," she said, without offering a reason. In fact, each time Mason mentioned some story she'd told him, she said the same thing: "But don't write about that." It reminded him of the more frustrating magazine assignments he'd been given: great sources who'd suddenly remember that this was going to be published, then start stammering and contradicting themselves. It seemed Sissy didn't want to give any individual tormentor the credit. And neither was she interested in figuring out the cause and effect—the tricky equation of her misery. She wanted those who read her note to experience awe and responsibility and a guilty pain. She wanted her memory and her act to burn on people like a never-healing wound.

Sissy's Letter—Take One

I've quit this world that treasures nothing so much as beauty (which I guess makes sense, considering all the ugliness out there). Sure, beauty's a rare thing—but really, I think most of you are digging in the wrong spots.

And that's not just because of men like my father—who think striving for eloquence is somehow noble enough to make them *good*. For all his poetic pursuits, higher and lower—"a man of the people and graceful

aspiration"—he never really could look his baby in the eye, especially when he said, "You're beautiful." He said it a lot, then finally stopped, because he couldn't think of anything else to say. A real poet would have figured out the words and how not to loathe his daughter.

But really, Dad, it's not just you.

It's Ms. Meir, who always singled me out (as if the rest of the class was paying attention): "Dreaming of pie again, Circe?" she'd say, then send me home because the safety pins I'd used to fasten the busted zipper on my jeans were "obscene." When skinny Dylan asked what *obscene* meant, she wrote it on the board, and we had to look it up in our dictionaries while waiting for the hall supervisor to come and take me away.

It's Alphonse Lader, who stopped me in the hall on Valentine's Day my first year of high school, got down on his knee, and presented me with a large heart-shaped box tied with a red ribbon. I knew something was up. I wasn't that stupid. His buddies were there, too, and I just stood there holding the heart in the hall. "Open it!" they said. I shook my head and started to shiver. "Please," said Alphonse Lader, "be my Valentine." I hesitated, then pulled off the heart-shaped cover—inside was a jar of diet pills surrounded by two dozen packets of NutraSweet.

Crossing a street on the way home, I thought, *I can't believe he went to all that trouble*, then almost got hit by a car with all my laughing and crying.

"Tell me about your mother," said Mason.

Sissy laughed.

Mason was kind of strung out, and although he'd brought them both coffees, she'd said she didn't drink the stuff, and then she'd started to sulk. But now a laugh—that was good, even if he was being serious.

"I was being serious. I know your dad's a famous poet . . ."

"And a jerk."

"Right, but what about your mom?"

Sissy couldn't come up with much. Her mother had the makings of an apparition: a waif-thin woman with incandescent eyes who died when Sissy was ten years old. It seemed like she'd never been there at all—omnipresent but totally absent.

"But it's weird," said Sissy. "I don't really remember one thing about her. Not anything that ever happened—just that she was always there, looking at me. I don't know how to explain it. I'm not even really sure what she died of. I guess you could say she was beautiful. And skinny, too. She got skinnier and skinnier until they put her in a coffin that was way too big. Maybe she had an eating disorder or something."

"Haven't you asked your dad about it?"

"My dad's rich," said Sissy. Not only was this apropos of nothing, but she'd already told him this shortly after they'd negotiated his fee. "Do you want to know why?" asked Sissy. Mason figured it had something to do with him being a famous poet. "Lattack," she said.

"Excuse me?"

"It's for getting rid of lice."

"And what? Your dad invented it?"

"Nope. He just wrote them an ad."

"And . . ."

"You don't remember."

Mason shrugged.

Sissy seemed excited. "Oh, this is good," she said. "He came up with dozens of slogans and catchphrases—but it was all too confusing, or self-aware, or just plain creepy. Lice is a tough sell."

"I guess so."

"So, finally, at like meeting number six with the guys from the company, he threw up his hands and said, 'I don't know! *Lattack. It kills the buggers dead!*'"

"Holy shit!"

"Yeah. Yeah! You remember it now?"

"*It kills the buggers dead!*"

"It kills the buggers dead!" It was nice, in a strange way, to see Sissy engaged in something. Mason wanted to keep it going. "That was huge!" he said. "It was like *I've fallen and I can't get up!* Your dad made all his money just from that?" "That, then *Chase. It cleans teeth white . . . AmiCard. It makes your money rich . . .*"

"Yeah, I get it."

"I figure I could take over the business. I've got a bunch of them. Check it out: *Gin. It gets you good drunk fast.*"

Mason laughed and took a sip of his coffee.

"*Coffee!*" she said. "*It fills you full of beans.*"

"That's pretty good."

"You try one!"

"I dunno . . . Okay, how about this: *Ex-Lax. It gets rid of all the shit.*"

Sissy held up her hand and tilted it—like it was almost good, but not. "The trick is not to just be super obvious. It's got to be redundant, too. Like *Ex-Lax: You can shit out all the shit.*"

"Yeah. I see what you mean."

Sissy beamed. "I got another one. *Trojan. It keeps the unborn out.*"

"Or should it be *in?*" said Mason.

"What?"

"Depending who you're marketing to . . ."

"Oh yeah!" said Sissy. She blushed then started to giggle.

"*Trojan. Keep the unborn right where you want 'em!*"

Sissy laughed so hard she almost fell off the bench, and Mason had to grab her, then he was laughing, too.

"Sissy . . ." he said as they regained their breath.

"What."

"Are you sure you want to do this?"

She looked down for a moment, at her large round knees. When she lifted her head, the joy was nowhere to be seen—just anger flooding from her eyes.

"Fuck you, man," she said. "You already took the fucking money!"

"No, I know . . ."

"I swear: If you get stupid like this, I'll fuck you up. I will *fuck you up!*"

"I'm sorry."

"Just fuck off, man . . . I mean it."

Mason put down the coffee. Sissy got to her feet, then turned and began to climb the hill, staggering up as though she were bearing the weight of a wounded comrade.

13. *Sometimes I feel like more than one person.*

14. *Given the choice, I would buy a dress with patterns on it.*

Sissy's Letter—Take Two

There are too many of you.

Hundreds of pretty girls who started giggling once they'd passed me by.

Two thousand peers who called me "Circle."

A half dozen skinny equestrians who fell into the sawdust laughing when I couldn't mount a horse.

Bus drivers, doctors, store clerks, pot dealers, and people walking on the beach, who looked at me then looked away.

But for God's sake, you're thinking, not everyone is such an asshole!

And that's true. But also this: In almost twenty-five years, the instances of kindness, fun, and caring have been so rare that I can't wait for any more of them—or rather, I refuse to fucking wait. And this, too: I can't help noticing that those nicest to me are always the beaten-down buggers with nothing left to lose. I guess ugly is more acceptable when you're surrounded by it.

Mason felt bad for having upset Sissy. He wanted to make it up to her with a decent letter, but it wasn't coming, and now he was almost out of blow. He flipped open his cell phone and gave Chaz a call.

The doorbell rang. Still holding his phone, Mason walked to the window, pulled it open. He looked down into the street. "Now that's fast!" said the voice on the phone. He could see Chaz on the sidewalk, mouthing the words into his handset. Mason hung up. A minute later, Chaz was in his apartment.

"'Bout time you dropped a dime. Started to worry you weren't a drug addict any more."

"Nice to see you, too." He was curious as to why Chaz had been standing outside his apartment, but wouldn't give him the satisfaction of asking.

Chaz sat down and started shuffling cards. "Oh yeah," he said, as if in afterthought, and pulled out a dime bag of coke. Mason handed him $200. Chaz arched an eyebrow. "What's up, Marlowe? Sell another story?"

Mason nodded, then peeled off eight more hundred. "Square?" he said.

"Like Steven."

Mason dumped some powder on the table and reached for a card.

"Before you get all sniffy," said Chaz, "there's something I want to show you."

"All right."

He waved for Mason to follow him: out of the apartment, down the stairs, and out onto the sidewalk. He took a few steps to the right and stopped in front of Harvey's, closed since 11 P.M. He pulled out a ring of keys and unlocked the door. "I didn't know you were in the burger business," said Mason. They stepped into the vestibule. To their left was the entrance to the restaurant, presumably still locked. Right in front of them, however, stood a steel gray door. "After you," said Chaz.

Mason pulled the handle. A bulb flashed on, and he was descending a staircase, turning, down into darkness. The door clicked closed above. The flip of a switch. "Holy shit!" Mason looked into the soft yellow light. "What is this place?"

"I call it the Cave."

25

THE CAVE was everything a rogue could want: a long, fully stocked bar; a billiard and a poker table (both with brand new felt); a rounded stage, a DJ booth and plenty of dark corners. The color scheme was classic dingy brothel—walls painted black and burgundy, the shadows of wine-colored drapes. There were hovering spots of yellow light—over the poker table, the pool table, the bar.

They walked together, boot heels clicking, across the floor.

"What can I poison you with?" said Chaz.

Mason, still in awe, reached for a stool and sat down.

The bar was fairly high, like in a saloon. Chaz ducked down and came up with a bottle. He rolled out two tumblers, three ice cubes, three fingers of whisky in each. Then, next to Mason's glass, he placed a disc like a coaster, but stainless steel—a straight line of coke, and a straw.

"I like this place," said Mason.

"I thought you would."

"Is it just for me? Or you thinking of inviting other people?"

Chaz took a drink. "Wouldn't be fair to keep it to ourselves." He looked around, grinning. "This place is too good—don't you think?"

"How you going to do it?"

"Nice and simple: cards, coke, and booze. Two A.M. till noon, seven days a week. No daylight, no bullshit—just safe, dark fun. We open on Friday."

"Who's *we*?"

"Could be you and me—if you weren't such a snowbird."

Mason inhaled through his nose, put down the straw.

Chaz laughed. "So really just me. But you know how it is."

Mason didn't, in fact, know how it was. He would have said so, if he thought Chaz would clarify things. But every time he tried to learn about the urban drug trade, it proved too complicated and too simple at the same time. Mason had been in enough dens of iniquity to know how much he didn't know. You either grew up understanding how it all worked, like Chaz or Tenner, or you got popped early, then learned it in jail.

"Your place, though?" said Mason.

"My place, all the way."

There'd be other people connected to this and that—taking a cut, making things smoother—not friends, necessarily, or even partners, still a part of it nonetheless. But if it was Chaz's place, then he was the boss. That much, Mason knew.

"Why didn't you tell me about this?"

Chaz shrugged. "Surprise!" he said.

"What about the cops?"

"The cops'll love this place. You know how it is: People gotta go somewhere when the bars close—keep 'em off the streets. Maybe a visit or two, but I doubt they'd shut us down. Not unless somebody dies. Here—check this out."

Mason followed him into the dark recesses. A light switched on, illuminating a large garage door. "The scatterhouse exit—for when the raids come. There's a ramp up to the loading dock."

"Cool."

"That's nothing."

They walked back to the bar, one on either side.

"You want to see cool?" said Chaz, pouring two more drinks. He raised his glass. "To the Cave," he said.

"To the Cave," said Mason. He raised his tumbler and took a gulp. Then, lowering his drink, he stopped, cocked his head. "Chaz?"

Standing up on the midrail of the stool, he leaned over the bar. Nothing but floor. He got off the stool and walked around to the other side, bent down. There were bottles, some blow, a baseball bat . . . but Chaz had disappeared.

26

"CHAZ?" MASON looked around the bar. Then back at the floor under his feet. He crouched down again, looking for what, he didn't know. Suddenly there was a noise behind him and he swiveled and fell on his ass against the bar, bottles clanking.

"Holy shit!"

Where a moment before the wall had been, there was Chaz. He was leaning back in a chair like he was waiting for the cows to come home—one of his feet sticking out through the opening in the wall.

"Holy fucking shit!!"

"Yeah, you said that already."

"What the hell?"

"Come on in."

The easiest way to get through was just to roll, like in that scene when Indiana Jones almost loses his hat. So that's what Mason did. As soon as he was clear of the entrance, the wall slid back into place—quiet but with a heavy click at the end. It sounded final.

"Reinforced steel," said Chaz. They stood up and he flipped a switch.

"Holy shit!" said Mason, yet again. "What the hell is this?"

"The cave within the Cave," said Chaz.

The room was the size of an average jail cell, with many of the same attributes: a bunk bed against one wall, a small table and chair, a latrine in the corner. On one wall, a few books and an old tape deck. The shelving on the opposite wall, however, contained things not found in your average pokey: twenty gallons of water, a hundred cans of food, three handguns, and eight large bricks of Peruvian cocaine.

"I call it the QT room," said Chaz. He sat back down in one of the chairs.

"Why's that?"

"Because it's on the QT."

Mason nodded. On the fourth wall, the one they'd come through, was a window. It was large—about the same dimension and shape as the horizontal door—at eye level. He stepped toward it as Chaz dimmed the light again. Through the glass they could see everything—the bar, poker table, dance floor—the Cave outside the cave.

"It's one-way," said Chaz, tapping on the window. "That's two inches of bulletproof glass, and the same again on the other side. Bash it with a baseball bat, and you wouldn't hear a pat out there— not a pitter. These walls are a foot thick. Doesn't it feel like a space pod or something—like out there is the universe? *Ground control to Major Tom . . .*" He pulled out his cell phone. "Look, no reception."

Mason walked over to the shelves. "How about radio?"

"Nope."

He flipped open the tape deck. "Gowan? So if you got trapped in here you'd have to listen to Gowan for the rest of your life?"

"Only for a few months. Eventually you'd run out of food and water."

Mason shuddered. He sat down in one of the chairs and gazed out the bullet-proof window. "How'd you do this?"

"That safecracker I went to find. Montana, remember? Old crony of my dad's—he owed us a favor. He's the only one knows about this, and he'll be dead any day now. Cancer of the eye."

"And why, exactly . . . ?"

"You kidding? It's perfect. One whiff of the bulls and I'm

through the rabbit hole. We get busted, I only lose what's on the floor. Plus, it's just plain cool."

"No, I know that. But why are you showing me? If it's on the QT, I mean."

"Couldn't keep it to myself. That's the problem with a secret room: you got to let someone in on it—or else it's no fun. And let's say they bust me—I'd need you to come get the stuff out of here, right?"

"If you say so." He looked at Chaz. "So how do I get in?"

"That's the coolest part." He got up, walked over to the window, and put his left hand against the wall. A tiny green light, and the door slid open. "Right hand gets you in, left hand gets you out. Think you can remember that?"

Mason nodded, his mouth agape.

"We'll have to scan your hands."

"Naturally."

"Oh, and here," he said, moving to the other side of the glass. "An intercom—in case you want to talk to someone. But remember . . ."

"It's on the QT," said Mason.

Chaz just grinned.

Back on the other side of the wall, Chaz turned the scatterhouse lights on. Mason stood looking at the mirror. There was no hint, nothing to suggest that anything lay behind it. The glass appeared bolted to the wall. On this side, the intercom was in the ceiling, with the hand scanner—practically invisible—at knee level behind the bar.

"There's a sensor," said Chaz. "As soon as you're through the door, it closes. That's another reason I told you: something goes hinky and I get stuck in there, no one would ever know."

"So you're saying if that happens, the Cave is mine?"

"Very funny." Chaz brought the lights back down. "If it's been awhile, and you haven't seen me—you know where to look. I figure that place could turn into hell pretty fast."

"Most places can," said Mason. "Let's drink to it."

"Right," said Chaz and reached for a bottle. "Demons with demons."

It was something Tenner used to say.

Mason spent hours going over all the bad things Sissy had been
through, most of them pertaining in one way or another to her
body. He didn't doubt she was clinically depressed and hated her
life every single day, and so she was suicidal. Fine. He was supposed
to do his job and write her a letter. That was the deal.

But he couldn't see her doing it.

There were all sorts of people he could imagine killing themselves. He just had to look out the window to see madmen covered
in scabs, limping hookers, junkies with half-shaved heads—all
shouting out loud to die. It wasn't hard to imagine them diving
into traffic, ripping themselves to ribbons with a steak knife, jumping off whatever they could, shouting the whole way down.

But Sissy?

He pictured her at home, at night, in an apartment her father
paid for. Alone. In pain. Utterly alone. Sad beyond belief.

But then what . . . ?

It had been one of his stipulations: *I don't want to know how.* But
now he did. He wanted to see it. Thought maybe it would help
him write. What a strange fucking thing to think.

15. *There never was a time I liked to play with guns.*
16. *My parents were too loving.*

"How do you plan to do it?"

They were back under fluorescence, in clouds of fry oil and
steam: Mason's penance.

"Do what?"

"Kill yourself."

"Oh my, Mr. Shakespeare! What if somebody hears?"

"What happened to Mr. Hemingway?"

"Slipped while cleaning his shotgun. And anyway, I thought you didn't want to know about that."

"You're smart enough to write your own letter, Sissy."

"But then you wouldn't get paid."

"I'll give you back the money."

"Hara-kiri."

"What's that . . .?"

"Ceremonial gutting of the self."

"Are you serious? You really want to commit hara-kiri?"

"*Commit* is such a great word, don't you think?"

"Look, Sissy. I'm at your service. I really am. I'm just trying to figure it out. You understand how that's important, right?"

"Right. Okay. So I'm going to commit to committing hari-kari. Have you read *Shōgun?*"

"You're in a hell of a mood today, aren't you?"

"Just upping the dose, Mr. Dante—or was that his first name? You really think I've gotten this far without knowing my meds?"

"So you're stoned is all?"

"No more than you."

"And that's it?"

"That's it. I'm going to plunge a large blade into my chest, pull it down, turn the handle, push it left, then draw it all the way to the right. After that, my stomach will spill out, along with some other gut type things. I figure I'll need a real long blade to get to all of that. What do *you* think, Dr. Faustus?"

"He's a fictional character, Sissy."

"And what are you, Mason D?"

28

"SO, YOU'RE a writer?" Dr. Francis was looking at his file again. "You going to write me into one of your stories?"

"Uh . . ."

Did it say it on his T-shirt or something? I WANT YOU TO BE MY CHARACTER.

"Just don't use my name, okay?" She smiled, as if it was a joke.

"You got it."

"Seriously, though. What you need to do right now is focus on yourself."

Mason looked at her. A wavy tendril of brownish blonde hair had broken loose from the tuck behind her ear. It brought to mind a highway sign, a squiggly arrow. He imagined her looking into the reflection of her own eyes in the morning, trying to seem older. Her throat was smooth, freckles on her collarbone—but there *was* age, if you looked closely, in the tautness of her narrow shoulders. "I'll try," he said.

"What kind of things do you write?"

"You know . . . got a novel I'm working on. Like everybody else . . . Oh yeah, and I wrote a poem the other day!"

"You seem happy about that."

"No, just amused."

"It's a funny poem?"

"Not at all."

"Oh."

"But it was funny writing it. I hate poetry."

"I see. Do you enjoy writing, though?"

"When I'm high, I do."

"Do you always write high?"

"Pretty much—that and drunk."

"What if you weren't?"

"What do you mean?"

"What if you wrote sober?"

"I don't know . . ."

"Well, let's try."

Mason looked warily at the doctor.

"Do you use a computer?"

"Yeah . . . for the most part."

"Okay, so you'll do it by hand. I'd like you to start a notebook."

"I've already got one."

"Do you write in it sober?"

"Not particularly . . . No."

"Okay then, let's try this again. I'd like you to start a *new* notebook. We'll call it *The Book of Sobriety*."

"That's a terrible title."

"So come up with a different one—you're the writer. Anyway, what I want you to do is this: Every way you usually write, you'll do it differently. So instead of typing, you'll write by hand. If you write at night, you'll write in the day. I want you to change where you sit, what music you listen to, everything you can think of. And, most importantly, when you write in that notebook, I want you to do it sober."

"I don't know," said Mason. "I really hate journals."

"Did I say the word *journal*?"

"Nope." They looked at each other. "So what do I write?"

"What did you write in your other notebook?"

"Notes."

Dr. Francis just looked at him.

"On my novel, mostly. On the novel in progress."

"So not that," she said. "For now, I'll give you a topic, and you'll write me a little something. Okay? Don't worry about how good it is, or how well crafted, or whatever. It just has to be sober."

"Should be a real page-turner."

The doctor waited.

"Okay," said Mason. "What's my first assignment?"

"Your first memory," said Dr. Francis. "You can make it a poem if you want. Maybe even a funny one."

17. *I'm scared of people knowing things about me.*
18. *If I were a tree, I'd be a cut-down tree.*

29

IT WAS a thing of beauty, this Cave. Mason wondered if he should have told the doctor about it. If he was even partially serious about detox or rehab or harm reduction, or whatever the hell they were setting out to do, having this place a hundred yards away from his door was going to be an issue. But even with doctor-patient confidentiality, it felt wrong to say anything. Like a betrayal. And anyway, there was a good chance she already knew about the place, it being right across the street. Most of these people were probably her patients.

A duo of well-dressed lawyers had abandoned the nine-ball game to messily grope each other, pissing off the punks who'd been trying to get some trash talk going. A large Métis man in a trench coat was looming over the SpongeBob pinball machine, attempting to beat high score while snorting a series of lines off the flashing Plexiglas. Vlad the DJ put the needle to "Baby's on Fire," and Kristen—the cute slutty bartender—sang along as she cracked a Bud for Christian, the petite Haitian stripper.

The poker table was full—a blue, green, and black monster in the center of the felt; tumbling stacks; cards snapping; thick lines of coke on metal discs; cigarette packs; forearms with fresh tattoos still leaking blood; a card burning, then turning to the river.

In all corners the shadows were full: skids, capos, trannies, nannies, boxers, traders, waiters, goths, hookers, dealers, doctors, DJs, addicts, assholes, punks, bikers, cabbies, teachers, dancers, drunks, dilettantes, dentists, and debt collectors—Chaz's patrons, getting blasted in the early morning.

A thing of beauty, just beneath the Earth's crust: Plato's good old Cave.

30

"HERE," SAID Mason. He put the manila envelope on the orange tabletop. "You can go ahead and read it."

"I'll do it when I'm alone," said Sissy.

Warren said something like that.

"There's a few options here . . ." said Mason. "One of them's a poem."

"A poem?"

"Kind of a response to 'Circe and the Stallion.'"

"I'm not sure how I feel about an homage . . ."

"It's more a *fuck you.*"

Sissy nodded. "Your eyes look weird," she said.

It seemed as if Mason was about to say something. But then he didn't.

"Are you going to be okay?" she asked.

"Yes," he said, then got up and left.

19. *People will never change.*
20. *I would rather be a bird than a businessman.*

Two loud and skinny prostitutes push through the open door. Sissy gets up and follows them to the counter. She orders two bacon burgers, medium fries, and a milk shake.

Sitting back down, she unwraps one of the burgers. A few large bites, and her eyes are glistening—with tears or fluorescence, it's hard to tell. She opens the envelope and starts to read.

SISSY AND THE FUCKING STALLION

How about this: I disregard your bullshit myths and care
Not a piss where the gods might keep them, cuz
I take the horses anyway
I can, and I can change
Any verse structure, just by sticking a knife in
To packaging bubbles or a belly, believing, my sweet lords, that plastic
 surgery
Or suicide, if done on the trot—one of necessity, the other not—is the
 exact same
Fucking thing.

I once had hope, apologies at the ready,
That someone would save me or just give a smile
Every day every minute every stride through the sand
Ideas and courage, sonatas and throwing stars, the beat of hooves
Racing though my head, the ocean in all directions, the terrifying
 promise of a universe.
I get rid of it now—the sea brine, island, hope, and just Be
Heavy on a horse, breathing on his back, following that thud thud
Thud across the earth, until we all feel the same weight
Dead on the back of a stunning horse, in a poem, and not sorry any
 more
I love and hate you all
Giddy fucking up.

Joe's run off to Fire Lake.

The
Fourth

Introducing:
Sarah, Soon, and Willy,
and the Ghosts of Gauguin

31

MASON WAS sitting on the deck among the debris of nests, surrounded by dead baby birds, when Sarah showed up. She was carrying a beach towel. She didn't say anything, just sat down next to him. Every so often a mourning swallow dove at Mason. He watched it coming, trying to stay steady. Eventually he turned to Sarah. "Why aren't you at the lake?" he said.

She shrugged. "It got boring."

"I'm having a rough day."

"I can tell. It's time to stand up now." She helped him to his feet.

He looked at her. "Have you been crying?"

"No," said Sarah. "Come on. Let's go inside."

"My boots . . ."

"Don't look down. Not just yet." She led him into the kitchen and put a beer in his hand.

"Thanks."

"I'm going to go clean that up, okay, before the others come home. Then we'll go for a walk."

Mason nodded.

Sarah was his favorite cousin, named after his mother. He'd gone out of his way to be nice to her in the past, and today she was making up for it. He had a beer ready for her when she came back in.

"Thanks," he said. "I lost it there for a moment."

"No problem." She took the beer. "That was pretty gruesome." She tipped her head back and glugged half the bottle.

"Slow down there, cuz."

She wiped her mouth. "You're one to talk."

"Are you even old enough to drink?"

"In some provinces." She finished the bottle. "I hear you broke up with Katya."

"Come on," said Mason. "Let's take that walk."

They got two more beers from the fridge and headed back outside, swallows diving at both of them. They walked alongside the paddocks, Warren and Zevon trotting along next to them. "Does Zevon like beer?" said Sarah.

"I'd assume so."

She gave the horse a slurp and laughed. "Can we go for a ride later?"

"Maybe." They walked through the trees for a while, came to a clearing, then a cliff that looked out over the pasture. "Check it out," said Mason. "What does it remind you of?"

Sarah walked to the edge and peered down the steep slope. "The prize colt," she said.

"Ha! I knew you'd know." He took a swig of beer. Sarah did the same. They both looked down.

The Book of Sobriety

I don't know
To talk, to walk
My feet from a flower in a vacant lot
In the lap of a woman
Her long hair, a blue dress
I don't know rippling
From the sky, its cool safe breath.

"What do you know, baby?" she asks
And waits.
I know babies' bodies don't rot in back alleys under trash.
Eighty-five-year-old men don't jump out of hospital windows.

Soldiers don't hold Gypsy children by the ankles
And swing them against pillars
Until their heads break off.
Sightseers don't videotape drowning mothers.
Gunmen don't stage massacres at funerals
Or in quiet Indian villages.
People don't starve to death
Or beat you for your boots.

And I will never leave
This summer field of flowers.
But I don't know
To talk
To write
To say all this.

Her hand strokes my head.
"You'll know some day," she says
and smiles
the kindest smile
I don't know from my eyes
Scares me
For the first time in my life.

32

HE JUST wanted to sleep but couldn't. It felt as if someone were hollowing him out with a ladle, body and soul. He gasped and shook, like some feeble antihero in a comic book—*Drugs not working! Must . . . correct . . . body chemistry . . . find a way to . . . survive . . .* For no clear reason he was rolling cocaine, tobacco, and marijuana together, but kept spilling it all over his lap. *Must . . . roll . . . better!* Finally he made a smoke of sorts and lit it, the flame licking his cheek. He inhaled and turned on the computer. It felt as if there were someone crying in his chest . . . *Too low. Must get higher!* He cracked open a popper, inhaling deeply. Then another.

For a brief but thankful moment, a faint high lifted through him. He clicked on the Internet icon, then his email. At that instant the marijuana, coke, and amyl nitrate collided in his bloodstream— opposing mercenaries with the same damn purpose. Demons with demons . . .

He awoke beneath the desk. His shirt was off, as was one shoe, but he was still wearing his sunglasses. He pulled himself up onto the chair. A message was open on his computer screen:

To: GhostMason@hotmail.com
From: Soontobe@gmail.com
Subject: Dear Sir

How very novel — a morbid scribe for hire! I require, for my own personal project, someone discreet, artistic, and hesitant to use exclamation marks. Does that sound like you?

I think it does! I think that you might be just the man I'm looking for.

Sincerely,
Interested in ending it all!

Mason found a cigarette, lit it, gagged, then hit REPLY:

To: Soontobe@gmail.com
From: GhostMason@hotmail.com
Subject: Dear Interested in ending it all

What the hell are you talking about?

Sincerely,
Not feeling too good right now!

He pressed SEND, looked for his other shoe, couldn't find it, took off the one he was wearing, then stumbled over to the sink for

a dozen glasses of water. He was only partly hydrated when another message came through.

To: GhostMason@hotmail.com

From: Soontobe@gmail.com

Subject: Dear Not feeling too good right now!

Sorry to hear you're not feeling too good right now. Happy, however, to see that you have a sense of humor. (Do you, though? It's hard to tell in emails.)

Now, to your question: I am talking about the possibility of hiring you for — as I said — a personal project: a rather morbid one. Would you like to know more? I sure would, including your rates.

Sincerely,

Interested to know more,

and also in ending it all!

Mason belted down three more glasses of water, took some Alka-Seltzer, brewed some coffee, forgot to pour it, lit another cigarette, gagged again, then typed out another response:

To: Soontobe@gmail.com

From: GhostMason@hotmail.com

Subject: Dear Interested

I appreciate your interest.

My sense of humor is actually hurting quite a lot today, and I seem to have lost a shoe. I still don't really know what you're talking about, and I don't discuss business details, including rates, via email. I may be willing to meet with you — once I'm feeling better.

Sincerely,

Not feeling any better yet!

Mason turned off the computer, took off his sunglasses, then climbed the ladder to his bed.

33

THE COD liver oil girl smiled down from the poster on the wall. The doctor finished reading and looked up at Mason. "It's not very funny."

"You asked for my first memory," said Mason.

"I'm not sure it's that either."

"What's that supposed to mean? I remember it: sitting in the lap of a woman, her blue dress . . ."

"Sure. But the rest of it—don't get me wrong, it's a clever device: the negation of these unspeakable thoughts in the mouth of a child who can't talk—but it's also very distancing."

"You told me just to write!"

"Which you did. And I just read it." She picked up the notebook and looked at it. "It's very sad."

"Okay. Enough already! Next time I'll write a funny one!"

"Well, that's just it: In person you distance yourself with humor. And yet, here . . ." she turned the notebook to face him, "you contorted. You found a way to bring sadness—all the sadness in the world—to your very first memory. What does that tell you?"

Mason glared at her. She stared back at him, waiting.

"I'm sad," he finally said. "Is that what you want to hear?"

She shrugged slightly, in a way that made him crazy.

"My friend just killed herself!" It came out before he could stop it. "So—so I *should* be sad, don't you think?"

The doctor blinked. "I'm sorry for your loss." Mason took a breath, then nodded. "Do you want to talk about it?"

He shook his head.

"It must have been difficult to write this sober." Dr. Francis tapped the notebook with a finger. Mason nodded. "That must have taken a lot of strength."

His shame felt visible. He tried to turn it outward, to make it look like anger—but she'd opened his file now. "Hmm . . ." she said.

"What?"

She flipped the folder closed. "How are you sleeping?"

He stared at her. "Not well."

"No. I can imagine not. Do you dream at all?"

"Yeah . . ." He looked at the desktop. "They're pretty intense."

"Coke dreams," said the doctor.

"Coke dreams," said Mason.

"How about, for next week, you write me one of those?" She handed back *The Book of Sobriety*. "Have you thought of a better title?

"Not really."

"Well, you can work on that, too."

Mason got up to leave.

"Good luck, Mason. I'm sorry about your friend."

The Book of Sobriety

She is a different kind of Circe: a warrior—nothing Sissy about her. She's on a horse—and her size is ferocious, her belly bare beneath a bra made of bronze. She is riding into battle alone—a thunder of hooves moving toward her through the dark. The horse rears, and she pulls out her sword.

The air is full of ash.

The ash turns to fog, a fog so thick, the approaching army, though deafening, is still invisible—the rumble like an earthquake.

Then, out of the fog appears a rider on a motorcycle, speeding straight for Circe. The liquid air funnels around him, and his mirrored visor flashes. He is the man in the black helmet.

And he is coming.

34

"I *love* this place!" said the man sitting across from Mason. They were in Kensington Market, in a bar called This Place. Above their heads a surfboard with *license plate* scrawled across it was hanging from the ceiling. On the wall were dozens of license plates. He pointed to the one in the center. It read *SRFBORED*. "I come here all the time."

Mason nodded.

He was slight, with large eyes and olive skin. His head was shaved, and he wore a purple T-shirt beneath a brown suit jacket. He smiled when the server approached, and they both ordered a beer, then Mason asked for a double Jameson.

"Drinker," said the man, as if taking a mental note.

"I'm Mason," said Mason, and held out his hand.

"Soon," said the man.

For a dodgy instant Mason thought the guy was declaring his unreadiness to shake hands. "That's my name," he said. They shook.

"Soon?"

"Soon Sahala—but I'm usually right on time."

Mason nodded, as if it were a normal name and the guy hadn't made a joke. The drinks arrived. "What can I do for you, Soon?"

"I'm interested in your business."

"You mentioned that."

"For a per . . ."

"A personal project. Yeah, I know."

Soon pointed a finger at Mason as if to say "You got it, brother." Mason drank his whisky, then said, "From your emails, it doesn't seem like you need a ghostwriter."

"Perhaps not," Soon said, grinning. "I was thinking we could work on the note together." Mason waited. "You know . . . the suicide note."

"Most people don't smile so much when they say that."

"I like collaboration."

Mason stared at him. He took out a cigarette, put it to his lips, then flicked it back out. "I don't have a clue what you're talking about."

"Art!" said Soon, with a grand sweep of his arm, as if they were drinking beer in the Louvre. "I'm talking about Art! . . . and Death of course."

As it turned out, Soon talked about Art and Death for a living. He taught a course by that name at the university. "I used to be a big deal," he said, with only a hint of irony, "at least in the Toronto art scene. My forte was the filling of public space."

He meant this more literally than Mason realized at first. For one project he'd selected sixteen outdoor pools (drained for the fall season) and filled them each with something different: goldenrod, dental floss, cupcakes (the birds loved it), stuffed monkeys with Velcro paws, blueberry jam, paper clips, beer (that one caused some problems in the neighborhood), baseball cards, Guatemalan worry dolls (picketed, for no apparent reason, by a suburban church group), cock rings (oddly, *not* picketed by a suburban church group), takeout menus, feathers, typewriters, taco shells, and breath mints. He called it *Swim in This!* and filled the last one with water.

In a less ambitious project, Soon drove around the city at night with his headlights off and filmed people trying to get his attention. For a week he projected the film, entitled *Hey, Buddy!* as a continuous loop on the side of the Manulife building.

Then there was *What God Sees*, a series of flat-roof murals, photographed via helicopter. The photos were placed in a bucket and lowered into a well before a live audience of six baffled onlookers.

"Then came the Pee-Wee project," said Soon, a bit too seriously. "That's when things started going south—both artistically and personally." He held his hand up like he didn't want to talk about it.

Mason waited.

"That was a real bad time."

Mason nodded.

"I'll tell you about it later."

"Okay then," said Mason. "What can I do for you?"

"I told you," said Soon, and glanced around the bar. "I'm looking for a collaborator."

"Or an accomplice."

"Call it what you will." Soon put a leather satchel on the table

GHOSTED

and pulled out a large file folder. "I want you to read everything in this folder and get back to me."

"Why can't you just tell me what you want?"

"You need to spend some time with the material."

If there was one thing Mason didn't like, it was people telling him what he needed. And anyway, he had that buzzing in the back of his throat that called for cocaine. "Bullshit," he said, and stood up.

"I'll pay you," said Soon. "Just to read it and meet with me after."

"How much?"

"Is $500 enough?"

"Six," said Mason, and headed to the bathroom.

35

THE FOLDER was full of files. Mason lit a smoke and pulled out the first one, labeled THE CONTEST. He turned to the first page. *Project Savior*, it read: *A call to Artists, Architects and Engineers to Plan and Submit Designs for an Artistic and Functional Jump-Prevention Barrier for Toronto's Bloor Viaduct.*

Following the contest guidelines was a rather overwrought history of the viaduct:

> Built in 1919 to unite the city of Toronto by spanning the Don Valley, its design was revolutionary—made to accommodate a subway line, even though no such thing would exist in Canada for another thirty years. And still, with all that foresight, they constructed guardrails only four feet high. By the time the first subway crossed the viaduct, the only place more people committed suicide in North America was the Golden Gate Bridge in San Francisco. To this day the Bloor Viaduct remains the second most popular suicide destination on the continent.

This first file was full of such facts. For instance, the Taft and the Duke Ellington bridges are only a block apart in Washington DC, but people only dove off the Duke. When they put up a jump barrier, the suicides stopped. Nobody went over to the Taft. In the

margin next to this anecdote was a handwritten note: *The music still matters!*

There was a story about Mount Mihara—an active volcano into which, in 1933, two Japanese classmates jumped, followed over the next couple of years by hundreds of others. It became a tourist destination until a barricade was erected. In the margin: *No better metaphor than a volcano.*

Under the subheading *Access Is Everything* was this: *After Sylvia Plath gassed herself to death, the British government replaced coal gas with a less lethal one, and immediately the suicide rate dropped by a third—the same percentage of Brits with gas ovens.* Scrawled below it: *or those who read Sylvia Plath?*

Even without these insightful notes it was obvious to Mason how this "call to artists" would have sounded to Soon: like *destiny*— redemption, profundity, and millions of dollars—the mother of all grant applications.

The contest deadline had been a year ago, and Mason knew they were already building the thing. He'd seen it: a nauseating mess of lines and crosses, cables and gables. It wrecked the bridge and blocked the view—the kind of thing that made people want to kill themselves in the first place. So either way, Soon had failed, whether he'd won the contest or not.

The second file was labeled THE PROCESS. Before he started reading, Mason did a couple of lines.

21. *If something's a challenge, it's probably worth doing.*
22. *I'd rather fold a napkin (or tablecloth) than unfold one.*

Despite whatever missteps Soon had made in the art world, his college decided to back the bid. They even gave him a team: two architecture students looking for credits and an engineering graduate preoccupied with "light in public space."

Any hopes the others may have had about a cooperative process should have been quickly dashed by Soon's working project title: Save Your Breath.

There were journal entries, photocopied. Certain sections had the ring of someone who expected future generations to study his diary:

I go there in the evenings to patrol the ramparts: "I will save you," I want to say to the lost souls of this city. I walk back and forth across the bridge for inspiration.

Inspiration! From the ancient Greek—meaning "to breathe; to give life to." The Greeks understood. They knew that art and life are one and the same. And breath created both—the whole universe—from the atom to the setting sun, the Acropolis to the A-Bomb. Art is the breath of God.

Mason sat back. He took a breath, then lit another smoke. Sure, it was self-involved, overdone, verging on mania. But one thing was clear: this *mattered* to Soon. He'd decided, as part of his journals, to compile a list of everyone who'd jumped from the viaduct—over four hundred of them. Some had earned whole paragraphs:

- On the evening of July 5, 1991, Constable Rick Terrain—veteran cop and gambling addict—is entrusted with $3,400 he helped raise for the Toronto Sick Kids Hospital. Instead of driving home he goes to the casino. In less than two hours, he's lost it all. At 7:15 the next morning, he jumps off the viaduct, and as he falls he shoots himself in the head with his service revolver.
- Just after 2 A.M., New Year's Eve, 1988, Joseph Andrew Selkirk is walking across the viaduct with three friends. They are all in the same biochemistry program at U of T and live in the same dorm. They are sharing a bottle of champagne and laughing about how Joe struck out with a girl they all like at a party they've just been to. Joe is laughing, too. Then he says, "It's going to be a tough year," takes a step toward the railing, and is gone.
- On October 10, 1970, two women walk through early twilight onto the viaduct—one from the east, one from the west. Tabitha Gault and Linda Delarosa don't know each other, but they've come for the same reason and meet by chance at the center of the bridge. Sitting twenty feet apart on top of the stone railing, they begin to talk. They speak for a while, until a police cruiser pulls up. The officer gets out of his car and approaches, asking them if they're all right and to please return to the sidewalk. The two women look at each other. One pushes off, diving backward into the air. Then the other does the same.

There were some who hadn't even made it to adulthood:

- June 6, 1988. Robert Eddie. 17 years old. Blind from birth. Abused by an alcoholic father.
- December 15, last year. Rebecca Lapin. 16 years old. Victim of a savage childhood rape. Years of reconstructive surgeries and near-constant psychiatric care.
- January 3, 1978. Geoffrey Grayson. 13 years old. Runaway. High on mescaline.

The list went on—the youngest among them not even in her teens:

- April 18, 1994. Sandra Pappalia. 10 years old. Bullied at school. Her pet puppy beaten to death by gang of neighborhood children.

Mason closed the second file and moved onto the third, entitled THE SUBMISSION. It consisted of the package Soon had given to the jury: eight blueprints; a twelve-page breakdown of materials, work schedule, and cost projection; a twenty-two-page description of the project; as well as a one-thousand-word manifesto.

The name had changed, from Save Your Breath to the Wings of Hope. The tag line read *If you're caught today, you can fly tomorrow.*

The "wings" would be made of a strong, translucent material—the same stuff they use to make parachutes—suspended from the sides of the bridge by airplane cables. They would angle upward. They wouldn't necessarily stop someone from jumping, but rather catch them if they did. And there was no real way to climb out of them. Once in the wings' embrace, there'd be little to do but wait.

"The wings will hold them, soft yet secure," wrote Soon. "Beautiful wings, shining in the sun—they'll lift the spirit of the entire city. And that troubled, heavy bridge will rise."

In his manifesto, Soon suggested that the idea for a barrier would never have been agreed to if it weren't for lobbying by the families of suicides and also by a rash of recent high-profile jumpers: a local midday talk show host; a freelance journalist on commission to

write the memoirs of a genocide survivor; a much-loved math teacher and gymnastics coach who, having just been nominated for Ontario teacher of the year, hurled his infant son off the viaduct, then dove after him.

He wanted to carve their names into the top of the stone railing:

Starting with Brigadier-General Reginald Bunt, who, nine months after the opening of the viaduct and one month after the Treaty of Versailles, marched the bridge in his uniform and medals, saluted the honking motorists, then stormed the Toronto sky.

After that, nearly four hundred more names. All the way to Samuel Ray Shelf—a seventy-six-year-old widower with a rebuilt hip, cataracts, and a monthly bus pass. On November 30 (just weeks ago) he got off the bus on Bloor Street, then walked the last mile slowly.

It was obvious that Soon, well-versed in the lexicon of suicide, knew there'd be resistance to commemoration of any sort.

You will no doubt balk at the engraving of names. But I want you to think about it again—about redemption—about the fact that some-times the fallen can rise, as can ideas once thwarted. And please remember that rethinking is an essential step toward meaningful creation—the blessing known as hope.

23. When a door closes, a window opens.
24. I'd like to be a fighter pilot.

The last file was labeled THE VICTOR. It did not refer to Soon. The first page was a letter congratulating him on being a runner-up. It had been torn into six pieces, then taped back together. The rest of the file was a copy of the winning proposal, titled "The Saving Grace."

For now, though, Mason had read enough. He felt bad for Soon and even worse for the thirty dozen people whose suicides he'd been forced to consider. He was jittery and anxious, out of booze, and almost out of coke. It was time to hit the Cave.

Uncle Fishy was working the door. There was supposed to be a $10 cover charge, but Mason rolled his eyes and pushed on through. Fortunately Chaz got to him before the bouncers did.

"You owe him hundreds of dollars!" said Chaz, grinning.

"I thought the door goes to the house."

"Well, you're into *me* for a lot more!"

"Sure. But there's no way I'm paying cover."

"Course not," said Chaz, his arm around him as they pushed through the curtains, Fishy left twitching in the doorway. "He thinks you're going to lose his Dogmobile in a poker game."

Mason laughed. "It hadn't even occurred to me." He pulled out the $600.

Chaz looked at him but didn't say anything—just went to get him chips.

The game was relatively steep: blinds of $5 and $10, no limit. You could feasibly lose $500 every few minutes, from 2 A.M. till noon, every day. This made some people edgy.

Mason sat down. He was loose and wound up at the same time. The combination of booze, cocaine, poker, and too much reading about suicide will do that to you. He decided tonight was his night. Of course, he decided that a lot, and in many different ways: his night to win, his night to lose, his night to find love, his night to overdose, his night to show these guys something they'd never seen.

Within an hour he'd lost the $600, plus another $400 he'd borrowed from the house. But he could feel his cards coming, his game hitting, just around the corner. He did rails at a quicker rate, to find more energy, to focus it—but then something messed with his focus.

Coked-up gamblers aren't easily distracted. The felt is a dark green galaxy. Even in the Cave, where every night was New Year's on Mars, Mason's attention rarely strayed from the game. But now he kept glancing at the girl in the wheelchair.

If he looked beyond the smoky solar system of the table, she

GHOSTED

119

was right in his line of sight. She'd been pushed there by another girl—and just sort of dumped. It felt like a while ago now, and the way time disappeared at the poker table it was probably twice that at least. It was hard to see her face out there, but it seemed as if she was watching him—a busted satellite, stuck in orbit, waiting . . .

And then Mason was out of chips again and needed another drink. He had to get by her wheelchair to reach the bar, but it lurched forward, and he stumbled into it.

"Are you okay?" he said.

"I'm paralyzed."

"Oh . . . really?"

"Yes, really," she said and smiled. "Are you getting more chips?"

"I dunno . . ." said Mason.

"You're not very lucky." She had a slow, deliberate way of talking, her head tilted to one side. Her right hand was on the wheel, rolling it back and forth. The left lay in her lap.

"Poker's not about luck," said Mason.

"I sit corrected," said the girl. "You're not very *good.*"

He was about to explain it to her, then stopped. "You want a drink? Let's go to the bar."

"I can only go around in circles."

"What?"

"Circles."

He pushed her to a table near the bar, then got them a couple of Jamesons.

They introduced themselves.

"What's Willy short for?" said Mason.

"It's long for Will," she said.

"You're kind of feminine for a Will."

"And short for a tall girl . . . shit happens."

They drank whisky, and Mason chopped some lines on the table.

"I like drug addicts," said Willy. Mason laughed and offered her a rolled-up bill, and she shook her head—slow and methodical, like a bird on a branch looking both ways. "Not for me."

Mason kept drinking and doing lines. He was buzzed, chatty, and the music was thumping, so it was a while before he noticed she'd stopped chatting back. "What's up?" he said.

"I have to pee."

"No problem."

Willy shifted in her chair. "My friend's supposed to be back."

"Oh," said Mason. "Oh . . . and you need to pee."

"I've drunk a lot."

"Oh . . ."

"You keep on saying that."

"Sorry."

She was staring at him intently.

"Do you want some help?" he finally asked.

"Sure," she said as Mason got up.

He pushed her through the crowded Cave and into the bathroom. It took a moment to adjust to the light. Looking in the mirror, he got his first clear sight of Willy. Her lips were red and full; her hair black, tied in a ponytail; her skin so alabaster white, it radiated blue in the shadows. Her eyes were green, her teeth pointed. There was a bruise on her collarbone. It reminded Mason of a sea urchin. Her breasts were large, pressing against the tight weave of a dark blue sweater.

"What are you looking at?"

"Your teeth," he said. He looked over at the stalls. All four were occupied and none accessible to wheelchairs. He hadn't noticed that before. He'd have to talk to Chaz.

"So. This friend of yours . . ." he said, and then one of the doors opened. A guy and a girl came out.

Mason turned to look at Willy. "How do we do this?"

"It's going to be awkward."

"*Awkward*'s my middle name."

Willy snorted. "You'll have to pick me up."

Leaning down to her, he felt how drunk he was. He curled an arm beneath her legs and the other beneath her arms. She smelled of bubblegum and ashes. He began to lift, and she gasped. "Sorry," he said.

"It's okay."

She was halfway out of the chair.

"What should I do?"

"Try again. You can be rough—especially on my right side. I've got no feeling there."

He yanked and heaved and eventually Willy was in his arms. He stumbled forward and her head smacked into the stall.

"Ow!"

"Sorry." They tumbled into the toilet. There was a thud and a splash. Most of her landed upright, somewhat on the seat. Mason was on his knees at her feet, his arm still wedged beneath her legs, his hand in the toilet water. "Well, *that* was easy," he said.

Willy laughed. "You know you're not done."

"The pants?"

"The pants."

"Should I just pull . . . ?"

"Well, undo them first. You've taken a girl's pants off before . . ."

The people in the next stall over started banging around and moaning. Mason undid the top button, pulled down the zipper. Her underwear was pink. Shifting the waistband back and forth, he shimmied her jeans down over her hips, down below her knees. There was soft golden hair on her legs. He reached up and, trying not to look, yanked her panties from under her ass: one quick movement, like whipping a tablecloth from beneath china.

"Okay?"

"Yep."

"I'll close the door, then. You okay?"

"Yep. Sure."

He backed out of the stall and closed the door behind him and went to wash his hands. He stood next to Willy's wheelchair. "I'll just wait here," he said, calling through the door.

"Okay."

He turned the tap back on—he thought the running water might help her pee. After a while she said, "You still there?"

"Yep."

Then there was silence again. He sat down in her chair.

"Are you sitting in my chair?"

"Yeah . . . Sorry." He moved to get up.

"No, it's okay. I kind of like it." Finally he could hear her start to pee.

He wheeled himself over to the counter and cut up some lines. The peeing stopped.

"I'm still going to be awhile," said Willy.

"Okay," said Mason. The stalls on either side emptied out—little punks and tramps sniffing and giggling, spilling forth like strung out clowns from a small stinky car. They looked at themselves in the mirror, then tumbled back into the Cave. Mason rolled over to the stalls. He faced the closed door. "I don't really get it."

"What's that?"

"I'm just confused about . . . um . . . what kind of paralyzed are you? Do you mind if I ask you that?"

"I'm hemiplegic."

"You're what?"

"I can only move half of me, split right down the center. Only the right side can move."

"I thought you could only feel your *left*."

"I can."

Mason rolled closer to the door, half a rotation. "Are you telling me you can only feel half your body, and it's the side you can't move?"

"Uh-huh."

"And . . . and the side you *can* move, you can't feel at all?"

"Yep."

"Are you fucking kidding me?"

"God's probably laughing his head off."

He thought of her face, her green eyes. "Can I ask you what happened?"

"I'm not going to tell you."

He imagined how the two of them looked from above—staring at each other through a blue metal door.

"I'm going to smoke something," said Willy.

"You can smoke it out here."

"I'm going to smoke some heroin."

"Oh. Okay." He heard a lighter spark. He took out a cigarette and lit it. The two lines of smoke rose, mixing in the air above the door.

"So what about this friend of yours?"

"Fuck her," said Willy, then inhaled and exhaled slowly. "I shouldn't say that. She takes care of me—most of the time. Then

there's other times—when I'm pissing on strangers . . ." She inhaled and let it out again.

"You didn't piss on me." He thought of her thighs, covered in soft downy gold.

"You got lucky is all."

They finished smoking.

"You all done?"

"Yeah, I am." The lock clicked. Mason pushed open the door and knelt down before her. He put one hand between her knees, gripping the soft pink fabric of her underwear. With the other hand he cupped her backside, lifting it gently, sliding the panties up along her thighs. She reached out her right arm, hooking it around his neck, and pulled. She held herself like that, slightly off the seat, as he reached in with both hands, his fingers under the strings of her underwear, stretching the pink cloth up, around, then snug across her ass.

"Oh."

"Okay?"

"Okay," said Willy.

25. *The weather that describes me best is rain.*

26. *Love is not meant to hurt us.*

Notes on the Novel in Progress

Writing is like a poker game. It takes patience, concentration, endurance, focus.

No wonder your book is a mess.

It also requires inventiveness and guts—flashes of bravery and risk. And . . .

The ability to read other people.

Things to beware of:

A novel full of people who only read themselves.

Narrators consumed with the act of narration.

The origin of characters.

Mirrored walls.

Rooms without belly dancers, windows, or doorknobs.

Open concepts.

Caves within caves.

To research:

Bridges. Bats. Wheelchairs. Subway tunnels. Harm reduction. Love.

Possible title:

The Book of Hangovers

36

MASON HAD slept badly, his dreams full of people falling, and he'd woken a number of times into that slipping terror that he was falling, too.

Now here he sat with his second cup of coffee and the winning submission: "The Saving Grace."

It was the work of Dr. Anders Christoph of Trent University, and in many ways it was similar to Soon's—poetic, hyperbolic. Christoph wrote about the confluence of geological, mythological, and historical forces; the ancient shoreline of Lake Iroquois; existential emptiness; and Michael Ondaatje's *In the Skin of a Lion*. He had gone so far as to compare his design to the character of Nicholas Temelcoff—the bridge builder who swooped out of the fog to save a falling nun. The whole thing depressed Mason. His stomach grumbled, so he packed up the file and went to get a burger.

He'd planned to go to his local Harvey's, but at the corner he kept on walking, all the way across downtown to the one known as Ho-vees. He ordered a burger and a milk shake, then sat down at a table against the wall to eat and read. Every time someone came through the door, he looked up.

That's not her.

He looked back down. Ketchup dripped on the page.

Christoph's manifesto was full of musical imagery. He described the barrier itself as "a virtuous harp with steel strings—to be plucked by passersby, strummed by the wind—a song of renewal carried through the valley."

Mason finished his burger. "Don't You Forget About Me" was playing on the radio. He scanned the restaurant one last time.

She's not going to come.
He left Ho-vees and headed for the valley.

23. *I prefer colorful paintings to dark ones.*
24. *Misery is indifferent to company.*

The Bloor Viaduct spans ten lanes of highway, two sets of railroad tracks, the city's primary power lines, a cycling path, and the shallow waters of the Don River. It is approximately five hundred yards across and two hundred feet high. Standing atop it on a clear day, you could see the valley stretching north into hills or south all the way to the lake. From the southern walkway you could see the downtown skyline, the CN Tower rising. Or at least that's how it used to be.

Today, as Mason walked onto the bridge, all he saw were lines. These were the strings of the virtuous harp. They'd started at both ends of the viaduct, working toward the middle on both sides of the bridge. About a quarter had been done so far, and over the summer the rest would be filled in, too—until everyone was safe. Saved from themselves and the pull of gravity. Saved by the Saving Grace.

The lines were strung vertically, from large metal crosses. If you tried to look through them while moving, the nausea was instantaneous. It was like looking at the world through an oscillating fan—not a good thing to do with a hangover.

He stepped up and put his head against the thick metal cables, so that now he could see the view: cars backed up on the parkway—never-ending lines in both directions—beside them the river, shallow and murky brown, its banks lined with sparse trees and bushes. There was a haze over the lake in the distance. The CN Tower looked flimsy in the bright sun. He stepped back, grabbed on to one of the taut steel strings, and tried to give it a pluck. Paul Bunyan couldn't have budged it. The whistling wind was like a failed transmission signal.

He kept his eyes on the pavement and walked toward the center of the bridge. As he came to the end of the lines his queasiness passed, the world opened up, and suddenly he could breathe again. Mason looked out. It felt like he was standing in the middle of the air. He thought of a passage from Soon's journals:

It's not the Golden Gate, but there is something: enough poetry, music, and active volcano; mix it with despair, the concrete, and shrubs below, and you've got a deadly sort of beauty. Standing on the viaduct I began to see them—my neighbors, students, the people of my city, stepping toward the railing . . .

And now Mason saw them, too—some hesitant, some manic, making a last cell phone call, blinded by tears—dozens, then hundreds of them, pushing forward, pouring over the edge, into the grip of gravity, then down. Their bodies exploding at the bottom.

He felt nothing but anger—at the Saving Grace, $4 million to make him nauseous, chicken wire would have done just fine; at Soon, his bullshit artistic envy; at himself, poor Circe, how right she'd been: We're all just a bunch of King Kongs, stupid, lonely, stumbling around trying to make harps out of bridges, dying for beauty.

The whole walk home Mason thought of one sentence, written by Soon on lined yellow paper: *Sixty-eight survivor accounts, and only one consistency: "When I started to fall, I changed my mind."*

37

"I'M NOT going to do it." They were back in This Place. Mason pushed the check across the table toward Soon.

"What is that?"

"It's your money. I'm not taking the job."

"I paid you in cash."

"Either way . . . I'm not collaborating with you."

"Why not?"

Mason looked around the bar, then leaned in. "After all that research—all that thought and energy trying to stop people from killing themselves—a couple of failures, and all of a sudden *you* want to kill yourself?"

Soon sat back and looked at Mason. He seemed to be sussing something out. "*All of a sudden* . . . I wouldn't exactly say *that*."

"What would you say?"

"How about *not at all*?"

"What does that mean?"

"*He wanted to kill himself not at all*—I know the syntax is weird, but . . ."

"What are you talking about?"

"Please sit down."

Mason did.

"I'm not saying I didn't think about it," said Soon. "When they announced the winner, I fell apart. The Saving Grace . . ." he spat it out as if there were something green and fuzzy growing on the words. "I was perfect for that project. My idea was better." He stared at the full beer in front of him. Then, for the first time in Mason's presence, he took a sip.

Mason said nothing.

Soon wiped his mouth. "It wasn't my first one."

"Your first idea?"

"My first breakdown." He looked at Mason. His eyes had a spark in them. "Isn't that a great image? Like we're cars that overheat and the gears just jam and suddenly there's smoke and coolant everywhere. You lose your cool. That's what happens in a breakdown." He took another, longer sip of beer.

They drank in silence.

Then finally Mason spoke. "Okay," he said. "So what happened the first time?"

Soon put his glass down. "The novel happened."

"Excuse me?"

"*The Ghosts of Gauguin*." He tipped the glass slightly and stared down into it. "It was a great premise—about this group of struggling artists who fake their own suicides, then sell each other's work on eBay for millions. They escape to a remote island in the South Pacific—rich and famous and supposedly dead." He gulped at his beer. "Then of course they end up killing each other. It was *The Da Vinci Code* meets *Lord of the Flies*."

"Huh."

"Yeah. Huh. I'd been working on it for years. Everything I'd learned about art and the drama of life was going into that book." He looked Mason in the eye. "It would have been a bestseller."

"So what happened?"

Soon drained the last of his beer, then swallowed down a belch. He thumped himself in the chest. "This movie came out: *Posthumous Island*. You ever see it?"

"I don't think so."

"Yeah, it wasn't very good. But it was my book—exactly!" He waved at the bartender, who poured them another glass.

"What did you do?"

"Nothing." The bartender put the beers on the table. Soon took a sip. When he spoke again, his voice was a little louder, his words slightly slurred. "What the hell *could* I do? I couldn't prove they stole it. And maybe they didn't even know they had." He took another gulp. "You know how one year there's like four movies about people switching bodies. Or dogs playing sports . . . You know what I mean?"

Mason nodded.

"But this was more than that!" He thumped the table, his beer sloshing over his hand. "It was so *specific!*" Soon took another sip. "Think of it! How long have people been writing books? Hundreds of years, right?" He stared at Mason.

"Right . . ."

"Right! So for hundreds of years nobody thought of this premise. Then suddenly—*wham!*" He slammed his hand onto the table, and both their glasses jumped. The beer was beginning to pool. "Two people think of the *exact* same story in the *exact* same year! Or *close* to the same year?"

"Uh . . . no?"

"No *way!*" Another sip. "Or maybe *yes!*" A bit of beer sprayed from his mouth. "Maybe that's how it works! Like there's these ghosts of ideas roaming the earth, diving in and out of heads." He mimed this happening, as if the ghosts were attached to his fingertips and dripping with beer. "Maybe that's what happened to me. Five years of my life, sanity, everything—sacrificed for what? Can you imagine what that's like?"

The bartender had brought over a stack of napkins, and now Mason was wiping the table. "So what did you do?"

"Oh, I did a lot of things . . . a *lot* of things! I yelled at God. I got addicted to sleeping pills. I even started drinking." He took another glug. "I'd never really drunk before that." Some beer

trickled out the side of his mouth. "I don't always react that well to alcohol."

Mason nodded, piling up the napkins.

"And then, of course, there was *Pee-wee's Big Mistake*." He laughed and shook his head. "That," he said, "was my real masterpiece! The original title was *If Pee-wee Ran Things*. It was a smart, kind of cheeky thing about civic duty and infrastructure and things like that, and I got a big grant for it. But *then*—between the conception and the realization—I had a breakdown . . . Isn't that a great word?"

"Yeah. Like a car," said Mason. "So what happened to *Pee-wee*?"

"Things got confusing . . ." He looked down at the table. "I set up these big speakers right outside the courthouse that blasted 'Right On for the Darkness' over and over—you know, Curtis Mayfield?"

Mason nodded.

"I had these floodlights that strobed in time with the music and a bunch of homeless people wrapping city hall in cellophane. And I can't really remember why now, but I painted a bunch of stop signs blue. It was a messy night. There was like $3 million in accident claims." He sipped his beer. "Eleven injuries."

"Whoa."

"Yeah. That's when I started teaching. But you know what?" He looked up at Mason, a glistening kind of hope in his eyes.

"What?" said Mason.

"In some ways, those failures—the novel, the viaduct—they're the best things that ever happened to me."

Mason waited.

"They're pure inspiration!" he said. "The kind that turns art into life! Which brings us to here!" He held up his beer as if to make a toast. "To our collaboration!"

Mason lifted his drink, warily. "What do you mean?"

"I'll do better than write *The Ghosts of Gauguin*!" He crashed his beer into Mason's. "I'm going to live the fucking book!"

29. I prefer solitary exercise to team sports.
30. Telling the truth is often foolish.

The Book of Sobriety

The man in the black helmet is coming.

He is riding out of the ashen fog, speeding straight for Circe.

His motorcycle is black. And so is her horse.

Her sword is glistening silver, soaring in the air above her head.

Just before they collide, the man in the black helmet pulls out a glowing red saber. And now there's fear in Circe's eyes—but it is too late . . .

The crash is ferocious. Sparks like fireworks, like strobe lights, a battle-star exploding. The saber cuts through Circe's belly, and as it does, her face changes—from fear to knowing: from Circe to Sissy to Sarah.

And as it does, her sword strikes his helmet. His visor cracks.

And then I wake up.

38

"Who is Sarah?"

"A girl I knew."

"Do you want to tell me about her?"

"Not really?"

"What about Circe?"

"Same."

"She's the same as Sarah—or you don't want to tell me about her."

"That second one."

"What about Sissy?"

"She's the same as Circe."

"Uh . . ."

"I mean she's the same person."

"You sure about that?"

"What do you mean?"

"There are a lot of amorphous identities going on here."

Mason said nothing.

"Is she the friend who killed herself?"

Mason said nothing.

"What about the man on the motorcycle?"

"The man in the black helmet."

"Have you dreamt of him before?"

"Sometimes."

"Does he ever have a face?"

"I'm sure he *has* one. Under the helmet, you know?"

"Uh-huh."

"I mean I know who he is."

"You do?"

"Not really his *identity*—but I met him once."

"When was this?"

"I was ten."

"Could you write about that?"

"I guess I could try."

31. The past does not affect me much.
32. It hurts behind my eyes when I pee.

39

BETWEEN ASSISTING a suicide and collaborating on a performance art piece (as Soon was describing his self-serving scam), Mason preferred the latter: less money up front but easier on the soul.

Perhaps it shouldn't have surprised him, considering Soon's previous endeavors, that aspects of the caper seemed less than airtight. The original plan had involved upstaging the Saving Grace. Mason had to convince Soon that faking a suicide off the Bloor Viaduct was impractical, if not impossible. The Don Valley was pretty much devoid of water, so when bodies fell, they were quickly found, often stuck in the middle of a windshield. They needed a bodyless suicide—a location that could swallow a corpse.

Still, it seemed difficult for Soon to put aside his bitterness. As such, they agreed to correspond "the event" with the unveiling of the Saving Grace—which was supposed to take place in early July. They'd chosen a new location: the Old Jackson Bridge, fifty miles northeast of Toronto. It was secluded and high enough, spanning tumultuous waters.

And the new plan was this: Soon would set up a video camera on the bridge and film himself delivering his final lesson, titled "Drowning in the Presence of Art," written by the two of them together. Soon would be wearing a long coat (color and style as yet undetermined) and, underneath it, a harness attached to a bungee cord (itself attached to the bridge). The last line still echoing, he'd turn and make the leap . . .

Then Soon would disappear, his legacy left in the hands of Mason. Mason would play a character based on the baser parts of himself—a disheveled drifter who thinks he's a writer, a directionless lover of art. Soon had already enrolled him in the summer class he taught. It would be Mason's job (apart from helping with the jump) to make sure the public put it all together: misunderstood genius, unappreciated artist, a savior who'd come in second.

He'd have the video in his possession—him having placed a last-minute call to his favorite student—and he'd put it out there for all to see. No matter how Mason tried to keep him focused on the money (Soon had promised him a cut of the windfall), the idea and the spectacle of the thing continued to distract him. He saw "Drowning in the Presence of Art" as the perfect showcase for his creativity and knowledge—a public phantasmagoria of art, death, art history, and the death of public culture.

"But they won't know it's Art."

"But *I* will," said Soon. "And what if one day they find out the truth?"

Mason didn't love that scenario. But compared to some of the things he'd done, the thought of owning up to Soon's devious art project didn't seem so bad. In the meantime, they both had work to do. They had to write the letter that Soon would recite, and Soon had to create the art that would eventually be sold on eBay. He envisioned a series of paintings that no informed collector could resist. The maudlin taste of prophecy would simply overwhelm them.

In addition to attending Soon's summer classes, Mason had a wake to plan.

In the Wake of Sahala would embody the sensibility of the moment. It would be an outpouring of grief and artistic recognition—without a body to mourn—staged in a public space. Ideally, it would feel

more like birth than death—the first spark of a movement: Soon-ism. The mourners would be known as Soonies—though Mason preferred "Saholes." He knew where to find a bunch of those.

40

MASON SPENT his nights and mornings in the Cave, playing poker and hanging out with Willy whenever her friend Bethany ditched her. He hated Bethany. She was a snarky, nasty, mean-eyed bitch with stringy hair pulled back in a pink scrunchy. She treated Willy like a burden. Until someone got too close, that is—and then Willy was her "precious." Mason called her Gollum.

Without Bethany, Willy couldn't move. She couldn't get a drink, or go to the bathroom, or shoot heroin. Bethany would disappear, then come back hours later, strung out or pissed off—ready to fight whoever had been helping Willy out.

"Sure, she's a bitch, but what am I supposed to do?" said Willy. "She cleans me, feeds me, gets me high . . . even braids my hair sometimes. Who else is going to do that?"

Mason said nothing. But it wasn't as if Bethany did it for free. Willy's disability check paid for a lot of smack, plus a small, subsidized apartment. Then there was the motorized chair Willy used to own. Bethany had sold it when they'd run out of money a few months back.

"Fucking Gollum," said Mason.

Willy laughed. "It's not just her," she said. "I was jonesing, too."

33. *I would rather spend money on shoes than a night out.*
34. *A major world catastrophe would not affect me much.*

During the day Mason slept or hung out in Ho-vees. He'd pretty much given up on hot dogs. Then there was the class he was taking: Art and Death 101. He enjoyed it more than he thought he would. Located in the looming Gothic castle in the middle of Spadina Avenue (half of which, it turned out, was allotted to the University

of Toronto's visual arts program—the other half to the making of prosthetic eyes), it was a great place to be hungover.

There was something both soothing and invigorating about sitting half asleep in a darkened room, images of beauty, passion, and discord flashing on a screen. And from the darkness Soon's voice was surprising, uttering the commanding narration of a beautiful nightmare.

It was a crossover course—on the cusp between art history and fine arts. So, while most of it was dedicated to Soon's slide-show lectures, students in the Fine Arts Department were also required to complete a creative project of their own. At the end of the second week, they began the presentations. A young lady stood in front of the class. She didn't smile. She didn't seem nervous. Her bangs were long, her voice thin.

"This is the Ghost Station," she said. "Other than video and recording equipment, my materials are all found. They are the environment itself—that of Lower Bay Station. It existed as a subway stop for only six months, in 1961. Since then it has been abandoned—as are the tunnels leading in and out of it. The sounds you will hear are at least partially due to the movement of surrounding subway lines, running alongside and above the Ghost Station. The rest is ambient, unknown . . ."

The lights dimmed, and the projector chugged on. For the next five minutes, the room became a virtual tunnel, a hollow, haunting projection of echo and shadow, then a sudden flashing—the reflection off an old sign or a mirror. The tunnel stretched on and on, into a black hole, both claustrophobic and limitless. When it was over, Mason approached the young lady.

"How did you find this place?"

"Spooky," she said, then smiled. And before he could rephrase the question, she'd left the room.

35. In my dreams I'm often falling.
36. I like finding shapes in the clouds.

Mason asked Chaz if he could use the Cave to rehearse a performance art piece, using some of the patrons as extras. Chaz looked at him sideways, then shrugged. And so Mason recruited a couple

of dozen Saholes—offering $50 each for the rehearsal. The actual performance (date and location to be announced) would earn them another $200. He chose carefully among the Cave-dwellers: those who needed money, rarely partook of sunlight (let alone street-level socializing), and never picked up a newspaper.

"First rehearsal's tomorrow," said Mason.

Soon looked pleased. "I'd like to be a part of it."

"Well, we haven't made the idol yet—so in its absence, you could represent that which will represent you in your absence."

"Perfect," said Soon. "I'll work on a costume."

41

THE REHEARSAL was a fucking disaster.

Mason had told Soon to get there around noon so they could start when the Cave closed. He had planned to get some rest, but by 10 A.M. he was still playing poker, popping poppers, doing lines. Willy was with him, and for a change he was stacking up chips.

Then Bethany showed up. "Let's get out of here," she said and put her hands on the back of Willy's chair.

"No," said Willy.

"What?" It came out like a gust of wind. Mason felt her breath on the back of his neck. For a moment all was quiet.

"He's winning," said Willy. Mason turned to look at her. She was smiling at him.

"*This* fucking guy?" said Bethany. "He ain't winning shit. Not with a pair of threes."

The table erupted into swearing, players slamming their cards on the table. Mason could see the bouncers across the Cave, busy with something in the bathroom. Chaz was out of sight. "Get the fuck out of here, lady," said the guy across from Mason.

"That's what I'm doing," said Bethany, and she tugged at the wheelchair. Mason grabbed a hold of it too. "She wants to stay," he said.

"Don't you speak for her!" said Bethany. Chaz was coming through the crowd.

"I want to stay," said Willy.

Bethany tugged, glaring at Mason. Then, "Fine!" she said. "*You* take care of her!" She shoved the chair forward.

Willy hit the table—chips, cards, and drinks exploding into the air. Chaz grabbed on to Bethany. Mason got a hold of Willy and pulled her away from the mess. Bethany was screaming now, the players were shouting, and the bouncers were crossing the floor.

"Are you okay?" said Mason.

But Willy didn't answer. She didn't say anything until Bethany was gone.

Chaz tried to avoid barring people. That was how booze cans got raided—some asshole, sore from being kicked out, went to the cops for revenge. But everyone agreed: wrecking a high-stakes poker game by throwing a handicapped girl at it was definitely a barring offense. But what to do with the game? Three thousand dollars in poker chips scattered across the floor? In the end they were redistributed, but to no one's satisfaction. Chaz gave the players drinks on the house, then agreed to stay open for two extra hours.

While all this was happening, Willy smoked her dope in the bathroom stall, Mason cutting lines on the counter.

"You okay?" he said.

The smoke rose, a thin cut above the door. "You were doing so well."

"It doesn't matter."

"It does to me. I want to see you win."

"All right," he said, and did a line. "Then I guess it's time to win." They went back to the table, and Willy sat beside him. He huffed and he puffed, and by noon there was fire on the felt.

When Soon saw the Cave, he almost fled. But he spotted Mason through the crowd and charged onward with trepidation, as only a sober, impatient artist in a midday speakeasy could do. Then he just stood there, looking at the gamblers. People started to grumble. Mason was intent on taking this pot down and didn't even recognize him: a long purple coat of leather and suede, dark eyeliner

beneath Buddy Holly glasses, a po' boy cap, and a Fu Manchu. Even for the Cave, Soon was sporting a creepy look.

Mason glanced up. "Play or walk," he said.

"It's time for rehearsal," said the weird purple stranger. Chairs scraped the floor.

"Soon?"

But Soon had begun to sweat. He opened his mouth to speak, and the Fu Manchu fell across his mouth. Someone yelled, "Narc!" and then, once again, things got messy.

Mason pulled him away from the table.

"Why the hell are you dressed like that?"

"You wanted a representation of my representation!"

"And this is it?"

"And also a disguise—so the Soonies won't recognize me."

Mason shook his head, as if trying to get bugs out of his brain.

"I thought about it a lot!" said Soon. "And anyway, you said this place was going to be closed!"

"I know. I'm sorry."

"Are you on drugs?" said Soon.

"Yes, a lot of them. But just relax, okay? I'm going to get you a drink. And then I'll round up the Saholes."

"Soonies."

"Right," said Mason. "I even made you T-shirts."

37. To give is a blessing.
38. I'm sure there's life on other planets.

Just after 2 P.M., Detective Flores descended from street level with two patrolmen. He'd known this place existed and wasn't going to bother with it. But now there were assault charges pending—laid by an angry girl with a pink scrunchy in her hair.

As he adjusted to the dark, Flores identified an illegal poker game, an unlicensed bar, open use of contraband narcotics and stimulants . . . but that was all in the background, barely interesting compared to what was going on right in front of him.

Twenty or so people in purple T-shirts, with SOON HAS ALREADY

HAPPENED on the front and !!! on the back, were chanting: *Sa-ha-la—Sis-boom-bah! Sa-ha-la Sis-boom-bah!* over and over, though apparently not quite loud enough . . . For in their midst, standing on the back of an occupied wheelchair, stood a young man (who Flores thought he recognized) bellowing this same chant and waving his arms like a conductor. The rhythm improved, and the young man shouted, "Cry! Now everyone start to cry!" The girl in the wheelchair beamed.

Then suddenly, above all of this, rose the opening verse of "Take My Breath Away" (which Flores *definitely* recognized from the *Top Gun* soundtrack). And into the spotlight on the stage came six stumbling men carrying a fold-up table, on top of which sat a bespectacled swami with a taped-on moustache.

"*Sa-ha-la. Sis-boom-bah!*" chanted the purple people.

"Cry!" shouted the young man on the back of the wheelchair. "You're heartbroken! Cry!"

When he finally saw Flores, Mason stopped shouting. The detective appeared to be mouthing something to him—something like, "What the hell, Mason? It's 2 P.M. on a Wednesday!"

Then there was a crash as Soon Sahala tumbled from the stage.

42

"IT COULD have gone worse," said Soon.

"How exactly?"

Two of the Saholes (even Soon was now calling them this) had been arrested for outstanding warrants. Booze, drugs, and poker winnings had been seized. Plus, Soon had sprained his ankle.

"Well," he said. "I could have broken it."

"True."

The cops had let them go after a cursory search. It hadn't been easy, getting Willy up the stairs with Soon limping like that. Once they did, she'd fallen asleep on the couch. Mason didn't want to wake her, so now here they were: out on the roof, keeping an eye on the back alley. Mason had left the wheelchair in the dogmobile.

Chaz, he assumed, was eating beans and listening to Gowan.

Soon began to sing:

First is the worst
Second is the best
Third is the nerd with a hairy chest.

Mason pulled out a dime bag.

"Can I try some of that?"

Mason thought about saying no, but he was high and wired, and eventually he just shrugged. He poured some out on his brand-new Ontario health card and passed it to Soon with a rolled-up bill.

"Plug your other nostril and draw in hard."

Soon did so, then caught his breath. "Just two more months," he said, and pointed at the downtown skyline.

"What?" said Mason.

"In two months the CN Tower will no longer be the tallest free-standing structure in the world."

"Dubai. Right?"

Soon nodded. "I had a plan, you know? To save it from second place."

"You had a plan to make the CN Tower taller?"

"No, not taller. It was about embracing things."

"What are you talking about?"

"I'm talking about Art," said Soon "Something for the entire city. I brought an idea to the lighting designer guy, and he actually liked it: the CN Tower of Babel—languages not of sound, but of light." He moved his hands in the air as if his fingertips were fireworks.

It occurred to Mason that Soon's third breakdown shouldn't be happening on his roof. "Go easy on that, will you?" Soon nodded and tried to do another line.

Mason looked at the tower. "So what happened?"

"When the Wings of Hope failed, I kind of blamed everyone. The collaboration ended. Who knows? Maybe he's still working on it?"

The sun was starting to set.

"What do we do now?" said Mason.

"About what?"

Mason took the coke away from him.

"About our plans."

"I like the T-shirts," said Soon. "And what about that chant!"

"Well, we can't do it now. My cover's blown." Mason took a hit.

"I can still do the jump."

"We'll see. We can figure it out when we're sober."

Soon appeared to think about that. "Can I have another coke?"

"That's not how you say it." Mason passed him the baggie.

Soon tried to take a hit, but ended up sucking air. Mason took it back.

"It's rare, you know," said Soon. "People who jump off bridges."

"Not rare enough," said Mason.

"No, I mean percentage-wise. It takes a special kind of person to do it that way. Most people kill themselves in really depressing places, like garages and alleys and things like that. That's just fucking sad."

Mason looked at him and started to laugh.

And then Soon was laughing, too. "Man," he said. "Cocaine is really good."

They looked at the skyline, laughing.

39. *The night sky is blue, not black.*

40. *Pain is a psychic construct.*

Soon was gone. Willy was awake. She was shaking. Mason held her in his arms.

"I'm scared," she said.

"Of what?"

"I don't know."

Sometimes everything is terrifying.

"What would help?"

"Water," she said.

"I'll get you a glass."

"No, I mean *being* in water. Do you have a bathtub?"

He didn't answer for a moment. He wanted so much to make her all right.

"How about whisky?"

"Okay."

He stood up to fetch a bottle and stumbled a bit.

"You're all fucked-up," she said.

"Yeah."

She was shaking so much. He spilled the whisky as he poured. He did a line and went to the closet.

"What are you doing?" she asked.

He unfolded the suit he'd worn to Warren's funeral.

"I'm taking you out."

Once she was dressed, he lifted her onto his back. It was a long, steep way down, and Willy wasn't light. "Reach out," he said. "Hold on to the railing with me." They started the descent.

Almost halfway, his body began to shake. His legs were burning. *You're going to lose her.*

You're both going down.

His heels slipped, and he grabbed at the railing, wrenching his shoulder as they dropped—but thank God, backward: just two stairs down, thudding onto the landing.

They sat there, crumpled, catching their breath. Mason felt trapped—it was down to the bottom, or all the way back up. *You can't do either.*

He muttered apologies, and they started the second flight on their butts, one stair, two stairs—a gutless midnight descent. *You haven't changed a bit.*

You coward.

Then, just like that, he was up with Willy in his arms and barreling down the stairs. She yelled with surprise and terror—much better than fear. They burst through the door and onto the sidewalk.

"Oh, my God," gasped Willy. "What the hell was that?"

He felt good all of a sudden. Powerful. And it wasn't just being high.

He sat Willy down in the alley, then collected her chair and a bottle of Dewar's from the Dogmobile. He put the bottle in her lap and buckled her in.

"You plan on racing?" she said, and then they were off—flying down the street.

What the hell was that?

It had almost got him, but he'd dug in his heels and leapt.

You're going to crash.

It was true. He'd been up for two days. But now he was flying. And feeling all right . . . At a steady run they were there in twenty minutes: up the ramp, across the rotunda, to the sparkling entrance of the Sheraton Plaza Hotel.

He nodded to the doorman, who had on a red coat with faux gold buttons, and the doors slid open. In the lobby he waved a quick hello to the desk, then headed for the elevators. He pressed the UP button, and a moment later they were in.

He pressed the button marked *R*.

"What does *R* mean?"

"Rooftop," he said, and they began to rise.

43

WILLY FLOATED naked beneath the night sky, thirty-one floors above the ground. Mason held her head and stroked her left side. The water was warm, the air cool, stars pulsing above them.

"What if someone comes out here?"

"We'll offer them a drink."

Mason felt at peace. He looked at Willy's body, laid out in the blue sheen, an alien landscape. Her right half, the one that felt nothing, was lush and pulsing and strong. Her left side was not withered, but utterly passive, moved by the shifting water. It was difficult to fathom, that everything she felt was inside of there.

"How do you feel?"

"Good."

Mason kissed her. It tasted like cantaloupe.

He pushed her gently to the side of the pool, then held her as they smoked some heroin, a cigarette. They sipped more whisky.

"This is the first time I've done it," said Mason.

"What? Swimming with a cripple?"

"Heroin," he said.

"Careful. It hits you harder if you smoke it. And I'll probably need help getting out of here."

"What happened to you, Willy?"

"What do you mean?" she said. And he didn't ask again.

He held her head as the water lapped against his chest. "I'll tell you something I don't tell anyone," he said.

"Why?"

He was close to flying, but not in a blissful way. More like he was rising through air, pulled by the sky—and at the same time in water, tugged gently downward by tides.

He thought he was going to tell her about Warren and Sissy and the awful things he'd done for money, but then he was talking about the swallows instead. He described it all—stomping down with his boot heels in the morning. And then the afternoon:

"I stayed angry long after they got back from the lake. I helped set up for Aunt Jo's birthday party, and I just got angrier. At dinner I sat at the kids' table. Everybody thought I was being sweet, but really they were the only ones I could bear to look at. My cousin Sarah sat with me—she was eighteen at the time—and we kept sending one of my nephews over for bottles of wine. I drank a lot—kept looking up at those fucking nests: the six of them left. Nobody even noticed—I'd killed them all for nothing. Anyway, I'd been drinking all day. Sarah was drinking too . . ." Mason felt himself slipping, the stars reflected in the water. "Have you seen *The Man from Snowy River?*"

"Yes," said Willy. "I love that movie." Her voice seemed far away.

"You know that scene?"

"With the horse, of course . . ."

"Down the cliff . . ."

"Of course . . ."

"Down . . ."

The cliff.

"Mason!"

The stars were shaking above him.

You've let go of her.

He felt himself falling.

You've let go of Willy!

It was only a few seconds, but by the time he had her in his arms again, he was crying. "I'm sorry. I'm so sorry . . ." She was gasping. He held her, crying.

They caught their breath.

"It's okay," she sputtered.

"I don't know what happened . . ."

Willy said nothing.

"I can't believe I let go of you. I'm so fucking sorry . . ."

"Forget it."

There was silence, then the rippling of water. "I'd like another hit," she said.

Mason pushed her slowly to the poolside and rested her swaying against his belly in the water. He reached his arms out, dried his hands on his black suit, scooped her pipe into the ziplock, and lit it.

"You're good at that," said Willy, then took a long drag. "You could probably shoot me up sometime." The smoke trailed from her lips, and he kissed her.

And now she was kissing him back. Her arm was out, and so was his, pulling them along the side of the pool, all the way to the shallow end.

The corner was long and sloping, like a submerged wheelchair ramp. Willy lay against it, legs in the pool, hips at the waterline, her breasts like the moon's reflections. Water shed from Mason as he rose, out of the pool and into Willy. He thought he might die, the pleasure was so great. She held him with all her strength—the side that felt nothing pulling him in deeper to the one that felt all. And then they were gone together.

"I don't think you're ready," said Willy.

"For what?"

"To tell whatever story you were trying to tell."

He gave a laugh. Willy smiled. They smoked some more at the edge of the pool, drinking whisky too, until Willy began to talk:

"It was 1985. I was six years old . . ."

Above twelve hundred hotel rooms, beneath twelve million suns, Willy floated in the dark as she told her story. Her voice, the heroin, letting her go, being inside her—Mason was focused like never before. And as she spoke he could see it happening.

It is 1985. She is six years old, in her daddy's apartment in Scarborough. She is sleeping—then suddenly awake . . .

There's something wrong. Her stuffed monkey, Randolph, is slipping off the itchy orange couch, and she pulls him back under the sheet—soft with a Bay blanket on top . . . Something else is wrong. The lights are on. It's bright, but not just from the lights . . . There's a fire—right where she's looking—through the door into the bedroom. His bed is on fire.

"Daddy!" she screams. And there he is, rushing through the door, right in front of the couch, across the room and back again. But it's as if he can't hear her. There is music playing—she can hear it now, and it sounds like the xylophones in music class, she's never heard them in a real song—with a weird voice yelling, "It's gone. Daddy. Gone—the love is gone . . ." It is the Violent Femmes. (She knows that now, but didn't then.)

"Daddy!" she shouts, as loud as she can—and he turns and leaps toward her, picking her up, into his arms. She's holding Randolph, and they're whooshing across the room. The breath is gone from her. She is relieved to be in his arms. They're whooshing back across the room the other way, and in front of them the whole bedroom is on fire. She sees flames like tentacles, reaching through the door, and her daddy isn't saying anything. He's turning again, back across the floor, and there's just the weird voice singing: "I can tell by the way that you switch and walk. I can see by the way that you baby talk . . ."

The xylophones are even louder now—and when she starts to scream it comes out like coughing. We have to get outside! She holds Randolph with one arm, banging on her daddy's shoulder with the other.

"It's gone, Daddy, gone. Your love is gone. It's gone, Daddy, gone. Your love is gone. It's gone, Daddy, gone. Your love is gone away . . . It's gone away . . ."

The fire is spreading. Willy is yelling and coughing in her daddy's arms. He stops and turns, not toward the door to the hall but past

Shaughnessy Bishop-Stall

the couch instead, to the rickety screen door out onto the balcony, which screeches as he pulls it open.

Willy gasps. They're finally outside, seven storeys above the ground. The night air rushes into her lungs, and suddenly, instead of a scream, she's got a question. Her daddy clutches her tighter— then lunges forward, over the railing.

"I don't know if he was trying to kill or save me."

Mason held her tight.

Notes on the Novel in Progress

You can explain it all later, for fuck's sake.
If things are moving, don't slow them down.

44

HE DROVE his fedora slowly. He wanted to be going fast, but the Dogmobile wasn't meant for highways. It only had three wheels, for Christ's sake. He turned down the country road. The cart bounced. He checked the time and switched on the radio. Stevie Nicks was singing "White-Winged Dove." He lit a cigarette, trying to calm his nerves. Whatever was happening, he was pissed off at Soon. His first sleep in days and he'd woken up to this:

To: GhostMason@hotmail.com
From: Soontobe@gmail.com
Subject: Soon rather than later

Cocaine's not as good the next day, is it?
Now's the time, I know.
I'll meet you on the Jackson.

Twilight cut through the windshield as he approached the bridge. There was no one to be seen. Ahead, a parked rental car and a camcorder, like toys plunked down by a giant hand.

He stopped and got out. Clouds moved fast overhead. He bit hard on the end of his cigarette. There was a Post-it note stuck to the tripod:

If you find this camera please don't touch it. If your curiosity is too great for that, I ask you to make the footage public. If you are Mr. D, then hats off to you.

I'll see you, Soon.

Mason didn't like this one bit.

The camcorder's battery was dead. He checked that the digital card was still in it, then stepped to the railing and looked down. Hundreds of feet below, white waves were churning, and he could see something purple snagged among the rocks: Soon's gypsy leather coat. That had been Mason's idea: *Unbutton as you turn so they can't see the harness. When you dive, the coat is a flourish behind you. It's a cape! It is wings!*

By the looks of it, he'd done it well: unharnessed on his own, then left the coat behind. Toweled off. Changed his clothes—the wet ones in a backpack with the bungee, then walked to Fort Jackson to take the Greyhound who knows where—the act of disappearing.

When Mason got home, Willy was asleep. He plugged in the camcorder, connected it to his laptop, poured a drink, and pressed PLAY:

The screen is dark, then flashes to light. No voice, but the sound of birds. Images come into focus, turning: the top of a railing, parts of a bridge, another railing, a vista of far-off trees and open sky, the roof of a nondescript car, 360 degrees. The bridge appears desolate.

A *kitcha kitcha* sound. Fingers. Then the camera is steady. Boot steps, a chest. A man walking backward away from the camera, flashes of light over his shoulder, his face . . .

And now Soon is standing in the middle of the screen. We see him from the knees up; a deep purple coat; his back to the railing; behind him, sky.

He stares for a moment into the camera. And then he begins:

They'll come for you. You're sure of it. When it comes down to it, they'll come for you—over the hill, bugles blowing, when the wagon is surrounded and the ammunition spent . . .

The ancient Greeks could have used linear perspective. They had the means—a hand sticking out of its frame. But they figured it was better, I guess, to leave the hand on the wall. The ancient Greeks could have painted in oil. Instead, they used it to coat the bottom of their boats. So their boats wouldn't sink. So they wouldn't drown.

They'll come for you. When the air is burning, when the flames reach the top window . . .

The most perfect frescoes we have from ancient Rome are on the walls of Pompeii. Preserved when the volcano blew—the destruction of an entire city: ash shadows on the sidewalk, burned black like Hiroshima, good-bye. But we have the art. We have the Art! Now we can see how the rooms, like Venetian works of the fifteenth century, open up—as if there's something past the surface, something beyond the walls, other than silhouettes framed, drowning in shadow.

They'll come for you. When there's no more time, and the eyes are staring in circles, your feet above the ground . . . They'll be there, through the town square, splitting the noose with an arrow, cracking the hangman's head with a rifle butt . . .

Trabeated architecture; post and lintel. A noose. Postmodern; doors open both ways. If it's abstract, you've got to ask yourself, abstracted from what? Is drowning an abstraction of swimming?

Buckminster Fuller built a geodesic dome over an entire Japanese city to control its environment. So it could drown in its own air.

They'll come for you. When you're going down for the third time and there's nothing but the waves overhead, crashing and rolling, the incredible weight of your own body, going down . . .

Rembrandt. The greatest portraitist ever. And everyone he ever loved— wives, children, they all died—until all that was left was statuary. He loved the stuff so much he would have sold his soul, his fingers, for Medusa's head. Paid for a shipload of classical statues: his entire life savings. The ship sank. Bronze and marble men clinging to each other, scratching at the crates, down and down . . . After that he painted his own face, a visual penance, reflected over and over until he died.

Ernst Ludwig Kirchner: His whole life in paint: nudes in the studio. Torn banners and empty mornings. His own self in soldier's uniform, his right hand missing, a bloody stump. The Nazis declared it degenerate art. Made him watch as they destroyed his entire collection, then left him alone to kill himself.

Mark Rothko lived for color. Painted every color to its fullest. Each producing its own light—a source, a well of blood. Every fucking hue. Then he began to run out. In the year before he committed suicide, all of his paintings were gray. Painted himself into a box, into an ocean.

They'll come for you. When you're going down for the fourth . . ."

As Soon speaks, he unbuttons his coat. Not turning. Still facing the camera.

The fifth . . .

His coat is off now. In a flourish he throws it—over his shoulder, over the railing, like wings into the sky, billowing, then falling, and out of the frame.

And there's nothing, not even the weight of your own body . . .

Mason holds his breath.

The T-shirt is white with black lettering. It says SOON. There is no harness. Nothing. He steps backward.

They'll come for you. You're sure of it.

Step.

Always have been.

A quick turn.

The back of his shirt says: NOW!!!

And he is airborne . . .

Mason shouts, smacks at the space bar. The image freezes on sky, cut by railing. Nothing else.

But no—there is a bird, caught swooping into frame.

Mason stares at the screen, the wings in half flap.

Who wants to brave those bronzed beauties
Lying in the sun
With their long soft hair falling
Flying as they run?

The
Fifth

**Introducing:
Seth, Utopia,
and the Lady of the Horses**

45

SARAH AND Mason have finally escaped the family dinner and are on their way to the lake, drinking from a bottle of Teacher's.

"Can you believe the moon?" says Sarah as they emerge from the forest. It is a giant silver hangnail among the million stars.

They've come to the fence. Mason is holding a flashlight. It illuminates gravel, then the cattle guard—a dozen iron bars, more than a hoof's width apart. "Watch your step," he says, keeping the beam steady as Sarah walks across.

On the other side, a sparse stand of birch trees lines the gravel road. The rest is pasture, all the way down to the lake. The light in his hand dances as he crosses over the guard. Then something hits him. A flurry of wings. Then another, and another. They scratch across his hands, grab at his T-shirt. He hears Sarah shriek, and his hair is being pulled. The beam of light is strobing. There is screeching all around. He throws the flashlight to the ground. His shirt is in his hands now and he's beating the air as he runs. He can hear Sarah running, too, and keeps on going, down through the fields.

Then above his breath and pounding heart, he hears Sarah laughing—her feet slowing down . . . and finally he stops.

"Fucking bats!" she gasps, doubled over, but he doesn't know what she means. His brain is still shouting:

They came this far.
They'll always be coming.

He wants to keep running, but Sarah is gasping now, her hands on her knees. She looks up at him still laughing. He's holding his shirt like a useless weapon, sweating and shaking. "Fucking bats," she says again. And finally he gets it.

Any time else, he would have been the cool one. He would have been the one laughing—whisking them away from the birch trees and bats—especially for his cousin who looks up to him so much. They both know this. They're not going to mention the swallows.

"They didn't like the light," she says, catching her breath.

"It probably fucks up their sonar."

"Echolocation," she says. Then he sees she regrets it, didn't mean to correct him. They begin to walk toward the lake: him swinging his T-shirt; her, the bottle of Teacher's. It's quiet. They look up at the overwhelming stars. "You know," she says, "aliens probably see this as the Bat Planet."

Mason laughs, though he doesn't know why.

"Seriously. One quarter of all species of mammals are bats. One quarter. And you know what else? Ninety-five percent of all seeds in the rainforest are scattered by bats. They're the ones saving the planet."

"How do you know this?"

She shrugs. "I just finished high school." And now she's running again, her long hair flying, down toward the dock.

When he gets there, the lake is shining, the reflection of a million stars. Mason kicks off his cowboy boots, then fumbles with his belt.

"I don't know about you," says Sarah, "but I'm skinny-dipping."

A bright naked body flies past him, into the water like a streaking ghost.

He dives in and glides to where she floats, then starts to swim. He keeps on going until he's halfway across the lake. He stops, treading water among the stars. He remembers what the swimming instructor told his mother when he was just a kid.

"Won't be going to the Olympics—but that boy of yours, he could tread water till the end of the world."

He takes a slow breath off the surface, looks toward the shore, and thinks, *What if I never go back.*

The Book of Sobriety

When I was nine or ten, it was all about peashooters. I know that sounds as if I grew up in the Great Depression or something, but that's the way it was; some of us had Ataris, and some of us had BMXs, but we all had peashooters.

We got them from a store on Broadway—which, in Vancouver, is what they call Ninth Avenue. It was a weird little shop—the shelves stacked with dusty cans of meat and shoe polish, displays of obscure plastic figurines, skipping ropes, and stamp books, as if the proprietor had bought his personal quota of wares in 1954 and never sold a thing, until we started showing up to purchase his bags of dried peas and thick, plastic, swirling-colored shooters. Little kids with just enough change. I still remember his deep-ringed, apathetic eyes: more like the devil than any dealer I know.

Do kids today have peashooters? They should. Peashooters are awesome! It wasn't just like, *ptoooie-ptoooie, I got ya!* You'd stuff a whole mouthful, then blast it like a machine gun. Or you could draw one all the way back almost into your throat and let it shoot like a rifle. Sometimes you'd draw in too much and swallow one. Writing this now, I can taste the peas in my mouth. It is a very particular taste, dusty with danger, drawing the saliva out of you.

And getting hit by a good shot—it fucking hurt. We had teams and garbage can lids for shields and belts we'd made that held the peas in a pouch. We ran through the alleys shooting at each other, and it didn't always end well—so of course our parents were freaking out, but they couldn't really do much. You had kids going to battle wearing their dad's sunglasses so they wouldn't lose an eye.

Eventually it got boring shooting at each other (although, writing this now, I don't see how it could . . .). One day we took it to the next level:

All the way down my block, there were cherry trees lining the street. They were fairly easy to climb, and so a half dozen of us got up in the branches on both sides of the road, waiting like snipers. I don't remember whose idea it was—maybe mine, maybe Chaz's—but it doesn't matter; we were all into it.

It wasn't that busy a street: a car every two or three minutes, and we got a few shots off at the first couple without much response. The third one slowed down after a decent barrage, and right away we stopped

shooting. Then it kept on going, and we laughed and howled like we'd blown up the Death Star.

I don't even know for sure if I shot at the man in the black helmet. I remember seeing him coming—the bike and rider gleaming black in the sunlight. I was in the tree right in front of my house, and as he passed beneath me, he started to brake—the peas like hail bouncing off his helmet. The motorcycle came to a stop, and then—as if they'd all been struck by the same gale—kids started dropping from the cherry trees, hitting the ground, and running. And I jumped, too.

For some reason, though, I ran away from my house—across the street, right behind his bike as he gunned it to the curb. I reached the far sidewalk, turned to the right, sprinting over lawns, then dodged between two houses. In my panic I must have thought there was an opening that led to the lane. But there wasn't. Just a tall pine fence. I turned around and there he was:

All in black—boots to helmet, a mirrored visor covering his face. I don't know why he kept the helmet on, but he did. It felt like forever, him just standing there, so huge in the sunlight that there was no way I could get past him. And I could see myself, tiny in his visor.

Then my memory starts playing tricks. I think he said something, but when I try to remember it's just absurd—Darth Vader and the devil kind of crap:

"Now you must join the dark side!"

Or, "You're going to hell, kid!"

And sometimes he speaks my name.

Whatever he said, he moved toward me. The last thing I remember is his big black boot. And that's all I've got—him coming, and the terror blasting through me like an explosion. I'd never felt a fear like that. I couldn't even imagine what was about to happen. I still dream about him, though: the Man in the Black Helmet.

And he's coming for me.

46

THE DOCTOR closed Mason's notebook.

"You missed our last appointment," she said.

"I'm sorry about that."

"We had an agreement. You come here once a week, and I'll get you into the program. Is that still what you want?"

"Yeah. I was having a tough time. I'm sorry . . . but what do you think?"

"About what?"

"About what I wrote."

"What do *you* think about it?"

"Give me a break!" He pushed his chair back and looked around the room—at the cod liver oil, her sign about nuts . . .

"Hey," he said, "Where's your diploma?"

"Excuse me?"

He pointed to the bare patch of wall.

"Getting reframed," she said. "This a place where things tend to get broken."

Mason nodded.

She picked his notebook up off the desk. "It's well written," she said. "If you wrote it sober, you did a good job. Is that what you want to hear?"

"I don't know . . ."

"Why weren't you here last week?"

"Because I'm fucked-up!" said Mason.

"Well, why are you so fucked-up?"

"You want a list?"

"If you're willing to give it to me."

He felt himself shaking. "Well, for one, I have a drug problem—that's been established, right?" They looked at each other. "I keep losing money. My novel is *not* going well. I'm alienated from my family. I'm fucked-up all the time, and my friends keep killing themselves . . ."

"What do you mean?" said Dr. Francis.

"What do I mean about what?"

"Have you lost someone else?"

Mason stared at her. "Yes," he said. "That's why I'm so fucked-up."

She studied him for a moment, then put the notebook down. "Is there something you want to tell me?"

"What do you mean?" said Mason. He knew, by the way she was looking at him, it was the wrong thing to say. "Can I . . ."

She pulled the Socratic statements from a drawer and placed them on the desk. "I expect you here next week," she said

He picked up his things and left. She hadn't told him what to write.

41. Silence is golden.

42. I usually want more salt.

47

THEY WERE difficult days. The only thing he liked about them was Willy—being with her in his bed, talking and making love. But that had its difficulties, too. She couldn't feel anything, and then suddenly she felt too much. It was tricky getting her drugs; Chaz disapproved of heroin and was edgy since the raid. Mason dodged conversation with him and avoided certain things with Willy. He told her Soon had shelved the performance piece for a speaking tour in Iceland, and she didn't push it. She was the same as Chaz that way, kept curiosity on a leash like a dog.

When Willy slept, Mason didn't. He hadn't slept for days. He went to Ho-Vees and drank milk shakes spiked with vodka, his heart rate spiking every time a fat girl came through the door.

He went to the library and searched for "Circe and the Stallion." Finally he found it, in *The Glimpse of a Bruise*—a collection of poetry by Jonathan Follow.

He started phoning various Follows.

He drove back to the Old Jackson Bridge and looked into the squalls.

And once, when the fog came in, he went down to the lakeshore—a random spot on the docks that was usually full of people. He imagined Warren hurling himself in. He stood there for a while, listening to the water as it slipped against the moss-covered moorings a dozen feet below, trying to make it seem deadly. All he could see was fog—or rather, the path of moonlight through it— all the particles of air and water together with the shimmering light

of a heaven moon. And he felt as if he couldn't breathe, because of the overwhelming ratio of water to air and all the unnameable beauty . . . Then suddenly the fog began to part, just slightly—a thin slice that made the moonlit air dance in swirls, reaching from the surface of the invisible lake straight up like an inverse funnel.

This tall swirl moved toward him, cutting wider through the fog with the moonlight dancing over it. And then, from the lake, he heard a voice . . .

"Quack," it said.

And he knew he had to sleep.

One morning—after a long night in the Cave—Mason and Willy emerged into the light of day. The air was warm. Still in the shadow of the doorway, Mason scanned the street. He was sure that Bethany was out there—making plans to take back her "precious"—but it wasn't going to happen today.

Then, through all those lanes of traffic, he saw Dr. Francis—across the street, just standing there in front of the MHAD building. She was staring right at him—or at both of them, it seemed. As he crossed into the sunlight Mason raised his hand, as if to say hello. The doctor's eyes were fixed on his. A streetcar came between them and stopped at the stop. When it pulled away, the doctor was gone.

"Why'd you do that?" said Willy.

"What?"

"Why'd you wave at that woman?"

"She's my addictions doctor," said Mason. He expected her to ask why his addictions doctor was standing out on the sidewalk, glaring at them across nine lanes of traffic, but she didn't. "She takes her job seriously," he said and coughed out a laugh.

Willy said nothing. He pushed her the fifty feet down to his building, then in through the door. It closed behind them. He sat down on the stairs facing her and took out a baggie of coke. He was getting better at the climb—but still, after such a long night, he could do with the extra energy. At this point it was a

matter of safety. He did a line, then lifted her out of the wheelchair and onto his back. Where moments before he'd felt hollow, weak, troubled, he was now unstoppable—moving up the stairs strong and focused. The hit lasted as long as it needed to. He got her up both flights—into the apartment, into the bed—and then he collapsed, his back against the three-step ladder.

Willy touched his head—the most generous sort of touch, from a hand that felt nothing. "I know her," she said.

"What?"

"Dr. Francis. I know her."

"How?"

"She worked at St. Vincent's. It's a woman's shelter I used to go to."

Mason breathed in. His body felt hollow. He was crashing now. It never got easier—more predictable, mundane—but never easier. That said, it was better like this: crashing with Willy's hand on his head—better than doing it alone.

"If I tell you something, will you promise not to tell anyone?"

He breathed out. "Of course," he said.

"She risked her medical license for me. Even jail time, probably. You know when Bethany sold my wheelchair?"

Mason grunted.

"Things got out of control. We'd been squatting in a room on the edge of Regent Park, and Bethany took off. When Dr. Francis found me, I was totally bugging out. She should have just taken me to emergency like that—let me suffer through it—but I was begging her, I was so messed up. So you know what she did?"

Mason held his breath.

"She went to the park and scored some smack."

He let it out. "Fuck," he said.

"She shot me up—right there in that room. And then she called the ambulance."

"How'd she even know where to find you?"

"That's Dr. Francis," said Willy. "She can do stuff like that."

"Then I guess I'm in good hands." Mason climbed the three stairs and crawled into bed.

Birds stood on the skylight, chirping.

48

DR. FRANCIS looked at him as she had through the traffic—clear eyes blazing out of such a young face. He shifted in his chair.

"I didn't really write this week," he said, lifting up *The Book of Sobriety*. "Wasn't really sober that much. And you didn't—"

"Leave her alone," said Dr. Francis.

"Excuse me?"

"Willy. I'm warning you to leave her alone."

"Me? You're warning me? I'm the one who got her away from that bitch . . ."

The doctor leaned forward. "So you saved her, did you?"

"No, I just think I can help . . ."

"What, fix her? Don't you think you have enough cripples in your life, Mason? Enough broken things? Why don't you try fixing yourself?"

"She's my friend," said Mason.

The doctor stood. "Okay," she said, forcing him to meet her eyes. "Then you have one chance: Explain to me why your friends keep dying. Or else you leave her alone."

"Excuse me?"

"Stop saying that!" said Dr. Francis. "You sound like a pussy!" She took a breath, then sat back down and took his file in her hand. "By your own summation, you have very few close friends. In the six weeks since you arrived here in your underwear, three of them have killed themselves. How do you explain that?"

"I never said any of that!"

"Actually, you did," said Dr. Francis. "You probably don't remember, but on your initial intake—when you came here in your underwear—one of the reasons you gave for your distress was this:" She opened the file. "You said a close friend of yours had just committed suicide. It's right here in your file. Then there was Sissy, or Circe, or whatever you'd like to call her," she flipped some pages. "And then last week . . ."

"So people die!" said Mason.

Dr. Francis closed the file. "If you don't have a better answer, I'm going to have to intervene."

Mason stood up. "What happened to confidentiality?"

"There is none," said Dr. Francis. "Not if I think you might harm yourself or someone else."

Mason was at the door now. "Then we may as well let everyone hear!" he said, throwing it open. He turned back, glaring at Dr. Francis. "But before you go threatening me, you should know: Willy told me what you did! So don't accuse me of endangering people—*or* trying to save them. Take a look at yourself, Doc!"

Then he strode out and into the waiting room. There was only one person there—a man in a hat, who looked slightly surprised. Mason nodded to him and carried on, out into the hallway. He punched the arrow pointing down.

43. *In my dreams I'm often falling.*
44. *I'd rather build a bridge than write a song.*

49

THERE WERE times when it was like he was watching himself. From outside of his body, or at least his consciousness—when he couldn't stop doing lines, making bad calls, digging a hole for himself, digging and digging. And the part of him watching didn't do a thing to stop him. Maybe it used to, long ago—but now all it did was watch. It knew he was too drunk, too high, and losing too much. It knew Willy was trying to talk to him—that she felt sick and sad and didn't want to be here, watching him dig. But even if it wanted to, it just couldn't stop him.

"I want to go home," said Willy.

"Then go home," said Mason.

"Please. You're not going to win."

He did a line, and he played the next hand. She said something else, but he tuned her out. He could see himself doing it.

"Do you want me to go?" he heard her say.

"I don't want you to do anything because of me. I can't take care of you. I can't fix you. I can't even help you."

"I don't want you to help me. I just want you."

He watched himself drink a beer, all the way down. Call $200. Do another line. "Well, you can't have me," he said.

And then she was gone.

And he couldn't even see himself anymore.

Notes on the Novel in Progress

It's all about point of view.

As long as his POV is engaging, we'll forgive the character's flaws.

Bullshit.

So what makes for empathy?

Struggle. Hopes and dreams. The collision of a painful personal past with an overwhelming present. Honesty. Humor.

What's so funny about peace, love, and empathy?

Fuck you.

Possible title:

Fuck You, Too

50

"WHAT THE fuck are you doing?"

He opened his eyes. He was on the floor near his bed. Chaz was sitting in a chair, looking down at him. Mason groaned.

"Why'd you treat her like that?"

"Willy?"

"Yeah, Willy."

"It's complicated."

"That's fucking bullshit."

"I can't take care of her, all right?"

"All right," said Chaz. "And I can't take care of you." He stood up. "That floor you're lying on costs $900 a month." He stepped over Mason and walked out the door.

Eventually Mason got up. He drank three glasses of water, took a long shower, got dressed again, and drank more water. He looked

out the window at the MHAD building, then turned on the laptop. He had one email.

Mason didn't get back to him as soon as possible. He was sick of people who wanted to kill themselves, or thought they did, or just wanted attention, and he didn't want to think about it any more. His first inclination was to delete the message—and to take his ad off that fucking website. But that seemed like a lot of work. So, instead, he made himself some coffee in his new coffeemaker and sat down on the couch to drink it. Then eventually, despite himself and his hangover, Mason started to think.

He thought of Warren, Sissy, and Soon, of Willy and even Sarah. He felt nauseous, hollow, and his brain was barely working. But he glugged his coffee and kept on thinking—of the things he'd done and the things he'd wanted, and the things he'd wanted to do. He barely felt, but he felt like sobbing. And then, like the stupidest kind of protagonist, he let himself think of redemption.

51

HE GOT off the streetcar at Prince and Mill, counted six doors down from the corner, and there it was: Tony's Happy Daze Bar and Beer.

You think that's funny, wait until you see the place.

It didn't look that funny—at least from the outside. The windows were blacked out with torn reflecting plastic, peeling at the corners. The word *cunt* (or maybe *cant*) was scrawled across the bottom of the door, as if some misogynist (or possibly an illiterate

philosophy major) had reached out with a spray-paint can while passing out on the sidewalk. He opened the door to the smell of fried rice and empty kegs.

At first glance, the inside wasn't very funny either. The floor was covered with dirty orange carpet and, in some parts, squares of cardboard framed with duct tape. The fluorescence had been mercifully lessened by the demise of several tubes. A pale green glow shone over a pool table in the back, and shimmering lights from a large fish tank illuminated the wall. There were a few shoddy tables. Directly in front of the door stood an elaborate, mahogany coatrack. *I guess that's sort of funny*, thought Mason, stepping awkwardly around it.

A skinny Asian woman was leaning on the bar, facing (yet seeming to ignore) her patrons. They were all men, in various degrees of slump, each separated from the next by a vacant orange stool. One of them had a cane by his side—the one on the end wore a hat.

"It's *hot* out there," said Mason, and glanced around. The man closest to him gave a snort, and the barmaid looked over as if she doubted it was worth the effort of turning her head. Mason tried a smile and a nod.

"You wanna drink?" she said.

"Please."

She rolled her eyes. "What drink you wan'?"

"Just a beer," said Mason. "Make it a Keith's."

As she poured the beer, Mason glanced at the men once more and cleared his throat. "It's friggin' *hot* out . . ."

"You say that before," said the barmaid, thudding the glass down in front of him. "It stupid."

The man who'd snorted now growled. "It's only sixty-three degrees."

"You drug smoker?" the barmaid asked.

Mason tried to laugh as if they were all sharing a joke. Then the man with the hat at the end of the bar called out, "What the hell do you expect? It's Toronto in the summertime." Mason picked up his beer and walked to the end of the bar.

He sat down. "You know what . . . ?" But the man in the hat interrupted.

"Mary! Can you turn it up? I like this song." "Sussudio," by Phil Collins, was playing.

"*Nobody* like this song!" said Mary, but she turned it up anyway.

"She's right," said Mason.

"I guess. But now they can't hear us."

"That was the worst secret code ever."

"Who knew the temperature would drop overnight? And anyway, you got it wrong. It was supposed to be *fucking* hot out there, not *frigging*." He sounded disappointed.

"Why didn't you just say, 'I'll be the one in the floppy gray hat?'"

"I wanted to check you out a bit first."

"So . . ."

"So you seem a bit weird." The man's voice was forlorn, like that of a stuffed donkey.

"*I* seem weird! 'Sussudio'! It's not even a real name!"

"You may be right." The man picked up his drink. "I'm Seth Handyman."

"Mason," said Mason. They clinked their glasses together.

"You play pool?" Seth asked.

As he racked the balls, Mason studied him. The hat was disconcerting—a classic fedora that had lost its shape. It cast a shadow across his face, making evaluation difficult: longish, grayish hair—almost to his shoulders. Sallow skin, gray cheeks, unshaven but not bearded, wet and lippy mouth, lanky arms and long hands that moved quickly around the felt. No real fix on the eyes. In general: midforties, a bit overweight, and probably not too bad at pool. Mason decided to let him win a few games. "Want to play for a beer?"

Seth looked up, eyes still shaded by the brim of his hat. "Don't drink," he said.

"Oh."

Seth flipped a quarter.

"Heads," said Mason.

"Nope," said Seth. He put the coin back in his pocket, then turned to select a cue. "I used to drink." He rolled out the white ball, then broke. It cracked like a rifle shot, one of each down. "I was good at it, too. These guys here—they drink like Finns."

"What are fins?"

Seth sank a solid, then sighed. "People who live in Finland."

"Right."

"You ever been there? Worst drinkers in the world. They're pretty awful all round, actually: dour, unattractive, dull as dirt; it's like their gray matter is actually gray—you know what I mean?" He had a way of talking that was incongruous with how much of it he was doing, as if it were a chore he had to finish. *Man*, thought Mason, *this guy is depressed*. And yet there was something else going on—as if this depression was a fairly new development, as if he'd spent his life in witty repartee, and now, though partially lobotomized, the banter just kept coming.

"They'll sit there staring at nothing, drinking fast. Get drunk quick, angry for like ten minutes or so, and then they just pass out." He missed his next shot.

Mason sank a stripe, then another, then flubbed one.

"Anyway, point is: These guys are like Finns."

"So why do you come here?"

"Be alone." He took the duck instead of the position shot, then a tricky combo. "Also, it's kind of a funny place."

"Like Finland?"

"Ha!" Seth missed a long bank shot and turned to Mason. "Get this: highest literacy rate in the world *and* the highest suicide rate. *That's* Finland."

And so they'd arrived at the subjects of the day: reading, writing, and suicide. Mason put his cue down. His newfound (heroic) purpose made it easier than before. He took a breath and spoke directly: "Okay, Seth—this is how we'll do it: I'll tell you what I can offer you, and you tell me how it suits you. Okay?"

For a moment the man seemed taken aback. He did, in fact, take a step backward. Then he leaned on his cue. "All right. If you've got something to say . . ." There was a challenge in his voice.

He doesn't know you're here to save him.

And so Mason explained his business—the same as before but with fewer stipulations—no cumbersome speech about last names and not wanting to know. The more he knew, the better.

When he'd finished his spiel, Seth looked down at the floor, then up again. "How do you live with yourself?" he said.

It felt like a gutshot. "Excuse me?"

"I'm just kidding, kid," said Seth, and laughed. "No, really—this is perfect."

"Oh . . . okay then."

"It's your shot."

"We keep playing?"

Seth leaned against the table as if thinking about it. Then, slowly, he tipped back the brim of his hat. His eyes were baby blue flecked with white. He looked at Mason. "I love games," he said, in that far-off mirthless voice.

"Sure," said Mason.

"Especially one-on-one." Seth studied him as he spoke. "Pool, tennis, poker, boxing. People say you play games, you play sports, but you don't play boxing—as if violence and pain can't also be a game. But that's bullshit, don't you think? You know what's one of my favorite things?"

Mason looked at him. "Brown paper parcels, tied up with string?"

A smile—a creepy one, sure, but the man actually smiled.

"Heads-up no-limit poker," he said, and looked at Mason as if they knew each other. But before he could respond, the moment had passed. "Come on," said Seth. "Let's finish the game."

"A tenner on it?"

Seth laughed. "God, I love gamblers." He said it the way Willy said she loved drug addicts. "Tell you what . . ."

"What?"

"Let's play for the truth instead."

And so that's what they did. One question per ball.

They racked again, and Mason broke.

One of each down.

"Do you work?" Mason asked.

"Sure."

"What do you do?"

"That's two questions."

"I sank two balls."

Seth squinted, then nodded. "Subway," he said.

"Restaurant or rapid transit?"

"Not the fucking restaurant."

One in the side.

"Why did you stop drinking?"

"It gets me in trouble."

Four down the rail in the end.

"Have you tried to kill yourself?"

"Nope."

Mason flubbed a bank shot. Seth took aim.

Eleven in the end.

"What's your last name?"

Mason hesitated. "Dubisee,"

Fourteen, same pocket.

"How many clients have you had?"

"Three."

Sixteen in the side.

"How many are dead?"

"At least two."

A crash. The mahogany coatrack fell to the floor as one of the old guys stumbled over it. Mary shouted, "Fuck you marbles!" or something like that, and the men started pounding their fists on the bar.

A bit funny, but not funny ha-ha.

"What's the deal with the coatrack?" said Mason.

"It's not your turn." Seth missed.

Mason sank the two ball, then asked the question again.

"It's a sort of sobriety test," said Seth. "You knock it over on the way out, you gotta give Mary your keys and buy the bar a round. You knock it over on the way in, and you don't get served—unless you buy two rounds."

"So we got a drink coming?"

Seth shrugged.

Mason took aim.

Down the rail in the end.

Instead of asking about the drink again, he looked at Seth straight on. "Are we going to work together?" he said.

"Oh, that was decided long ago."

Eight in the end.

"Another game?" said Mason.

"That's your question?"

Mason nodded.

"Sure," said Seth, and racked up the balls. "We've got a lot to answer for."

The Book of ~~Sobriety~~ Confession

Forgive me, doctor, for not being sober. That is my first confession.

The word *inspire* means, literally, "to breathe life into." I stole that from a person who's most likely dead now. That is my second.

I have done the opposite of inspire. I've stolen breath away.

Fourteen swallows. One horse. A few human beings.

And how did this happen?

I used to be a writer, and I needed inspiration. I searched the world for it, did all sorts of things, both good and bad, but couldn't always find the natural stuff. I started using the chemical kind, until eventually that's all I had.

I confess to using unnatural inspiration.

One day a man asked me to write something for him—a love letter. He paid me well, I did my best, and then he killed himself—leaving the letter as a suicide note. The idea confused me, upset me, angered me—and then it inspired me.

I decided to advertise my skills. (I confess to poor judgment.) Like the man in fake love, my next client was a dishevelment of lines, blank spaces, discomfort, sadness—a bit part in her own story—huge yet deflated. She wanted me to fill her in, and she was willing to pay. (I confess to being an unexemplary gambler.) And so I did. I tried to breathe life into her—to make her more real—so there'd be something for her to leave behind.

I confess to remorse.

I confess to being a pussy.

The next one had to trick me, but it wasn't hard to do. He just told me what I wanted to hear—that it was about art rather than death, the trick of creativity. So I signed on for fraud and got suicide just the same. This fucking writing is a deadly pursuit.

Is that good enough for you, Doctor? Or do you need to know about Willy?

I confess: I like her for dishonorable reasons. I like her breasts and her mouth and her proclivity for drugs. And I'm sure you're right—I like that she's broken more than I am, the idea that I could fix her. And maybe I can't save her, but I wasn't going to hurt her.

I confess that I miss her—and all the dishonorable things we did together.

I confess that I'm a derelict.

That I spent my best years in narcissistic wandering.

That glory meant more to me than goodness—and maybe still does.

That my hunger controls my heart.

That I am self-indulgent, self-destructive, and my own worst narrator.

That I said things I shouldn't have said, wrote things I shouldn't have written.

That I let the world get smaller.

And forgot to look out for people.

But I want you to know: I plan to do better.

To be what I should have been.

I just hope it's not too late.

To: JFollow@FollowMe.com
From: MasonD@hotmail.com
Subject: Urgent

To the poet Jonathan Follow,

There is a matter both urgent and delicate that I need to discuss with you. It pertains to the well-being of your immediate family. I tracked your address down off an internet site that may not be reliable. I hope this message has found the appropriate reader. I'm sorry if it alarms you. Please contact me as soon as possible.

Sincerely,

Mason D

Name: Seth Handyman.

Gender: Male.

Age: 44.

Place of work: Subway (not the restaurant).

Drug and alcohol use: Abstinent. Heavy past use likely.

Appearance: Medium height, slightly overweight.

Hair: Almost to his shoulders, graying, thinning. Wears a floppy gray fedora.

Eyes: Pale glassy blue, with white flecks—like robin's eggs.

Hangout: Tony's Happy Daze Bar and Beer.

Likes: Games.

Dislikes: Finland.

Family: Parents deceased. Brother estranged.

Risk to self: High.

Risk to others: Unknown.

Depression, hopelessness: Apparent.

Fear, anxiety, panic: Unknown.

Mood swings, unstable moods: Unknown.

Uncontrollable, compulsive behavior: Unknown.

Impulsive, illegal or reckless behavior: Unknown.

Manic, bizarre behavior: A little.

Openness to being saved: Unknown.

Would like to belong to several clubs: Probably not.

52

TWO DAYS later they were back in Tony's Happy Daze Bar and Beer, shooting pool and asking questions.

Twelve off the ten in the side.

"Do you have fear, anxiety, or panic?"

"Right now?" said Seth.

"Generally."

"No. Not generally."

Mason miscued. The four went into the side.

"It's still a ball . . ."

"My ball, my question."

A shrug from Mason.

"Where is your family?"

Mason hesitated. "The other side of the country."

Seven cross-corner.

"What was the name of your first client?"

"Sorry," said Mason. "That's confidential."

"Oh, yeah?"

"Yes."

"One of the rules of suicide assistance?" Seth turned and put his cue back in the rack. "Interesting. Very ethical."

"What are you doing?"

"This game has rules, too. So apparently we've got a conflict." He picked up his jacket. "I'm leaving now." He walked toward the coat-rack.

He's getting away.

"Warren," said Mason.

Seth turned. "Before you tell me his last name, keep in mind: I can just go online: the *Globe* obituaries cover the past two years."

He wanted to tell him, *Stop making this so goddamn difficult. I'm trying to fucking save you!*

"Why do you want to know?"

"So we can trust each other," said Seth.

Just fucking tell him!

"Shanter," said Mason. "Warren Shanter."

Seth walked back and picked up the cue. He smacked carelessly at a cluster of balls. The ten went down.

"My ball," said Mason. Seth stood back. "Did you bring the money?"

"I will next time," said Seth. Mason looked at him, then he missed a cross-side.

Seth took down the six.

"Have you started on the letter?"

"I will when you pay me." They looked at each other.

This is a dangerous game, kiddo.

Seth glanced down at the slate. "It's a messy table."

Mason's balls were all trapped on the rails. And Seth had no shot. Mason looked at him. "You forfeiting?" he said.

Something flashed across Seth's face. Then he just looked tired. "I'll give you one question."

"All right," said Mason. "Why can't you write your own letter?"

"Writing's like drinking. I used to do it, but now I don't."

"That makes no sense."

Seth shrugged. "It's the truth, though." He turned around and headed out the door.

Mason paid his bill, then followed him. A half block away, Seth's gray hat bobbed. Mason walked toward it.

Seth turned left on Sudden Street. A minute later, Mason turned too, then crouched behind a parked car. The sidewalk was clear, and Seth was only about thirty yards ahead of him, just standing there. He was staring at a tree.

After a few minutes he began walking again. Mason moved slower, still in a crouch behind the row of parked cars.

Three blocks down, Seth stopped once more, in front of a large old house, two plots wide, painted a dark brownish black. There was a chest-high wrought-iron fence surrounding the yard. He pressed something on the gate, then waited a moment before pulling it open. He walked up the front steps onto the porch, waited again, then stepped inside.

As Mason studied the large dark house, the door opened again. Two men walked out onto the porch and lit cigarettes. They began to smoke in silence.

To: MasonD@hotmail.com
From: JFollow@FollowMe.com
Subject: Urgent

Dear Mr. D,

Unfortunately I'm not the J. Follow you're looking for (I am less famous). The good news is I think I can help you. This has happened before (we are distant relatives but have met only once). Here is a phone number that may work: (915) 822-2131.

All the best,
Jeffrey (not a poet) Follow

53

ONE WEEK after his ill-fated meeting with Dr. Francis, Mason returned to her office. He didn't say anything—just bowed his head and handed her *The Book of Confession*.

45. *I prefer candlelight to lamps.*
46. *There are angels here among us.*

He sat in the Cave, three lines of coke and a twenty-sixer on the bar in front of him. The DJ was playing a remix of a Nina Simone song. Mason looked in the mirror—imagining someone behind it watching him. He studied himself that way—trying to see what the man in the safe room saw: a self-conscious loner, a drunk, a sucker, a guy staring at himself in a crowded boozecan. He changed his focus and, still looking in the large, bulletproof mirror, searched the room around him, all these faces in the flashing dark and light.

Chaz came down the bar and stood in front of him.

"What?"

"You've only got yourself to blame."

"Thanks, Chaz. I'm doing fine."

"You kidding me? You're over the cliff with the buffalo."

"Nope." Mason did a line. "Things are good, actually. I've got purpose now."

"You got what?"

"Meaning, a reason to live . . . you know: purpose."

"Well, you look like bat shit. What's it called . . . ?"

"Guano?"

"Yeah, you're all guano-looking. How much did you lose last night?"

"Some."

"And the night before?"

Mason poured himself another glass. "Also some. What's your point?"

"What's your purpose?" Chaz waved toward the card table. "Putting vampires through college?"

"Nah, it's something good." His heart was palpitating a bit. He took a long drink and did another line. Chaz turned to leave, but Mason stopped him. "Can you find an address from a phone number?"

"Possibly."

Mason took a napkin, wrote down the number, and slid it across the bar. "Oh," he said, pulling it back. "There's also an address I want a number for." He wrote *68 Sudden Street*.

"Why don't you just visit the one and phone the other?"

"It's a long story."

"Anything to do with Willy?"

"Not directly."

"Well, it should," said Chaz.

Mason looked at him. "You seen her?"

Chaz didn't answer. There was a ruckus at the poker table. Chaz put the napkin in his pocket and headed down the bar. Mason did a line, lit a smoke, and stared at the mirror again.

54

Combo cross-side.

Boom.

Seth was *on* today. He was in the zone. His voice had a bit of cut to it. Even the questions were sharper.

"How long since you've seen your family?"

"About five years."

Six in the end.

"What are you hiding from?"

"Myself, I guess," said Mason. He'd meant it to sound trite, to undercut the question. But his voice had gone too high. Seth let the silence stretch, then took another shot.

Mason hadn't yet decided what to do with the information he'd got from Chaz, but questions like that last one made him want to beat Seth—still save him of course—but bring him down a notch at the same time.

Seth rattled the corner.

Mason took aim.

Fourteen in the side.

"Do you live with anyone?"

"Nope."

Mason stepped back from the table. He looked at Seth, who was chalking his cue. "We're playing for the truth," he said.

Seth looked up at him.

"You live in a halfway house," said Mason. "With sixteen other ex-cons."

They stood there for a moment. "Why don't you shoot?"

"It's not your turn for a question, Seth." He lined up a combo. The nine skidded and missed the pocket.

Seth stepped up to the table. No assessment, he just leaned in— and *boom*, he hammered down the four ball.

"How long you been a drug addict?"

No time to answer. *Boom.*

"And a drunk?"

Boom. "And a lousy gambler?"

Boom. "And a fucking pussy?"

He stood up, pushed back the brim of his hat, and they looked at each other. Mason didn't like what he saw.

He's still worth saving.

Is he, though?

"About five years," said Mason.

Boom. Eight ball in the end.

Seth grinned. "Who's the Man in the Black Helmet?" he said. Then he turned to put his cue away.

Mason just stared at the back of his head.

"By the way," said Seth. "I don't have your money." He pulled something out of his jacket pocket, turning back around. "I brought you this instead." He tossed it onto the table, the balls scattering sadly. A brown notebook. On the cover, in raised hokey font, it read NOTEBOOK.

Mason walked over and picked it up. Seth was already out the door.

55

THEY ARE in the paddock, drunk, hair still wet from the lake—saddling up beneath a silver moon. The Big House is dark: Aunt Jo and three more generations sleeping off the wine. Mason holds the reins for Sarah. She gets up on Warren and he pulls the cinch tight. Warren starts to prance.

Mason swings onto Zevon's back and the long gate falls open. They ride through it, a line of trees on one side, the fence then the steep hill down to the land on the other. He angles toward the high road, digs in his heels and they're off, hooves thundering over the earth. When he turns back he sees Sarah's hair, like wings, shimmering in the moonlight.

56

The Book of Handyman

This is my notebook. Like a diary, but my new counselor, Mr. White, said I didn't have to call it that if I don't want to. He is the one who wants me to right in it. I don't like to right very much because when I read it out loud it doesn't sound like it should. It sounds like I'm a little kid or something.

But Mr. White says it doesn't matter if its good or not and I should do it even if its bad stuff. And nobody else will look at it. Its private. Even he's just gonna look fast at the pages—to see that I'm doing what he asked.

Mr. White wants me to right about what happened to me when I was attacked and what I feel and what my thoughts are. He says jail is for thinking about all kinds of stuff. He calls prison *jail*. He says I should right about what bothers me and what makes me angry. Also, he said I should call him Larry.

So! Do you want to no what bothers me? One of the things is I feel like people don't care to much. Even people who are supposed to help you—like doctors. They didn't even give me drugs when I left the hospital. Can you believe that? If your in jail they don't care about you. They don't give you pharmacuticals for the pain, and they didn't even try to fix my head. So now I'm basically a freak. Thats something else that bothers me!

The doorbell was ringing. Mason put the notebook down and looked at it.

What the fuck?

This was not the man he'd met. He thought about this as he walked to the intercom.

It was Chaz. "I got something for you."

"Why don't you come up?"

"I've got to open the Cave," he said. Mason pulled on a shirt and headed down the stairs.

Chaz held out a piece of paper and Mason took it:

Jonathan Follow. 10 Apple Road. Utopia, Ontario.

"Is this a joke?"

"Nope," said Chaz. "It's a real town. Real road, too. Go ahead and Google it."

"Thank you," said Mason.

Chaz nodded. "I've got to open up."

The Book of Handyman

Now I'm going to tell you about Mr. White—oops, I mean "Larry"!

He has glasses. And he's already like a friend to me. He said I can tell him anything in the world! Even if it's really bad! And also he kind of looks like a woman. But not like a hot one. More like a fat one with no breasts, you know? Like a fat, flat bitch. I know thats sort of mean—but I don't mean it that way. Its just true. (I sure am glad he's not going to read this!) And another thing about Larry—that fat bitch is fucking patronizing. He thinks everybody is as stupid as he is, poor fucker. But really, there's not much to do here. So if Larry White wants me to write—I'll guess I'll write . . .

It reminds me of that song. How's it go?

If Barry White saved your life

Or got you back with your ex-wife

Sing Barry White (Barry White)

Sing Barry White (Barry White)

It's all right (It's all riiiiiiiiiight . . .)

Mason closed the notebook. It was weird all right, but he didn't have time for this shit, kept thinking of Sissy Follow.

Saving people is a matter of minutes.

He picked up the piece of paper and the Google map he'd printed.

You know what you have to do.

He knew what he had to do.

57

IT WAS four in the morning when he left the city limits. He crossed onto Route 7, a two-lane back road, heading northeast at thirty miles an hour. There was no one else on the highway.

When you opened her up like this, the Dogmobile got loud—three small wheels with a Smurf-like engine. He switched on the radio. At first he thought it was between stations—but then he heard it: the low spooky opening of "State Trooper." It made him shiver. They hardly ever played this on the radio. He turned it up and lit a smoke. The sky was full of stars.

On the last of Springsteen's mournful howls, begging and defiant at the same time, Mason slowed down to twenty and poured some coke onto the stainless steel counter. It was going to be a long night. He cut with one hand and steered with the other. He did a line and looked out from beneath the poppy seed brim. For a moment he had the same feeling as when he'd been in the QT room, staring out at the darkened Cave. He was right here and, at the same time, light years away—floating and trapped where no one would ever know—all-seeing and never seen, his visor a one-way mirror. But then the feeling was gone. It was hard to stay anxious driving a Dogmobile, the stars all shining bright.

He lit a smoke and pressed down on the gas, easing back up to thirty. At these speeds he'd be lucky to get there by daybreak. On the map it looked tricky—a ways off the highway, with an old train track running through. Apple Road was probably gravel, or even just dirt. At least he wouldn't be conspicuous, bouncing along in a motorized, fiberglass, big-city hat.

But how did Seth know? About the Man in the Black Helmet?

He turned up the radio.

It was the first gray of morning. The Dogmobile crept through the outskirts of Barrie, past its belching, slumbering form.

The light turned silver, shimmering from the horizon, and the sides of the highway began to take shape. Mason drove west on County Road 18, the sun rising behind him—the first hint of warmth like animal breath on his neck.

He'd been doing lines to stay awake, and now the dawn made him feel twitchy and aching. He wanted a drink.

Will Utopia have a bar?

What time would it open?

"Rain Dance" by the Guess Who came on the radio. Another anomaly. It felt as if he was coming onto something—what with the coke and the sunrise and the songs they never played. He stepped on the gas, and the Dogmobile stopped.

Not all at once, mind you. First it stuttered, shook, skidded, and banged. After *that* it stopped. There was a hissing sound that made Mason want to run for the hills. He turned off the engine, wiped the coke off the stainless steel counter, then stumbled out of the hissing hat onto the highway.

He walked up the side of the road for a minute or so, then turned and looked back. Left to right: spooky tree in the middle of a barren field, mess of chicken wire and vines, dilapidated barn, gravel, ditch, giant fedora on wheels, the faded center line of County Road 18, ditch, log fence, another barn, then fields into infinity. He waited until the Dogmobile stopped making that unsettling sound, then walked back toward it.

No point in looking at the engine. He wasn't even sure where it was. "Probably a gasket," he said. "Or a hose. Or maybe . . ." He noticed he was talking out loud and stopped. After trying the ignition a half dozen times, he took out his cell phone.

No reception.

He did a line, then set to work. He stuffed two bottles of water, a package of chicken dogs, three bags of chips, sunglasses, and Seth's notebook into a plastic bag. He put the clutch in neutral, dropped the bag on the side of the road, then began to push the Dogmobile off the highway.

This was awkward. The chrome made it heavier than it should

have been; the fiberglass made it lighter, and tippy. And the odd number of wheels didn't help with the balance. Control was a delusion.

When the Dogmobile hit the gravel, it slowed down a bit—but didn't stop. It was a singular sound—a giant chrome and fiberglass fedora tumbling into a ditch. Three hundred ravens alighted from the surrounding fields. They dispersed in the air like awakened souls.

Mason stood at the side of the road, waiting for a car to come. He drank some water. Then, to kill time, he pulled out the notebook.

The Book of Handyman

The Day I Was Degloved,
by S. Handyman
Dedicated to Mr. Larry White
(Sing Larry White)

It was a Tuesday afternoon and I was in the exercise room for my trice-weekly constitutional. You should know, dear nonexistent reader, that prisoners in my position—for our own safety—do most things separately from the general prisoner population. On this day I was on my own, but for a guard named Jacob, and I was working on my triceps and forearms. Lying face-up on a padded bench, I was holding a barbell above me, doing vertical curls. My forearms are particularly impressive, and young Jacob was watching closely—until suddenly he wasn't. Within a second of realizing I was alone, no longer was I alone.

I don't know why, with all the equipment in there, they bothered to fashion a weapon; men become bored in prison. From what little I could gauge in that awkward moment, they'd made a hatchet of sorts—heavy and pointed, but also dull. It struck the top of my head, denting but not splitting my skull. The blade, however, caught beneath my scalp. Scalp is very thick—five separate layers of skin and flesh—adding up to almost an inch. But should something get through a few layers with sufficient force at the right angle, they lift right up, like peel from an orange.

That was, in a life full of fascinating sensations, the most memorable. It felt as if my brain—though still connected to my nervous system—had

been ripped from my head. The sound was like amplified Velcro. I didn't lose consciousness. In fact I sat straight up, hurling the barbell across the room. The top of my head was flipped back but still attached, so that it stuck up in a semicircle, like a blood-red sun rising above the Earth. I shouted, and my attackers fled.

If Larry White makes you write
About getting scalped in a jailhouse fight
Sing Larry White (Larry White). . .

A car was coming. Mason stuck out his thumb, trying to make eye contact with the driver. Smiling. And then it was gone.

The sun's been up a while.

Mason looked down at the notebook. Seth was emerging, but he'd have to wait.

Every minute counts.

He stuffed the notebook back in the bag and headed down the road.

47. I've never had a favourite color, or animal, or tree.
48. The world is what we make it.

How many roads had he walked like this before? Hundreds. Maybe thousands? It had been a while, though: his boot heels on gravel, the sound of crickets and wires humming overhead, the crackling of someone making a phone call, the distance stretching out in all directions. It was like being home—the side of the highway in the early morning, comforting and intense. He hadn't known he'd missed it so much. Sure, he was high as a satellite, but there was no mistaking this feeling—completely alone, yet connected with everything. He took it all in: the tennis shoe on the fence post, golden flashes on the silos, the dragonfly threesome buzzing through the grass, bullet holes in the speed limit sign, the smell of dry dirt and rotting wood, the shimmer of a car approaching. *What have you been doing all this time?* He stuck out his thumb.

This one didn't stop either. He pulled out his phone and checked the little bars on the faceplate. Still nothing. He turned and kept walking, the Save-On Foods bag swinging at his side.

Finally he came to the sign: UTOPIA 6 KM. There was an arrow pointing south down another road. It was paved but potholed, with no dividing line. The sun was a quarter way up in the sky. Mason bent over, digging into his cowboy boots to pull up his socks. He put on his sunglasses and headed for Utopia.

58

IT WAS high noon when he got there. Or rather, he was high and it was noon. Utopia didn't look like much of a place—not any more, at least. There was a railway track, a small station house, and a church, but the grass around it had grown high, and the sign sticking out of it read THE LAK—OF FIR—IS REAL. The stores were boarded up but for the gas station, which looked like a giant corrugated tin can, cut in half, laid on its side with a store front nailed on where the lid used to be. There was a large cardboard ice cream cone with three scoops and, next to that, a placard that read THE BEST DARN CHIPS—EVER!!!" Gas cost fifteen cents less here than it did on the highway.

There was a quick ringing, like Tinkerbell descending. A heavy-set woman came out of the store and put her hand up, shielding her eyes and squinting at Mason, as if he emanated light.

"Hey there," he said. When he heard his voice he realized how fucked-up he was.

"Yup. What can I do you for?"

A tricky question at the best of times.

"Just passing through," said Mason, which was a silly thing to say.

"How 'bout something to drink?"

"Actually, I've got water."

"You want food?'

"I've got hot dogs and chips."

"Well, *you* come prepared, don't you?" She kept her hand up as a visor and looked at the sky. He walked toward her.

"Do you want some?"

"What's that?" She squinted back at him.

"A hot dog? Chips?" He didn't know where he was going with

this. As he came into the shade, she dropped her hand and raised her eyebrows—as if only now she saw the city in him. He took off his sunglasses. "I sell them."

"What, chips? You're a traveling chip salesman?"

Mason laughed. "I own a hot dog cart. I'm a hot dog salesman." He opened his hands, as if to illustrate: *I, too, am in the roadside food industry.* "In fact," said Mason, "my cart broke down, back on the highway there."

"You're selling hot dogs on the highway?" Apparently this was where the humor had been lurking. She said it slowly, emphasizing *hot dogs* and *highway*, then started to laugh, with little ascending *hoo-hoo-hoo*s.

"Not exactly." said Mason. He looked around while she laughed it out. There was a sign hanging from the railway house. It said CONSTANCE.

"I thought this was Utopia."

The woman caught her breath. "It is."

He pointed at the sign.

"Well, it used to be Constance, when the train stopped here. Then, after that, they changed it."

"To Utopia?"

"Come in," she said. "We'll get you some lemonade."

"Anything stronger?"

She laughed again and Mason followed her into the store.

49. I mostly remember happy things.
50. Hospitals are better than parks.

By one o'clock he was back on the road. He'd traded in the plastic bag for a small backpack with a Canadian flag on it. In one hand he carried a beer, in the other a tiger-stripe ice cream cone. The cocaine made eating unpleasant, and the ice cream was rapidly melting, his arm now streaked with orange and black stripes. Once out of view of the gas station, he tossed the cone over a fence. He poured beer onto his arm to wash away the ice cream, then some water to wash away the beer. The sun beat down.

He opened another can, then pulled out the map that Gas Station Joanie had drawn. "Google can't help you here," she'd said

as she sketched: only two lines, but a half dozen reference points. She'd said them aloud as she wrote them down: "The signpost with no sign . . . Gary's old Ford . . . that electrical transformer thingy . . . the Chalmers place (it's got a busted swimming pool out front) . . . the start of the woods . . . a wet woodpile . . . the turnoff to Apple Road . . ." Mason stopped. At the mouth of the road, leading into an old-growth deciduous forest, was a signpost that read APPLE ROAD—the one marker she hadn't included. It made the rest of them pointless.

He folded the map, put it back in the bag, and turned down the road into the forest. He looked around at the thick, looming trees. *No Lack of Fir* here, he thought. That was a good one. Gas Station Joanie would have liked it: *hoo, hoo, hoo.*

Apple Road was long. Mason's reborn love of travel receded, replaced by a tired nervousness. After a half hour he stopped, opened another beer, did another line. His thoughts had been running away from him, disappearing into the dark parts of the wood.

What the hell are you doing?

Do you even have a plan?

He tried to stop considering things, drank down half the beer, and kept on walking.

Finally he arrived at 10 Apple Road. The address was singed into a glossy piece of wood, chest high. Beneath the sign, hanging from gold chains, was another piece of wood in the shape of an apple. It read THE FOLLOWS.

The driveway was winding, so Mason couldn't see the end of it. He drained his beer and put the can in his backpack.

What if no one's home?

He stood there for a while, then looped the bag over one shoulder and headed down the driveway. He thought of doing another line, but his heart was already racing. And then he was there—out of the wood and into the clearing.

The house was large and rustic in a well-kept way. He could see roses on an arbor. In front of the house was lush green grass, then a gravel area where a dozen cars could park. Beyond the gravel— all the way to where Mason was standing—everything was bark mulch. To the left was a paddock, a barn, and stables. Elm trees stood like quiet soldiers.

A woman emerged from the stables. "Hey," she said.

Mason almost said, "Hey is for horses," but he stopped just in time. He didn't say anything.

She was tall and slender, in riding pants and a tight violet tank top bearing circles of sweat like dark, stylized hearts. There was dirt on her face. Again she said, "Hey."

"Hey," said Mason, and took a breath.

"What can I do for you?"

The syntax was normal, but still he thought of Gas Station Joanie. The beautiful woman was waiting. "I'm here to see Jonathan Follow," he said.

"Oh, shit." She tilted her head back and the tendons in her neck formed long shadows in the sunlight. "You're the guy who called, aren't you?"

"I . . ."

She turned toward the house. "I left a message. I told you not to bother. He's not even in the country right now."

Mason followed. "You didn't say . . ."

"I said not to bother. How'd you get this address?"

He was sweating, could feel it through his shirt. "It's about his daughter."

"What?" She turned to face him. Her tank top was like the two of hearts.

Mason stammered. "I . . . I'm really sorry, but it's really important. I know his daughter."

"Who?"

"Sissy."

"*I'm* Sissy."

"Circe!"

"*I'm* Circe."

"No." His feet shuffled loudly in the gravel.

"Uh . . . yeah." She looked at him as if he was stupid. Or crazy. Or stupid and crazy and high.

He tried to check himself—pointed at her, then away, into the elms. "Circe Follow," he said, his voice dropping at the end. The tree branches seemed to do the same, reaching lower.

Elms . . .

"I'm sorry, but you're going to have to tell me what this is about."

"Jesus." Mason looked around. Everything was closing in. "Do you . . . do you have a sister?"

"No." Her hands tightened at her sides.

"I'm . . . this is important!" There was a wind picking up. Snorting from the paddocks. "You have horses."

"What is this about?"

"Do you . . . do you teach riding?"

"I used to, yes. Now what do you want?"

"There was a girl here. Sort of fat, with lots of acne, and orange hair. Or, I don't know what her hair was like before . . ."

"What are you talking about?"

Mason looked around, the wind lifting wood chips, dust rising from the paddocks, the heavy smell of horses.

She was here, once. And now she's gone.

The scent like fresh mourning overtook him. His chest was constricting.

"Right here! She was right fucking here—but she couldn't get up! You're the one. You helped her up!"

Which is more than you ever did.

Mason's arms were out, as if he were lifting something.

"She started to cry! Right here!" He pointed at the dark, hooved earth. "She was crying right here!"

"Who are you talking about?"

"Sissy!"

"I'm sorry, I . . ."

You're too fucking late.

"Sissy!" He was looking around now, as if maybe she was hidden, behind the trees, in the paddock. His heart was racing, his head rushing with blood. Five years since the smell of stables.

She hasn't been here for a decade.

"I'm worried she might be dead!"

"You're going to have to leave," said the beautiful lady of the horses. Her hands were clenched at her sides. She was moving backward toward the house.

Mason followed her.

She's scared of you. Look at the fear in her face.

"Stop," he said, "You've got to help me!"

The woman looked blurry now, as water welled in his eyes. He

reached out and she took another step back, still staring him down. "If you don't leave," she said, "I'm phoning the police." The mares were whinnying. She opened the door and shut it behind her. The thud of a deadbolt.

Mason dropped, cross-legged in the dirt. He was still shaking from adrenaline but exhausted. Too high. Too low.

Can you stand up, sir?

If I could stand up, I would have climbed the fence.

He let out a laugh. No doubt she was watching him through the window, the phone in her hand. Or maybe a hunting rifle. Sissy Follow. The beautiful daughter of a poet.

He sat there for a while. But he knew at some point he'd have to stand up again. *And then what?*

The wind shifted.

The scent of horses was overpowering. It shook him to his heart.

Oh they smile so shy
And they flirt so well
And they lay you down so fast
Till you look straight up and say
Oh Lord, am I really here at last?

The
Sixth

No more introductions

59

The Book of Handyman

At the hospital I learned a satisfying acronym:

Skin

Connective tissue

Aponeurosis

Loose areolar tissue

Pericranium

The doctors didn't even try to save mine. They said there'd been so much blood loss that the flesh—though still attached to the back of my head—had died. It would have to be removed. What they meant, of course, was that it just hadn't been worth the effort. Instead of letting it die, they'd have had to wash it, sterilize it, and sew it all back down. And who the hell cared? My legion of fans? Johnny Cupcake in Cell Block 6? Nah, they'd keep on love-love-loving me anyway.

"You can wear a hat," said the man-child of a doctor, as if that might never have occurred to me. Then he brought in some colleagues to gawk at my open head.

One of the doctors—by the looks of it, a twelve-year-old Chinese boy—had seen this happen before: A woman in a car crash—and the steering wheel sliced her scalp in a line across the front, peeling it right to the back of her head. He said it was called "degloving."

I said, "Wouldn't 'detoqueing' make more sense?" The Oriental kid

laughed, and the others looked like they hadn't realized I was conscious. "So what happened to her?"

"We spent like hours cleaning under her scalp with soap and water, then it took forever to sew it back down . . ."

"Aha!" I said, looking at my doctor, who, minutes earlier, had been holding my scalp in one hand, a pair of scissors in the other. He avoided my eyes. "So there we have it: A soccer mom's scalp is worth more than mine?" The Chinese doc laughed nervously, someone else coughed. "Or maybe the other way round, hey?" I turned to Doogie Houser: "What were you planning to do—sell my scalp on eBay? Mark my words, kemosabe: When I leave here, the top of my head's coming with me."

And that's what happened: Two days later they gave me a paper to sign and put my scalp in a ziplock bag, then a cardboard box. One of the guards held it in his lap as we drove back to the prison. He thought it was medication. I was wearing a Kingston-issue toque, and halfway to the pen I said, "That's the top of my head you got there." He looked at me like he was bored. I said, "Go ahead and take my hat off: You'll see." After a few moments he put the box on the floor at his feet. I looked at the top of his head, trying to figure out how best to scalp him. It had never occurred to me how fun that would be.

S-C-A-L-P, find out what it means to me!

Sock it to me, sock it to me . . .

Mason shivered beneath the hot sun, felt his own scalp crawling. Gas Station Joanie was inside the store, calling the tow truck driver again. She came out, two cans of beer in one hand. "Whatcha reading?"

"You don't want to know."

She shrugged and passed him one of the beers. "The tow truck guy's being complicated. Says a Dogmobile's not a real kind of car, and he doesn't know when he can get here. Whatever happens, it'll cost you."

"Figured it would," said Mason. He'd tried to talk to the tow truck guy himself, but it hadn't gone very well. "Isn't there someone else?"

"Round here? You got somewhere to be?"

Mason opened the can of beer. "No idea."

"That's a weird answer."

He tipped the can toward her.

"Cheers," she said. "Don't worry—I won't bug you. We'll have us a drink, then I'll leave you to your reading."

The Book of Handyman

Although Larry says he's not reading this, he seems right fucking edgy about something.

I handed it in for his "perusal." At our next session he put it on the table between us and tried to look me in the eye, but his gaze fell fast and he was staring at my chest. "What's up, Mr. White," I said to him. "You checking out my titties?" I said it in that same voice I'd been using since the day I met him—kinda stupid, sort of naïve, almost accidentally rude. We'll call it my first-page voice.

He took a moment, then said, "Remember—you can call me Larry."

I've got to hand it to him; that was just great: "You can call me Larry!" He started babbling about how it was good to see that I'd taken his advice, and that writing was a constructive thing to do. But I had this vision forming:

Larry the Fat Bitch is in his office. He's taken off his jacket and is looking particularly ugly in a sweaty beige checkered shirt. He stops for a moment to contemplate his likeness to a hideous overweight woman. Pushing the thought away makes him twitch. He reaches down and pulls a brown notebook from his briefcase. He starts to read. And now, in my vision, his thoughts form in a bubble over his fat head, as would those of a particularly ugly comic book character:

"Ah, yes. Poor Seth Handyman. Can't write any better than he talks: the semicoherent, childish ramblings of an idiot. Maybe with a bit of time, though, and my help of course, he can learn to access things, process his thoughts. I could write a paper about it. Oh look, there's my name!" And then Larry turns the page.

And oh, what's this?

Fat Larry starts to shake.

The sweaty patches spread across his ugly shirt. He breathes quickly— and then, reading on, the words fill his brain like smoke fills a lung. He coughs, then retches.

When he's finished there are two thought bubbles over his head. One says "Holy shit, that man can write!" The other says "He's going to scalp my fat ugly head!"

If Larry White knows what's right
He'd better keep his mouth shut tight
Sing Larry White (Larry White)
Sing Larry White (Larry White)
It's all right (It's all riiiiight).

The thing about reading this fucked-up crap—it took his mind off Sissy.

But is the book going to last the rest of your life?

The sun was starting to sink in the sky.

"Still nothing." Gas Station Joanie was leaning in the doorway. "There's a bus goes by the junction to 18. It'd take you into Barrie."

"Just leave the Dogmobile?"

"They got other tow trucks in Barrie."

"Well, why don't we call one?"

"Not their district." She came out of the shadow and looked at the empty road.

"What time's the bus at?"

"Five thirty," said Jeannie. "It's almost five now. I'd give you a ride, but I've just got the scooter." She pointed at it, parked beside the tin can building—small and orange. He couldn't imagine how she fit on it.

And so Mason gave up on the tow truck man. He said good-bye to Gas Station Joanie, paid her for the beers, and headed back to County Road 18. He'd been up for thirty-six hours, killed the Dogmobile, stranded himself—and all for what?

For nothing.

When he got to the highway he checked his cell phone again. Still no reception, and it was past five thirty—no bus to be seen. His mouth felt full of sawdust. He sat down and drank a bottle of water. His hollow body ached, the air around him dry: naught for company but the ramblings of a disturbed convict.

The Book of Handyman

A few notable things have happened of late: Firstly, our dear friend Larry has greatly impressed me—so much, in fact, that I will refrain, for the time being, from referring to him as Larry the Ugly Bitch (that he remains

Shaughnessy Bishop-Stall

200

an ugly bitch is, for now, unimportant). I assumed that he was a coward and that upon "perusing" my latest journal submission he would: (1) hand it over to the warden, (2) refuse to counsel me anymore, (3) quit his job and spend his time wetting himself in lieu of jacking off.

But wrong I was, on all counts. Fat Larry has handed me back this notebook—which suggests one of two things: (1) He was honest about not reading what I wrote, or (2) He is being a man for once in his girly life. Either way: Good for him. Although nervous, he managed to mumble for a while, then said he'd like me to "go back further now—and write about other things."

Which brings me to notable thing the second. In this prison—a terrible, shitty place, filled with ugly passion but no succulence—I've rediscovered something I really enjoy: I like to write. It feels fucking good. And for that I thank Larry.

Thirdly, there's this: According to the charter, my internment is meant to be rehabilitation rather than punishment, yet I've been here four and half years, convicted of horrible crimes, and it wasn't until someone lopped off the top of my head that I was deemed fucked-up enough for personal therapy. It's wondrous, really; the system understands exactly how I feel: more for my scalp than for my sins.

And the final thing to note is our calendar:

In just two more months I'll be up for parole.

It was past six o'clock. The bus hadn't come, and Mason was having trouble reading. His brain was boiling from the heat of the day, the drugs, and exhaustion. A car drove by. Ten minutes late another, and neither of them stopped—as if he weren't even there.

But he knew that he was—he could tell by the mosquitoes. They were feasting on him now—buzzing around his ears. He slapped at them, blood streaking his fingers. His scalp was crawling, his skin burning as they swarmed.

The lak—of fir—is real!

And now he was up and running, back toward Utopia.

51. I would rather do karaoke than sing in the shower.
52. Good things never come in threes.

The scooter was gone, the gas station closed. He looked at the sign on the door:

He'd never seen a business referred to in the first person singular before. And now it occurred to him: He hadn't asked her a thing about herself—just kept on taking her beers, listening to those *hoo-hoo-hoo*s—couldn't say if she was happy or dying of loneliness. He sat down next to a gas pump—a lamp buzzing overhead, the deep yellow glow. Did the bus even exist? He couldn't say why anybody ever did anything.

At least the mosquitoes were gone. Maybe the smell of gasoline kept them away.

Maybe, maybe, and fucking maybe.

Who fucking knows?

He leaned against the pump awhile, waiting for sleep or nothing. He thought of Sissy. Soon and Sarah. Warren and Willy. Then he pulled out the goddamn notebook.

The Book of Handyman

> *If Larry White's butt was tight*
> *I'd fuck it hard with all my might*
> *Sing Larry White (Larry White)*
> *Sing Larry White (Larry White)*
> *It's alright (It's aalllriiight)*

Aw, I'm just kidding. But that's a fucking great word, isn't it? Alllriiiight. You listen to good rock 'n' roll—say some Velvet Underground—and there is no greater attainment than alright. That's all you can hope for, and you'll do anything to get it—drugs, sex, and violence all night, and then anything at all to feel alright, more and more till Nirvana. Nirvana feels alright. I feel alright. Lou Reed feels alright. Steve Earle feels alright. And finally Kurt Cobain feels alright.

But sometimes it takes a lot.

Okay, picture this: It's three o' clock in the afternoon, April 8, 1994. I'm sitting in my brother's living room, drinking beer and listening to In Utero. I've been doing this since I turned off the TV. No one else is home. This morning an electrician found Kurt in his own guesthouse. On the floor next

60

THE SAD drunk stranger had left hours ago, staggering up the road, but now Sissy Follow heard something outside. She opened the front door. There was a commotion in the stables—the beating of hooves, whinnying. She went back to get the rifle, then headed toward the barn. The sky was dark, just a faint glow on the horizon, stars appearing like pinhole cameras.

She pulled back the barn door and could see right away what was missing: a blanket, saddle, and bridle. She entered the paddocks. Silver, her shining white stallion, was gone. In the sawdust lay a piece of paper: *I am sorry, Sissy, for everything*

61

HE WAS riding a white horse, leaving Utopia behind.

There are a number of ways to see it, and just as many to say it:

You could say he'd been galloping like this for five long years, a ghost rider chasing him. You could say he had a monkey on his back, or an albatross or a drug-addled chimpanzee. You could say he was on the back of a stolen horse, carrying a bag of secrets.

He can see Sarah's hair, shimmering in the moonlight as they race across the plains. He leans forward, thumping the horse's broad neck with his open hand. He feels a great love for the animal, the night sky, the dizzying, rumbling speed—chasing something and also chased. This is where he is supposed to be, racing in the silver light—ready to fly or fall.

You could see it as a metaphor or a cheap cosmic joke. But this much you'd *have* to see: the branches *were* whipping his face, the stirrups *were* a bit uneven, the hooves *were* thundering beneath him. He *was* on the back of a white horse—five years ago and now again—drunk, high, and full of purpose.

He pulled out his cell phone.

Still no reception.

On his back was a pack.

In the backpack, a notebook.

He had read it front to back.

Faster, man!

Turning his head, he caught a glimpse of wings. He leaned forward and dug in his heels.

Giddy fucking up!

The Book of Handyman

I'm worried about Larry the Fat Bitch. I might have judged him too highly. He did return this notebook to me, but with hesitation. And I'm pretty sure I could see little Becky the Bunny in his eyes.

That always cracks me up: as if my situation has anything to do with her. It didn't even have to be a little girl. It might have been anybody that day—a fat girlish-looking man with pit stains, who just happened to waddle into the light at the right time—a short necktie instead of red socks . . . Or not a person at all; a new drug could have fallen from the sky, God might have risen up and licked my balls with a tongue of pure sensation—any of those things might have worked right then. It was a small fucking moment.

Fatty's eyes are only full of little Becky since she's who I chose to write about—and that's only because I was busted for that one. It's not like I'm copping to anything new or threatening anyone—that would be stupid, especially so close to my parole hearing.

Speaking of which: I'm sure, despite his worrisome sputtering, Larry will testify courageously on my behalf. There's really no reason not to; they'll let me free eventually. They tried to kill me and failed, might even try again—but someday I'll walk out of here, my fucked-up head held high.

I trust he'll remember that.

It's hard to think when you're moving like this. A misstep in the moonlight can send you flying. But he is already flying—so that, too, is hard to keep in mind, and eventually he stops trying. What good is thinking? Better just to keep moving. Every moment he holds on is another he doesn't fall. That is the meaning of everything: the bliss of adrenaline, gambling, horseback and drugs.

The white horse whinnies. He can feel it, too.

Mason held the reins in one hand and his cell phone in the other, still riding through the dead zone. There were too many races being run—he could feel the aching of a distant satellite, his animal tiring, the battery dying. Ahead was the city, the cellular network—but before that, a cliff. He could sense it in the moonlit darkness. It was as real as Sissy or Circe or Sarah, as real as the Man in the Black Helmet, as real as those evasive cellular waves, as real as Willy's left side and right. It was *time* that was false, or at least horribly skewed.

You're running out of time.

The Book of Handyman:

Dig it:

> In seven days, Prisoner Seth xxxxxx shall be released into the custody of Sudden Street Halfway House where, for the next forty-two days, he will be confined. During this time he will begin a med/psych program. If after forty-two days Prisoner xxxxxx is responding favorably to treatment, it may be deemed acceptable to begin curfew, to general parole.

So says the Man.

The week before Christmas I will walk out of here. And in a bag I'll carry two things: this notebook and the top of my head.

Oh, happy day . . .

Maybe even without the danger ahead, the waves of adrenaline, the volatile speed of horseback—without the horse's breath like wisps of fog, the sleep deprivation, and all the drugs and booze—maybe even without all that it would have been dreamlike: he had been riding, after all, for five long years, or maybe forever. He tried to think clearly.

Text requires less.

He flicked open his phone.

Less power, less reception.

As he rode, Mason typed with one thumb:

WILLY'S LIFE IN DANGER! GET HER SOMEWHERE SAFE!

But he couldn't send the message.

Get out of the dead zone.

The battery was dying.

Send the fucking message!

He couldn't get reception. He closed the phone and gripped the reins, his boot heels digging in. They hit another speed, racing through the night—horse and rider, demons on their backs.

The Book of Handyman

Things I've done
by Seth Handyman

I was born, as were most of us, from a bloody shitty cunt.

I opened my eyes, still dripping.

I saw everything.

I did things typically, unknowing, and it felt fucking good.

I spent part of my allowance on budgies and tore off their wings.

I spent the rest on candy and ate it.

I watched everything carefully.

I stole baking chocolate, gum from purses, magazines from doorsteps.

I worked on my muscles, lured dogs from neighboring yards, and cut off their ears, then testicles. Learned fast I'd be shunned–didn't mind the cliché: just the getting caught, and more the fucking punishment. That felt like losing.

I turned ten, pushed a whiny boy named Brian off the jungle gym headfirst down the hole for the fireman's pole. He was concussed, I cried, people took care of me. It was the best birthday ever, and a week later I got another—for mine had been ruined. Sadly Brian survived and became even more neurotic.

I killed two swans and tried to tie their necks in a knot—it was tougher than you might think.

I beat a crossing guard's daughter with her own shoes, blackening her eyes.

Went to juvenile detention.

I did a lot of drugs, sold a lot of drugs, and mixed them together—into new drugs, then sold those. I convinced a male nurse to fuck me, then I beat him with a flashlight.

I traveled. I read books. I wrote. I dove into canals. I threw empty bottles from rooftops, cars colliding in the street below.

I stopped traveling, became a DJ, raped a girl with red socks, rediscovered rock 'n' roll, decided not to kill her, then hit the road again.

I studied Buddhism.

Drank a lot.

I tied a boy named Jeffrey to a furnace and peed on him for three days while eating strawberries, drinking gin, and raping him.

I rolled drunks to buy drinks for drifters. I singed their eyelids with cigarettes.

I loved life, took what I could, was imprisoned for it, yet remained optimistic.

Then, all of a sudden, I was released.

And moved to a place called Sudden House—I became once more, for the most part, free. Free to be me, to live and love and write.

I enjoy the writing more each day. In fact, I came on this page.

And now I'll try it again.

For I am an optimist: Coming, coming … Oh, I am a poet.

On a quiet night, there is profound rhythm to the hooves and breath of a strong horse. It moves upward through the rider's gut and changes the beat of his heart, the tenor of his own breathing. Wind made of speed rushes past their ears. The horse and rider breathe together, drum rolling across the earth—hooves thudding and clicking—until the sound is like a message:

Down the cliff. Down the cliff
You'll never make it.
Down the cliff.

Hooves and breath. Hooves and breath.

A book on your back like a monkey junkie.

And the dark rider knows: Somewhere out in front of him, the Earth gives way to nothing.

The Book of Handyman

~~I think what's funny is people trying to figure things out. They try to figure me out as if I'm like them. Pathetic. I don't give a fuck, as in I got no empathy, asshole! Get it? But they try to get me by trying to relate to~~

me. I don't fucking relate! I do what makes me feel good. Period. Empathize with that, you pussy! If I were someone else, I'd just beat the shit out of me—if it made me feel better—instead of trying to understand. But people are just pussies and assholes. And I fucked them.

Fuck!

62

The Book of Handyman

You may notice that the last few pages have been torn out. There is a reason for that—just as there is a reason I have not written anything for the past four months. There is also a reason that I am writing this now—and it is *not* because I enjoy it. In fact, I find this painful. It has taken me almost half an hour to write these fucking sentences, and they're not even good. I am no longer a poet. But I will persevere, and explain all of this, for the sake of reason. I'm not saying this will be an engaging read. The writing is not good. But you must pay attention. I am writing this for you.

And keep in mind: Even poorly written words can change your life. These are the ones that changed mine:

"Condition of Parole, Medical: Progesterone treatment (injection q 14 days) under force of law."

At first glance the sentence doesn't seem too bad—other than it is incomplete and some of the words are confusing. But don't be fooled, it's a doozy—full of ugliness, hopelessness, and death. It can be found in paragraph 4, page 11, of Seth Handyman's "Conditions of Release," a work I should have read more carefully.

Progesterone is a female sex hormone that suppresses androgen through shutting down the pituitary axis. This, in turn, stops the production of testosterone.

The side effects of progesterone are as follows: Decreased libido. Decreased creativity. Extreme depression. Simply put: I have been legally, chemically castrated.

And as it turns out, the key to life is not acceptance or love or balance: It is testosterone. Without it there is nothing: no sensation, so no desire, so no reason to do anything—to eat or drink or fuck or write. No incentive

to choose one word over another. But it's more than that—or should I say less?

If I look out the window, what do I see: a tree, two squirrels, a plastic garbage container, a brick, a man with a brown cap, three cars, a woman in a blue dress, an orange pylon. To me they're all exactly the same. It's not just that my sense of competition is gone—it's that all competition is gone from the universe, so that nothing vies for attention. The woman is the pylon is the tree is the brick. And so why write, when one word describes it all: *ugly.*

U-G-L-Y.

You ain't got no alibi.

Yer ugly. Yer ugly.

And it's all yer fault.

So you see, with that one incomplete sentence—"Condition of parole . . ." I was robbed of everything: music, books, sex, power, pomegranates, women, pylons, trees, and bricks.

In the end, fat Larry fucked me—gave me freedom and took away my life. I, Seth Handyman: brought down by a girl's sex hormone.

Mason took the stairs two at a time. The apartment was empty. He plugged in his cell phone and called Chaz. No answer. He ran down the stairs and out—then down again, into the belly of the Cave. And there he was, his oldest friend, wiping down the bar. He looked like someone strange.

"Did you get my text?" said Mason.

"What happened to you?"

"I fell off a horse. Did you get the fucking text?"

"Yeah."

"And . . . ?"

"And Willy's safe," said Chaz. "What do you mean you fell off a horse?"

Mason looked at the mirror, trying to look through it. "Is she in there? Is she back there right now?"

Chaz nodded. "You want to see her?"

He thought for a moment. "What time is it?"

"What?"

"I need a gun."

"Your head is bleeding."

"So?"

"I'm not giving you a gun."

"Fine!" Mason took off his knapsack and slammed it down on the bar. He held the edge of it, wobbling. "Then how 'bout a drink?"

Chaz poured him a glass of Jim Beam. Mason did a quick succession of lines.

"What the fuck's going on, Mason?"

"What time is it?" said Mason

"Almost time to open."

"I gotta go."

"Oh, you do, eh?"

He took Seth's notebook from his backpack and handed it to Chaz. "Hold on to this. And keep Willy safe."

"Anything else?"

"I could do with a gun."

"You mentioned that."

"Just a small one . . ."

"Sit the fuck down, Mason."

Mason stared at the mirror. "I gotta make last call," he said.

"*That's* what you gotta do?"

"Yeah," he said, then killed his drink and exited through the curtains.

The Book of Handyman

It was so bad I thought of killing myself.

And then, one day, something happened:

I was waiting for the doctor. As if a prescription of despair and emptiness isn't enough, I have to go and wait to have it filled. So I was sitting in the doctor's waiting room, trying to plan my suicide, when suddenly I heard a voice.

"Willy told me what you did!" it said.

I looked up and there you were, standing in the open doorway, shouting at Dr. Francis. I don't know if you saw me. You were mad and self-righteous, fucked-up and wound up. It was like listening to my very own God: "Don't

you accuse me of hurting people—*or* trying to save them! Take a look at yourself, Doc!"

And with a nod to me, you left. You didn't know me—but I knew you: My lucky star. My resurrection.

Yes, you, Mason Dubisee, are going to be the one who saves me.

Mason came fast through the door, right into the mahogany coatrack. He hit it with his face, and down they both went, crashing to the floor. Mary, behind the bar, howled with glee. The men banged their fists: an explosion of sound, laughter like shrapnel. "For the *houuuuse!*" shrieked Mary.

He got up quick, a fresh flash of red across his nose. His clothes were heavy with dirt and sweat, hair stuck in a gash on his head. "Fuck the house!" said Mason. And then he saw Seth.

He was fifty yards away, on the other side of the pool table, a cue in his hands. They looked at each other.

"Where is my notebook?"

Mason shrugged.

"I warned you," said Seth.

"Oh wait," said Mason, his heart so fast it made his words feel slow. "What's this . . . ?" He looked down at his right hand. No one moved.

Then he lifted his middle finger.

In the time it took five men to thump the bar twice, Seth was past the pool table, Mason running straight at him. The men pounded the bar once more—Seth swinging his cue, Mason airborne.

They collided with a breathless crunch, the cue splitting as they tumbled over the corner pocket, into a row of chairs. Seth scrambled to his feet, but Mason drilled him down with an elbow to his face, punching and pushing him away at the same time, trying to make enough distance for a cross to the head. And that's when they grabbed him.

Fucking Finns, thought Mason, as they pulled him up, an elbow tight across his throat, his arms bent behind him. A cane smacked against his thigh. His ankle twisted. Someone stomped on it. Through the pain and loss of air, he heard Mary squeal with happiness. He wished he'd bought a round for the house.

Then Seth stood up.

Maybe it was because things had been moving at all different speeds, all that galloping, cocaine, and adrenaline—or that his collapsing windpipe created the effect of time slowing down—but it seemed Seth wasn't just standing; he was *rising* before him . . .

In each hand was a half of the splintered cue. Where once there was pudginess, now there were muscles—veiny arms stretched at his sides, low and taut, as if lifting *weight* and *menace*. His pale eyes glowed like fluorescence. His hat was on the floor, and his scalped head, full of horror, rose like a nightmare forming.

What hair remained was stringy and gray, like the cut of a disheveled monk. The crown looked nothing like the top of a man's head: instead of hair, or even skin, there was a shining cap of red-purple flesh, like an organ exposed. The men holding Mason gasped, and he realized they didn't know Seth from Adam—could have just as easily stayed out of this. Backlit by the aquarium, Seth now stood before him.

As Mason ran out of air, he saw the circle of gray hair shining—a silver halo surrounded by fish, pale blue orbs, a broken cue raised like a flare. Something whistled by his head. He thought of plums. Then, in superslow motion, he saw a red three ball spinning—mirrored, for an instant, in aquarium glass. The tank exploded.

In the moment before he passed out, there was a shining flood—a wall of water, the crystal blue wave rushing toward them, fish flying over the head of Seth, glistening and baffled into the world.

The Book of Handyman

What do you believe in, Mason?

Me, I believe the universe is controlled by two things: competition and coincidence. Not God, nor the devil nor fate nor logic.

The Big Bang, the splitting of an amoeba, evolution, ice ages, the harnessing of fire, the creation of the wheel, war, vaccination, every new life, every new path—they're all the result of competition and coincidence, neither profane nor divine. That's what *we* have, Mason: will, and the intersection of instances. And you'd better fucking believe it.

You're in *my* universe now.

Mason came to, surrounded by pieces of glass, seashell, porcelain figurines, and a half dozen fish flopping—baby birds crashed on a deck. The floor was wet with blood and water. Looking up, he saw a man in a black helmet battling atop a pool table—swinging his cue like a lightsaber. *Right on*, thought Mason, then passed out again.

The Book of Handyman

It's cosmic, ain't it—that of all the doctor's offices in all the world, you'd be shooting your mouth off in mine—about how you know the sins of our doctor. And not only would you be a hack, a gambler, and a fuckup, but you'd be a fucked-up hack who writes suicide notes to cover his gambling debts. And then you come to me, unrecognizing—tell me all this before I can even bribe you—and shoot some crummy pool. I do believe my universe loves me.

I believe in offers that can't be refused.

I believe our doctor will replace the progesterone with a placebo, allowing me to live—free and free, alive and alive.

I believe you will convince her to do this to save yourself. Or, if that's not enough, to save your Willy—so to speak.

I believe I dream in color.

I believe in rock 'n' roll.

I believe in so many things now, thanks to you.

This faith—it is the making of a great new game.

And you, my man, must play it. So listen well to the rules:

You must return to Tony's Happy Daze Bar and Beer before last call tomorrow, alone and unassisted.

Should you fail to do so, these are the penalties: (1) I will send the authorities the specifics of your business. (2) I will hunt down Ms. Willy and convince her to help me in your stead.

It's really no bother; I'd love to ride a crippled mare.

And by the way, you needn't worry about my letter. You might want to write one for yourself, though. Just in case.

Ciao for now,

Seth Handyman

P.S. If you don't bring this notebook, you'd better come ready to fight.

When Mason next awoke, the fish were gone. His face was wet with beer, and Chaz was standing over him, an empty pint glass in his hand. "Let's go, Dorothy," he said. "We got to get out of here."

Mason tried to lift himself, shards of glass, shell, and porcelain cutting into his palms. Chaz hauled him up and leaned him against the pool table. There were two unconscious men slumped in a corner. Neither one was Seth. Mason tried to ask his whereabouts, but all that came out was "*Cahhhhh . . .*" It felt like his throat had been stomped on. He tried to lie down on the table.

"Now," said Chaz. "Before the cops get here." He put Mason's arm over his shoulders. They staggered across the wet, beach-strewn floor and made it out the door. The streetlights were bright. Chaz's motorcycle was parked on the sidewalk. Mason got on the back. He tried to ask what had happened to the fish—but all that came out was "*Cah- ahhhaaahhhhhh . . .*" He could hear the sirens as they pulled away.

63

MASON LAY on the floor of the Cave making pitiful scratchy sounds.

"He's got no head?" said Chaz. "What do you mean he's got no head? He held a glass of whisky, salt, and lemon juice and poured a bit down Mason's throat—trying to open up that windpipe.

"The top of it . . . is gone," Mason croaked. "You didn't notice?"

"I was kind of busy saving your ass."

"Thank you."

"So let me see if I've got this right—come on, try to sit up: You quit your job selling hot dogs and started writing suicide letters instead."

Mason nodded.

"For psychos."

"I didn't . . . know."

"Of course not—how could you? Only well-adjusted people hire a guy to . . . Is that even a thing? How do you think of something like that?"

Mason tried to speak, but nothing came out.

"Forget it. I don't want to hear." He propped Mason's back against the bar, then sat in a chair and looked at him.

"So. Since starting this new job of yours, you've—let me see . . . you helped somebody jump off a bridge, you wrecked the Dogmobile, you stole a horse . . ."

Mason was nodding.

"You stalked a convicted psychopath, took his journal, then attacked him in front of several witnesses who came to his rescue, forcing me to assault pretty much everybody in the place . . . But before doing any of this, you told him all your secrets, and even spelled your last name for him . . . Have I got this right?"

"We did *quid pro quo*."

"You *what*?"

Mason tried again. "*Quid . . . pro quo*. I ask . . . a question, and then . . ."

"I know what *quid pro quo* is, you moron . . ."

"But we had to . . . *aaaach*, sink a ball."

"What the fuck are you talking about?"

"Quid . . ."

"If you say *pro quo* again, I'm going to strangle you too."

"It's . . . moot anyway."

"Moot? What could possibly be moot?"

Mason tried, but all that came out was "*caaaaahhhh* . . ." He started to mime something. Chaz leaned forward with the glass. Liquid gurgled into Mason's mouth.

"I think he read my file."

"Your what?"

"We had the same therapist."

"The same what?"

"She's a doc—"

"So the horse thieving, the psycho assaulting . . . that started *after* you got professional help?"

Mason nodded.

"You should look for a new therapist."

"She's in danger," said Mason.

"Of course she is," said Chaz, standing up. He walked behind his chair.

"Read the notebook."

"First things first," said Chaz. "We gotta get you cleaned up."

Mason nodded.

"I mean all the way clean," said Chaz, looking Mason in the eye. "You're no good to anyone like this."

Mason stared at the floor between his legs. He took a moment and raised his head. "The doc . . . can help." As Chaz circled the chair the room began to spin.

"Why would she do that?"

The Cave tilted. He felt his body sliding, his throat closing up again.

"Just read the fucking book . . ."

Who wants to play those 8s and aces?

Who wants to raise?

Who needs a stake?

The
Seventh

Demons with Demons

64

THEY ARE beautiful.

And fucking scary, too.

There is a bridge with blue and silver wings, and people are jumping off—limbs stretching in all directions. Some are falling, some diving, some grabbing hold of the wings and flying.

There is a man clutching a bird in his upheld hand—trying to save it from drowning as he sinks into a lake. His fist is tight, pinning the bird's wings to its body. They are both trying to rise.

There is a woman cutting off her own head with a black and silver saber. At her feet sit a dozen dirt-streaked children, their bellies distended. Blood drips onto the white plates before them.

There is a man on a silver horse, sliding down a sheer cliff in the moonlight. He is leaning so far back—one arm stretching up behind him—that they look like an extension of each other, horse and rider. The bit in the horse's mouth is flashing, pulling its head so far back that its neck is breaking. The head of a young woman, her face awakened in surprise, is bursting through the horse's throat.

They are works of art. Dreams. Memories. Hallucinations. It doesn't matter. Yet. Nothing does. He shakes. Awake. Then asleep. Then awake.

53. *You don't need drugs to have a good time.*
54. *The lak of fir is real.*

G H O S T E D

He thinks he's in a bathtub or a womb. But it's just sweat, and as he realizes this, the sensation turns from warm to cold. He is lying on his back. There are words above him, white paint against a dark sky. Or are they in his head?

Stay as you are.

He thinks about this: To stay as he is, he must be in a specific way . . .

He's quite sure he is naked, covered with a wet sheet. It feels like he's up high, on the edge of a cliff. It's difficult to move his body—he does it slowly. There are tubes in his arms, and as he turns they tug at his flesh. He thinks of E.T: the empathetic extraterrestrial. The tubes are attached to a metal stand. It reminds him of the mahogany coatrack. He thinks of fish, then nestling swallows. The light is dim, but as his eyes adjust, he sees images on the walls around him: a bridge with wings, a man holding a bird, a woman with a saber, a horse down a cliff. He crawls to the edge and looks . . .

The light is coming through a large window. He blinks long and purposefully, and when he opens his eyes again, he can see them out there. They're doing the things that earthlings do: drinking and smoking, kissing and dancing, winning and losing—probably talking and laughing, too. But he can't hear a word, not a sound. Watching them hurts him physically. Something inside him says:

You'll never do that again. That's all over for you.

He wonders if he is dead, or perhaps just deaf.

And then he hears something. "Mason." It is Willy's voice, coming from below—as if she's at the bottom of this goddamn cliff. He tries to answer, but no sound comes out. *Not deaf, but mute.* "Mason," she says again, and now it is too much for him. He pulls out the tubes and hurls himself into the darkness below.

He opens his eyes, but sees nothing. A voice is shouting in his head.

Water!

Water drips from above. He feels it on his skin, but his throat won't open to drink.

Water, you asshole!

It pools around him as he pushes against the floor. His ankle is burning, and the pain makes him feel alive, even as he thinks he's dead. He is naked, on all fours, struggling to get up—and then he sees her, right in front of him. It's as if she's floating on her back—like when he held her in the pool. There are tubes in her arms. He reaches out and touches her. "Mason," she says. Never has he loved his name so much.

He climbs in next to her. Their bodies entwine, slippery and warm. They slip in and out of consciousness, sweating beneath a damp white sheet.

55. I am often too hot or too cold.
56. My dreams are always awful.

There are children, in trees, all down the street. Then suddenly they're dropping from the boughs. But they never land, just keep on falling. He's in the air alongside them—and now suddenly on the ground, looking up as they plummet toward him. He's got a net in his hands, but it's all tangled up. It's made of razor wire, and it rips through his flesh as he tries to stretch it open. And now there's a *thud*. The earth quakes: a *thud*, a *thud*, and a *thud*—as they hit the ground around him.

57. Life is a pale imitation of art.
58. I prefer the bottom bunk.

He wakes again—the deep sweat, the tubes, the dim light—but this time he knows where he is. And suddenly there's nothing but sadness—a hollow in his chest. He's felt it a thousand times before, coming down in the light of day, but now it is burrowing—larger, emptier. And the overwhelming sensation is this:

It has barely started to dig, to empty you out. It will get worse and worse, and then you'll be hollow forever, here in the half-light.

He hears Willy breathing in the bed beneath him, and wants to be down there with her.

How did I get back up here?

He tries to move, to get these damn tubes out of him.

"No," says a voice in the darkness, or maybe just in his head:

Stay as you are. You need to heal. You need some fluids.
He wants to protest, but he's got no voice.
Don't worry about Willy. She's doing all right.
Alllriiiiiight.

59. Anyone lived in a pretty how town.
60. It kills the buggers dead.

He awakes to her screaming beneath him. He doesn't think, just jumps. His ankle buckles, but he doesn't notice. He grabs on to her. A light flashes on, arms reaching over him, laying their hands on her writhing body—half of it yanked by the other.

Why is this happening?

Her screaming loses volume. Her head turns toward him. He sees Willy's face.

Then Sissy's, then Circe's . . .

This makes no sense.

And now it is Sarah.

No sense at all.

He holds on to her hand, unable to help in any way.

65

WILLY IS sleeping. Mason sits on a chair beside her. He can hear her breathing, but nothing else. It could be any time, any day, any universe. The air is close in this cave within the Cave. It smells of their breath and body fluids, and oil paint. He looks around at the canvases like dreams leaning on the walls. He closes his eyes. Then he opens them again—stares straight out through the bulletproof window, at the Cave outside this cave.

And there they are: his best friend and his doctor, sitting at a table on the other side of the bar—their mouths moving, a candle flickering between them. How long has it been?

Five days? Five months? Five years?

His legs shake as he stands. He falls against the wall and presses the intercom button.

The sound of a scratchy record fills the room: piano and guitar, a slow backbeat. Leaning into the speaker, he tries to say something, but all that comes out is "*Caaaaaahhh . . .*" drowned out by the music—and then, above it a voice:

"Have you seen *The Man from Snowy River?*"

He takes his finger off the intercom button, but the voices keep on coming.

"No. Is it good?"

He presses hard and then releases.

"Sure. This Aussie kid—his father dies, his horse runs off with a wild herd, and he goes and becomes a ranch hand, falls in love with the rancher's daughter, pisses off her dad. That kind of stuff. But there's this scene at the end—a couple dozen cowboys chasing after this wild herd. The rancher's prize colt is with them now, too, and whoever catches them gets to be a hero."

He jabs at it, but the QT room is filling with music—and Chaz's rising voice.

"So they get to this cliff—not a sheer drop, but enough that it's a cliff. The wild horses go down, and the cowboys pull up. Except for him, of course—the Man from Snowy River. He doesn't even hesitate." Chaz takes a breath. "The kid, he just goes for it—over the edge and down."

Mason bangs on the intercom.

"He digs in his heels and does it—leaning so far back, his head's almost touching the horse's tail . . ."

Mason sees it happening. He looks at them through the window.

"It's a death-defying leap, but of course he makes it. He rounds 'em up, gets his horse back, the girl . . . It's a great fucking scene."

"Cool," says the doctor.

Chaz lifts his glass, "Mason used to watch it over and over when we were kids. That's what he wanted: blaze of glory, over the edge—the whole fucking bit. Problem is . . ." and Chaz takes a sip, "the guy never grew out of it."

The fucking guy*!*

"Did he tell you about Sarah?"

Dr. Francis opens her hands—indicating confidentiality.

Chaz nods, as if he understands.

Mason wants to strangle them both.

"The way I see it," says Chaz. "He had a shitty summer. He turned twenty-five, his girlfriend dumped him, and he still wasn't a famous writer—just drank like one. But we were all having a tough go of it."

"Isn't that the summer your father died?"

Chaz nods. "Anyway. His mom sold the house in the city and bought a ranch. He was working on his lonesome cowboy bit . . ."

Mason punches the intercom.

"They had a family reunion or something. I don't know. I wasn't there . . ."

"Because of your father . . . Tenner, right?"

Chaz takes a drink. "This is about Mason," he says.

"Well, don't you think it affected him, too?"

Chaz looks at her. "Sarah idolized Mason. Thought everything he did was cool."

"Sarah, his cousin . . . ?"

Chaz nods. Mason gives up on the intercom. Holding the wall, he crosses over to where the scanner is. He puts his hand on the panel. Nothing.

He tries the other hand.

Nothing.

"She'd have followed him anywhere."

He slides down the wall, sitting with his back to the window.

He can see her now as she circles in the clearing, Warren's dark mane flaring out. They turn, then straighten. She looks once at Mason, who is on the back of Zevon, grinning at the edge of the cliff. She digs her heels in. "Yahhhh!" she shouts, but the sound is swept back as she charges. There's no expression on her face. Her eyes flash silver, and Warren just gallops—straight past Mason, into the air.

The noise is awful, like an avalanche of horse—the hooves cutting downward through rock and soil, the whinny a desperate wail. But Sarah is silent.

Mason sees the fall—Warren tumbling, hooves over head over Sarah—a monstrosity of limbs, hair and eyes flashing in the moonlight, the sickening crunch as the whinnying stops.

He slides off Zevon's back—then down the cliff on his ass, a gutless moonlit descent.

61. I'd like to see myself through someone else's eyes.

"You know what I think?" says the voice of Chaz. "It's not about Sarah at all. She was in the hospital for a while. They thought she might be paralyzed, but it turned out better than that. She's not going to be in the Olympics or anything, but she can walk. The horse died, but it's not that either. It's all about him."

"How?" says the doctor.

"You spend your life jumping off little cliffs, but there's not always someone watching, and then you're landing badly, and it starts to hurt. Finally, after years of busting yourself up, you get to the big cliff—but it's someone else who goes over. And then everyone pays attention, but now you're not the hero. Not by a long shot. So then what happens? You start busting yourself up for real."

Chaz takes a drink—a long slow one. Then his voice is lower.

"Mason's been going over the edge since the day he didn't. But it would have happened anyway."

The doctor speaks: "What do you mean?"

The song is almost over.

"The swallows, Sarah, Warren going over the edge—they're all real, but they're also a story. Without them, there'd be a different story. Sooner or later, he'd have found a way to fall. Antihero is a lot easier than hero. And if those are the only choices you've given yourself . . ."

The doctor cuts in. "Is this what you'd tell him, if you were his doctor?"

There is a pause. "You know what I'd tell him?" It sounds as if Chaz is taking a sip. "You're fucked-up and haunted, but not by what you think you are. And if you ever get clean, you might have a chance."

"Ghosted," says Dr. Francis.

"What?"

"He's been ghosted . . ."

There is a *boom*, and then it all goes quiet.

Mason is on his feet, a dented can of beans in his hands. There is no more talking, no more music. The intercom system is pulverized. He stands there shaking.

And then a voice behind him:

"Come here to me," she says.

He turns and walks toward her. He drops the can and climbs beneath the sheet, curling into Willy.

"It's going to be okay," she says.

He shivers.

"What song was that?"

"Fire Lake," he tries to say.

66

WHEN THEY talk it sounds like ghosts having a conversation—slow, ethereal, disjointed—but ghosts who like each other . . .

"What happened . . . to your throat?"

"Crushed windpipe . . . stupid bar fight. Are you all right?"

"Yes."

"How did Chaz find you?"

"You're the one who left, silly . . . I've been here the whole time."

"Here . . . behind the wall?"

"Here behind the wall."

"I thought you were . . . with Bethany."

"I wanted to get clean for you."

"Me, too . . ."

"We can do it together."

"All right."

"You seem sad, or angry."

"Not at you . . ."

Their voices move in the dark together, stumbling and drifting along.

67

THIS TIME he is standing and partially dressed—jeans and cowboy boots, holding on to the bed. "I demand our release!" he announces.

"You got your voice back!" says the doctor.

"Then I guess you heard what I said."

Chaz laughs, but Mason doesn't look at him.

"He's angry," says Willy.

"You're not a prisoner here," says the doctor.

"Well, we can't get out of here. So what do *you* call it?"

"Jesus Christ!" says Chaz. "I had to reset the scanner so she could get in and out." He nods toward the doctor. Mason just glares.

"You've been through a lot," says Dr. Francis. "It's normal to feel anxious, confused, even scared. It happens during detox."

"I'm not fucking scared."

"Would you rather not be here?"

"I don't fucking know."

"For Christ's sake!" says Chaz. "You're injured. You're both sick. The psycho's out there, and he's got your address. But if you want to leave . . ."

"No," says Mason. He looks at the doctor. "But things are going to change . . . You'll scan our hands—both of us." He looks down at Willy, who smiles. "And what the hell is she on?"

"Sedatives," says the doctor. "Both of you are. It's a difficult transition . . ."

"Well, give her less," says Mason, "so we can have a conversation. Like normal people."

Willy nods in agreement.

"And give me fucking none! No more drugs at all!" He looks at Dr. Francis. "We're in a fucking cave for Christ's sake! Can't you lose your license?"

"We've all things to lose," the doctor says.

Mason waves a hand, then takes the other one off the bed. He steadies himself and looks at them both. "From now on," he says. "I'll be the one looking after her."

Chaz steps toward him. "Are you fucking kidding me—?" But the doctor cuts him off.

"All right," she says, looking at Mason, who is having trouble standing. "You're through the worst of it now—physically at least. If you want to play doctor, I'll show you what to do." She turns to Willy. "Is that okay with you?"

"Yes," says Willy.

The doctor fixes Mason. "And you—are you committed to this? To getting clean and helping Willy?"

"Yes," says Mason.

62. I like the smell of burning rubber.

It feels like an alien ceremony—the scanning of the hands. No one knows just what to say. "Remember," says Chaz. "The right hand gets you in. The left one gets you out."

And after that they're left alone, Mason and Willy, in their cave within the Cave.

"I love you," says Willy.

"It's going to be all right."

Their hands seem to glow as they hold each other tight.

68

HE IS still in the woods but catches sight of the road ahead. He sees what it'll be like: painful, shameful, remorseful, lost, scared, grieving, and just plain sad. In some ways the road will be worse than the woods. But there will be good things, too. Even now there are moments of elation—and then just an emptying, water flowing from his eyes without any emotion at all: a pure physical purge that makes his muscles burn and his head pound, like vomiting without being able to stop. He knows Willy feels it, too—though hers is different. At one point, in her delirium, he hears her humming "Fire Lake." It is lovely and haunting. He presses against her, and the emptying subsides.

When he's sure she's deep in sleep, he sets himself a mission— his first one out of the QT room. He locates the Sony tape deck— on a shelf with the cans of beans. He picks it up and presses his

palm to the panel on the wall. The door slides back, and he rolls on through.

He's on the other side now. But for a moment he doesn't move—curled up behind the bar. Then he stands and turns and looks at the mirror. His own face shocks him—drawn and bloated at the same time. His eyes look intent—but on what, he doesn't know. He tries to look through, to see Willy behind the glass.

But of course he can't. Wouldn't know if she was screaming.

He limps across the floor. At the DJ booth, Bob Seger's *Against the Wind* is still on the turntable. He plugs in the Sony, takes out the Gowan cassette, and finds a roll of masking tape. Thank God for old technology. PLAY/RECORD. He drops the needle in the groove.

Scratch, scratch. Piano. Then acoustic guitar.

When the singing starts, he starts to get dizzy: the heavy scent of booze and cigarettes, sweet sensory metal dripping down his throat. Five years, and this is the longest he's been sober. It hurts like fucking hell.

But man, this song is good.

The wall slides back, and he gets up off the floor

"Where have you been?" says Willy.

"I got you something." He plugs in the tape deck.

"I wish you hadn't left."

"Just listen," he says, and presses Play.

Scratch, scratch. Piano. Then acoustic guitar.

She is smiling, and when the song is over, he kisses her.

He looks into her eyes. "What do you want to be when you grow up?"

She pushes him away with her hollow right hand. "That's mean," she says.

"Why?"

"I don't really know."

"You don't know why it's mean, or you don't know what you want to be?"

"Both."

"Same here." He tries to kiss her again.

"It's embarrassing," she says.

"What is?"

"When I was a kid I wanted to be an actress."

"Why is that embarrassing?"

"Because," she says. She tries to turn away, but her body makes it difficult. "I never got to grow out of it. I was a kid who wanted to be an actress, and then suddenly I was paralyzed." She looks straight at him. "So now all I ever wanted to be was a stupid actress."

"You still could be," says Mason.

"It's easier to act like a cripple than the other way around. Show me how to act like I'm walking?"

"It's not about that . . ."

"You're not even getting it. It's a stupid thing to want to be."

"Like being a writer?"

"You don't want to be a writer, Mason. Admit it." She grins at him. "You want to be a cowboy."

"Fuck you," he says, and starts to smile.

"Fuck me," she says, and pulls him in. They kiss each other deeply. It's been so long since he felt like this—it starts to make him high. He tugs at her hair. The air is thick—it tastes like them but somehow sweet. He runs his tongue down the left side of her neck—the side that can feel—over her breast to her rough left nipple. She begins to gasp, then stops. "I want to feel you everywhere."

"How?" says Mason. He tugs on her hair, her mouth opens wider.

As he gazes in, she snaps her teeth. "First," she says. "You'll have to hurt me. Do you think you can do that?"

"I . . . I don't know."

She slides her right hand in between his legs and breathes into his ear. "I think you can," she says.

"Tell me what to do."

"Go and get your belt."

Scratch, scratch. Piano. Then acoustic guitar.

She is on her front, quaking in the half light. There are welts across her back and ass, a film of beading sweat. He presses hard against her, leaning over, his mouth near her neck. He whispers, "Steady."

She tries to breathe it back to him. It sounds like steam. He

rises once more, drawing the leather strap from the center of her shoulders, down her spine, over her ass, and between her legs. He lifts his arm, the belt snaking, catching her as it flicks into the air. Her breath catches—belt folded, the buckle in his hand, he strikes downward again. *Left side, then right. Left side, then right.* She writhes underneath him, nerves firing beneath her skin. He's inside her and can see the same stars. *Left side, then right. Left side, then right*—until she feels them both the same, ecstasy and pain.

And by the time they finally come, their bodies are long gone.

69

IT IS a strange sort of purgatory: watching it all—the drinking and drugging, the cards and dancing, the fighting and laughing—through a one-way mirror, surrounded by paintings of imminent death, lashing the woman he loves, "Fire Lake" playing over and over and over . . .

All he'd have to do, of course, is roll through the wall. He'd have all the booze and coke he could want—and get some smack for Willy. But he is through the withdrawal now and chooses not to give in. This act of free will makes the torture complete, almost sacred. Willy loves and hates him for it.

Mason considers some makeshift curtains. He could put the paintings over the window, the other way around.

Those fucking paintings.

They're fucked-up, sure, but also beautiful. He leaves them as they are. He thinks he knows where they came from—but not how they came to be *here*. He'll have to ask Chaz about that—about a lot of things.

It's been weird watching Chaz on the other side, going about his business, but Mason is still not ready to see him, to sit down and talk. For now he's faced enough. And eventually the Cave beyond the cave, like a TV left on too long, no longer holds his attention. The hollowing out becomes everything, the dream of filling up.

At noon each day there's a delivery—food, meds, and Gatorade—left out on the bar. Soon even Willy is able to eat. He massages her

legs—gives her painkillers and Valium. She won't detox fully this way, but neither will the pain hit full capacity. Then one day there is something else: a small cup with a screw-top lid and a label reading METHADONE 100MG.

For a moment he thinks of not showing it to Willy.

But when he does, her face transforms. "Oh God," she says, and just like that he gives up on a world without narcotics—at least for her. It makes him feel separate from her—which is simply fucking terrifying. He thinks of life beyond this cave and trying to live it without any drugs. The thought is too painful, which makes him feel like her again—so then he holds on to that.

And Willy holds the cup.

"But what if I take it," she says. "And tomorrow there's nothing?"

"She wouldn't do that to us," says Mason.

"Okay," says Willy. And her smile comes back, full of life and thirst.

Mason unscrews the cap. He takes a whiff. It is mixed with juice, so they can't inject it, and the smell surprises him.

"Sports Day," he says.

"What?"

"It's that weird juice they used to have at McDonald's, and on Sports Day, too. Remember?"

"I wasn't big on Sports Day."

"But you had the juice, right? Here, try some . . ." He holds it to her lips, tilting the bottle carefully. She sips and sips, then drinks it down. He wipes her lips and kisses her.

"Sports Day!" says Willy.

"I hated it, too," says Mason, then wishes he hadn't. There is no way the potato sack race was as tiresome for him as for ten-year-old Willy, watching from her wheelchair—nothing to do but suck weird orange juice from a straw, the science teacher holding a Fudgsicle for her to lick—her chin streaked brown and orange while the other kids yelped and shrieked.

"Fuck it," says Willy. "We got the juice!"

63. My hands can do things without me knowing.
64. There is nothing that can't be broken.

The next day there is no lunch. Not even a Gatorade.

They wait until after one. Then Mason begins to get dressed.

Willy looks scared. "What if something happened?"

"Like what?"

"I don't know. What if you don't come back?"

"I'm coming back," he says.

"But what if you don't? How do I even get out of here?"

"The left one gets you out," he says, pointing at her hands, trying to make it sound funny.

"That's fucking great!" says Willy. "My only way out is a hand I can't move!"

"You can lift it with your right," says Mason, then stops and kisses her. "I'll be right back. I promise."

70

MASON EMERGED from the Cave, into the blinding light. He inhaled deeply, holding the air in his lungs, taking a step as he let it out. The man with the invisible kite was on the far median, where the southbound streetcar stopped, keeping tension on the invisible string.

Mason walked to the corner. The world was unbelievable and finally real. The air was cool, the sun shining. The traffic made him feel as if he were inside something enormous. He held himself together, breathed, and waited for the light to change.

When he'd crossed Spadina, his body and soul wanted to keep on walking, down the street, through the neighborhood, just to take a walk—but he thought of Willy and turned into MHAD, through the sliding doors.

He took the elevator to the sixth floor. The waiting room was empty, the door open.

"He has arisen," said the doctor, as Mason walked into her office.

He looked at her. "Why did you do that?" he said.

"I figured you needed some air."

He held her gaze.

"I needed to get your attention," she said.

"What about Willy?"

"She'll be good on the methadone," she said, and motioned for him to sit down. "I think it's the best thing for her."

"Why are you doing this?" said Mason.

"What exactly?" Dr. Francis leaned forward. "Risking my job just to get you straight?"

Mason took a seat.

"I need you better," she said. "To help me fix the mess you've made."

"Which one?"

There was a file on her desk. She opened it. "Setya Kateva."

"Excuse me?"

"Seth," she said. "That's his real name. It's Finnish."

"So that's it?" said Mason. "He's a self-hating Finn."

"I wouldn't say he's a self-hating anything, not without progesterone." She looked at Mason. "We've got to get him back. And soon."

Mason saw Soon dropping beneath the railing, that bird swooping into frame. He shook it off. "He's still out there?" he said. "Isn't it time to call the cops?"

She closed the file. "He wouldn't be out there if you hadn't attacked him. Just him being in that bar was a breach of his . . ."

"Hey!" said Mason "It was *you* he was trying to blackmail. And he threatened Willy's life!"

The doctor sat back in her chair. "All right," she said. "But is that really why you attacked him?"

"Would you stop being a fucking shrink?" He stood back up and paced behind his chair. "What difference does it make? If he breached his parole, then the cops should be on him already, right?"

Dr. Francis shook her head. "Parole officers are swamped. They use doctors like me as a de facto check-in."

"What about Sudden Street?"

She flicked her hand through the air. "Told them Seth missed an appointment, so I called it in. And seeing as he hadn't come home, I'd call the cops again. Save 'em some work: APB and everything."

"But that's not what you did . . ."

The doctor shook her head.

"So he's running but no one's chasing him!"

"Pretty much."

"What the hell are you doing?"

"There's something I should tell you, Mason."

"There's a *lot* that you should tell me."

She looked at him straight and took a breath. "Seth knows everything about you. He has your file, and he has your notebook . . . He has your confession, Mason."

"What the fuck are you talking about?"

"He broke into my office."

Mason steadied his gaze. He tried to steady his breathing. "It doesn't matter," he said. "I don't care what he's got on me. The guy should be locked up."

"Even if you get locked up, too?"

Mason shrugged.

The doctor shook her head. "Jail's too good for Seth."

"What's that supposed to mean?"

Dr. Francis leaned forward. "We'll do this ourselves," she said, then pointed a finger at Mason. "He's got something of yours. You've got something of his."

"His stupid fucking notebook?"

The doctor nodded. "It's up to us," she said. "We can take him down."

Mason sat in the chair again. "There's something you're not telling me."

"There's a *lot* that I'm not telling you." She looked him in the eye. "Do you want redemption or not?"

"I'll think about it," said Mason, and put his hand on the desk. "Now give me the goddamn juice."

It felt like someone else's apartment, or as if he'd lived there in another life. There were wisps of cocaine on the table, and the room still smelled of whisky. His bed remained unmade.

He sat down and turned on the computer. There was an email

from Seth—and only now did he notice the *To:* line. He'd been too high, or too something, to see it:

To: MasonD@hotmail.com
From: Handyman@hotmail.com
Subject: You

Owe me, bitch.

S. Handyman

Truth be told, he'd been expecting something creepier. He pressed REPLY.

To: Handyman@hotmail.com
From: MasonD@hotmail.com
Subject: I

Was expecting something creepier. You once had a way with words.

M. Dubisee

The phone rang. He hit SEND, walked over, and picked it up.

"What are you doing?" It was Dr. Francis. "He knows where you live."

"You're the one who's watching me." He hung up the phone. Then he took the ad off that website, killed his other account, packed up his laptop, and left.

"That doctor is crazy," said Mason, as Willy drank down the methadone.

"We're all crazy. It means that we're alive."

Mason took the cup. "I'll go out soon and get us some food."

She lay back down. "Are you going to be out all the time now?"

"Not all the time."

"Is something wrong?" She turned her head to look at him. "You seem like something's wrong."

"I have to tell you something, Willy."

She nodded. And then he told her everything: about Warren and Sissy and Soon—about Warren, Zevon, and Sarah—and then about Seth Handyman.

When he finished, she let out a sigh, but her eyes were shining bright. "Are you going to beat him?" she said.

"I'm not sure how to do it."

"Well, *get* sure," she said. "Get sure, get better, and beat him. Live happily ever after."

"Aren't you even scared?"

"Not for you," said Willy. "Just don't forget I'm down here. I hate it when you're gone."

Notes on the Novel in Progress

It will always be in progress.

Read it again when you think you're clean; if it still makes sense, you're not clean enough.

Kill all the semicolons.

Possible title:

Stop If You Have the Chance

71

NOT BEING high made him high. He knew one day that would end, and then the normalcy might crush him. But right now he felt pretty damn good. The strength and clarity was intense. He went for walks, and then his walks turned into runs—a limping run, because of his ankle. He knew it was a manic thing to do, but his lungs and heart just felt so strong.

He focused his energy on Willy, massaging her curves and straight-aways. And he read to her: *Papillon, The Collected Works of Billy the Kid, The Moon and Sixpence*—bits of each until his throat was raw, and they listened to "Fire Lake." They fought each other's cravings—that's how they tried to do it. As one of them got triggered (and it was hard

not to, in this cave within the Cave) the other took on the struggle, howling and swearing until they set in to each other again. His libido had returned with a vengeance.

For most of Mason's life it had been overwhelming—a driving hunger for love and sex—a thirst that could feel like a curse. He'd been trumped: by girlfriends, affairs, romances, and ravages, flesh upon flesh. But eventually he'd overwhelmed it—with a new kind of thirst: a stronger, bloodless one—for ash and powder and pure adrenaline. And then he was dry as a bone, nothing but hunger, words, and dust. He'd still had sex, more as a measure of time, waiting for the drugs to come.

But now it was back: love for love, sex for sex. And it felt like a fucking blessing. They gave it their all and overdid it—chewing up the cave, whipping and gasping and screwing themselves blind until, finally, sweating and bug-eyed, their craving was a beautiful farce. They lay there exhausted, and Mason lost feeling in half his body. But he didn't tell Willy that—just curled himself into her, singing them both to sleep.

"I can give you something to help stabilize your mood," said Dr. Francis.

"Do I want that?"

"It might help with the cravings."

He looked at her. She'd changed her tack. "Why are you being so nice?"

The doctor stood up. "Tell me, Mason—do you think you understood?"

"Understood what?"

"That suicide business of yours." She walked to the window. "Why they'd do it? *If* they'd do it? Who they actually were? Either you thought you understood—that you could relate and empathize—or else you didn't care. It's one or the other."

"I don't know.

"That's a lame answer. Come here."

Mason got up and stood next to her.

"See that girl there, the Asian girl with green shoes . . . ?" She was pointing down into the street. "She's one of my patients. I adore her. She always flirts with me . . . She's got this thing where she swallows razor blades."

"What?"

"She swallows razor blades. She wraps them in bits of toilet paper so they can get down her throat, and then the paper dissolves . . . Her insides are torn to ribbons. I've sent her to surgery six times now. They hate her at the hospital."

"Jesus."

"She's started breaking her own fingers with a hammer. She came in yesterday and was like, 'Can you look at this?' Her left hand looked like—well, like someone had been hammering it."

"Can't you put her somewhere?"

"Now that's interesting. I was just thinking about how weird that is . . ."

"What?"

"There's this room we've got on the ninth floor: White walls, nothing in it. If someone's on suicide watch, you check them every five minutes. But sometimes even that's too long. You'd be surprised how many people can beat that clock, hanging themselves off a doorknob—can you imagine what kind of will that takes? So anyway, this particular room, it doesn't have a doorknob—nothing but a mat on the floor and a one-way window so we can watch you."

"I was in one of those," said Mason.

The doctor nodded. "You know what we call it?"

"What?"

"The TQ room."

Mason felt the breath go out of him.

"Most hospitals have one. It stands for 'therapeutic quiet.'" She was still looking down at the street. "Problem is, I can't put anyone in there for more than a day. Someone like her, she'd need twenty-four-hour surveillance—for as long as it takes—and there's nowhere like that. The best was when she was in jail. We're kind of trying for that right now—but even then, I don't know . . . It went well last time until something happened. She pulled her own teeth out—then she started cutting her tongue."

He almost gagged, looking down at this girl on the corner.

"I kind of love her. Anyway, my point—one of them—is that she's not suicidal." She flicked her fingers like a gun at the windowpane. "Even *her* I can't diagnose as suicidal—not honestly. She's self-harming, self-destructive, and eventually what she does will probably kill her—but it doesn't make her suicidal." She turned and looked at him. "You should meet her. She's awesome! She gives me the oddest presents—things she's shoplifted, always useless things. She's an inspired person. She might even survive—if her mother doesn't."

"What does that mean?" Mason was watching her—the girl with green sneakers, who swallowed razor blades, beat her own hand with a hammer, and pulled out her teeth. She was crossing the street toward them.

"Her mom pimped her out till she was big enough to fight. And still she keeps in touch with her. But every time they talk, she ends up doing something." Dr. Francis turned and looked at him. "The point is, if she's not suicidal—and she's not—you don't get to be."

The girl in green shoes had vanished into the building.

"You had another point, too?"

"Right. That girl coming up to see me right now—you know why I love her?"

"Why?"

"She barely bullshits me at all. Do you know how rare that is? Ninety-nine percent of everyone I see—the thing they have in common? They're full of shit. That doesn't make me dislike them. I get it. But there's a result, right? You get so used to bullshit and deception, and omission, that you see it in the air like rays of light or something. And eventually you don't care any more, until you do by accident."

Mason thought of Sissy—or whatever her name was. The doctor was silent.

"You haven't asked me about Seth."

"You said you'd think about it."

She walked over to the minifridge in the corner, unlocked it, and pulled out a paper bag.

"Take the methadone," she said, "and give me your answer tomorrow."

He stood in the hallway. Both elevators opened at the same time. Mason got into one as a green shoe stepped out of the other.

He walked down Spadina, into the Market, then over to Busytown Park. It was a sunny day. He sat on the grass with his legs crossed, then he swiveled around and did some push-ups—his shoulders felt unused, but strong. He went over to the small jungle gym, kids climbing all over the place, and did a dozen chin-ups. When he dropped down on the sand, his ankle stayed firm. He drank some water from the fountain, then headed back to the Cave.

He decided to enter through the alley. He hadn't been back there since he'd taken the Dogmobile and headed for Utopia—that ill-planned journey, ending in a country ditch. So it was a surprise to see the fiberglass fedora parked in its usual spot. He walked up to it and reached out his hand, as he would to a skittish horse. Lines from a Springsteen song sang through his head:

Everything dies, baby, that's a fact.
But maybe everything that dies some day comes back.

He went down into the Cave.

72

To: MasonD@hotmail.com
From: Handyman@hotmail.com
Subject: I

want my fucking notebook back.

S. Handyman

Now Mason knew for sure: There was only one copy of *The Book of Handyman.* Seth's hubris hadn't allowed for Xeroxes. He wanted the book. But he *knew* he'd want the book, and that's why he gave it. If something was taken from him, he'd get it back—his freedom, his strength, his mojo—*all* the fucking marbles. Now there was the taste of challenge on his tongue—like blood and vodka mixed with honey. Mason could taste it, too.

"What did you just say?" Dr. Francis rose from her seat.

"I challenged him to a game of eight ball . . . but then he suggested poker instead. I knew he would. But I wanted it to be his idea."

"What the hell are you talking about, Mason?"

"Playing pool for your soul isn't as cool. With stakes like these, poker's more intense. It's more cinematic. Plus, he's sure he can win."

"Stakes like what?" She was looking at Mason as if he'd always irritated her—but now he was a guy who irritated her and happened to be holding a bomb.

"If he wins, he gets his notebook back. Plus he gets his freedom."

"His freedom?"

"Like he wanted from the beginning: You stop the treatment without anybody knowing, and you keep him out of jail."

She moved fast across the room. "I will *not*," she said, so close to him that he could feel her breath.

He looked her straight in the eye. "You won't have to."

She rocked back on her heels, changed her focus. "So what? You're going to win?"

"I won't lose," said Mason.

"In which case . . ."

"He's back in prison."

"I told you, Mason . . ."

"You told me there was a lot you weren't telling me."

She took a moment. Then shook her head. "If he loses, he kills himself."

"Why would . . .?" But then Mason stopped. "You know," he said, "that might just work."

73

"I HATE it when you're gone," said Willy.

"You were asleep. I was just out there in the Cave."

"What were you doing?"

"Emailing Seth." He stroked her head. "You can't get reception in here."

"Oh."

"How do you feel?"

"Half-'n'-half," she said. He pinched her ass on the feeling side. "When do we get out of here?"

"I just got to beat the psycho. Then I'll take you back to my place."

"I love it when you talk like that."

"Everything's going to be okay." He kissed her shoulders.

"I'm scared about something," she said.

"What?"

"You're so much better now. Without the drugs and the booze and everything. You look better, you sound better."

"Isn't that good?"

"I don't know. It scares me."

"Why?"

She looked away. "I'm never getting better. You know that, right?"

Mason smiled. "Deep down, I'm still a mess."

Willy didn't smile. "It's hard to explain," she said.

"What is?"

"I kind of feel like a fake sometimes."

Mason waited.

"It's like when you asked me what happened . . . People always ask me that. And I know they mean why am in a wheelchair but they also mean why am I a junkie—or they *don't* mean that!"

"What do you mean?"

She punched him with her senseless fist. "I told you it's hard to explain."

"Sorry."

"It's like everyone assumes they're the same thing—that this is why I do drugs . . ." she pointed at her body. "Or why I *did* drugs or whatever. You know why *I* think I'm fucked-up?"

Mason shook his head.

"The stupidest reason ever." She looked up, at the bottom of the top bunk. "Some stupid guy broke my heart. I loved him a lot, and he broke my heart. Same as everybody, right? And when he left, I couldn't even go after him—so maybe in that way, yeah: I'm fucked because I can't run after them."

There was silence for a while.

Finally Mason spoke. "Well, you know," he said. "It usually doesn't work."

"What?"

"Running after them."

Willy took a breath. "But sometimes it does, right?"

"Maybe."

"You know why I liked Bethany?"

"No," said Mason. "Not at all."

"Because I didn't like her." She turned her head and looked at him. "I'm scared you're going to leave me." And then he could see she was crying.

Dr. Francis was at her desk, Chaz in the corner like her bodyguard or something. She lifted her head and looked at Mason, who had chosen not to take a seat. "He says you're not as good as you think you are."

"I said he's terrible," said Chaz.

"Well, he can go fuck himself," said Mason.

"If you don't win, we're screwed."

"I'm going to win."

Chaz came out of the corner and stood in front of Mason. "I don't think you understand. If Seth wins, he's not walking out of there. We're not just letting him go."

"So."

"So what then? I shoot the guy?"

They looked at each other. "Sounds good to me."

"Jesus, Mason!" Chaz sat down in the chair where the patients sat. He looked at Dr. Francis. "Jesus . . ."

Dr. Francis turned to Mason. "I'm worried you think Seth will be easy to beat."

Mason went over and stood by the window. The doctor kept talking:

"Don't assume sociopaths, just because they lack empathy, aren't good at reading people. Usually it's the opposite. That's their currency—other people's weaknesses. They can see them like . . . like stink lines in a cartoon. It's what makes them so good at manipulating." She pointed her finger at him. "You won't get anything from him, Mason. But Seth—he'll read you perfectly."

"Ha!" said Mason, turning away from the window.

"What?"

"You're fucking right. He's the Warrior Monk." He looked at Chaz, a half smile on his face. "Seth is the fucking Warrior Monk."

"It's why he agreed to play . . ."

"Why he *chose* the game," said Mason.

"He knows he can't lose."

"He *thinks* he'll win," said Mason, now leaning against the windowsill, "but it's not a given. If it was, he wouldn't be interested. He wants the highest stakes there are *and* a meaningful adversary. That's always been missing for him. And now look at this, it's perfect: He already hates me, but he trusts me as a gambler. If he wins, he's got my humiliation—your humiliation, too—his notebook, his freedom. And if he loses, he's dead." Mason walked toward them. "The doctor was right: It's *way* better than prison. It's exciting to him. He thinks the odds are in his favor, but the stakes actually shake him. They shake him all the way. He couldn't *design* a better game."

"The odds *are* in his favor!" said Chaz. "Even if what you're saying made sense, how are you going to beat him? You play to lose." He stood up. "I love you, man. But you're a terrible poker player. You play with heart and no brains. You like the rush too much. You're good at the game, but not at *winning*. You think that's going to change?"

Mason faced Dr. Francis. "Why does everyone know me better than I do?" He looked at Chaz. "And since when do you talk like a normal person? What happened to Chaz the goombah? Life start getting him down?"

Chaz shook his head and walked out of the office.

Dr. Francis sighed. "Why do you do that, Mason?"

"What?"

"You make people feel stupid for caring about you."

"Really?"

"Yup."

"Interesting . . ."

"You heard us in the Cave that day, didn't you?"

"What do you mean?"

"The Man from Snowy River."

"I don't remember *you* saying much."

"He loves you like a brother."

Mason looked out the window. Chaz was crossing the street.

"Yeah," he said. "It's a fucking curse."

"For you or for him?"

Mason turned to her. "I've run out of statements," he said.

To: Handyman@hotmail.com

From: MasonD@hotmail.com

Subject: The Rules of the Game, Draft #4

The game will be heads-up no limit Texas hold 'em, tournament style.

The purchase of a sealed deck must be witnessed by both players.

Each player will have $1,000 in chips. Blinds 5 and 10.

The blinds will be raised every half hour.

The deal will alternate every hand.

After shuffling, a cut must be offered by the dealer.

All other rules of the house apply.

The stakes have been agreed upon and are fixed.

They must be paid in full.

M. Dubisee

To: MasonD@hotmail.com

From: Handyman@hotmail.com

Subject: RE: The Rules of the Game, Draft #4

Shuffle up and deal.

S. Handyman

Notes on the Novel in Progress

If you're going to have a big climactic scene, at least have a break before it—time for the reader to think:

What has happened? What are the stakes?

Okay. That should be enough.

74

DR. FRANCIS sat on Willy's bunk in the QT room. She and Willy were talking, some of it medical, some of it not.

On the other side of the glass, the Cave was empty but for Mason and Chaz. They sat at a table near the bar.

"You know what you're doing?"

"Yeah," said Mason. "For the first time in a long time."

"That's not how it works, you know?"

"What?"

"You get sober and that's it—like taking a pill and suddenly you're an invincible genius or something."

Mason grinned. "Then why do I feel like one?"

"Because you're an idiot."

It was five minutes to nine. Mason finished his soda water, nodded at the ladies through the looking glass, then headed for the door.

65. *The thought of dancing makes me nervous.*
66. *I have no favorite number.*

Mason stood with his back to the wall, outside the Lucky Save—as if waiting on some normal dude: *maybe grab some beers, play some poker . . .* Then there he was, coming out of Harvey's—a black hood over a baseball cap—like any guy on the street. It was a strange moment, standing there, as if they were about to shake hands or something.

"You look like shit," said Seth.

But Mason looked sharp: clean-shaven, in a pressed suit, collar open, no tie. And the detox had done him good. He grinned and held the Lucky Save door.

It felt unreal: Seth Handyman in the Lucky Save Convenience—like going for lunch with Darth Vader. Mason pointed at the cards, hanging on the wall next to the batteries. "A pack of Bicycle, please. The blue ones."

"Red," said Seth. Mason shrugged, and so did the Lucky Save proprietor. As the man turned around to get the cards, Seth took four vials of poppers from beside the register, put them in his pocket, and walked toward the door.

The man put the cards on the counter. "That's $5.25."

Mason was suddenly nauseous. He paid and left the store.

"Okay," he said. "A couple things you'll want to know . . ."

"Don't worry," said Seth, ushering Mason into the Harvey's vestibule. "I've been here before." He pulled open the door to the Cave. "Your buddy runs this place, right?"

They descended in the dark, Seth behind him on the stairs. His nausea felt cold now—icy vomit waiting in his guts. They pushed through the curtains.

The Cave looked cool like this—open for business but empty, the dim light, black and burgundy, shadows and candle flame. Chaz was standing behind the bar like a saloonkeeper, wiping out a highball glass. Seth crossed the room toward him.

"Howdy," said Seth.

Chaz nodded, still wiping the glass.

"You're the guy who broke my nose." He sat down at the bar.

"Yeah?"

"With a motorcycle helmet, I believe."

Chaz nodded, like that sounded about right.

Seth flipped back his hood, the cap still on. His face looked leaner in the light.

"Double Jack on the rocks," he said. "And one for my buddy."

Chaz looked to Mason.

"Soda water."

Seth laughed. "Oh, how the worm has turned!"

Chaz poured. Mason hadn't expected this: having to watch Seth drink whisky.

"I thought you didn't drink," he said, and immediately wished he hadn't. *Weakness.*

"Only when I'm on parole." Seth leaned over and pulled up his pant leg. There were red lines where the tracking bracelet had been. "What's your excuse?"

Mason took a breath.

"You're playing over there," said Chaz. He was trying to sound casual, as if he were assigning a lane in a bowling alley, still wiping that fucking glass.

At the table were two chairs and two stacks of chips. Mason walked over and put down his glass of soda water.

"No way," said Seth.

"What?"

"I'm not sitting with my back to him—*or* to that mirror."

Mason glanced toward the bar. "Your call," he said, switching his drink to the other side. There was no angle from the mirror. He felt eyes on his back, and Chaz just trying to stay calm.

Seth walked around the table and unzipped his hoodie. He pulled it off as he took his seat, under the yellow light. He was wearing a dark blue T-shirt, the sleeves rolled up tight over cut, sinewy muscles. Mason's glass was almost empty. Chaz came over to get it.

"Is he going to be here while we play?" said Seth.

"It's his place," said Mason.

"It wasn't in the rules. If *you* have someone, *I* get someone."

"What?"

"It's only fair."

"How are you going to . . . ?"

Seth got up and drank down his drink. The pudginess had disappeared. He looked lean and mean. "Back in a minute." He crossed the Cave and went out through the curtains. Mason looked at the unopened deck of cards. Chaz brought his drink over. "He's been here before."

"So it seems."

"You think he's coming back?"

Mason shrugged.

"He looks different, right?"

Mason nodded. "He's stopped the progesterone," he said. "It made him fat and bloated."

"It's only been a week."

"A very long week."

Chaz went to the bar to watch the monitor. Mason concentrated on his breathing.

They stayed like that for a while, then eventually Chaz spoke: "He's got someone with him." The curtains parted.

Seth walked to his chair and sat down. The other man stayed standing, to the right of Seth's chair. He was facing Mason, but looking over him, past him—his hands in the air circling each other slowly—like he was reeling out line, or invisible string.

"Jesus!" said Mason.

"You want something to drink, buddy?" said Seth. The Kite Man said nothing. Seth held up his glass. "Another for me, Chaz." He looked at Mason. "How's that soda water treating you?"

Mason picked up the deck.

"Let's crack 'em open," said Seth.

The plastic foil put Mason's teeth on edge. His mouth was dry. Another sip, and his drink was empty again. Seth heard the clink of ice in his glass and laughed. Mason felt his anger rising like quicksand around his shoulders. The Kite Man's stare had shifted—the same line, just farther away. Mason took a breath, began to shuffle. Seth watched him, his eyes flicking with the cards. Mason placed the deck in the middle of the table: "Cut for deal?" he said.

Seth nodded with a smile, then reached out and cut the 10 of clubs—Mason, the 6 of diamonds. Chaz arrived with the drinks. Seth began to shuffle: a classic waterfall for a while, then he triple-cut one-handed, drinking from his glass with the other. Mason stacked his chips into five piles. "Small blind," said Seth.

Mason tossed a $5 chip into the pot. Seth put in his $10 and placed the deck next to it. Mason cut the cards, then watched as Seth began to deal.

67. There is no try—only do and do not.
68. It's sometimes hard to breathe.

Mason looked at his pocket cards: a suited connector—10 and jack of hearts. He put them down on the felt. They felt good beneath his fingers. "Plus twenty," he said, sliding the chips into the pot.

"All in," said Seth.

To Mason it felt like a giant had grabbed him, picked him up, and slammed him back into his chair.

Seth picked up his chips in two large stacks and placed them in the center of the table. He looked at Mason, his face blank.

Mason's mind stumbled, from gear to gear, his thoughts chugging out, then racing over everything—all the possibilities. The more he thought, the less it made sense: Seth ready to end it all—right now, on the first hand—with so much at stake. Not only

life and death, but the game itself . . . The bet was insane. It was
ludicrous . . . Wondrous. It was the kind of bet Mason would make
on a grand or so—but on his *life*?

An awesome move.

And then, before he realized what was happening, Mason smiled
at his opponent—an impressed, heavy grin, full of awe and respect.

Just fold the fucking hand!

"I fold," said Mason.

Seth nodded and gathered up the chips. Mason sat back in his
chair. He'd lost the first hand—not a lot of chips, but that stupid
smile: a victory for Seth he hadn't meant to give.

For a while they traded hands, big blind picking up antes, maybe
$40 on the flop . . . nothing made it to the turn. Mason was focused
on two things. One was keeping their stacks close to even.

It wasn't until the seventh hand that they went all the way: from
the flop, to the turn, to the river. But still the betting was low,
$180 in the pot: Seth turned over three 6s, beating Mason's two
pair. But Mason was feeling okay: The game was young; they were
finding their pace.

"What time is it?" said Seth.

Mason shuffled.

"Nine forty-five," said Chaz.

"Aren't the blinds supposed to go up?" said Seth.

Mason kept on shuffling.

"Blinds are ten and twenty," said Chaz.

As if on cue, Seth pulled something from his pocket.

"Can you pass me one of those?" he said, pointing at the bar.
Mason didn't turn around, just shuffled. Seth got up from the table
and came back with a metal coaster in his hand. He sat down and,
without looking at Mason, dumped a pile of white onto the shiny
chrome in front of him.

"No fucking way," said Mason, trying to swallow the words as
he said them.

Seth glanced up at him, some poor sucker's credit card in his
hand. He pressed it down—that crunching sound. Mason's chest
constricted, he fumbled the shuffle—and now Seth was chopping;
chop-chop-chopping . . . little piles, thick white lines . . .

As Chaz came around the table, the Kite Man lifted his hands quickly, as if trying to avoid snagging him.

"Sorry," said Chaz. "No drugs at the game."

Seth looked up. "Oh," he said, still chopping away, "that's actually not true." He nodded at Mason. "Ask your buddy there. The rules of the house apply."

"It's *my* house," said Chaz.

"And it's our game," said Seth. "Should we take it somewhere else?"

They both looked at Mason.

Mason looked at the pile of coke. Never in his life had he wanted a line so badly. He dropped his gaze and shook his head. As Seth turned back to Chaz, a look of satisfied innocence on his face, Mason—halfway through a shuffle—stretched his arms across the table, the cards in an arch between his fingers. Then he let them go.

"Oops," he said, as the cards riffled down. Cocaine blew across the table, into the air like a cloud. "Sorry about that."

Seth turned to him. "Don't worry, buddy." He smiled. "There's a lot more where that came from.

Seth snorted a rail before every hand—sometimes between bets—and he was sharp with it, too: cutting lines, cutting cards, his hands flashing in perfect practiced motion. He hit the coke, then popped a popper. He drank down his bourbon in long gulps, struck a match one-handed.

The man knows how to do it.

Seth played and drank and drugged and smoked—like the Mason of old, just better. Lighting a cigarette, his eyes shone in the flame; this is what they said: *It's* worth *it—even if my judgment falters—to drink so well, to get so high, to watch you suffer so.*

And the Mason of new could but sit and watch. He fumbled the cards. His hands shook as he sipped his soda water. He dropped his chips, gritting his teeth as if in pain. But in truth, Mason wasn't suffering.

Inside he was Zen.

It had happened four hands ago. Surrounded by triggers—the snap of the cards, the click of the chips, the strike of the match, the clink of the glass, the cut of the chrome, the pop of the poppers,

the inhale, the long lovely drawing in, the exhale, everything he'd lost—and forced to face the end, the never again . . . *not ever*, he'd thought, as violent a thought as losing the game. Then suddenly it had disappeared. And in its place a gentler one:

Not now.

He'd breathed this thought in deep. *Not now.* And then he'd breathed it out, aimed at all his triggers, and it blasted straight through them. He saw clearly, with focus. He kept on fumbling, just for show—shaking, dropping his chips. And now, six hands later, they were almost back to even.

There was $60 on the table, and a flop, but nothing on the board: 9, 4, queen—all different suits. Mason checked.

"Sixty," said Seth, betting the pot.

Mason hesitated, then mumbled: "Okay, plus $200."

A moment of silence, then Seth slammed his cards down—a violent fold. "You're kidding me!" he said, and glared at Mason.

Mason, still futzing around with his chips, lifted his head—and then he grinned. The air left the room—backdraft in a burning house. Seth burst out: "You're *fucking* kidding!"

Mason swept the pot toward himself. He was the chip leader now—not by much, but it meant a lot. If, say, in this next hand, they both went all in and Mason won, then Seth was done, Seth was dead. Mason stacked his chips. By the way he'd played it, his cover was blown—Seth knew he was strong and had been for a while. But the grin, too, was worth a lot. It said that Mason was more than strong. He took the cards to shuffle.

"All right," said Seth. He did a last thick line, then swept the rest onto the floor. "You think you can get into my head? Is that what you think?" He pulled off his cap and threw it. The Kite Man flinched, pulling back with his forward hand. "Take a look!" said Seth, and bowed across the table, giving Mason a bird's eye view. The purple flesh seemed to pulse. "Get right in there," he said, then lifted his head and stared into Mason's eyes.

"Cut," said Mason.

Seth tapped the deck. Mason began to deal.

They looked at their cards.

"Fifty," said Seth, bumping up the blind.

Mason nodded and put it in.

He burned a card, then dealt the flop: 8, 8, 2. He always liked the way two 8s looked—like infinite snakes.

"A hundred," said Seth.

Mason looked at him, then down at his cards. "Plus $100," he said, and reached for his chips.

"All in," said Seth.

It is a particular kind of stillness when even an invisible kite stops moving.

Mason took a breath. "All in," he said.

Chaz was coming out from behind the bar.

Seth turned his cards over: an 8 and an ace. He smiled.

"Oh, God," said Chaz, in the voice of someone watching death.

Mason flipped his cards: a jack and an ace.

Chaz sat down. His mouth hung open. "Oh, God," he said.

Seth grinned. "What the hell were you thinking?"

Mason didn't answer. He looked up at the Kite Man and shivered. He turned back to the table, then looked at Chaz. "I was pot committed . . ."

Chaz said nothing, still staring at the cards.

"Burn and turn," said Seth. "Burn. And. Turn."

Mason reached out. He burned a card. Then turned a jack.

There was a quick inhale and Seth laughed. "Not a chance in hell," he said.

Two running jacks is impossible.

Like finding God . . . well, anywhere.

Mason burned the last burn. Only the jack could save him.

"Hey, Chaz," he said, his hand still shaking. "I think I could do with a drink."

Then he turned the final card.

75

"Show me again."

They were sitting at each side of the bar. Mason did a wash, spreading the cards in all directions. Then he gathered them up and started to shuffle every which way: waterfall, chopper, one-handed.

He split them one last time, then dealt the cards: Mason a jack and an ace, Chaz an ace and an eight. Then came the flop: 8, 8, 2.

"Booyah!" said Chaz.

Then a jack and then a jack.

"Holy fucking crap."

"It's not as easy as it looks," said Mason. "First you got to get ahold of 'em—all nine cards—and nick 'em like so. It takes a lot of hands."

"That's why you were playing so tight."

"Yeah, sure. But that's just the start." He picked up the cards. "You got to shuffle the same every time and get the guy to that special place—rile him up just right." Then he snapped them together and put them down.

"So he taps the cut," said Chaz.

"So he finally taps the cut."

"What if he never did . . . or you couldn't get the lead?"

Mason shrugged. "Then I'd just become the Warrior Monk."

"That was your backup plan?"

"I did get worried a couple of times."

"You're fucking insane."

He shrugged again and grinned.

Chaz shook his head. "Why that hand?"

"I guess it ate away at me a bit," said Mason. "That was a bad fucking beat you gave me."

"But you still should have told me the plan . . ."

"It works!" said Dr. Francis, pushing through the curtain. She looked happy, waving her hands in the air. "I can see him wherever he goes! You should come to my office and take a look."

Chaz got up to pour her a drink. It occurred to Mason he'd never seen Dr. Francis excited—in an enthusiastic way. "Give me a double," she said, and sat down at the bar.

She'd bought the GPS microchip and software online. The puncture gun she got from the vet who looked after her cat when she went away on vacation.

"I still can't imagine you on vacation," said Mason.

She held up the glass, then drank it straight down. Within forty-eight hours Seth was supposed to kill himself. And now they could track his every move.

She hadn't said a word to Seth. It was like watching a gangland hit. She came out of the darkness, took a hold of his head, and pumped the chip with a blast—up through the back of his neck, past the base of his skull. A brain surgeon would have trouble getting it out.

"I can't believe he just sat there," said Chaz.

"Actually," said Dr. Francis. "Neither can I."

"You wanted death," said Mason. "So we had to renegotiate. The stakes went up at the end."

They looked at him.

"To what?" said Chaz. "What do you put against a chip in your head?"

"It should be obvious," said Mason, and lifted his hands. "You put up your goddamn scalp."

76

THIS WAS to be their last night in the QT room, and Mason and Willy were happy.

"In some ways I'll miss this place," she said.

"Yeah," said Mason, though he didn't exactly agree with her. Even now the knowledge lurked: how easy this room could turn— if your friends disappeared, if the door refused to open—from a hideout into hell.

"I still can't believe you bet your scalp! Your hair's so thick and nice!"

The nervous energy of watching the game through a one-way mirror had made Willy giddy, then just tired, and soon she fell asleep. Mason lay with her awhile, looking out through the bulletproof window. The Cave would be opening in an hour or so. He got up, put his left hand to the wall, then rolled on out.

Chaz was alone at the bar, still holding a deck of cards. "So tell me," he said. "How'd you learn to do it?"

"Fifteen years of practice," said Mason. "And a lot of shuffling."

"Yeah, but how?"

Mason sat down and looked at him. "I had a good teacher."

"No way . . ." said Chaz.

"Yup."

"You're kidding me."

"Remember what he said that night?"

"Boom, boom . . . and boom."

Mason nodded. "Yeah. Then he said, 'If you're going to stack the deck . . . '"

"So he taught you how? Why didn't you ever tell me?"

"He told me not to."

"That bastard! Why didn't he teach *me*?"

Mason shrugged. "I guess he just liked me more."

"Okay. Well if you're so good at cheating, why do you lose so much?"

"I won today, didn't I?"

"Yeah. You did."

"To Tenner." Mason raised an empty glass.

"To Tenner . . ." There was silence as Chaz swallowed down his drink. Mason watched him.

"It was hard to play sober—I guess a lot of things are going to be hard."

"You played better."

"Maybe. Cheating helps."

"I guess so . . . You think he'll do it?"

"We'll see. At least we got him tagged."

Chaz picked up the bottle and gestured to Mason. Mason shook his head. "I got a question," he said. "Those paintings in there. They're Soon's, right?"

Chaz poured a glass. "I found them in the Dogmobile."

"What do you mean?"

"I needed somewhere to store things. Didn't want you detoxing in a room full of coke and guns."

"Good thinking."

"I'd got it towed back here—nice driving, by the way."

"Sorry about that."

"So I thought I'd stash it all in that big empty hat. I took down the drop ceiling, and there they were . . ."

"*Hats off to you . . .*"

"What?"

"A note he left."

"Well, he left you another one, too." Chaz dug into his jacket pocket, pulled out an envelope, and put it on the table.

Mason stared at it.

Chaz looked at his watch. "The rabble will be here soon."

"Thanks," said Mason. He picked up the envelope and headed back in, to the cave within the Cave.

Dear Mr. D.,

I have entitled the series *The Ghosts of Soon*. Enclosed is a signed letter of provenance, so that no one will debate either authorship or ownership of these paintings. They belong to you, and as long as I am held in the public consciousness, they should be worth something. It is in both our interests that I am well remembered.

I'm sorry I misled you, but I also misread you; I didn't expect your conscience to kick in quite so fast. Thanks for caring. You're a good man.

Soon Sahala

Fishy was supposed to have been watching the monitor. As it was, Chaz was on the wrong side of the room when he heard the thunder: Detective Flores and fifteen other cops in flak jackets, six of them holding shotguns.

Willy was still asleep, but Mason saw it happening—drinks and chips scattering, Chaz hurtling over the bar. Then that was it—he didn't drop to the floor, didn't roll through the trap door. Instead he stood up. Mason could see what he was thinking: His friends were safe, and that's all that mattered. Why push his luck? He and Mason were facing each other now, and although Chaz couldn't see though the glass, they found each other's eyes. He gave him a smile, then turned around with his hands up—shotguns trained on his generous grin.

Who wants to take that long shot gamble?

And head it out to Fire Lake?

The
Eighth

Beneath the Black Helmet

77

MASON STOOD on the subway platform. There was hardly anyone around, even here at St. George station, where the university line crossed over the Bloor. His hands were shaking, he was looking down at the track. Air rushed in and out of the tunnels, the distant sounds of metal on metal, radio buzz, fluorescent humming.

At 12:07 A.M. the sound system clicked on: a low hiss from the speakers in the ceiling, a computerized bell: *bong, bong*—two notes deemed suitable for getting people's attention—and then a level, vapid voice *Attention TTC commuters. At this time, travel both east and west on the Bloor line has been suspended until further notice. We apologize for the inconvenience. Attention TTC commuters . . .*

Mason stood there another minute, until the air shifted. The southbound train came screeching out of the tunnel.

He stepped in, the doors closed behind him, and he was off. As the train flew through the darkness, an image of a man came into his head. He was in a business suit, running through a field. There was a look of exhilaration and fear on his face. Then Mason realized what it was: a Monty Python skit he hadn't seen for years, the voice-over something like "God gave this man the rare opportunity to choose the manner of his own death . . ." And at this moment, cresting the hill behind him, came a legion of naked buxom women. Mason could see them now, their long soft hair flying as they ran. They chased the man right off a cliff.

God knows, with all those options out there, why Seth would choose the subway. But apparently he had.

Mason got off at Queen's Park and walked the rest of the way. Near his apartment, he cut through the alley. There was still police tape around the loading dock, and the Dogmobile was gone. He was pretty sure the cops hadn't found the QT room. Flores and his men had emptied the Cave while he and Willy watched from behind the glass. They'd waited all through the day—then, in the evening, he'd carried her out.

They'd left everything behind—including *The Book of Handyman*; *Notes on the Novel in Progress*; seventy Socratic statements; the letters he'd written for Warren, Sissy, and Soon; Soon's research; and anything else incriminating Chaz had found in Mason's apartment and transferred to the QT room, believing that would be safer.

His laptop was down there, too. But still, he wasn't in a hurry to go back—especially considering the bag of cocaine. Mason had found it tucked down between the bed and the wall. Chaz must have dropped it there while moving his cache out to the Dogmobile. All that time detoxing, Mason had been locked in a room with a pound of pure Peruvian. He salivated thinking about it. Unless the cops had miraculously found the entrance to the QT room, the coke was down there right now—along with *The Ghosts of Soon*—that and a tape deck that played only one song, over and over and over . . .

Mason climbed the stairs to his apartment. He liked the feeling of opening the door, knowing there was someone inside.

"Hey there, cowboy," said Willy. She was propped up in the captain's bed.

"You're awake."

"I wasn't uncomfortable," she said. "Just waiting for you . . ." He could see she was nervous. She didn't know how to ask the question.

"He did it," said Mason.

"Seriously?"

"The subway stopped running right after midnight. We'll know for sure tomorrow."

"Holy shit," she said.

"Yeah."

78

MASON'S ALARM rang at 8:45 A.M. It was the first time he'd ever set it, his first day with rules: awake before 9 A.M.; breakfast, lunch, and dinner; at least an hour of exercise; no drugs; no gambling— and for the time being, no booze—to bed by 1 A.M. He'd even decided to look for a job, something that didn't involve hot dogs, suicide, or writing. Let other people write books.

Willy stirred. He told her to sleep a bit more, then got out of bed and climbed down the steps. He shaved, ate some granola, then called Dr. Francis.

There was no answer at the MHAD office. He tried her cell phone.

"Dr. Francis speaking." There was noise in the background.

"It's me," said Mason. "Where are you?"

"I work at the shelter on Tuesdays."

"Oh. Do you have any news?"

"The prognosis looks good!" she said.

Mason realized he'd been holding his breath and let it go.

"Come to my office tomorrow, and we can talk about it."

"Willy needs her medication," he said. It had been over forty-eight hours. Had the doctor forgotten?

"Right . . ." she said. "Why don't you meet me here at noon."

In the hope that she could sleep through most of the day, Mason gave Willy some Imovane. "But if you wake up in pain," he said, "take a Valium. And you call me on my cell." He put the phone next to the bed.

"Don't worry," she said. "I'll be all right."

Except for the trip to the St. George subway station, he hadn't gone farther than a city block in weeks—the Cave, the MHAD building, the market, the park. When had the world gotten so small that he could see the breadth of it from his window? It was time the universe started expanding again. He took long strides and a roundabout route: through the university, around Queen's Park, down into the financial district, then back up Yonge Street. The air was cool, the sky was clear, and he figured this counted as exercise.

He arrived at the Sherbourne Shelter around eleven thirty. It was in the basement of a stone church that had become more and more secular over the years—an old men's shelter for the "hard to house" over the age of forty-five. Mason had spent enough time on the streets to know that if you managed to live to fifty, you weren't so much put out to pasture as turned into prey. Towering office buildings stood on either side of the old church, looking as if they were about to steal its lunch money. There were a half dozen guys smoking on the steps. Mason considered walking a few more blocks to kill the time, but his ankle had started to throb, so he took a seat on the stairs.

A stocky, red-faced man in a cat burglar toque sat down next to him. "Got a smoke?" he said.

"You're smoking one," said Mason.

"Yeah, but for later."

"Nope. Sorry."

"Huh!" said the man, then leaned back a bit, as if studying him from a different angle. He took a long drag on the filter. "So what's up with you, man?" The others were looking over now, too—like they were trying to figure out whether Mason was worth trying to figure out. Any other day he might have fit right in, but this was the new Mason—the one who shaved and crossed things off lists, and it seemed they could see it in him.

"I'm here to visit my friend," he said.

"Who'd that be?"

"The doctor."

"The who?" One of the old men with hard eyes was lumbering toward them.

"Dr. Francis. She's the . . ."

"Watch what you're saying 'bout Frannie," said the old man, leaning in close. He smelled of cherry cough syrup and fresh urine.

"I said she's my friend," said Mason.

"Saved my life, that lady did!" said the old man, as if they were arguing. "No one says nothing bad about her!"

"Fair enough." The rest of the old guys were shuffling over now, too. Mason took his hands out of his pockets. "How'd she save your life?"

Shaughnessy Bishop-Stall

"*Ah . . .*" He flicked his hand in the air as if Mason wasn't worth the trouble. "Had one of my attacks right there on the floor. I was legally dead . . ."

"You weren't dead, Wilf," said a man with rheumy eyes.

"*Legally* I was. But Frannie—she's smart! She knew right away what the problem was. Gave me a shot right in the thigh. Turns out . . ." he lifted one of his fingers, like this was the crux of everything, "I'm allergic to shrimps."

"You didn't know that?"

"Never had a shrimp before. There's a first time for everything. Point is, I been around doctors my whole life—*they* never knew I was allergic to shrimp. To them I'm no more than a dog. But Frannie—she's different."

Mason did his best to follow the logic. "She's allergic to nuts," he said.

Wilf sat up a bit straighter. "To nuts!" he said, and looked around at the others, who actually seemed impressed. "I told you! She could see that we're the same—she's got that empathizing gene, makes her care about people. She saved every one of us . . ."

"Didn't save me," said the rheumy-eyed one.

"Bullshit," said Wilf. "You're full of shit is what you are. Who got you morphine? Who got you housing?" He turned back to Mason. "It's true! He doesn't even live here! Just comes on Tuesday to see the doctor." The guys on the stairs started to laugh.

"I didn't say I didn't like her," said the one with rheumy eyes.

"You're in love with her!" said Wilf.

"*I'm* in love with her! You're the one with the shrimps and nuts and all the empathizing!"

"What the hell does that mean?"

All of them were laughing know—even the cat burglar, who handed Mason a smoke.

69. I know the constellations.

70. My heart is just an organ.

At noon, Mason said good-bye to the guys on the stairs and went into the shelter. It was like a hospital in an old war movie where they'd managed to keep the soldiers alive but never quite healed. They were

propped in doorways, lying on a bench, curled up in a corner, reading on a cot, walking around in circles, their hands buzzing at their own ears. They wore modern-day civilian rags, but the war was still with them—in their eyes, in their hacking coughs, their shaking hands, in the stiffness of their walk. The war was the cold of the winter, the heat of the summer, the violence on every corner, the never being able to relax, the pain of memory, the loss of memory, the crack, the Lysol, the smack, the booze, and the new weapons, too: the meth and the oxy and the giant TV screens attached to high-rise buildings. The war was foster homes, halfway houses, residential schools, jails, prisons, shantytowns, soup kitchens, and shelters. It was never getting a real night's sleep, hands grabbing at your belongings, men coughing sickness right into your mouth. It was abusive fathers, dead mothers, cruel foster parents, crowded jail cells. It was TB and scabies and hep C and AIDS. It was bedbugs and kerosene fires and cuts that never got clean. It was cops and gangbangers and bikers and bashers and pimps and your brother passing out on the streetcar tracks. It was schizophrenia, bipolar disorder, borderline personality. It was rage, isolation, mourning. It was self-deception, self-hatred, self-harm, self-destruction. It was your old lady loving you, your old lady leaving you, your old lady dead. It was missing everyone you'd ever known. It was nothing ever changing and no one to depend on. It was a code that changed every moment, a war that never ended. It was suicide. And Mason, walking through the shelter, felt like a man who'd barely dodged the draft.

Dr. Francis was talking to an old-timer in a trucker's cap. "Would you take me fishing sometime?" she said.

"Y'alright," said the old-timer. "But it ain't gonna be easy. We go for the big fish." He glared at Mason.

"All right then, Flash. I'm gonna hold you to it."

The old-timer nodded.

Mason followed her to a small office in the corner of the room. "You fish?" he said.

"I'm a quick study." She sat down in front of a computer and started clicking with the mouse. "Come here. I want to show you something." Mason pulled up a chair and sat down beside her. "There." She touched the screen with her finger, where a red dot pulsed in the middle of a street map. "That's where he is."

Mason felt his muscles tightening. "I thought he was dead."

She turned around. "Look at the intersection."

Mason leaned in. "Bay and Bloor."

"At precisely 12:02 this morning," said Dr. Francis. "A westbound train pulling into the Bay subway station struck and killed an unidentified male. Even the cops will tell you that. What they won't tell you is that, although the body was severely mangled and partially decapitated, the early autopsy report suggests the man had no scalp. You need a coroner friend for that kind of detail."

"So why is that dot still flashing?"

"Well, I'd assume that there in that tunnel, among all those bits of flesh and bone . . ." she turned back and tapped the screen once more, "is one bloody little microchip."

"Yuck," said Mason.

Dr. Francis nodded once, slowly, like she was accepting a compliment, then closed the screen. "Come on," she said. "It's my lunch hour. Let's take a walk."

There were a few guys smoking crack in the alley, including Wilf of the shrimp and nuts. When they saw Dr. Francis they looked embarrassed. She waved, then carried on to Bloor Street.

"They like you," said Mason.

"It took a while."

They walked along Bloor, and soon the viaduct could be seen up ahead. Dr. Francis looked to Mason, who gave a shrug. He was curious to see how the Saving Grace was coming along, but still he felt anxious as they walked toward it. Conversation seemed difficult. There was little that wasn't complicated between them. Of the three people they had in common, one was in jail for drugs and guns; one was on the doctor's methadone, illegally; and the third, thanks to them, was splitting his time—or at least his body—between a coroner's office and a subway station.

Dr. Francis gave it a shot. "That girl you went looking for . . . what was her name?"

"Oh," said Mason. "Well, I really don't know what her name was. That's sort of the problem."

"Yeah. Of course."

"I thought it was Sissy."

"Sissy. Right. I've been thinking about her. It's a very specific need, to become somebody else—like a psychological survival instinct."

"Do you think she killed herself?"

"Dunno. But if she didn't, she's probably someone else by now, since Sissy wasn't working. Best scenario, she'd mix the memories she could live with into a character who has never actually existed. The way I see it, that could open her up to possibility—like a door to the future."

"I should have done something before she disappeared."

The doctor said nothing.

They walked until they came to a barricade of orange cones and striped wooden horses. There were arrows diverting traffic north and south to alternate bridges and a large octagonal sign that read CLOSED FOR OPENING.

"Good title," said Mason.

The doctor grunted. "How's the book going?"

Mason stepped over one of the horses and walked toward the bridge. There were trucks, pallets, and a crane, but no one was working at the moment. A banner blew in the wind: THE SAVING GRACE—COMPLETION JULY 11.

"Just five days left to jump," said Mason.

"It was a serious question," said Dr. Francis. "About your book."

"I know," said Mason. He walked onto the bridge.

"So . . ."

"What do you mean *so*? It's done."

"It's finished?"

"No. Just done . . . Listen, do you think I can stay off the drugs?" Dr. Francis stepped onto the pedestrian walkway. "That's up to you." She touched the first strand of the Saving Grace.

"Well, I can tell you this," said Mason. "My chances go up if I don't write. Even with the whole *Book of Sobriety* thing, I can't imagine doing it sober, not really . . . What would happen if I started using again?"

"At the same rate? There's a good chance you'd die."

"So if I never write another word, then that's okay. At least I'd be alive.'"

"What makes living so important—all of a sudden?"

Mason's hands clenched. "What the fuck?" he said, then walked away from her. It was like that feeling when somebody makes a racial slur—your throat constricts, the world looks instantly ugly, and you don't know what to say. The difference here was she had a point.

He turned and took hold of the Saving Grace, tried to look at the skyline through the strands. "What do you think of this?" he said.

"What?" said Dr. Francis, catching up. "The harp strings?"

Mason nodded.

"It makes me sick to my stomach—literally."

"Yeah. Me, too."

"You can't walk and look at the world at the same time without wanting to throw up . . . there's something wrong with that."

Mason started to laugh.

Dr. Francis stood next to him. She held on to the wires and leaned back. "You know what I hate: People say suicide is cowardly, and no one ever objects. It's a lot of things, but I can't say it's that. Take suicide bombers—for some reason we all have to agree they're cowards. Evil, sure, but people are so scared of being gutless that automatically they equate the two."

They held on to the cables and tried to look through, to the distant great lake.

"Tell me," said Mason. "What did you mean when you said that I've been *ghosted*?"

Dr. Francis tried to pluck one of the metal strings. It made no sound. "Most of us actually. We've got these ghosts in us. And I'm not talking about souls. We're not born with them. You for instance . . . What did you want to be when you grew up?"

Mason thought of Willy. "A cowboy," he said. "Or a Jedi. A Jedi-cowboy, I guess."

Dr. Francis nodded. "And then what?"

"And then? I don't know . . . an explorer, an ambulance driver. Then a freedom fighter . . . a revolutionary poet—a seductive one, with an edge. Oh, and a rock star, of course—the lonesome, tough kind. And Gandhi, but a bit more kick-ass. A Sandinista Gandhi Hemingway Indiana Jones kind of thing . . ."

"Is that all?"

Mason laughed.

"No. It makes sense," she said. "You probably had a strong imagination—a hundred future selves. And then you got older, got out into the world, and saw all the possibility out there. So you just kept adding to them. It would have been overwhelming."

Mason remembered being drunk on his own capacity for adventure and greatness. He'd careened across the world and thought it would never end.

"And then," said Dr. Francis, "something happened. You stopped creating lives, and you didn't even know it. Not until one day when it hit you—dread, fear, maybe even panic—because finally, at some level, you realized that you'd stopped. And now this: you, standing there—or, more likely, hunched over and puking—were who you were, who you *are* . . . all the men you'd envisioned were never going to be."

Mason could see them now, slipping through the spaces in the Saving Grace—a hundred small men who looked like him but better: virtuous, chiseled, poetic, powerful, visionary, adored—the cowboy, the rock star, the philosopher-king—all tumbling into the valley below. And here he stood, not even a writer. It felt as if his legs had given out and he was just hanging there, holding onto the unplayable strings of a giant stupid harp.

"But you know what I think," said Dr. Francis. "When those ideas of yourself die, their ghosts persist. And they cause all sorts of trouble . . ."

He wasn't listening any more. He'd turned and started walking again, a hand stretched out, fingers bouncing on the taut metal wires.

Dr. Francis followed. They walked until there was no web—a twenty-foot section in the middle of the bridge still free of cables and crosses. Mason leaned forward against the low concrete wall and looked at the Toronto skyline—the CN Tower: no longer the tallest free-standing structure in the world. "What about you?" he said. "You got ghosts inside you, too?"

"I'm sure most people do. I've got patients who think they're spies, superheroes, doctors . . . Others got blindsided so young it's too evident to bear: Willy, for instance. I'm sure she lives every moment with the ghost of a girl whose father didn't drag her off a balcony."

Mason pictured her—that little bitch—sticking out her tongue and yelling, doing cartwheels through Willy's brain. "I should get home to her," he said.

They turned and started back across the bridge. "You're sort of opposites," said the doctor. "You and Willy."

Mason was going to ask what she meant, but he was tired of being told things. He walked and thought about it and then he saw: Willy had lived her whole life with her ghost right there—it inhabited half her body. Whereas Mason had dreamed up so many selves, for so long, that when he finally collapsed into the man he was, he was already old. But his ghosts were young and mutinous. He saw them as angry birds, diving for him, scrabbling for a perch in his chest.

"I think you need them, though," said Dr. Francis, "if you're going to be fully human."

"What?"

"The ghosts. People who don't have them—they've got no conflict. Take Seth: He always knew what he wanted and went about getting it. He was a hard man to beat. But it's interesting what we did—don't you think? We found a way to *ghost* him—or as close as it comes with a man like that: take away his libido, his cravings, and eventually he becomes ineffectual, barely an idea."

"So you think there's a difference," said Mason, "between being ghosted and just having them inside you?"

"I think so. Look at Chaz. There's a guy who's embraced his ghosts. He likes them. When he's happy he even talks like one."

"The ghost of Jimmy Cagney."

"Yeah. The kind of guy his dad would have liked."

"You think that makes him *less* fucked-up?"

The doctor shrugged. "How's he doing?" she said.

"They've got him at the Don," said Mason. They were nearing the end of the bridge. "I'm hoping to visit in the next couple days."

"He'll be all right," said Dr. Francis.

"And what about me? You think there's any hope?'"

The doctor laughed. "You're so dramatic."

"I'm serious."

"Some people," she said, "if they live long enough, their regrets turn into skills."

"What's that supposed to mean?"

"Boom, boom, and boom."

"At least I can cheat at cards?"

"Tell you what," said Dr. Francis. "When you see Chaz, ask him about it."

"About what, exactly?"

"The Man in the Black Helmet."

They'd reached the end of the bridge.

79

WHEN IT comes to certain things, movies tend to be right: the two chairs, the old phone receivers, two inches of Plexiglas between them. It occurred to Mason that the last time he'd seen Chaz was also through bulletproof glass. He was about to mention it, and then he thought better.

They might be listening in.

"What's the rumble?" said Chaz. "You hitting okay?"

"Me? You're the one in jail!"

Chaz looked around as if surprised. "By Jove, I am!" Then he leaned into the glass. "Tell me about our good friend Seth."

Mason looked him in the eye. "Gone," he said.

Chaz grinned.

"Ungracious final act, though," said Mason, looking around. "We'll get you out of here, I promise."

"What, this?" said Chaz, still smiling. "This ain't the work of Handyman."

"What do you mean?"

"The songbirds are singing."

"Why are you talking like that—is it because they're listening?"

"Just happy is all."

"You're in jail, Chaz."

"Right as fucking hail."

"Well, can you talk normal for now? Please?"

Chaz took a breath and nodded.

"So who do you think set you up?"

Mason could see the effort it took: Chaz rewriting the words in his head—getting rid of all the *stoolies*, *pigeons*, *songbirds*, and *rats* . . . Finally he just said, "Fishy."

"You're kidding me?" said Mason.

"Yeah. Who'd ever think it? If you can't trust a guy named Fishy . . ."

Mason just glared at him.

"I know, I know. You told me so . . ."

"How the fuck could he do it?" said Mason.

"It's funny really: His one contribution—the Dogmobile—was in my name. And that's where they found the stuff. Everything else belongs to the family. So in exchange for me, the guns, and drugs, he gets to keep the buildings."

"But *why* did he do it?"

"Aw," said Chaz. "He just wants to be the big man. It's kind of sweet, really . . ."

"It's not fucking sweet! I'm getting you out of here—the paintings are still down there. They're worth a lot if I do it right. I'll post bail. We'll get you a lawyer . . ."

"Stop," said Chaz.

"What?"

"Don't go down there. If himself or the cops ain't found it, just leave it alone, okay? Don't you worry—Fishy's going to get his. And I don't want you bailing me out. I kind of like it here."

"You're kidding me?"

"You got to get another line, Pancho. I just ain't kidding you. I know half the guys in here. It'll be good for me—it'll be good for business. It'll make me a better gangster. I really fucking believe that."

"That's touching, Chaz." Mason put the phone down, then picked it up again. "Will you at least get a lawyer?"

"Oh yeah, sure . . . I don't want to *live* here."

"Just a working vacation."

"Exactly."

They looked at each other. Mason thought of the glass. "You shouldn't have done it," he said.

"What?"

"When they raided, you should have . . . you know." Mason looked around. "You should have tried to get out."

"You mean in."

Mason nodded.

"You would have done the same."

"I don't know about that."

Chaz laughed. He looked at the clock on the wall.

So did Mason. Then he looked at Chaz. "The doctor told me to ask you something."

"What about?" said Chaz.

"The Man in the Black Helmet."

Chaz put the receiver down. Mason watched his mouth forming the words *What about him?*

"I don't know," said Mason, shrugging. "That's all she said."

Chaz picked up the phone. "Well, what do you remember?"

"I hit the ground. I looked around, then ran across the street . . ."

"Why?"

"What do you mean why?"

"You ran away from your own house, right behind his motor-cycle, and you don't remember why?"

Mason shrugged.

"It was because of me," said Chaz. He looked down at the steel counter, then up. "I was still there: just ten feet over and ten feet up. You hit the ground, looked up, and saw me there. And then ran the other way."

Mason squinted at Chaz, as if trying to see him twenty years ago, stuck up in a tree. Chaz squinted back and smiled. "He had you cornered, right?"

"Yeah," said Mason, looking at Chaz through the ages and branches.

"Did he say anything?"

"His helmet was on . . . I can't be sure of what I heard."

"What do you think he said?"

Mason looked down at the stainless steel. Then he mumbled something, the receiver away from his mouth.

"I can't hear you," said Chaz.

Mason looked up. "*You've done it now, you little prick.* Something like that?"

"Anything else?" Chaz was grinning.

"Yeah," said Mason, and took a breath. *"Now you must join the dark side.* And he was talking through that helmet. There are times I can hear his voice. It sounded like . . ."

"Like James Earl Jones with asthma?" Chaz was almost laughing.

"It isn't fucking funny! I remember him stepping toward me—those motherfucking boots. I could see myself in the visor. I thought I was going to die. He said something else . . . and then I think I fainted."

"You did," said Chaz, barely containing his laughter. "I saw it from the tree. But before you passed out, do you remember what you did?"

Mason shook his head.

"You gave him the finger."

Mason said nothing.

"You fucking gave him the finger, man. And you know what he said, before you passed out? You know what the man in the helmet said?"

"I don't know . . ."

"Come on, you really can't remember?"

Mason grabbed the phone and shouted, *"You're going to hell, kid!"*

"You're a hell of kid, Mason!"

"What?"

"That's what he said: *You're a hell—*"

"He did say my name! He did! That's when I passed out . . . How did he know my name?"

Chaz was shaking his head. His eyes were moist with tears and laughter. "Jesus, Mason," he said. "For a smart guy, you sure are stupid. That was our street. It wasn't another galaxy."

Mason looked at his best friend through bulletproof glass.

"Who do you know owned a motorcycle?"

Mason felt faint. "You're kidding me," he said.

"That's right, young Jedi: He was my father."

Mason put the phone down. *"Jesus,"* he said. He stood up, then picked up the phone again. "You told the doctor, but you never told me! All those fucking years!"

Chaz just smiled.

"He told you not to, didn't he?" He sat back down. "That god-damn bastard!"

"He said it was more important that *I* knew." A guard appeared behind him.

"Knew what, exactly?"

"What a good guy you'd be."

Mason said nothing.

"Tenner was a complex dude," said Chaz.

"And kind of crazy."

They nodded at each other, and then they said good-bye.

Mason was a half block from his door when an old blue Nova pulled up alongside him. The passenger window rolled down. "Hop in," said Detective Sergeant Flores.

"I'm almost home."

"You're always almost home."

"You don't understand," said Mason, leaning toward the window. "I got a guest staying with me . . ."

"Well, can't she take care of herself?"

"That's the thing," said Mason. "She's hemiplegic. Do you know what that is? It's crazy, actually—half your body's paralyzed, half of it's got no feeling, but . . ."

"But they're two different halves. Get the fuck in."

Mason did and they pulled away from the curb.

Flores took a right on College. They drove past the university. A few more blocks, and then he spoke. "I was contacted by some-one," he said. "She told me you'd kidnapped a hemiplegic girl. She described it pretty much the same way you did."

"Oh," said Mason. "Well, there you go."

Flores turned to look at him. "You didn't, did you?"

"What, kidnap a hemiplegic girl?"

"Yeah."

"No. Not at all. I mean she's staying with me but . . ."

"Yeah. That's what I figured. The woman who made the complaint—she's known to us, if you know what I mean . . ."

Mason nodded.

"And then there's you . . ."

Mason said nothing. They crossed over Bay Street.

"Me and you," said Flores. "We've had our share of run-ins."

"I guess that's life."

Flores glanced at him. "I guess," he said. "But in this job, certain people just tend to pop up—you know what I mean?"

"Sure," said Mason. "Like in any job. I guess."

"Perhaps," said Flores, then took a right on Yonge. The sign said you weren't allowed to. "I guess you heard about your hot dog stand—the Dogfather Cart or whatever you call it."

"The Dogmobile," said Mason.

"Yeah. It was full of drugs and money. Strange, don't you think?"

Mason tried the window, but it wouldn't slide down.

"Same guy who owns it, he ran that booze can next to you. I'm guessing you might know him."

They were heading back along Dundas. As they passed the Art Gallery of Ontario Mason thought, *I've never even been in there.*

"Sure," said Mason. "I visited him in jail today."

Flores kept on driving. At Spadina again, he took a right. Another block, and he pulled to the curb. "You call me, Mason," he said. "If there's something you want to tell me." He held out a card, and Mason took it.

"Like what?" he said, and pictured a big white horse, standing beside a gas station.

"I couldn't even imagine," said Flores.

Mason got out, and the Nova pulled away.

He walked quickly up the street. He'd left for the Don at noon and now it was early evening. He hated Willy being alone so long.

He went into the building, up the stairs, but when he reached the top, it was gone—that feeling of someone there, waiting for you to come home.

He opened the door and stepped inside.

The Book of Sobriety

Where the hell are you? I'm going crazy here. I've been out looking for you all night. And now I'm back here alone.

My body's screaming to get hammered, my brain's swearing at me to get high—but then I'll be smashed in some alley, and you'll still be God knows where, alone.

I started out in Regent Park, in Bethany's old place—broke down the door, and there was nothing but a yoga mat, three coffee cups, and a lamp with no cord. I went to the women's shelters, but they won't tell you anything if you're a guy. "That bitch is worse than any guy," I told them (referring to Bethany, not to you). Still they stayed firm.

I went to the men's shelters—Seaton House, Jarvis, the Good Shepherd—to talk to the guys, get some info. A pretty young captive in a wheelchair should be noticeable. But nothing. I even went to Sherbourne and talked to the Thursday doctor, but she couldn't help me, and I could see what she was thinking—the same as Sergeant fucking Flowers: "Impressive, Mason. It takes a certain kind of guy to lose his paralyzed girlfriend." He's a fucking riot.

Where the hell are you?

I went into strip joints and dollar-beer bars, even visited the safe injection site. It's amazing how many people I know—from the streets, from the Cave. But no one has seen you. I even went to the shantytown down by the docks. They tried to help me out. A little dwarfy guy took me across the tracks to the old rail house, where there was a girl—not you—in a beat-up wheelchair. I gave him ten bucks anyway.

Dr. Francis finally picked up after the one-hundredth ring—all pissy because it was so late and I'd been calling her so much. In the end she was kind. She made me promise to stay sober until we find you. I'm going to see her tomorrow morning. What the fuck am I supposed to do till then?

"Write," she said.

Are you fucking serious?

"But do it sober."

I don't feel like writing.

"Come on: We practiced for just such an emergency. You can do it, Mason. Write something for Willy."

So that's what I'm trying to do. I'm trying to write something for you, Willy.

But it's like everything's competing now: a thousand moments banging at the edge of my brain, as if they all want to be thought, remembered, written—as if this is their one chance to live again. But because they're all trying at the same time, nothing makes it all the way through—just weird glimpses: my father shaking beneath a tinfoil blanket—he's just run his first marathon; the spiky shadow of a cactus; my mother taking her glasses off and smiling; a blue dress; sunshine; a scene from the movie *Gandhi*; a red barn; wind in the trees, horses . . . I've never told you about the good things. I did such a job of forgetting them—and now they're only fragments, here to bug my brain. I hope that you're okay.

Every month I send my mother an email:

"I love you. I'm okay."

Every month for five years: I type those words and I feel sick.

Because I more than love her, and I never am okay.

I thought I was okay last week. But now look at me. I just want to get drunk. I just want to get high. I just wish you were here. I need to talk to someone. I need to talk to you—about everything. Writing doesn't do it. Or, rather, I can't write. I miss you. I'm worried that you weren't taken away. I'm worried that you left me. I feel hollowed out. Empty. Scared.

I more than love you, Willy. And I never am okay.

80

"You made it through the night."

"Sort of," said Mason, and paced across her office. "Fucking Bethany. She took the methadone, too. I found this." He pulled a pink scrunchy out of his pocket. "It was on the floor by the fridge.

"What are you worried about?" said Dr. Francis. Mason glared at her. "I mean *precisely*. What are your precise worries?"

Mason sat down, but his knee kept going. "That she's hurt," he said. Dr. Francis said nothing. "That she's back on the stuff. That she's scared. That she'll think that I'm not looking for her. I don't know . . . I'm worried about everything."

The phone rang. Dr. Francis reached to answer it, and Mason

got up again. He walked to the window, turned . . . then he saw Dr. Francis's face.

She pressed a button. A voice came out of the speaker.

" . . . *never at home. I thought he might be there—not that I don't want to talk to you, Doc . . . Are you there, Mason?*"

Mason's breath caught in his throat.

"*Oh good. That sounded like a gasp. I'm glad I caught you then . . .*"

"Where is she?" said Mason. His voice felt locked inside his head.

"*No, Mason. No questions.*"

Dr. Francis was tapping at her keyboard.

"*In fact, I don't even have any questions for you . . . Earlier, yes—I wanted to know things: like where I might find my notebook, or how you managed to beat me, or how best I could make you suffer . . . little things like that . . .*"

Dr. Francis spun the laptop so Mason could see the screen.

"*Funny thing is, the more time I've spent on it—on her I should say—I began to realize something . . .*"

The red dot was flashing, but not at Bay and Bloor.

"*The satisfaction is never in the answer—it's always in the asking.*"

It was here at Spadina and College.

"*And with that in mind, I do have one question for you, Mason . . .*"

Mason spun around, as if Seth might be there—right there in that very room.

"*How does it feel? To know I spent last night with your gimpy girl-friend—and that she's never screamed so much . . .*"

"Where the *fuck* is she!" Mason rushed at the phone. And then he saw the number.

"*No!*" shouted Seth. "*You do* not *get to ask any questions . . . For one: You didn't sink a ball. For two: You cheated. And three: Well, I've got someone else to play with now.*"

Mason moved toward the window.

"*That's boom, boom . . .*"

He looked out, across the street.

"*And fucking BOOM!*"

The window of his apartment blew out.

Mason turned and ran. Through reception, into the hall. He pushed the elevators once, waited two seconds, then dashed into

the stairwell. Down six floors. Through the main lobby, the sliding doors, the sidewalk, between parked cars, one lane, two lanes . . . As he hit the median, before the streetcar tracks, he saw it in the road: the strewn wreckage of his new coffeemaker. Something snagged like a fishing line beneath his chin. His feet flew up. He was airborne, looking at the sky.

If he had to describe the last thing he saw, right before the streetcar hit:

It looked like an invisible kite.

Who wants to go to Fire Lake?

Head out, out to Fire Lake.

Yeah, who's going to do it?

(Repeat)

The
Ninth

Saving Grace

81

ANYONE ELSE would be in hell.

It is dark—just enough light to see the blistered ceiling, ancient steaming pipes, hollow tanks like metal bulls, the flash of a long blade. The sound is both constant and fluctuating—miles away, then suddenly right on top of her, the sound of his breathing. She is used to this kind of dark, echoing terror. Part of her has lived inside it almost as long as she remembers. And this noise, the screaming hum, fading in and out—it isn't so different from the voice in her head. It's as if her singular world has finally become manifest.

She is naked, on her back, strapped to a table. It is redundant, she thinks, to tie down the likes of her.

He has a sword with a dog-faced dragon on the blade. When it cuts into her, she sees flashes of light—and part of her begins to long for the blade. *A flash.* She sees saliva drip from his mouth onto her skin as he leans into it, carving up her flesh. Her own scream is so loud that the rest of the darkness goes quiet.

She knows her screams excite him, and so she gives it her all. She opens her mouth and howls. She can taste and smell her own blood. It begins to pool beneath her.

The more he tears her apart, the more she is complete and strong, using everything she's ever learned. It feels good to know she's tricked this slobbering, joyful beast, and he doesn't even know it yet. She's found a way to finally free herself and hopefully

save Mason, too. This thought makes her happiest, and she screams with all her might, because she loves Mason—more than anyone she's ever known. More than anyone since her father.

And realizing this—at this flashing bloody moment, she knows this, too:

He was trying to save you.

From the fire. From the demons.

And so he jumped.

They got a hold of her anyway, of course. But now she has them—or at least this one—right in the palm of her hand, so to speak.

The right hand gets you in.

He asks her questions, basking in what he thinks is her pain. But she's already won. It had been difficult at first: not to flinch when he struck her left side. It took more than mere acting, but she managed it, then screamed out so painfully when he slashed her right breast that his joy was overwhelming. And now she's bluffed him so well that he leaves her *left* alone.

The left hand gets you out.

"Where is my book?"

She screams, gasps, then screams again. He digs in deeper. A flash and she sees his face—the ecstatic brutality of a fucked-up child.

He isn't so tough.

For all the talk: how *inscrutable*, how *perceptive* the sociopath—how beneficial the lack of empathy—it won't be beauty that kills the *real* beast but lack of imagination. He wanted to carve up the living, most precious side of her—but couldn't make the necessary leap: The body that *moves* is not always the one that *feels*.

"Where is my book?" he says, cutting into her breast again. She screams and gasps and finally she tells him.

And he knows she is telling the truth.

"How do I get it?" he says. She sobs as if about to pass out. Then he slices downward, gouging out her nipple. She is wailing, half her body writhing.

"How do I fucking get it?"

And finally it comes out of her, like a burst of breath—and both of them go quiet. They turn and look at her hand. It seems, suddenly, like its own entity—clenching against the restraints, blood between the fingers . . .

Willy repeats the words. "The right hand gets you in." Her voice is broken, lost and hollow, and he is sure she is telling the truth. Could a stupider lie ever be told? His joy is overwhelming. He begins to sharpen the blade.

82

WHEN MASON came to, he was lying on the floor beside the captain's bed. It looked like a meteor had crashed through his window. He tried to get up, but the pain stopped him—that, and a hand on his chest. And now Ms. Pac-Man was staring down at him, smiling gravely.

"Ms. Pac-Man?" he said.

"Her name is Barbara," said a voice. It was Dr. Francis. It sounded as if she was over by the window. "She carried you up here."

Barbara nodded. She'd retrieved the beach towel from where Mason had tossed it by the door—weeks or months ago, he didn't know. It was tied around her neck once more. She leaned down, her mouth against his ear. "*She's* the one," whispered Barbara, her eyes looking across the room at the doctor. "She eats the ghosts."

"Carried me up here . . . ?" called Mason.

"You were knocked unconscious," said the doctor's voice. "She's very strong." Barbara smiled again, and it started to come back to him . . . "Oh, Jesus! Willy!" He struggled to his feet. He could see Dr. Francis by the window. He took a step and crumpled.

"We don't have time for this," said Dr. Francis. She walked over to Mason's new position on the floor and crouched down, holding her laptop. "Look," she said, "this makes no sense."

"What am I looking at?"

"Nothing," said Dr. Francis.

"Where the fuck is Willy?"

"Listen to me very carefully. The cops'll be here any minute." She cocked her head toward the broken window, and only now did he notice the noise—idling sirens, backed-up traffic, a streetcar full of bitching commuters. "We've got to figure this out!"

"Then don't tell me I'm looking at nothing!"

"Bay and Bloor," said Dr. Francis. "The Bay Street subway station. This was the location of the GPS, right? When we thought that Seth was dead."

"Okay . . ."

"After you saw it that day, then the signal got weaker—the same spot, just weaker, until it was gone. I assumed the trains had run it over. But then today, he shows up and so does the signal. You saw it, right?"

Mason nodded. "So where is he?"

"That's the thing. I was watching the screen while you went after him. But then you collided with that streetcar . . ."

"Where the fuck *is* he!"

"The last I saw, he was *here*," said Dr. Francis pointing at the screen. "Back at Bay and Bloor. But now the signal's gone again. It doesn't make any sense . . ."

"I know where he is!" said Mason. He jumped to his feet. Barbara caught him as he fell.

"You've got to stop doing that!" said Dr. Francis. "You can't go anywhere."

Mason twisted around and jabbed at the computer screen. "He's right there," he said. "But deeper! He's playing the fucking depths!"

"What do you mean?"

"The deeper he goes, the weaker the signal? But I know where he is! I've got to call Flores!"

"What are you going to tell him?"

"He's not at *Bay* Station. He's at *Lower* Bay!"

She handed him the phone. "What the hell is Lower Bay?"

"It's a ghost station."

83

MASON LOOKED up from his hospital bed

"You look like hell," said Detective Sergeant Flores.

"Can I see her?" said Mason.

"Not now. She's in surgery."

"How bad is she?"

"Bad," said Flores. "But for some reason he kept to her right side."

"You're saying she didn't suffer?"

Flores walked toward the window. "Are you aware that there was a second victim there—in that *ghost station* of yours?"

Not my *ghost station.*

"A girl by the name of Bethany Strohl."

"Dead?"

Flores nodded. "She *definitely* suffered."

Mason didn't know what to do here—in this limbo—this private room with a cop, waiting for Willy to come out from under anesthesia. He had a separated shoulder, two broken ribs, and his ankle was sprained again, but he wished the pain were more intense.

"Have you caught the guy who did it?"

Flores looked at him. "We found this at the station," he said, and pulled a ziplock bag out of his jacket. "Do you know what it is?"

"A scalp?" said Mason.

"That's right! And do you know who it belongs to?"

"Seth Handyman?"

"Who?"

"Setya Kateva?"

"This scalp belongs to a man named Larry Weib. He used to work as a counselor in the Kingston Pen and was recently run over by a subway train."

"White," said Mason.

"Excuse me?"

"I knew him as Larry White."

"Oh, you did," said Detective Flores. "I think you'd better tell me about it."

And so he did.

Mason told him about Warren and Willy, Soon, Sissy, and Seth. He didn't mention Chaz or the doctor, the QT room or the chip in Handyman's head. But he came clean on everything else. He even confessed to stealing the poet's daughter's horse.

"That's a helluva story," said Flores, writing in his notebook.

Mason just nodded. It was the least he could do—Willy still under the knife—confess and keep confessing.

"So this Handyman," said Flores. "He hired you to write a suicide letter?"

"Yes."

"But you have no idea where he might be now?"

Mason thought about it. "Aren't there more ghost stations? I'm pretty sure there are."

Detective Flores wrote something in his book. "Do you own a motorcycle?"

"No. Why?"

"Just trying to figure things out. That bar fight you mentioned . . ."

"Tony's Happy Daze Bar and Beer."

"Exactly. Was there anybody with you?"

"What do you mean?"

"Well, I took that call. The fish tank was busted."

Mason nodded.

"And do you know where we found those fish?"

He shook his head.

"In a motorcycle helmet." Flores paused. "Just swimming around inside. Now what kind of thug, fleeing a crime scene, would stop and save the fish?"

"That *is* weird."

Flores flipped his notebook closed.

"Are you going to arrest me now?"

"I'm going to look into a few things first. "But don't worry; I know where to find you. Oh, and I take it back . . ."

"What's that?" said Mason.

"For a guy who's been thrown from a horse, beat up in a bar, and hit by a streetcar, you don't actually look so bad."

"Must be the detox," said Mason.

"Right. I forgot about the detox." Flores turned to go, then stopped. "I hope she pulls through. I really do."

84

IT HAD been a whole day and she was still unconscious—in the ICU, in a room made of windows across from the nurses' station. There was a blue hospital sheet pulled up to her chin. Mason sat

by her bed, scared to move—scared to ask anyone anything. The whole unit was far too quiet.

He leaned forward and spoke into her ear. "I love you," he said. "More than you can know."

He paused, then said, "I'll kill him. I promise."

"There's a policeman here to see you." Mason jumped at the voice, then turned.

He saw Detective Flores waiting in the hall behind the nurse. He wondered where the doctor was.

"Ask him not to arrest me until she wakes up."

"I'm not arresting you," said Flores. Mason whispered something else to Willy. Then he got up and walked down the hall.

"Must be difficult to look at," said the detective.

"She looks peaceful."

The detective said nothing. Mason followed him into a small room with a large soda machine.

"Did you find Seth?"

"Not yet. But we will."

"He'll surprise you," said Mason.

Detective Flores took a photo out of his pocket and handed it to Mason. Then he started fishing in his other pocket for change. "You know that guy?" he said.

It was a man with dark skin, wearing a sweater. "He's vaguely familiar. I think I might have sold him a veggie dog once."

The detective walked over to the pop machine. "That," he said, "is Joseph Batt." He stooped slightly to peer at the buttons.

"Who?"

He made his selection. A *kachunk* sound came from within.

"He's the man who killed Warren Shanter," said Flores, a root beer in his hand.

71. Everything dies, baby. That's a fact.
72. Everything that dies, some day comes back.

"Mozambique," Mason said.

"He regrets it," said Flores. "Ten years looking for the man who killed his son. And all he got was remorse."

"And Warren . . ."

"Just another hopeless romantic, I guess."

"So what does that mean?"

"On the one hand, you didn't assist his suicide. On the other, you came up with that business model all by yourself."

Mason looked at the floor.

"But we got nothing that matches the fat girl. Not yet."

Mason nodded. He could see Sissy's face. He wished he knew her name.

"I found a fair amount on Soon, though. Did you know he came here as a refugee in 1978 after his family was killed in East Timor? Hacked to bits . . . But if, as you say, he hired you for an art project, well, I don't see a problem—or a body, for that matter."

The nurse appeared in the doorway. "Your friend is awake," she said.

85

THERE WERE doctors and nurses all over the place now, as well as detectives and policemen. A possible murder victim suddenly awake was an exciting thing. There was a grave intensity in there. Mason did his best not to hear what they were saying.

Eventually they let him in, and finally they left. He knew they were still out there, watching through the glass—but it didn't matter. It was just the two of them now.

"Hey there," said Willy. Her voice was thin, but she was smiling.

"Hey," said Mason. "I love you."

"I know."

"*More* than you can know."

"All right," she said. "*More* than I know. I love you, too."

He sat down and looked at her face. It was bruised but strong. There was life in her eyes. "You look good."

She laughed—a distant, eerie sound. "You haven't really looked."

"Do you want me to?"

"Only if you can see what's there."

"What should I look for?" said Mason.

"Victory . . ." It seemed she was going to say something else, but then she didn't.

Mason leaned forward. He kissed her lips, took hold of the blue sheet, then pulled it back.

The shock was so severe it was like his windpipe had closed again. He didn't gag or gasp for air, just couldn't breathe. The only thought he had was more like an image: a paper snowflake.

He was trying to make a snowflake.

But he didn't fold the paper.

Somewhere back there, in the land of oxygen, he could hear her voice. "Don't you see?" she said.

So he tried to look again, and now the snowflake was gone—replaced by Willy, half her body carved, so much cut-up meat.

"Don't cry," said Willy. "We won."

"Look at you," he said.

And Willy did. She looked down at herself, then up at Mason. She smiled, as if there was happiness somewhere. But Mason felt blown apart, because now he knew. He pulled the sheet back over her. Willy would never leave this room.

"It's going to be okay," she said.

"I don't know what to do."

"Why don't you tell me a story?"

Mason tried to rein in his thoughts. "There once was a little girl . . ."

"Not me," she said. "How about your dad? I've got an unhealthy interest in fathers . . ."

"What do you want to know?"

"I want a story." She smiled, and Mason saw that she was doing this for him.

"Okay . . ." Mason thought. "My father almost killed me—"

"Mine, too," said Willy and laughed.

"—on the day that I was born."

"Fucking fathers!" said Willy.

Mason got up from his chair. "He didn't mean to. It was a hospital room, like this one—except the walls weren't made of glass." He glanced out at the people looking in and limped around to the

other side of the bed. "I'd just been born." He lifted up the sheet and climbed underneath. As soon as his skin touched hers, everything else stopped.

He felt her body, her death ahead of them. Then it all just broke inside him. Not gradually, but all at once. The world was her voice, the thought of her as a child, her terror, her fall, her half getting up, her wondrous strength and kind crafty eyes, her life before he knew her, her warmth and paralysis, the hum of her butchered flesh, how she needed him and he needed her, her goodness, how she made him feel, and he finally felt it—the world right next to him, and it was about to be taken away. He grabbed for her body, pulling her arms around him. And then he felt it—her right arm there, without a hand.

"Oh, fucking God," he said, looking at nothing.

"I told you," said Willy. "We got him."

"No," he said, "I love you," and began to sob.

"I do know," said Willy, her voice steady, as he curled against her chest. "Now please, baby, tell me the story. I want to see you on the day you were born."

He was tiny. She was everything. His tears flooded down as he spoke. He didn't have to think of the words. They'd been told so many times, always different—always the same.

"My father came into the hospital room. He was smiling. They called him Johnnie Walker Joe, but today it was champagne. He held it in his arms like a baby. He tore off the foil and cranked the wire. Aiming the bottle heavenward, he pushed with his thumbs . . ."

And as he spoke, Willy grew lighter against him, giving up the ghost.

When the cork hit the pillow, she was gone.

Mason tried to go with her. He fought with all his might. But those docs and cops, they held him down. And she was left to rise.

86

YOUR FRIEND is awake.

Your friend is dead.

You have no friends.

You have no hope.

That's why you are here.

Where?

In the QT Room. In the TQ Room. In the White Room with black curtains near the station. The station is abandoned, and so are you, my friend. Silver horses run down moonbeams in your dark eyes.

What?

It's a song. You've gone crazy—and that's what crazy people do: They sing. How about "Fire Lake." You know how it goes, don't you?

Yes.

It was your father's favorite song. And we'll tell you something now, because you deserve a break.

What?

It's not about going to hell—unless you want it to be. It's about facing risk. He said so himself.

Who?

Bob Seger of course.

How . . . ?

How do we know? The same way we know that Warren gave Carolina one of your letters. The same way we know that Joseph Batt was crying when he struck Warren on the head and pushed him into the lake. The same way we know who Sissy is. And she's not the only one who changed her name.

The same way we know that Soon wanted to help people, but he had no gift for it—except when it came to you. We've seen his body floating in the dark river.

The same way we know that Willy saved your life.

The same way we know where Seth is—and so does the doctor. In fact, she's watching him right now.

The same way we know you, Mason, what you could have been, what you've chosen to forget . . .

All this we know, and more.

But how?

Isn't it obvious? We are semiomniscient.

Like a narrator?

Like narrators. Like ghosts. Like the ones who tell your story.

Can you change it?

We're not your fucking authors, Mason.

Well, can you help me?

Most of us don't even like you. We could have done a better job. Lived a better life. Had a better story. And now you've gone insane.

The doctor was right—there are far too many of us, stuck in your busted body, your broken brain. You should have listened to her. *She* has a gift for saving people. She eats ghosts for breakfast (and still we like her).

Can you at least get me out of here?

A question, Mason: What is the date?

Just get me the hell out!

What's wrong with where you are?

There's nothing here!

This is a place where things tend to get broken.

Not even a doorknob!

When the room is empty the story's over. Why do you think we're talking to you? There's nothing left for us to do.

Can you get me out of here or not?

Why?

What do you mean, why?

What exactly would you do?

Don't you know?

We're only *semi*omniscient.

Then I guess you'll have to wait and see. But I'll let you tell the story.

The door clicked open.

87

MASON STEPPED out of the room. He limped down the empty hall and came to a bank of elevators. He was on the eleventh floor. He pressed the DOWN button.

The inside of the elevator was mirrored. He looked at himself, and an unexpected Mason looked back: blue hospital gown, bruised eyes, bare feet. Not exactly inconspicuous. There was a *ding* as the doors opened.

He crossed through Emergency and made it outside. The sky was growing dark. He turned and looked at the building: Western Hospital. Just eight blocks through Kensington Market to his apartment.

A skinhead on stilts was chasing small children. A woman was standing on a large rock, playing the trumpet. The statue of Al Waxman had daisy chains around its neck. Dogs were running in circles. No one paid Mason the least bit of attention. He limped past the taco stands, the fishmongers, the cheese shops, all the way to Spadina, then up.

And there she was, in front of the MHAD building. "I need your help again," he said. Barbara nodded, tightening her cape.

It was a bit over the top—like someone purposefully causing a distraction. She jumped and raged and spun her arms and howled—an earthbound, unhinged superhero.

It took all of security just to get her attention, by which time Mason was in the elevator.

He got out at the sixth floor. Dr. Francis's office door was closed. He knocked and knocked again. It was locked. He stepped back then hurled himself into it. The frame cracked. It felt like his shoulder did, too. He took another run and the door broke, pain shooting up his leg as he crashed to the floor.

He pulled himself up on the desk, then sat down in the doctor's chair. He pressed a button on her keyboard and the screen sprang to life—the aerial map of downtown, homed in right here: at College and Spadina. There was nothing now, but Mason saw where the beacon would have been. And the doctor would have been watching it— that pulsing red dot, growing fainter on the screen, until it was gone.

A question, Mason: What is the date?

He looked at the corner of the screen: 7:36 P.M. July 10th.
Saving people is a matter of minutes.
And she's not the only one who changed her name.
He lifted his head.

YOU ARE MY SUNSHINE!

The diploma was back on the wall:

THE ONTARIO COLLEGE OF PHYSICIANS CERTIFIES

GRACE LAPIN

AS A REGISTERED DOCTOR OF MEDICINE,
GENERAL PRACTICE

NO NUTS ALLOWED!

He looked at the screen again, then back at the wall—until finally the words clicked into place.
This is a place where things tend to get broken.
There was a soapstone paperweight on her desk. He picked it up, limped around to the small fridge, and bashed at the lock until it broke.
Three cups of Sports Day methadone, 100 milligrams each.
What are you doing, Mason?
He pulled a bag out of the trash bin and put them in it. Then he left the building and crossed the street, hopping like an injured idiot—with a death wish and a bag full of methadone.
Before entering his building, he went into the Lucky Save to make one final purchase. Then he dragged himself up the stairs to the door of his apartment. He stopped. He had that feeling——that someone was in there, waiting for him to come home. He opened the door, and something flew past his face, then he limped to the center of the room. A bird was circling near the ceiling. It swooped low then rose again.
He pulled out the cups of methadone and put them on his desk. Then he found his cowboy boots, wincing as he pulled them on, and his leather jacket. He drank some Jim Beam, then grabbed his

cell phone and sat at the desk. Looking out on Spadina through a broken window, he dialed the doctor's cell. Once. Twice. Nothing. He opened a drawer and pulled out a pad of paper. A pen.

What the hell are you doing?

He tried to calm his mind. The bird flew overhead. He crumpled up the paper and threw it, then drank some more Jim Beam. He tried again. And again. Nothing. And nothing. He dialed her number once more, then put the phone in his pocket.

"He didn't leave a note." He opened two of the cups. "Boom and boom," he said, then drank them both down.

You're a fucking idiot!

He turned around. "For some people, if they live long enough, their regrets turn into skills."

So was that long enough?

And have you even lived?

The bird swooped as he got to his feet. It looked like a swallow . . . or maybe a sparrow. He'd never been good at birds.

He made it across the room and down the stairs. His limp was almost gone. He was in the alley now, and there was Chaz's motorcycle. Before he got on, he paused for a moment. Beneath his feet was the QT room, the cave within the Cave—never to be opened. He imagined everything inside it, the story that could be told. Then he got on the bike and hit the throttle.

Okay, then.

If that's the way it's going to be . . .

While Mason drives to our certain death, we'll tell you something he "forgets." His father rode a motorcycle, too. In fact Mason's dad and Tenner used to ride together, and drink together, too. Joseph Dubisee was a neighborhood hero—the only knock-around guy without a blue-collar job. He told stories for a living. Didn't make much, but everyone loved him. At family picnics he walked on his hands while reciting e. e. cummings. He ripped phone books in half and sang along to everything. Johnnie Walker Joe, one of the last real men.

As Mason speeds through the streets, a fog is descending. It rolls across the city and up around his neck—as if downtown is drowning and all he can do is tread water. Then he finds a new gear, in

GHOSTED

both himself and the Norton. He kicks it faster, and the motor roars. Illuminated in the headlight, the thick air streams around the bike—an X-Wing flying through strafing fire. He bears down, lowering his head against the rush, and hurtles onward—the streetlights suns in another galaxy.

When he turned thirty, Joe Dubisee ran his first marathon. After five hours, he'd smoked four cigarettes and was somehow still running. After six hours, it was more like a limp, and his animal brain had taken over. A cop on a motorcycle came up alongside him. He said they were opening the streets again—he'd have to move to the sidewalk. Johnnie Walker Joe growled and gave him the finger.

It is hard to control a motorcycle with one good leg and one good arm while overdosing on methadone, especially in the fog.

And it's a strange sensation: the chemicals shutting you down, slowing your heart rate, your breathing, your circulation, even as the darkening world speeds past you, faster and faster. You are pulled in two directions: downward by gravity, narcosis, and death; forward by velocity, necessity, and death. The ride and the drugs are the fastest route to both. So you just keep going.

After six and a half hours, Joe crossed the finish line. The front of the paper the next day was a photo not of the winner but of the loser—flanked by two dozen motorcycle cops, his arms held high in victory. Five months later he killed himself.

That's not what happened.

Five months later he drove his motorcycle off a cliff.

There's more to it than that.

Five months later his oversensitive little boy got scared at a sleepover and called his drunken daddy to come and pick him up.

That is not what happened!

Either way, Joe Dubisee killed himself on a motorcycle and now his unimaginative son is doing the same.

That's not what's fucking happening . . .

An unexpected turn. The back tire slips out, and now the ground is gone. That slow flying, the endless skid, the airborne descent.

Mason feels the wind through his hair. *Oh, God*, he thinks. *I was trying to do something!* It takes that long before he lands.

88

FOR THE first time in years, Mason landed well. *Relatively*, that is: He came down on the same side that was hit by the street-car—so that his injuries didn't multiply, just deepened: his shoulder became more separated, his ribs more broken, his ankle more sprained. Despite not wearing a helmet, his head actually fared quite well. He even managed to break his nose—that fourth time lucky, cracking it back into place.

The immense pain and adrenaline helped stave off the effects of the methadone—so that he didn't pass out or die. That was coming, of course—just around the corner—and now the bike was unridable. But as Mason's newfound luck would have it, he'd crashed near the Sherbourne Shelter. It took him a moment to get his bearings. He staggered up the street, around the corner, into the alley—and then he saw it: the glow of a crack pipe through the fog.

Mason called out: "Hey, Wilf!"

"Who's that?"

He staggered toward them. "Hey, Wilf! Hey, guys!"

"Stop yer yammering!"

"Who the hell is that?"

"It's me," said Mason. "Frannie's friend. I need some crack."

They flipped a lighter to take a look.

It might have been the arm hanging four inches too low, or the blood-spattered hospital duds tucked into his cowboy boots, or just the look in Mason's eyes—whatever it was they all agreed: The man needed some crack.

With each toke Mason grew stronger. And although the fog remained, the life-crushing darkness started to lift. His heartbeat, barely a waltz, began to quicken. His lungs expanded with cocaine breath. Blood rushed through his veins—from head to heart to liver to legs. And then he was off.

* * *

It was *kind* of like running: the way a smoking, drinking marathoner who'd hit the wall four hours ago or a drugged-up madman with half a working body might do it, and the pain kept Mason somewhat straight. It was hard to tell in the fog, but it felt as if he was getting somewhere.

Then finally he could see it: the finish line. There were floodlights on the banner: THE SAVING GRACE — COMPLETION JULY 11.

Just one more night to jump.

Go fuck yourself.

Mason hit the barrier: CLOSED FOR OPENING. And he tumbled to the pavement.

It was pure will that got him to his feet again—the fog so thick that he couldn't see the ground. Out onto the bridge, it felt as if he were stumbling through the air. After a while he saw a light ahead, then a giant lamp—the beams refracting in the fog, bouncing off the taut metal wires.

Mason pushed on, into the dark mist. Then after a while, he saw another light. For the longest time it got no brighter, until finally he was upon it, staggering into the translucent glow: on one side, the center balustrade, the crosses, and wires; on the other, a breach in the barrier, no Saving Grace, the fog alight, swirling around the profile of a woman.

She couldn't be sure he was real, even though he spoke: "Please come down from there?"

The voice was both hoarse and ethereal—like words wrenched from a body.

"No," she said.

He limped toward her through the fog, a ghostly apparition. "She's dead."

It was unclear just who he meant, but that his heart and soul had finally broken.

"I know," said the doctor, because either way it was true.

"You may as well come down. You're not going to jump." He

stepped toward her. "If you were, you would have done it by now. Instead of waiting for someone . . ."

"Ha!" She fixed him with her gray eyes, her hair shimmering as it waved. "You think I was waiting for you? You get things wrong all the time, Mason." She turned her head. "I was just hoping the fog would lift, so I could see. But I guess I've got to go." She lifted her leg over the railing.

"I know what happened," said Mason. "She's on the list: *Rebecca Lapin. 16 years old. Victim of a savage childhood rape* . . . Becky the bunny. She jumped the week that Seth got paroled. Then he was put in your care—the man who raped your sister."

"The man who killed her," said Dr. Francis, once Lapin. "The fates served him up to me."

"How much were you giving him?"

"A triple dose each time." She turned her head and her voice was clear. "I was torturing him to death. He was living in hell—until you came along."

"Well, he's back there now. Willy made sure of it."

"I know. I saw."

"So why don't you come on down, Grace?"

"Don't call me that."

"It wasn't your fault."

"I was supposed to be looking after her, but I was talking to my boyfriend on the phone. She was attacked and torn apart. That's sort of my fault—wouldn't you say?"

"No." Mason moved toward her.

"One more step, and I'm gone."

He stopped.

"You can't do this, Frannie."

"Why's that, Mason? Because I don't have a letter? You can write me one. Just leave it on my desk."

"I wouldn't know what to write."

"No. You wouldn't. But that's not my problem. You're the one who thinks words are so important. Tell me, Mason. What did your father do?"

He said nothing.

"I mean what did he do for a living?"

"He was a writer. He used to tell me stories when I got scared."

"And how did he die?"

"I think you know."

"I think he drove off a cliff, drunk. And you blame yourself, because you were scared and you wanted him to come and get you. And if that's enough to put you on this bridge—then I can definitely be here."

"No," said Mason. "You're listening to the ghosts."

"Tell me, then."

He took the cup of methadone from his pocket, popped off the lid and drank it. She watched him.

"My mom was out of town. I think they were fighting. I was staying at Chaz's house. I didn't call my dad—he called me. I don't know where he was, but he was crying. I'd never heard him cry before. He told me he was scared, and he was coming to pick me up."

"So in a way he might have saved you, by driving off that cliff."

"In a way. But you're not saving anyone."

"Nope."

"But you could if you get down from there—dozens, maybe hundreds. You're good at saving people."

"How do you know?"

"I've been listening to the ghosts, too. Sometimes they get it right."

"I think you've got a brain injury, Mason. You should have that checked."

"Just tell me why you're doing it."

"I thought maybe I'd feel better when Seth was gone. But I didn't." The fog was lifting now. "I've got patients beat up constantly by the people who should love them. But I worry more when they finally get the courage to leave. That's when they overdose, hang themselves—it happens all the time. Suddenly it's quiet—no one to beat them up but themselves." Behind her, the night sky became a canvas, speckled with stars, the headlights of cars, distant amber windows. "So Seth is gone. The fog is lifting. And now I've got nothing to do."

She turned and rocked forward, lifting her elbows to push with her hands.

"See you, Mason . . ."

He lunged toward her. Then suddenly she stopped.

"What the fuck is that?" she said.

From the heart of the city rose a tower of colored light. It was flashing and spinning, illogical and stunning, garish, ridiculous and beautiful—a born-again phoenix, a disco ball in its beak.

"It's the CN Tower of Babel!" said Mason.

They stared at it—the doctor on the wall, Mason behind her. "Soon did it, and he didn't even know . . ." It was the second-tallest freestanding structure in the world: And suddenly it was awesome. The streaming, pulsing lights, every hue known to man—it seemed both random and patterned, controlled, blissful chaos—like watching someone laughing on the surface of the moon.

"Too bad he's dead," said Mason. "He would have liked this."

"I'm still jumping," said the doctor.

Mason didn't look at her. He looked at the tower instead. "If you do, the bastards win. Seth is victorious and Willy died for nothing."

"Everyone dies for nothing. That's what dying is."

"Fuck you," said Mason. His knees were shaking now. He was starting to go down.

"You're not talking me out of this, Mason. You're not smart enough." She rose to her feet, turned, and looked at him—her body silhouetted against the flashing night sky, Soon's unknown masterpiece. "You don't have the words. I doubt anyone does."

"I know," said Mason, his legs finally giving out. "I knew that from the start." He dropped to his knees and pulled out his cell phone. "That's what the backup plan is for." He dialed 9-1-1.

"Ambulance," he said.

"Call a hearse," said Grace.

"It's not for you." He focused on her eyes and spoke into the phone: "Please listen carefully. There is a man in the center of the Bloor Viaduct. No, he is not going to jump. He's injured. He has multiple fractures, but that is not what he will die of. I need your full attention. Thank you. Approximately fifty minutes ago he drank two hundred milligrams of methadone. He has no tolerance. In order to delay loss of consciousness he ingested a large amount of crack cocaine. That was approximately half an hour ago. Within the last ten minutes he drank another one hundred milligrams of

methadone. At the end of this conversation he will inhale a vial of amyl nitrate, which will counteract any remaining stimulant. He will collapse and his breathing will cease. Are you listening? There is a doctor nearby. She has, attached to her belt, a shot of epinephrine. With this and CPR she may be able to keep him alive for a few minutes. I have faith in her—she is a very good doctor. But there are barriers on either side of the bridge. Please tell them to run. He does not want to die."

Mason hung up the phone. Still looking at her, he pulled a small brown bottle from his pocket. He flipped off the cap and held it up.

"See you on the other side," he said, and took a deep breath in.

THE OTHER SIDE

THE DOOR opened and a round girl with downcast eyes entered the store. A soft bell sounded as the door closed behind her. It was a small store. There was a tall woman behind the counter at the far end, and they glanced at each other as the girl began to browse the sections: comedy, suspense, drama, action, horror . . .

When she came to the last aisle—classics—she saw there was someone else there: an Asian girl with green shoes. She skipped that section and arrived at the counter. The tall woman was quite lovely, a delicate mole on her upper lip. The girl became self-conscious and started to sweat, but still she managed to ask, "Do you have *The Man from Snowy River?*"

The woman smiled. "I hope so," she said. "I'll take a look." She turned and entered the alcove behind her. The girl looked at a rack titled NEW RELEASES. The bell sounded again, the door opening, closing.

When the woman reappeared, the girl was holding a box, just staring at it, like there was a ghost in her hands.

"Whatcha got there?" said the woman.

She showed her: *The Last Word.*

"Oh yeah. It looks pretty crummy—about a guy who writes suicide letters for people. Wynona Rider's in it. Never made it to theaters."

The girl nodded.

"I found *The Man from Snowy River*." She pointed at *The Last Word*. "Do you want that one, too?"

"No," said the girl and put it back on the shelf.

"Do you have an account?"

She shook her head. The woman tapped at a keyboard.

"You got ID?"

The girl looked up. Taped to the monitor was a handwritten note:

> *Carolina behind the counter:*
> *You make me feel like Rambo, before the crummy sequels.*

The girl pointed. Her hand was shaking. "Where did you get that?"

"That?" she said, leaning out to look. "One of our customers gave it to me. I like it a lot, but he never came back." The girl looked into her eyes. Cat eyes. The woman held her gaze. "I guess it's for the better—he wasn't really my type."

"I don't have I.D."

"That's okay," said the woman, and tapped the keyboard again. "What is your name?"

The girl hesitated. "Constance," she said.

"That's a beautiful name. I'm Carolina." She held out her hand.

For a moment the girl didn't know what to do. Then she took it.

And like an e. e. cummings poem, what's-her-name fell in love.

The girl with green shoes decided to cut through the Market. It was getting late, but even as the sky darkened a man flew a kite in the park. He moved his hands quickly, trying to avoid tree branches and power lines. The kite danced against the dark blue sky.

She walked among the stalls, the smell of fish and pomegranates in the air. A breeze blew, and it wasn't too cold. Winter was over at last. At Spadina she turned and walked up to College. Outside the MHAD building, she nodded at Barbara, who whispered something to her. The sliding doors slid open.

* * *

It was dark when she came out again. The doctor was with her. The CN Tower was doing its thing—colored lights dancing above the city. The doctor pointed at it and said something. The girl with green shoes smiled, then turned and headed up Spadina. The doctor crossed the street.

Beside Harvey's was the entrance to a new subterranean restaurant: the Scatterhouse Grill. Inside, a gentleman in an ill-fitting tuxedo took her coat, then ushered her down the stairs.

He saw her come through the curtains, then stop and take in the room. It was an oddly decadent place—like a bordello mixed with a bistro—a bit of speakeasy, too. The waitresses moved quickly, trays held high. People were enjoying themselves, but it wasn't too loud. Velvet curtains absorbed the racket, just the lilting sound of laughter left.

She spotted him, seated at a table near the bar, and smiled. He stood up.

"Hey there," said Grace.

"Hey," said Mason.

He opened his arms and they held each other.

"It's good to see you."

She sat down, glancing at the bar—or at the wall behind it. There was a fish tank in front of a large mirror. She turned to look at Mason. "This place is alright."

"I'm surprised, too," he said.

"What are you drinking?"

He held up his glass. "Light beer. Harm reduction."

"Live a little," she said, and turned toward the waitress. "Gin and tonic for me." Then back to him: "How was your trip?"

"Good," he said. "I spent most of the time with my mom. We figured some things out."

"Did you see Sarah?"

"Yeah. We can talk about that later. How about you?"

"Things are good, actually. And guess what? The girl with the green shoes—the one who swallows razor blades—her mother died."

"That's great."

"It is! And look what she brought me." She dug into her purse and took out a VHS box. "*Breathless*, the original French one. The tape's not even in it. She just stole the box."

"That's sweet."

"Isn't it?"

The waitress came back with her drink, and Grace addressed her: "Can you do me a favor? Can you find the proprietor and ask him to come over here."

The waitress left. There was silence for a moment. They looked toward the bar. "How's the book going?" said Grace.

"Almost done . . ." said Mason.

She smiled at him. "That's one more thing to celebrate."

"But I think I'll change the ending."

"Your prerogative . . ." said the doctor.

A man walked up to the table.

"Nice place," said Mason. "You got any hot dogs on the menu?"

The man said nothing.

"Actually," said Grace. "Can you bring us a bottle of your finest champagne? It's my friend's birthday." She reached across the table and took Mason's hand. "He's thirty-one today."

"And I just got word," said Mason, "my buddy's getting out of prison." He looked at the proprietor. "I think he'll like this place."

The man turned and walked away.

"Is that true?" said Grace. "Is Chaz getting out?"

"Not for a while," said Mason. "I wanted to see his face."

"It looked kind of fishy."

"That it did."

She excused herself to go to the ladies' room.

Mason sipped his beer, then got up and walked to the bar, still limping slightly. He sat down on a stool and looked at the fish—then through the water and further. He stayed like that for a while.

When he refocused he saw someone behind him in the mirror, aiming something at his back. There was a popping sound. He ducked and the cork hit the glass. Then it bounced into the fish tank.

On the other side was a room. Light shone through the window, refracting through the water. The floor was covered with empty food cans and water jugs. The shelves were almost bare. There were paintings on canvas, books, and stacks of paper strewn around a laptop on the desk. There were bunks against the back wall. On the bottom one, holding the severed right hand of a woman, sat a very thin man.

He had a beard and long straggly hair except on the crown of his head, where the flesh was dark and red. He looked like a monk who, for a very long time, had been trapped in a forgotten space pod—or a moribund submarine.

When the fish scattered, the castaway looked up. There was a young man out there. That was not unusual—*everyone* was out there—but this one was looking in.

And now from behind the young man, a woman appeared, holding two glasses of champagne. She was laughing. The young man stood, so that his head rose above the water. The woman put her arm around him and said something. They had about them the toughness and grace of people who had saved each other. Clinking their glasses together, they turned toward the man in the room.

The man in the room rose, still holding the severed right hand.

Mason and Grace looked right through him.

He stood there for a while after they turned away. He watched the two of them dine—on the other side of the water, across the universe. Then he took a deep breath and two steps to his right. He hit the tape deck and picked up the bag. "Fire Lake" began to play. He moved to the desk and poured out some powder. Next to it, he placed the hand. It was lifeless, rotting. It meant something to him. The champagne cork bobbed in the water, as if attached to a lure. He did a line, then growled and howled—a sound of ecstatic suffering that no one would ever hear.

He sat down to write.

Acknowledgments

MY LOVE and thanks to Bob Stall, Jacqui Bishop, Kate Greenaway, Anne Collins, Mike and Nick Wasko, Samantha Haywood, Marci Denesiuk, Paul Quarrington, Lee Gowan, Ernest Hillen, Anne Perdue, Lisa Norton, Bob Seger, my sisters Cassidy and Reilley, my brother Josh, and *This American Life*.

My deepest gratitude to Denise Oswald, Anne Horowitz, Carrie Dieringer, Warren Zevon, Krista Muir, Colum McCann, Timothy Taylor, Janine Kobylka, Saskia Wolsak, Josh Knelman, Maggie Haywood, Adrian Kinloch, John Fraser, Anna Luengo, L. Arthur English, Louise Dennys, Michael McRobb, Mark Sumner, Scott Sellers, Bruce Springsteen, Max Lenderman, Jason Gladue, John Greenaway, Nancy Greenaway, the Greeneri clan, all the Bishops, the Stalls, and Zev Johnny Bishop Greenaway.